Cheap Diamonds

"*Cheap Diamonds* is a dazzler. . . . Vivid, real, and written with heart and scope, *Cheap Diamonds* is anything but—it's the real deal."
—Adriana Trigiani, author of *Lucia, Lucia*

"*Cheap Diamonds* is just plain fun to read. There's humor, there's heartbreak, and there's an answer to a question almost every woman asks at some point in her life: What's it like to be one of those damn models? The answer will surprise and entertain you."
—Elizabeth Berg, author of *The Handmaid and the Carpenter* and *Dream When You're Feeling Blue*

"A captivating weekend read . . . [*Cheap Diamonds*] sparkles with the style and voice that can come only from firsthand experience in the fashion industry."
—*Detroit Free Press*

"Entertaining . . . [The] social commentary, drama, and sadness packed into the book . . . keep the reader turning pages."
—*The Providence Journal*

"I love everything about *Cheap Diamonds*—the vibrantly drawn characters, their brilliantly woven stories, the riveting plot that absorbs interest and sustains suspense every step of the way, and the richly detailed rendering of the ever-fascinating world of high fashion. It is a complete triumph—a masterly and entertaining work."
—Doris Kearns Goodwin

Also by Norris Church Mailer

Windchill Summer

CHEAP DIAMONDS

CHEAP DIAMONDS

A NOVEL

Norris
Church Mailer

BALLANTINE BOOKS • NEW YORK

Cheap Diamonds is a work of fiction. All incidents and dialogue, and all characters, with the exception of some well-known historical and public figures, are products of the author's imagination and are not to be construed as real. Where real-life historical or public figures appear, the situations, incidents, and dialogues concerning those persons are entirely fictional and are not intended to depict actual events or to change the entirely fictional nature of the work. In all other respects, any resemblance to persons living or dead is entirely coincidental.

2008 Ballantine Books Trade Paperback Edition

Published in the United States by Ballantine Books, an imprint of
The Random House Publishing Group, a division of Random House, Inc., New York.

BALLANTINE and colophon are registered trademarks of Random House, Inc.
RANDOM HOUSE READER'S CIRCLE and colophon are registered trademarks of
Random House, Inc.

Originally published in hardcover in the United States by
Random House, an imprint of The Random House Publishing Group,
a division of Random House, Inc., in 2007.

LIBRARY OF CONGRESS CATALOGING-IN-PUBLICATION DATA
Mailer, Norris Church.
Cheap diamonds: a novel / by Norris Church Mailer.
p. cm.
ISBN 978-0-8129-7270-2
1. Young women—New York (State)—New York—Fiction. I. Title.
PS3563.A3824C47 2007
813'.54—dc22 2006037986

Printed in the United States of America

www.randomhousereaderscircle.com

246897531

Book design by Susan Turner

For my mother, Gaynell Davis,
and the sweet memory of my father, James Arthur Davis

CHEAP DIAMONDS

1

CHEEKBONES AND AIRPLANES

There just simply wasn't any such place as 830 Broadway. It went down to 860 and dead-ended at Union Square Park, and that was all she wrote. I checked my appointment book to see if I had misread it, but no—in the nine o'clock space it said, *Ron Bonetti, 830 Broadway.* I stared at the numbers on the building again, then looked around the corner to see if they might for some reason continue down that way. Nope—860 was all there was.

Great.

On top of running out of Broadway, I was practically crippled from walking twenty-two blocks in new patent-leather gillies that had rubbed blisters on both of my heels, my right eyelash was off-kilter, and I was sweating in my mulberry Bobbie Brooks crew-necked sweater and box-pleated miniskirt. I never thought New York would be this hot in September, as far up north as it was. All I remembered from the news was big snowstorms, but then in Sweet Valley there never was a whole lot about New York on the news unless somebody got shot in a restaurant or thrown onto the subway tracks and run over, which seemed to happen a lot. Cabs cost a fortune and subways were faster than buses but I can tell you right now, I was leery of going down into them. I have a little problem with being underground anyhow, and most of the stations were not very well lit and had an odor like mothballs and dirty bathroom. Plus, I was shocked when I saw that homeless people *lived* down there, and I didn't like myself for the way I reacted to them. Part of me was disgusted that human beings could smell that bad and carry on their life right out in public the way they did, and another part felt sorry for them and un-Christian if I didn't give them money. Like what if they were the old angel-in-disguise beggar from the Bible story, testing my compassion? I would flunk big-time, because I really needed every quarter I had. The subway was thirty cents, and that added up if you had to go several places in a day. Which was another reason I had decided to walk it this morning, since the day was pretty and sunny, and I didn't know exactly how far it was. I was going to have to study a map of Manhattan, and soon.

I crossed the street to Union Square Park, found a bench near a statue of Abraham Lincoln, and sat down to reglue my eyelash and try to figure out what might be the best way to go to find more Broadway. My blistered feet didn't want to make too many detours. I made a mental note to carry Band-Aids in my purse from now on. Thank goodness I had gotten up early and left myself a lot of time, having already found out the hard way how long it took to get anywhere in this town, and another little phobia of mine is being late.

Sitting in the park under green shade trees with the cheeky pigeons pecking on the ground right by my feet, I still had a hard time believing I was really in New York City. I'm not sure what I was expecting, but it wasn't what had gone on in the last crazy week. Everything had happened so fast that, like Alice, I felt I was running as hard as I could just to stay in place. Up until last Saturday, I had never been on an airplane in my life, or out of the state of Arkansas, for that matter, except for a couple of trips to Vian, Oklahoma, to visit my aunt Juanita's family.

"I just can't understand why you want to go to New York and try to be one of those models, Cherry," Mama said for the umpteenth time. "It's a big old dirty city, and there are young girls in the papers every day up there who get killed or worse. I won't get one good night's sleep worrying about you in that place. I thought you wanted to be an art teacher!

That's what we paid for you to go to college and do. Is all that money wasted? And what are we supposed to do with that big box of expensive oil paints and brushes you brought home? Your daddy and me sure can't use them. I couldn't paint a straight line with a ruler."

Daddy just said flatly that I wasn't going, and that was the end of that.

But that's what *he* thought. I talked to them until I was blue in the face. I had done a lot of research in *Cosmopolitan* and *Vogue,* and they said the model agencies took good care of their girls—why would they want anything to happen to their moneymakers? And I wouldn't be all alone up there. I would make friends. I was good at that. If an agency didn't take me on, I'd come right back home, I promised. If one did, I would call every week and write a lot. I was twenty-two years old, for Pete's sake! A college graduate. Half my friends were married with kids, including my cousin Lucille, who was younger than me and already had a baby more than a year old. Her mother and daddy didn't treat her like she was a child. I had never in my life done anything drastic that they didn't want me to do, and I know I was their only child and they would miss me, but I really, *really* wanted to go to New York and I just couldn't go if I didn't have their blessing. Or at least their saying it was sort of all right.

It took a while, but I wore them down. Mama, I think, even got to be a little excited about it. She'd never had a chance to do anything but be a wife and mother, since she had married Daddy the summer before her senior year of high school and had me the next July. She even confessed that at one time she'd dreamed about going to Hollywood, but didn't have the money or the nerve. At forty, she was the mother all the boys my age voted the hottest-looking mom; blond and beautiful and slim, she always dressed like a movie star to the best of her ability. She wore filmy nylon negligees around the house, and high-heeled satin slippers with marabou feathers on the vamps. I think her feet were permanently arched, like Barbie's, from always wearing heels, and flats weren't comfortable. She didn't even own a pair.

"There's no reason to pad around the house in flip-flops and a ratty old robe, like some fat housewife who has given up. Just remember, Cherry, if you let yourself go, your husband won't be far behind."

She always said that, but she and I both knew she had Daddy wrapped around her little finger. And when she finally came around to my side, Daddy had to throw up his hands and quit.

"I can't fight the both of you," he said. "But I'm buying you a round-trip ticket, Cheryl Ann, and you get on that plane and come home the first time you even smell trouble, do you hear?" I heard. I heard he was buying my ticket!

Watching out the thick round window of a plane as the ground falls away and the cars on the highway become the size of Raisinets is not the most comforting of feelings, especially after the stewardess made a big point of showing us what to do in case of emergency, how to blow up the life vests and breathe in the little yellow cups and all, and I couldn't help but notice there was a booth that sold flight insurance right by the counter where I got my ticket. I thought about buying some, but figured my parents would be too grief-stricken to spend the money if the plane crashed, so I saved my seven dollars. They were plenty unhappy as it was, and waving good-bye to them from behind the rope at the airport gate was one of the hardest things I had ever had to do. We were all teary-eyed, and I thought for three full seconds about turning back and forgetting the whole thing, but there was that little siren voice in my head that kept calling out to me—*Cherrrry . . . come to New Yorrrrrk . . . yoooou can be a model . . . you kno͏ooooow you can*—so I took a deep breath, blew them a kiss, and got on the plane. In spite of how much I loved Mama and Daddy, Sweet Valley was not the place for a girl with stars in her eyes, and I had stars big enough to blind me.

Plus, I needed a change of scenery, big-time.

It's a long story, but a lot had happened to me since last year. The *Reader's Digest* version is, I had sort of fallen in love for the first time in my life (and finally lost my virginity!) with a guy named Tripp Barlow, and then it ended, which, as it turned out, was all for the best, since he had a wife he neglected to tell me about that he had married in Vietnam. Although he thought they were separated, *she* had other ideas, and now they had a baby girl named Mai.

I went, in the spring, up to St. Juniper's Catholic Boys Academy in the Ozarks to do my practice teaching, then came back and graduated from DuVall University, B.A. in art, class of 1970. I was out of school and the sixties were over. I'm optimistic by nature, but the last couple of years strained it, with several of my friends getting messed up in Vietnam, a couple of them killed. President Nixon promised he would end the war, but he sure was taking his good sweet time about it. It looked like his plan was to bomb them until there was nothing left to fight over—burning down the village to save the village, as the government is fond of saying. Like the Vietnamese are deader when the Communists kill them than when we do. And the ones they put to doing the shooting and burning are boys like my friends. It was getting crazy, especially after the National Guard shot those kids at Kent State last May. A lot of students across the country kind of lost it, rioting and taking over the administration buildings of colleges, but we hadn't done near that much at DuVall. We had a rally and everyone lit candles, but that was about it. I felt like I had done all the protesting I could, though, and needed a break from it all.

It was bittersweet, watching Arkansas disappear beneath the clouds as the plane carried me away. I felt light, like I was leaving everything behind—the war, the ex-boyfriend, Du U, and the schoolwork, but I felt a little lost as well. I was also leaving everything I loved, my family and friends, especially my best friend, Baby, who I hadn't been apart from since we were four years old.

But, like the angels in heaven, Sweet Valley and all I loved was still there; I just couldn't see them for the clouds.

The plane landed without crashing, thank the Lord, and after I called Mama and Daddy collect, I took a taxi to the Barbizon Hotel up on Lexington and Sixty-third Street, which *Cosmo* had said was a good, safe place to stay until you got your break. It was for women only and Grace Kelly and Lauren Bacall had once stayed there. Hopefully, I would be taken by an agency and could get an apartment soon, which would be a lot cheaper. I figured I had enough savings to last two months, if I was careful, and that seemed like enough time to make a start.

The room at the Barbizon was tiny, with a closet that barely held five of my outfits, so I had to leave the rest in suitcases, stacked around the bed, which didn't leave much room to walk. I shouldn't have brought so many clothes, but you never know what you'll need and the season was changing, so I pretty much brought everything I had.

Sunday, I spent the better part of the day trying to pick out what to wear for my interview at the model agency on Monday. All my clothes seemed hicky and wrong to me here in New York, even the few good outfits from Millie's, the best store in Sweet Valley, which Millie copied from the latest magazines as close as she could. I had sewn most of the rest myself, and although I used *Vogue* patterns, I had gotten a C in home ec, which, sorry to say, was deserved. As hard as I tried, I wasn't good at zippers, and the stitching on my hems could make you seasick looking at it. Plus, everything I had was a miniskirt, and all the fall magazines were showing midis. So be it. I would get some new clothes when I started making money, and maybe the midi was just a fad anyhow and wouldn't last. If they couldn't see past what I wore at the agency, it was their loss and they could just lump it.

Brave words, said into the mirror.

Given everybody back home warning me about muggers, I was a little nervous about walking around in the city by myself, but finally I got hungry and bored of the Barbizon café, so I ventured out and bought a slice of real pizza at the closest place to the hotel on Lexington Avenue and sat at a little table on the sidewalk watching the people pass by. Not every woman was beautiful and chic, as I thought they might be, which was somehow cheering, and there were lots of women pushing baby carriages. How dangerous could it be, finally, if the streets were full of babies? I relaxed. After dreaming about it for years, I was really here, on the street in New York City! Eating pizza!

I lay awake most of the night, too excited to sleep, thinking about tomorrow and listening to the noises of the traffic and police sirens and the muted voices that drifted up to the third floor of the Barbizon. It was strange and magical. Even the air was different in New York, like every breath was jammed full of electric currents that tingled my nerves.

I drifted off to sleep and dreamed I was climbing hundreds of stairs to get to the top of the Empire State Building. The higher I went, the more stairs kept on appearing, and I woke up at six o'clock, worn out and feeling alone. I wished somehow Baby had managed to come with me. Baby was nearly as upset as Mama and Daddy about me going, but she had already signed a teaching contract, and even though she was the most beautiful girl I knew, she wasn't the type to be a model, being four feet ten, and you had to at least be five-seven. I came in at five feet twelve, or even five-thirteen if I was honest. Although Baby and I got a lot of Mutt and Jeff jokes, we had been best friends ever since her family moved from the Philippines to Sweet Valley when we were four. We promised to write a lot and call when we could, but it wasn't the same.

I wished I could get her opinion on what to wear. Her zippers were always perfect.

Finally, I put on one of my Millie outfits and went out for my interview at the Suzan Hartman model agency, praying she would take me on, which obviously she did, or I wouldn't be out here now hunting for a photographer named Ron Bonetti who had a studio at nonexistent 830 Broadway.

Suzan Hartman was one of the biggest models in the 1950s and had started the agency several years ago when she turned thirty and the modeling jobs started drying up. She was originally from Arkansas, too, which is why I even thought about being a model in the first place. She grew up in Little Rock, but her grandmother lived in Sweet Valley, and Suzan's mother moved back there to live with her after Suzan left out for New York when she was barely seventeen and Mr. Hartman died of a heart attack. I'm not clear if Suzan's leaving caused the heart attack or not, but I'm inclined to believe it did, if my own father's reaction was any clue. Anyhow, Suzan's mother, Mrs. Hartman, was my sixth-grade teacher. She used to bring magazines with Suzan's pictures into class, and she pinned her covers on the bulletin board. There were a lot of them. We hardly had any room for our artwork. Suzan (pronounced Suz*an*) had started out life as Susan, but changed it when she became a model, although her mother still called her Susan. Mrs. Hartman seemed to have a soft spot for me and said once that I had the makings of a model, being tall and skinny with a little nose, which thrilled me no end, since usually the boys made fun of my long legs and called me Snipe. She even gave me the part of the Fairy in a Christmas play we did, and let me wear one of Suzan's old dresses. I was a good-size girl already by the sixth grade, and the dress was none too big. It was blue net with a gold top that itched like the dickens and flaked off, trailing glitter in the air like pixie dust. Suzan had worn it to her high school junior prom. I couldn't imagine how she danced all night in that dress. Her skin must have been scraped raw and bloody. In spite of all that, though, I did feel pretty glamorous, and from then on I was a little obsessed with Suzan, who didn't seem to come home to visit much. I only saw her in person one time, when I bumped into her and her mother at the county fair. I was in high school by that time, and she was not getting covers anymore. In any case, I had switched my allegiance to Lauren Hutton, Jean Shrimpton, Veruschka, and, later, Twiggy, who were so mod and great-looking and all a little offbeat, especially Veruschka, who, unlike me, *admitted* to being six feet one! I wondered what she had been called as a kid.

At the fair, Suzan was classically beautiful, in the fifties Grace Kelly style, her blond hair up in a perfect French twist, not one single hair sticking out. Among a crowd of blue jeans and plaid shirts, she was like somebody from another planet, wearing a simple sleeveless orange shift, no jewelry, and leather thong sandals with little gold coins dangling from the straps. I wanted those sandals so bad I could taste them, but they looked expensive and it was doubtful any store in Arkansas would carry them. Even if one did, they more than likely wouldn't come in my size, which unfortunately was eleven.

I sinfully coveted her small feet as I leaned against the corner of the fried-dough booth and watched her across the cow lot. She looked really bored, gazing at the prize FFA calf, smoking a cigarette, and eating a candied apple. Or rather, let me say, she was *holding* a candied apple. I never actually saw her take a bite, but the deep alizarin-crimson color of the apple looked really good against the cadmium-orange dress (painters always think in paint colors; it's a habit of mine), and she stood with one toe pointed out like she was waiting for someone to take her picture.

Finally, I got up the nerve to go say hi to Mrs. Hartman, who was happy to see me, and proudly introduced me as one of her favorite former students.

"Susan, this is Cherry Marshall, the one who wore your dress in the play."

"Su*zan,* mother."

She looked me up and down and didn't smile or say a word to me, not "nice to meet you," or "kiss my foot," or anything. I felt like a moron and mumbled something about going for another ride on the Tilt-A-Whirl.

Still, as rude and cold as Suzan was, seeing that face I had only known in magazines right there in the flesh at the Sweet Valley fairgrounds made being a model seem like it really could happen. After all, Helen Gurley Brown, the editor in chief of *Cosmopolitan* magazine, the bible for all us girls, was also from Arkansas! Arkansas girls didn't necessarily have to stay down on the farm. That's why God invented cheekbones and airplanes.

Even so, I was sure there were hundreds of other girls thinking the same thing, and for years I didn't dare tell Mama and Daddy I even dreamed about it since we were staunch members of the First Apostolic Holiness Church of God, and I knew they, especially Daddy, would be horrified by the sinfulness of it all. They would have preferred me to be a nurse or something helpful to humanity with a steady paycheck, but the smell of hospitals makes me gag and I fainted once when I tried to give blood. The only thing I was really good at was painting and drawing, so they finally agreed to let me study art if I would become a teacher. Teaching art isn't healing the sick, but I think it is nearly as important. Think how *beige* life would be without it. Art is the icing on the cupcake of life. Well, that sounds stupid, but you know what I mean. While I was doing my practice teaching last semester at St. Juniper's, my supervising teacher, Father Leo, who was not at all like you'd think priests were, took a few pretty good pictures of me. I also met Cassie Culver, whose boyfriend—or unhappily, ex-boyfriend—a cute guy named Lale Hardcastle, had actually run off to New York and to everyone's astonishment became a big male model.

One of the pictures Father Leo took of me got printed in the *Log Cabin Democrat,* which gave a boost to my dream, and my entire outlook changed. Instead of applying for teaching jobs after I graduated in May, I worked all summer as a salesgirl at the Family Hand, a great head shop in Sweet Valley where Baby and I had once painted murals on the walls, and I saved my money for New York. I know it's shallow to want to live a glamorous life and have your picture in magazines, and it isn't even helping humanity as much as teaching art, but I just had to try. I would always wonder, like Mama, if I would have made it and regret it if I didn't go.

I had no illusions that Suzan would remember me from the fair, and frankly hoped she wouldn't, but I got her address from Mrs. Hartman and sent her copies of Father Leo's pictures. She sent me back what looked like a form letter saying that I could come in for an interview and gave the times they saw new girls and a phone number to call for an appointment, but she didn't send me an airplane ticket or give me any encouragement or indicate that she knew I had been the favorite student of her mother. In fact, I doubt she even read the letter or looked at the pictures herself. It was probably some secretary. Well, she wasn't the only agent in town. If she said no, I would try all of them.

I was so nervous I could hardly breathe when I went into the agency Monday morning at ten. The waiting room was painted a sophisticated dark gray with lighter-gray carpet and plastic (but good plastic) molded chairs lined around the wall. Track lighting focused a beam on each of Suzan's framed covers, and there were enough to stretch all around the room.

The receptionist barely looked up, checked my name off a list, and told me to take a seat. There were several other nervous girls sitting around, all of us with manila envelopes on our laps. While I waited, girls and guys came in and out, not even glancing our way, heading back somewhere down the hallway, all of them beautiful, all of them relaxed and laughing and joking around, like the in-crowd in high school. They were the anointed ones. They had been taken. They had their pictures in magazines. All of them carried expensive-looking leather portfolios, and I recognized quite a few faces, although most didn't have on much makeup and tried to give the impression they had just rolled out of bed. But they made even blue jeans and a sweatshirt look chic by adding an armload of bracelets or a concha belt slung low, a scarf tied around their heads like Ali MacGraw or threaded through their belt loops. I felt really out of place, like 1966, in my mint-green miniskirt with matching tights and too much makeup.

The secretary called my name and I went through the door.

I guessed Suzan was pushing forty by now, but still so gorgeous it made you ache to look at her: a thin, delicate blonde with big blue eyes. She hadn't changed much from my first impression of her, though. Underneath all that delicacy those eyes were chipped out of the heart of an iceberg. She was a chain-smoker, and wielded her cigarette as a weapon when she talked. Her office was hazy with smoke; she had one in her hand and one burning in the ashtray.

Some people are surprised when they see me for the first time, but most try to not be so obviously shocked. Suzan didn't even try. I guess she never saw the pictures I sent or remembered me from the county fair.

"My, you're a big one!" she said, as she looked up from her desk, her eyes practically bugging out. "How tall are you? Five-eleven?"

"Closer to five-twelve."

"That may be too tall for us."

"Yes, ma'am, but Veruschka is over six feet, I think." Her eyes narrowed as she pulled more smoke out of the cigarette.

"Hmm. Yes, she is. What do you have for me?" I handed her my manila envelope with my few little photos, which she flipped through in three seconds and tossed on the desk. That stung. I was proud of them. Father Leo had a reputation as a real artist and even had shows of his pictures. One of these had won an award. It was of me standing in a woodsy brook in the early-morning mist, wearing a white net bathing suit. I looked like Venus on the clamshell rising from the water, with my river-bottom green eyes glowing, as a beam from the morning sun cast a light on them.

"These are totally wrong. You need to get some real pictures made, not bad artworks. They're not even in focus." I felt like I'd swallowed a small rock.

Then she stood up and walked around her desk, checking me over like I was a horse or something. I waited for her to pry my mouth open and look at my teeth. She was on the smaller end of the model chart—maybe five-seven, maybe a hair under—and had to look up at me, which I don't think she liked.

"How old are you?"

"Twenty-two."

"That's old. You should have started in your teens. You've lost several valuable years, and it might already be too late. We don't even take girls older than twenty-three."

It was too late to lie. I had skipped from feeling like a child with my parents to feeling like I was already over the hill.

"Well, I only turned twenty-two in July. I was in college and graduated this year."

"A college girl." She made a noise deep in her throat, which could have meant she wasn't impressed, or was impressed, or was trying to dislodge phlegm. "Where are you from? You have quite an accent." She had totally lost her own accent, but I could see a little flash of surprise and recognition when she first heard my voice.

"Same place you are. Sweet Valley, Arkansas. Your mother was my sixth-grade teacher. I met you once down there when y'all were at the county fair."

"Really? How interesting. You need to lose the accent, the first thing being 'y'all.' It is going to hold you back. I can recommend someone to give you speech lessons." She scribbled a name and number down on a piece of paper and handed it to me. That, at least, gave me a ray of hope.

"Thank you. I'll try."

I really kind of liked the word *y'all*. It was handy. What would I replace it with? "You guys"? "All of you"? My grandmother used to say "you'uns," but I somehow doubted Suzan would think that was better.

"Why do you bleach your hair white like that? It's all wrong with the dark brows. Although it really is a perfect job." She reached up and pawed through it with her red lacquered fingernails, like a chimpanzee checking for lice. "I can't see any roots at all. You must have had it done this morning. But we'll have to tone it down. Maybe a deep shade of gold. Lighten the brows. They look like they were stenciled on. Too fifties. And you have to get rid of the perm."

"I don't bleach my hair or perm it. That's just the way it is. It's natural." A lot of people, when they first meet me, think I might be an albino, although I am *not*—their eyes are pink and mine are green—because my hair is stone white and is also so curly that it looks like a bunch of corkscrews exploded out of my head. I have done everything including ironing to make it long and straight like Cher's, but ever since a year ago, when Lucille, my cousin I mentioned earlier, who was in beauty school at the time, tried to chemically straighten it and most of it broke off, I've given up and just let it go natural. My brows and lashes, ironically, *are* dyed. My mother started dying them with sable-brown Dark Eyes when I started school in the first grade, because they were white, too, and made me look rabbity. I've kept it up ever since. I hadn't seen the real color in so long I wouldn't know what it looked like, but I don't think it would be too attractive.

"Natural?" she said, her voice rising. "It's freakish. With that white hair and skin you look like you have been dipped in bleach. You need some color. It has to be blond. And we'll have to do something about the curl. It will just be too hard to work with."

My heart rose at her talking about "we," then sank. I went through too much the last time it was straightened, and I didn't want to dye my hair. Freakish though it might be, I was used to my white hair and really sort of liked it. As much as I complained about it, it was different. It was me.

As I was trying to figure out a way to nicely say I didn't want to dye my hair, a man walked into the office. He was tall and thin and his skin was the color of ash. He looked like a peaked version of Jimmy Stewart, only his face was not as nice. He also had a cigarette in his hand. The air in the office was beginning to make me woozy.

"Freddy, don't you agree that . . . what is your name?"

"Cherry."

"Cherry . . . nice name . . . should dye that hair and straighten it out? No one has hair like that in the business."

Freddy looked me up and down.

"No one in the business looks like this girl. And that is not necessarily a bad thing, Susan."

"Su*zan,* Freddy." She bit the words with her sharp white teeth.

"Su*zan*." He bowed his head, heavily accenting the last syllable, mocking her. She ignored it.

"I don't know. I'm not so sure she will sell."

"Blondes always sell, and she is more than a blonde. She's an über-blonde. Look at those legs. They're a mile long."

"She's too exotic."

"So is Veruschka. So is Pat McGuire. My God, Diana Vreeland is mad for exotic. There isn't one editorial outfit in *Vogue* this month that a secretary could wear. They're not into reality. They're into fantasy."

"But the California look is going to be the next big thing. The new ones coming up are more wholesome. More girl-next-door. Like Cheryl Tiegs. This one is just . . . just . . ." She couldn't think of a word for me. "Strange." She'd thought of one.

"Put her on the testing board and let's see. You never know."

He was smiling at me, in sort of a creepy way. His gray eyes looked liquid, like there might have been a few drinks sloshing in there behind them. He had on an odd aftershave I couldn't identify, sharp and sweetish, and I knew them all. I had a feeling it might be gin. She examined the pictures again, this time with a little magnifying glass, took another drag on her cigarette, and exhaled.

"All right, Cherry," she said at last, putting the pictures back into the envelope. "We'll give it a try. We'll put you on the testing board. You need some pictures. Go back and meet with Gina. She'll do the paperwork and give you to a booker, who will make some appointments with photographers who test new girls. And tell her to get Lana to show you how to put on makeup. You have a good blank canvas, but you don't know how to use paint." That was ironic, since I *was* a painter, but it was clear she wasn't into hearing my life story.

She handed the envelope of pictures to me, turned her back, put out the cigarette she was holding, and picked up the other one. Freddy leaned against the door frame, watching me, blowing more smoke into the air. My eyes were beginning to water.

"Thank you so much, Miss Hartman, Mr. . . ."

"Collins. But you can call me Freddy. I'm Mr. Hartman." He pointed to Suzan and winked.

"Um, thank you, too, Mr. Collins, uh, Freddy. I'm really excited you're giving me a chance."

"You can call me Suzan," she said briskly. "And you can thank me by succeeding and making me lots of money."

"Great. I will. I won't let you down, Suzan. By the way, your mother said to tell you hi—I called her before I left, and she was really happy I was seeing you."

"That's nice. Now do me a favor. Let's don't get all mushy about Arkansas. We're not two little girls from Little Rock. Got it?"

"Yes, ma'am. Got it."

"And drop the 'ma'am.' Besides being insulting to anybody under eighty, that's a dead giveaway. Nearly as bad as 'y'all.' "

"Right. Okay." I clutched my envelope and went out to meet Gina, who had an office down that hallway where all the glorious anointed were going. I was going to be a model, just like they were! If I could have, I would have jumped in the air and clicked my heels.

Gina was plump and on the edge of middle age, at least in her late thirties. She had a pretty face and I wondered if she had been a model when she was younger. She gave me a smile, and after Freddy and Suzan, it was a relief to see someone who was friendly. And not smoking.

"Welcome to Suzan Hartman, Cherry," she said, shaking my hand. "Sit down and talk to me." I sat. "For starters, let's fill out a card with your sizes and measurements. Do you know your measurements?" I knew some of them, but not glove size or head size, so she took out her tape and measured me. I was really ashamed to write eleven down for shoe size, but that's what it was.

"Well, shoes are probably out. The standard is nine. Bras, you won't be doing—the customary size is thirty-four B—but that's all right. Don't think your hands will make it—your fingers are too long and bony and you'd have to get nails—but you have great long legs. Good shape. Probably do well with hosiery ads. You're a size six, which is perfect, and with that lanky height you'll make out like a bandit on the runway. We're just starting the runway division here, and we'll put you in class to teach you how to walk. Love your coloring. It's natural, isn't it? Pretty face. Good teeth. You could slice bread with those cheekbones. Did Suzan say anything about your makeup?"

I told her about Lana.

"I don't think she's here now. I'll let her know, and you can meet with her later this week. We'll put it on your schedule. Your booker will make up a list of photographers for you to go see tomorrow. I think we'll give you to Liz. She'll set up appointments, and you'll call her every day to get your schedule. Or call her if you have problems or questions. Call her a lot. She'll be your mother superior. If you have nothing else to do, hang around here. You never know when a job will come in, and if she can't reach you, someone else will go for it. You can learn a lot from talking with the other models. You are going to be testing until you get enough pictures to fill your book and get your card, but you might luck out and get a job. You have a special look that someone might latch on to. I think you'll do well. Any questions?"

I was so ignorant I didn't even know what questions to ask. Frankly, my head was kind of foggy. I had never been dissected like that, so matter-of-factly, like I was a prime cow at an auction. I didn't know what a card was or how I got one or anything, but I figured I would learn it all in time. Then a question occurred to me.

"Just one. Do you know if there is a male model by the name of Lale Hardcastle here? He's from Arkansas, too, and I was just wondering."

"Not that I know of. He might have changed his name, though. A lot of models do. You have a unique name already, no Cherrys working that I know of. Although you'll have to drop the Marshall professionally. There's a model-turned-agent in England named Cherry Marshall, and we wouldn't want there to be any confusion."

"Are you serious? Really? Another Cherry Marshall? That's amazing!" I couldn't imagine there would be two Cherry Marshalls in the world, but England was far away, and whatever she looked like, I bet it wouldn't be like me. "All right," I said after considering it for two seconds. "In that case, I'll be just Cherry." I would probably have said yes if she wanted me to call myself Esmeralda McGonagall.

So I joined the ranks of one-name models. I hoped I could still use my last name on my driver's license and things. My real name was Cheryl Ann, but I had been called Cherry ever since I could remember, unless my parents wanted to emphasize something to get my attention, like, "Cheryl Ann, what's the matter with you, thinking you can go to New York and be a highfalutin fashion model? You're gettin' above your raisin', girl!"

I couldn't wait to call them!

Gina gave me a contract to sign, and I floated out of the office and back to the Barbizon, stopping off in Saks Fifth Avenue just to look around and breathe the fragrant air of expensive stuff. It was the most beautiful store I had ever seen in my life, and I spent a couple of hours riding up and down the escalators and touching everything, fluffy cashmeres, soft Italian leather shoes and bags, not daring to try any of it on.

2

GO-SEE

Dear Baby,

Sorry to call you collect—your landlady is probably still mad at me—but I had to let you know Suzan Hartman took me! When the phone bill comes in, tell me how much it is and I'll pay you back. I'll have to write letters until I get my own phone.

I know I've only been gone a week, but I miss you so much I can't stand it. I wish you were here to go with me on some of these crazy go-sees, as they call them (because you *go* to the photographers and they *see* if they like you), and do stuff, like movies or museums. There are so many! The Museum of Natural History has a whole dinosaur skeleton and a huge *whale* hanging from the ceiling! (I'm sure it's mostly plastic. Otherwise it would stink.) I am going to the Metropolitan Museum this weekend, but it won't be as much fun to see all the famous paintings we've studied in class without you.

How is the teaching job going? Are you getting any painting

done? Set up an easel in class and paint when the kids are busy. They'll get more out of watching you than painting themselves.

Is that sleazy Mr. Bachman still trying to get you to play hide-the-weenie? I hope you stay out of the supply closet when he's around, or take a student with you, after what he tried to pull last time. You should report him, but you're right—it would be your word against his, and he *is* the principal. I bet you're not the first teacher he made a pass at, though. And him with six kids! His poor wife. What about Coach McClellan? Has he asked you out yet? I don't know, though. He looks good now, but I bet in five years he will have a huge gut. Those athletic types always get fat when they stop working out. And he isn't smart enough for you. You need somebody who you can talk to. Like Father Leo, only not a priest! What a waste of manhood. Have you seen him since I left? Tell him I miss him and the guys. Suzan didn't think his pictures were really fashion shots, so I have to get a whole lot of new ones. Don't tell him. I still love them.

Just being in New York is pretty exciting but there is so much I have to learn, including finding my way around, and I haven't made any girlfriends yet, much less met any guys who are interesting. Most of the male models are too beautiful to even talk to. You know how I feel about pretty boys (remember Tripp?!). They're *trouble,* and these ones that model are the prettiest. I've noticed a lot of them have really plain girlfriends—isn't that interesting? Like they don't want to walk down the street with someone better-looking than they are. Their girlfriends just live to wait on their every need and look at them with cow eyes, poor things. I think some of the guys might be homosexual, or gay, as they call it up here, but I'm not sure. Anyhow, it seems like most of them are too much in love with themselves to love anybody else. Like Narcissus. Remember that story from humanities class? I'm not being fair, and I could say the same for some of the girls. I just don't feel like I fit in with all these perfect specimens. I am the farthest thing from perfect, but then some of the famous girls have their little quirks, too, so we'll see. One of the biggest ones has sort of a weird eye that sometimes looks east when the other one looks west! But if they photograph her from the right angle you can't really tell.

At first it felt awkward, but now I'm getting used to going out by myself to eat. Usually I take a book to the coffee shop near the hotel. For breakfast, I can get scrambled eggs and bacon for a dollar, with a buttered bagel, which looks kind of like a doughnut, but is bread that they *boil* and then bake, if you can believe it, and they always give you hash browns to boot. Nobody up here can understand anything I say, though, which makes it hard to even order a meal. The other day when I ordered a salad with ranch dressing, the waitress asked me if I said "French," and I said, "No, *ranch*," and she said, "That's what I said, *French*," and we went back and forth for five minutes, her screaming, "FRENCH?" at me like I was deaf, and me saying, "NO, *RANCH*," until finally I just gave up and said, "Blue cheese." I don't have as much trouble understanding them, I guess because of TV, but I am going to go and get speech lessons to lose my accent when I get some money.

I am still at the Barbizon, but Lana, one of the models who showed me some makeup tricks, said that when she first started she lived in a house owned by an old lady in Greenwich Village who rents rooms to actors and models and people like that, and she knew of a girl who was leaving. That would be a lot cheaper than the hotel, so I'm going to try and get it this week. Lana did a great job with the makeup, and showed me how to put eyeliner on just the outside half of my lid, sweeping it up and blending it with a smoky shadow so my eyes look slanted and the green really pops. She deepened my colors, which makes me look a lot more dramatic. I am totally another girl when it is all done up—I didn't recognize myself when she got through. AND, I have stopped plucking and am growing my eyebrows out to their original white—don't faint. Suzan's orders. She hates the dark neat brows for some reason.

Lana is quite a character. You would recognize her face—she's been on the cover of *Cosmo*, and she is almost as gorgeous as you, black hair and amber-colored eyes like a big cat, and she moves like a cat, too, sort of lounging on furniture rather than sitting, but I never heard anybody use swears in everyday conversation like she does, and I am ashamed to even write them down, so you'll just have to imagine the worst words you can. She goes by the one name, and when I asked what her last name was, she said, "Just Lana. The last is too hard to pronounce." She is from Serbia (I had to look at a map to find it) but came to New York with her family and learned English when she was fourteen, so her accent is even weirder than mine. A lot of the girls use one name, like Twiggy and

Apollonia and Veruschka, and now I am added to the list. They're having me go by just "Cherry," but I'll use my real last name anytime I need to. I don't think Daddy would like me giving it up, and it is too confusing when you are introduced to people if you don't have a last name.

You wouldn't believe the week I have had. I've been going out every day seeing photographers to try to get them to use me for tests, which would give me pictures to put in my book, and give the photographers a free model to try out shots or lighting or whatever. Out of about twenty photographers I saw, only one wanted to test me at all, and that was a total disaster, which I'll get to in a minute.

I'm gradually learning the subway, and it's not really as bad as we thought it would be. The first time I rode it I stood way back from the edge of the platform, though, in case some crazy person tried to throw me onto the tracks, but then I was so far away from the train that everyone rushed on in front of me and I had to fight to get on before the doors closed. Forget about getting a seat! I went out early in the morning and there were so many people going to work that there was hardly room to stand. We were all mooshed together like a can of Vienna sausages, pretending to read the ads above the windows, as if some stranger didn't have his nose practically in our armpits (*Aren't you glad YOU use Dial? Don't you wish EVERYBODY did?*), and every time the train went around a curve we all grabbed at each other to keep from falling. It was amazing how many people thought my rear end was a hand-hold or something. I have had boyfriends I wasn't that close to! Finally I got a seat when the person sitting right in front of me got off, but I couldn't see out the window for all the people standing, so I went past my stop and had to walk back ten blocks. Even so, I was still a few minutes early for my appointment, because Lana told me you have to allow an hour to get anywhere in this !@#$%&* town, (pick your own word) and you know how I am about being on time. I wish I could just get in the VW and go, like at home, but keeping a car in the city is a lot of trouble, with the parking and traffic and all.

The first place Suzan Hartman sent me was an ad agency on lower Fifth Avenue. I don't really even know what kind of ad they were doing, because nobody tells you anything. You just show up. It must not have been one of the big ones, though, because it wasn't exactly a ritzy place. Dirt-colored indoor-outdoor carpet.

Plastic plant. It was so crowded with girls there was no place to sit. A woman at a desk pointed to a sign-in sheet when I came over to tell her I was there, and I signed my name. A girl came out of a door and the woman told whoever was on the list next to go in, and somebody did. Finally, after ages, it was my turn. I had to find my own way to the office; it was weird, like the place was totally deserted except for the girls and the woman in the waiting room. I went down a dark hallway, and the last door on the left was the only one open, so I went in. A chubby woman with hair dyed that purplish-red sat behind the desk. She didn't ask me to sit down.

"Hi," I said, big smile. "I'm Cherry from Suzan Hartman."

"A southern girl, huh? Let me see your book."

Everybody up here always says, "Oh, what part of the South are you from?" or something like that. I am already trying not to say "y'all" or "ma'am," and at least not give them that satisfaction. They really treat southerners like they think we are subpar mentally. Added to that, when you say you're a model, then they think you are a *real* dimwit. I just can't stand it.

"Well, I don't really have a book yet, but I have some pictures," and I gave her my envelope with the beautiful shots that Father Leo took, which was all I had.

"How long have you been modeling?" she asked, squinting at me as she lit up a cigarette and tossed the match into a blue glass ashtray. I swear, every single person I have met smokes. Not to nag you, Baby, but I hope you are trying to quit.

"Actually, this is my first day and you are the first person I've seen," I said brightly, like the moron she thought I was. I don't know what I was expecting her to do—congratulate me? I can't believe myself. Maybe we *are* subpar mentally.

"Really? Thank you for coming. Tell the next girl to come in."

The appointments all week were more or less the same. Call back when you have more pictures. Drop off your card when you get one. Come around when you get some experience. Don't call us. We'll call you.

Then, the disaster. I went to this photographer named something Greek—I have blocked it out, but it sounded like Stasso Vendikas, or something like that. He looked kind of like Yul Brynner, bald and everything, only not as good-looking, and his place was smaller than most of the photography studios, which are usually in big open lofts. He had some framed pictures on the walls of Maud Adams and Evelyn Kuhn and Karen Graham, so I know he at least had photographed some big models—unless he just got the pictures from somewhere else and hung them up, which I didn't think of until later. Anyhow, I was a little impressed. He looked at my pictures and asked me if I had time to do a test right then and there. I tried to act cool, like I did this all the time, and called my booker, Liz, the girl who makes my appointments at the agency, and she said, sure, go ahead. I was done with go-sees for the day anyhow.

"You're in luck!" he said. "I'm doing a catalog. Go in the dressing room and put on the orange pantsuit hanging on the rack."

Wow! I was so excited. This might be a real job, not even a test! I was so naïve I didn't know you had to be booked through the agency for work. I really thought I would be in the catalog.

I had stripped off my dress and was about to put on the orange pants, when he came right into the dressing room without even knocking.

"Uh, Mr. Vendikas," I said, "I'm not ready yet. Could you please go out until I change?" He not only didn't go out, but he came over and took away the pants from me that I had been holding in front of myself, leaving me in my bikini panties, my pink jelly beans sticking out of my flat chest.

"Ah, you're lovely," he said. "So tall. Like a white long-stemmed rose. How tall are you, my dear?" He only came up to the bottom of my neck, and had really bad breath, like he had never brushed his teeth in his life. I tried to put my dress on, but he snatched it away. "Don't be embarrassed. You have a lovely body. You'll have to get used to showing that body off." I tried to push him away, but he grabbed at me and tried to kiss me, getting slobbers on my face, which was really disgusting. I pushed at his arms, but he was strong, and I couldn't get him off me.

"Stop it! Leave me alone!"

"Oh, you like it—you know you do. All of you like it." Sweat had popped out on his bald head, which made him even more disgusting, if that is possible.

"Are you trying to rape me or something?" I said. Baby, I was really scared. We were alone in the studio. I always thought if somebody was going to rape me I could scream or kick him in the balls or something, but men are a lot stronger than girls, even big ones, and I couldn't do anything. If I screamed, there was nobody to hear me. I would just have to get raped, I guess.

I stopped struggling and waited for him to do it. I hoped it would be quick and he wouldn't hurt me too much.

"*Rape* you? I don't have to rape girls!" he said, backing off, a little huffy. "Do you know how many women are waiting in line to have me make love to them? Did you see the pictures on my walls? Those girls are more famous than you will ever be! I have made love to every single one of them, and they beg for more!"

Yeah, sure, I thought. I just bet they did.

By that time, I had managed to get my dress on, grabbed my purse and pictures, and shoved past him to the door. He followed me out to the elevator, yelling, "You are a silly little girl! Don't you know you have to cooperate if you want to get ahead in this business? You will never make it! You, you . . . *virgin*!" It was the ugliest word he could think to call me.

I got out of there and called Liz from the phone booth on the corner. She wasn't as upset as I thought she'd be, which kind of upset me.

"Calm down, Cherry," she said. "You're all right. He didn't actually rape you, did he? Or hurt you?" I had to say no. "Good. I'll keep an eye on him and if we get any more complaints, he'll be out of test girls. Take the rest of the day off."

And that was my week. So no tests. No new pictures. But at least I didn't get raped. Please don't say anything to anybody about this, not Cassie and especially not Mama and Daddy. I know you won't, but I don't want them to try to make me come home. Maybe the guy is right, that models have to sleep with photographers to get any work, but I am not going to sleep with anyone, especially an old bald guy with bad breath, to get a test picture taken! There must be somebody in this town who will want to work with me for just me. But I learned a lesson—don't take your clothes off in some strange studio if you are all by yourself.

Have you seen Cassie? How is she doing? Has she heard anything from Lale? I asked at Suzan Hartman, and they had never heard of Lale Hardcastle, but then he's probably with another agency, or he might have changed his name. In fact, I bet that is just what he did. He should have realized, though, that if he was going to get his picture in magazines that somebody from home was going to recognize him. Even with his face half hidden behind the girl in that shampoo ad, Cassie jumped right on it. She would have recognized him, though, if it was just his little toe! Tell her if I run across him, I'll call her, although I have no idea what I'll say to him if I do meet him. I'd like to punch him in the nose. Wouldn't that be funny, to meet somebody who has never laid eyes on you, say, "How do you do?" and then punch them in the nose?!

I miss you so much. Please write soon.

I love you,
Cherry

3

830 BROADWAY

I felt like such an idiot. Of course there was an 830 Broadway. You just had to get around Union Square, walk on down a few blocks farther, and find where it started again, which I did with a little help from a nice woman walking one of those yappy little dust-mop dogs. I wasn't too hopeful that this Ron Bonetti meeting would turn out any better than the ones I'd had the last few days, though. After a whole week, not one person had offered to take my picture, except ol' Stasso. I had a feeling Suzan was just itching to get rid of me, especially since Freddy went out of his way to talk to me when I was at the agency, and if I couldn't even get a test, that would be a great excuse.

Liz was great, though, even if she had been a little casual about my almost-rape, and maybe I did overreact to that. She said not to worry, just keep plugging away, that lots of girls took a while to get going, and one day, bingo, they hit. Liz was from the Bronx with a real New York accent that I loved to listen to, had frosted hair, and chewed Juicy Fruit gum all the time. At least she and Gina seemed to like me, and while I couldn't say Lana was a friend, she smiled and talked to me.

830 Broadway was not any different from the other buildings I'd been in all week. Old. Creaky elevators with worn linoleum floors. Not the cleanest places. That was one thing about New York—everything was old. Some of the buildings, like up on the Upper East Side, where I was staying, had doormen and were clean and fancy with polished brass, but it seemed like the farther downtown you got, the less well-kept they were. The city had many neighborhoods, vastly different from one another, as I was finding out, and I was staying in one of the nicer ones. So far, most of the photographers I had met were downtown, trying to make it to the big time but not famous, and most of them probably never would be. I was beginning to understand that I wasn't going to be sent up to Avedon and Scavullo and Penn right away. In fact, I was beginning to get a little discouraged. Maybe I *should* dye my hair golden blond. I hated the thought that Suzan might be right. I tried to stay out of her way when I went in every day to get my schedule, because she always looked me up and down, like she didn't like what I was wearing, and said something, like "When are your eyebrows growing back to normal?" In fact, the white hairs were beginning to come in, salt and pepperish, but I brushed mascara over them to even them out. When all the dye came out I would see what they looked like then. I wouldn't promise not to dye them again, but she didn't know that.

I had fixed my eyelash while I was sitting on the bench beside Honest Abe in Union Square Park, but it still felt a little funny, so I took out my compact in the lobby of 830 to adjust it, touched up my new mulberry-colored lipstick that Lana thought looked better than my old pink one, then found Ron Bonetti's name on the list by the elevator and punched the number for the eighth floor. The elevator door opened directly into the studio instead of a hallway, and I stepped out into a little waiting room with an old leather couch and a couple of chairs. A great big spool that some kind of wire cable had been wound around was being used for a table, with magazines arranged on it. There didn't seem to be anybody around.

"Hello?" I called out. "Ron? Ron Bonetti?" There was some noise in the next room, so I went to the door and looked in.

Four guys were scattered around, lying on old couches or flat on the floor, sound asleep, as naked as picked birds.

"Uh, uh, uh, excuse me! I'm sorry!" I said, hypnotized like a mouse staring at a snake, so to speak. One of them opened an eye and sat up, rubbed his hand over his face, looked at me, and said, "Bonetti's not here, honey, but I can take a look at your book."

He started to get up, his hand outstretched, but I said, "Ohhhhh, that's all right. I'll come back later."

I ran to the elevator and punched the button, thinking more and more that my daddy might have been right about New York. It seemed like it took forever for it to come back up. When the door finally opened, I ran smack-dab into a short guy, probably just a couple of years older than me, with dark hair and a close-cropped beard, wearing yellow aviator glasses.

"Hold on—where's the fire?" he said, picking up my pictures, which had been knocked out of my hand. The elevator door rolled shut.

"Are you Ron Bonetti? What kind of a place is this? There are four naked guys in there!"

"What! Hey, Axel! What are you guys still doing here? You were supposed to be out of here last night!"

"Hey, man, give us a break. We shot all night and just needed to get a little shut-eye. Be cool." The guy who had talked to me earlier came out, zipping up his jeans. His hair was long and wild, and he had a black beard and mustache.

"Aw, man, look at you. Get those guys out of there! I'll take this lovely girl out for breakfast. We'll talk later."

Axel went back and I heard grumbling. We stood in silence while we waited again for the elevator. I clutched my pictures, which were beginning to get a little bent. Another one of the guys stuck his head around the door. His hair was sandy blond and he had the most amazing blue eyes. His shirt was still off, showing chest muscles carpeted in dark-blond hair, but at least he had put on his pants. He grinned at me with a perfect set of white teeth.

"Morning, ma'am," he said. "I apologize. My mama raised me better than that."

I did a double take. He looked familiar and had a thick accent, which had to be Arkansas. Maybe Tennessee or Texas. Before I could say anything, Axel came back out.

"Come on, Zack. We got to get out of here. Bonetti has business to do." He pointed at me and they disappeared.

The elevator door opened and Ron and I got inside.

"Those guys are making a student film, and I let them use the studio last night. I'm really sorry about that. Let me buy you some breakfast."

"You don't have to do that. It's okay. I just never saw that many naked men at one time before. They couldn't have been comfortable, on the floor like that without any blankets. I wonder why they weren't sleeping in their clothes?"

"I'll have to ask them that." We had walked out the door and stopped in front of a coffee shop on the corner. "Is this okay?"

"You don't have to buy me breakfast. Really. I can come back some other time. I'll just go on . . ."

He took me by the arm and ushered me in.

"Please. It's the least I can do."

I *was* kind of hungry, so I went along without too much arm-twisting. Like most coffee shops, the place was narrow, with six or seven red booths, a counter with stools, and air that sizzled with bacon frying. The cook was flipping eggs and pancakes as fast as he could, a big pile of hash browns mounded up over to the side of the griddle, and the waitresses rushed around, putting down plates and clearing dishes nonstop as a stream of people came in and out. We had to wait a couple of minutes for one of the girls to wipe our table, leaving us, unluckily, standing right in front of a case full of muffins and pastries. I eyed the cheese Danish, which I'd had for the first time in the coffee shop in the Barbizon and had gotten kind of addicted to. I'd never really thought about what I ate before, being naturally skinny, but Suzan had told me, in one of her brief, pointed comments, that I had to watch my diet because she didn't want to see me gain even one pound, so I decided not to have the Danish, especially in front of a photographer.

"Coffee?" the waitress said, putting down menus and two glasses of water after we got settled in a booth.

"Yes, please. Thank you," I said, trying not to sound too southern. She filled both our cups. Ron glanced at the menu.

"What'll you have?"

"I guess I'll have scrambled eggs. And a sesame-seed bagel. But I'll pay for it." He shot me a look, and I knew I shouldn't have said that.

"My friend will have the number one, sesame bagel instead of toast. I'll just have coffee. And the check." She flashed him a quick smile and rushed to give the order to the harried cook.

"Have you already had breakfast?"

"I never eat breakfast. Just black coffee and a little gasoline to kick-start the day." He pulled a small bottle of vodka out of his pocket and poured some into his cup.

After the last week, nothing surprised me.

"So what's with the accent?" he said, sipping his coffee like it was just coffee. "Where are you from?"

"Arkansas."

"Arkansas! I never met anybody from Arkansas."

"Well, now you have."

"Do they all look like you?"

"No, some of them are really tall." He laughed.

"Who was that blond guy in the studio?" I asked. "He sounded like he might be from Arkansas. The one Axel called Zack."

"Beats me. Axel is an old buddy from college who is going to film school. He drags in anybody who'll work for free to be in his movies. Why? Did you know that guy?"

"No. His voice just sounded kind of like home, and I was curious."

The waitress put down an oval plate piled up with scrambled eggs and hash browns, the bagel on a separate little dish. It had taken all of three minutes. They don't fool around in these coffee shops—you're in and out before your shirttail has time to hit your rear end.

"So. Arkansas, huh?" he said after a pause. "I see you're wearing shoes."

He grinned, like he had said something really witty. I wanted to like this guy, but he was making it hard.

"Yeah, well, they make us rent them at the border when we leave, and we have to check them in when we come back."

"You're pretty funny."

"So are you. Funny like an iron lung."

"Is that an old Arkansas expression?"

"Must be. We used to say stuff like that in the seventh grade. Funny like a three-legged dog . . ."

"Funny like a dead kitten?" he countered.

"Funny like a squashed baby duck."

"Funny like a putrid . . ."

"You want to see my pictures, or should we just try to think up some more funny Arkansas stuff? I know a joke about two possums crossing the road."

"I would love to see your pictures."

I handed them over with a little attitude. They had been tossed back at me a few too many times.

"I know these aren't real model pictures, but they're all I have. I've just been here . . ."

"Wow! These are incredible! Who took them?"

"Father Leo, a priest in a place called St. Juniper's, up in the Ozark Mountains. He was a friend of mine. I mean, *is* a friend of mine."

"A priest, huh? Well, he sure knows photography. These are really fine." He took his time, studying each of them. He finally put them down. "So, you a Cat'lic like me, then?"

"No, I belong to the First Apostolic Holiness Church of God. In Sweet Valley."

"Oh, yeah? Is that like Baptist?"

"Kind of."

"What's different about them?"

"Well, we're noisier. We speak in tongues and do healing services and shout when we're filled with the Holy Spirit and . . . and . . . stuff like that." I ran out of steam. It sounded bizarre in my own ears, and I was trying not to be embarrassed, because we're supposed to testify to sinners and be not ashamed—not that I knew for sure Ron was a sinner, even though he was drinking vodka at nine in the morning—but I had never been much good in the testifying department, and I was flustered.

He was staring at me like I'd grown another nose. Bad for my soul or not, I was embarrassed and I know my face got red.

"So. Okay. Let me get this straight," he said after a minute. "You belong to an Arkansas church that shouts and speaks in tongues, whatever that is, and then you had some hot pictures taken by a Catholic priest, and now you're in New York modeling for Suzan Hartman."

"Well . . . yeah. That's about it." It sounded weird when you put it that way, I had to admit. For a flash, I saw it all through my father's eyes. He'd seen the fashion magazines, the swimsuit ads, the models posing half naked in bra and girdle and stocking ads, and all. He was no dummy. He knew what men were like. But I couldn't be his little girl forever, and he knew that, too, and finally he had let me go. A little pang went through my heart, like I had lost something precious.

I had changed a lot in the past year, and frankly, going back to the summer a year ago, when I lost my virginity to Tripp Barlow and smoked pot without being struck by lightning, I'd kind of stopped believing I was going to burn in hell for every little bad thing I did, like Brother Wilkins said. I hadn't once thought about finding a church in New York. I guess I was close to being what we call back-slid. Still, even though my mind said not to worry, I knew deep down that I could never really get away from feeling that whatever I was doing was the wrong thing.

"How long have you been at it?"

"At what?"

"Modeling."

"Oh. A whole week. And not one person has wanted to do a test with me. One guy started to, but he only wanted to see me naked when I was changing and grab my boobs, which is kind of impossible since I don't have enough to grab. Don't laugh. Please don't laugh."

He had been ready to laugh, but his face changed. All of a sudden my bravado had run out and I was on the verge of crying. He reached over and took my hand. That made it worse, and to my horror, tears started running down my cheeks.

"Hey, sweetheart, don't do that. Come on. Everybody has to start somewhere. I have a fine-arts degree from NYU. I wanted to be an art photographer, but I couldn't get a gallery or make any money at it, and now I take pictures of food."

"You do?" I sniffed. "Food? Like in *Good Housekeeping,* when they give the recipes?"

"Yes, exactly like *Good Housekeeping,* and I'm really good at it, but what I want to do is fashion. I want to be the next Avedon, work at *Vogue* and *Bazaar.* So here I am. Reaching for the same gold ring as you." He fumbled in his pocket, looking for a handkerchief while I wiped at my eyes with my fingers, trying not to dislodge my eyelashes again. "Tell you what," he said finally, pulling a napkin out of the chrome holder and handing it to me. I blew my nose. "Let me do some pictures of you. You have something unique, and so do I. We'll start this thing together, and we'll wind up big stars, you and me. You wait and see."

"You want to take pictures of me? Are you sure? You don't have to, just to pay me back for Axel and Zack and them, you know. I've seen a naked man before. It was no big deal," I lied.

"I'm sure I want to photograph you. I'm not paying you back for anything."

He smiled and took a swig of his coffee.

"You know, if we're going to wind up big stars together, you'll have to tell me your name."

"Cherry. Just Cherry. Well, it's really Cherry Marshall, but they don't want me to use Marshall because some other, older model in England has it."

"Cherry. That name is going to be in the pages of *Vogue,* Cherry Marshall. You wait and see."

4

FLYIN' JACK'S

I couldn't believe that guy named Zack in Ron Bonetti's studio. That had to be a made-up name. The chances were he wasn't Lale—that would have been too much of a coincidence—but that accent sure did sound down home, and he looked a lot like the pictures Cassie showed me, only his hair was shorter now. Coincidence or not, I had to find out. Maybe I'd get Axel's number from Ron or something, but that could wait a while until I did the test and got some pictures out of him, if he didn't back out on me.

To tell you the truth, I wasn't in all that much of a hurry to find Lale. What I would do if this Zack was Lale, I didn't know. He had done a real number on a sweet girl who had become a friend, and when Cassie found out I was coming to New York she made me promise I would look for him. I couldn't say no, and I figured if somehow by chance we ran into each other, I would just start a little conversation and try to find out why he had done what he did. I mean, I sort of already knew *why* he had done it—that wasn't hard to see—but maybe I could convince him to call or at least write her. As ugly of me as it was, though, I kind of wished

I had never promised. I hated to be in the middle of things that were not my business. On the other hand, I wanted to help Cassie. It was a real predicament.

As I thought about Cassie and all that, it hit me how one teensy little decision can change your whole life. If I hadn't taken a wrong turn and got lost in a snowstorm, thereby coming into Buchanan on the wrong road, I wouldn't have stopped in at Flyin' Jack's, where Cassie was a waitress, and I might be teaching art somewhere right now, like Baby was. More important, Cassie might be dead. In fact, two people might be dead.

Mama always says there are no coincidences in life.

It seems like so long ago, in another life even, but it was only back in late February, and I was on my way to do my practice teaching at St. Juniper's, which was a slow four-hour drive from Sweet Valley up through the Ozark Mountains. It had just started snowing when I left, but as I climbed higher, it got heavier, and those winding mountain roads are tricky, even in good weather. Off to the left was a sheer drop-off with a breath-sucking view of the valley below, all silent and misty with snow, like a Japanese painting. My trusty little Volkswagen was doing its best—thank goodness Daddy had put on chains—but the wiper blades were old, smearing the windshield, and it was hard to see.

As if the worsening weather wasn't enough to make me nervous, I rounded a curve and there up on the rocks, somebody had hung a big homemade sign that said in crooked letters PREPARE TO MEET THY GOD!!! The words screamed out underneath a black paint-dripped cross. Not the most reassuring thing to see right at that particular moment because while I was trying to figure out how they had gotten up there to hang it, a Mack truck whipped around the curve, half over in my lane, and came within two feet of smashing into me. The blast of air as it passed blew my little car sideways, and I had to swerve to keep from going into the rocks. It shook me up to the point that I crawled along at five miles an hour until my heart stopped hammering. I could see him in the rearview mirror barreling toward the next curve, spraying up snow, oblivious to what was around the bend. I had no doubt he would plunge off the mountain and kill himself or somebody else before he made it to the bottom. Truckers are crazy. The stress of all those long hours of driving, not to mention the gallons of coffee and stay-awake pills they all take, must do some permanent damage to their nerves.

Unhappily, this near-miss made me remember the time when we

were in the sixth grade and the state troopers came to our school in their uniforms with Smokey the Bear hats and real guns hanging on their hips and all, to show us a film about traffic safety. It was actual home movies of car wrecks, if you can believe it. One was of a big truck carrying a load of pipes. The guy had been going down a mountain (truth be told, it looked a lot like the one I was on) too fast to make a turn, and went flying off the road; the truck wound up perched half on the road and half in the top branches of a tree. The pipes had crashed through the back window of the cab and jammed the guy's head clean through the steering wheel. They showed a good tight close-up of it, all bloody and purple.

We all had nightmares for weeks. I don't know what they were thinking about, showing stuff like that to kids, or why I had to remember it now, driving up this steep, narrow road in a snowstorm. There was no way I was about to turn tail at this point, though, so I just kept going and tried to see through my bad wipers as the snow came down and the knot in my stomach grew bigger. I had only been to St. Juniper's the one time, when I went for my interview, and although I thought I knew the way, everything looked different from the way it had back in the fall, when I had come on a bright sunny day and the leaves were red and gold.

The road split into a fork, which surprised me. I didn't remember any fork at all when I came up here the last time. Well, I would just have to trust my instincts. After a few miles, there was another fork, and then a while after that, another one. Just when I was beginning to wonder if I might have made a couple of bad choices, the road began to sharply slope up, and finally I topped a hill. It was snowing so hard I couldn't see more than a few feet ahead of me.

I took a breath and started down the other side, my legs shaky from practically standing on the clutch and the brake, when the car fishtailed and the right tire went off the road. I spun my wheels and desperately tried to remember any *National Geographic* articles that told you how to survive in the cold woods without freezing to death if you only had a nail file and two Snickers bars in your purse. I made a mental note to read the articles in the future instead of just flipping through and looking at the pictures.

After a hairy slide, miraculously the car bumped back up on the pavement, and soon, thank you, Jesus, I saw a sign that pointed toward Buchanan.

As I got to the edge of town, I passed a neat little café painted cheery robin's-egg blue snugged up next to Flyin' Jack's Truck Stop and realized

I was starving. I was so grateful to be back near people that I decided to turn around and have a little bite to fortify myself. Lunch would have been long gone at St. Juniper's.

Christmas bells still hanging over the door jangled when I came in, and the smell of good food hit me in the face and made my eyes water. It was a small place—just three red Naugahyde booths and five chrome stools lining the counter. Perched on one of them was a woman in tight blue jeans and a T-shirt with the sleeves rolled up over a tattoo that said CHARLIE on her not-insignificant bicep. She was leaned back with her elbows on the counter, smoking and talking to a man hunkered over a coffee cup who was wearing a plaid shirt and an oil-stained green billed cap that said L&B TRUCKING. She waved her cigarette at me. Her hands were big and square, like a man's, the nails neatly clipped.

"Come on in, darlin'—take a load off. Sit down anywhere you want to. We got room for everybody today." Her voice was rough, like it had been left out in the rain and rusted.

"Thanks. It's good and warm in here." I smiled at her and slid into the booth farthest from the door.

"Cassie, darlin', get off the can! You got a customer!" she yelled, then turned to me. "She'll be right out. I'm Bernadette, the chef and proprietor of the joint, so when you figure out what you want, I'll go back and cook it for you."

"I'd take the burger, if I was you," the man said, flicking another ash onto a mound of butts in a big ashtray. "That's edible. Either that or the beans and corn bread. Bernadette's a fairly decent corn bread maker. Little on the heavy side, but good and solid, and it sticks to your ribs."

"I'll heavy side *you,* Snuffy Simmons!" she said, poking him in the ribs. "You would've done been dead if it wasn't for my grub, so I don't want to hear any complaints out of you."

A waitress probably not long out of high school came out from the back room. She was heavyset and big-busted, with silky fine honey-brown hair, long and parted in the middle, cornflower-blue eyes, and white, even teeth set across a wide smile. Her nose was a little on the large side with a bump in the middle, but it didn't really matter. She was the friendliest face I had seen since I left Sweet Valley.

"How're you doing this lovely day?" She put a glass of water and a menu down in front of me.

"Not too bad now. It's been a rough one, though, and I'm hungry. What's good?"

"Everything's good. Depends on what you feel like. Burgers. Fries we make ourselves—real potatoes. Chili's good and spicy. Beans and corn bread, ham hock cooked in the beans. Fried catfish. Sandwiches. You name it."

"I'll try a bowl of beans and corn bread, since it comes so highly recommended. Side order of slaw," What did it matter if I ate beans? I was going to be sleeping alone, anyhow.

Cassie picked up the menu and went back to the kitchen. The man in the trucker hat, Snuffy, I guess his name was, nodded his approval, stood up, stretched, and rolled a toothpick out of a holder on the counter.

"Well, I ain't getting any younger, so I might as well get going. I got some doing around to do before I take off tonight. You take care, Bernadette, and try not to poison nobody while I'm gone to the big bad city."

"You take care *yourself*—and try not to starve up there. You won't get good cooking like mine up in Yankee land."

"You got that right." He turned to me. "In New York, they don't even know what chicken-fried steak is, nor red-eye gravy, neither. I stay just as long as it takes to unload my truck, and then I hightail it back here to civilization."

"You're going all the way to *New York City*?"

Outside of my one meeting with Suzan Hartman at the fair, I'd never met anyone who had actually been to New York City.

"You wouldn't like it," he said, picking a piece of meat out of his teeth and spitting it onto the floor. "Lot of big tall buildings, so many people crowded together you have to stand in line just to walk down the sidewalk. You have to look straight up to even see any blue sky. Too much garbage. Too much traffic. Too much noise. Too much everything. The side streets are one-way and narrow, and it takes a genius of a driver to maneuver an eighteen-wheeler down them, which fortunately, I am."

"There's no conceit in *his* family—he got it all," Bernadette put in.

"New York cabdrivers are all nuts, too. You gotta look out for them. It's a miracle more people don't get run over, as crazy as they drive. I wouldn't get in one of those ol' yellow things if my life depended on it. In fact, *all* New Yorkers are crazy. You need to carry a gun just to protect yourself from getting mugged."

Snuffy laid some money on the counter, picked his jacket off the coat tree.

"Y'all take it easy. I'll see you when I do." He swatted Bernadette on her tight rear end and winked at me.

"That old Snuffy sure is a card," Bernadette said as the bells jangled and Snuffy slipped on his jacket as he walked toward his pickup. "Best durn truck driver L and B has, though, and not too bad at everything else, if you know what I mean." She stubbed out her cigarette. "I'll get you your dinner," she said as she went back to the kitchen. "Just kick back and relax."

It was so warm and comfy in the restaurant that I did finally begin to relax. My feet were half frozen since I hadn't had the sense to wear thick socks, so I took off the rubber boots I was wearing and rubbed my toes through my silky tights, which is kind of gross, but there wasn't anybody else in there to see me. I had just put the boots back on when Cassie came back with a big bowl of steaming brown pinto beans, rich with pieces of ham, pink and juicy, and a basket of hot corn muffins.

"Here you go, darlin'. Perfect meal for a day like this. Where'd you come in from?"

"Sweet Valley. Know where that is?"

"I think so. Down southwest from here in the River Valley?" I nodded. "That's a pretty far drive, especially in this weather. You must be worn out. If you don't mind me asking, what made you go through a snowstorm to get here?"

"I'm going up to St. Juniper's to practice teach. Classes start tomorrow."

"No kidding. My mother is the head housekeeper up there. She runs the place, if you want to know the truth. Her name is Annie Culver. We go to mass up at the abbey, too. My name is Cassie Culver, by the way." She stuck out her hand, and I shook it.

"Cherry Marshall. Good to meet you."

I dug into the beans, but Cassie obviously didn't have a whole lot to do. She sat on the stool and leaned back for a chat.

"So what teacher will you be working with?"

"Father Leo. The art teacher."

"Oh, you'll love him! He's the best teacher they have. He lets me come up and use the wheel and the kiln sometimes on the weekends. Art was the only thing I was good at in school. I graduated from Buchanan last year, but we live not far from St. Juniper's. Our family grows grapes for Freyaldenheimer's winery."

"That's great. I heard they made wine up here. Are you going to college?"

"No way. I've had enough of school. I'm going to get married." She held out her left hand to show me her ring. I squinted and just about picked out the glint of a tiny diamond in the middle of a fancy gold setting.

"That's really beautiful. Lot of fire in that diamond. Who's the lucky guy?"

"Lale Hardcastle. We been going together since tenth grade."

"That's a good long time. What's he like?"

"Good-looking. He was voted Most Handsome every year of high school. It'll be one wedding where the groom is prettier than the bride."

"I don't believe that for a minute."

"You've seen me, but you haven't seen him."

"Well, maybe I'll get a chance to. I'll be here for the rest of the semester."

"You have a boyfriend?"

"Not at the moment. I just broke up with somebody, right before Thanksgiving. Or he broke up with me. He was a good-looking guy, too, and I hate to tell you, but most of the time, those are trouble."

"Yeah, I hear you, but Lale's not like that. Maybe you'll get back together."

"Afraid not. He's married to somebody else."

"Oh. That's awful. Well, you'll find somebody better. You're too beautiful not to have a boyfriend for long."

She seemed a little embarrassed. I shouldn't have blurted it out about Tripp like that, but it was the truth, so why hide it? And frankly, I'm not sure Tripp and I would have been together anyhow. I thought I loved him, enough that he was the first guy I ever slept with, but a lot had happened since I met him last summer, and although it was a big shock at the time when I found out about Faye, his Vietnamese wife, it wasn't like I was all that devastated. If I'm honest, part of me felt relief that I didn't have to make a decision about marrying him myself, because I was in no way ready to tie myself down like that. One thing about Tripp, though—he always made me feel beautiful. Most of the time I felt like a tall, gawky freak who could never find a place to put my legs and arms, but Mama drilled into me that when somebody gives you a compliment, you don't need to spend a lot of time denying it and shuffling your feet. All you have to say is "Thank you." Otherwise, you insult their taste.

"Thank you."

"You look like you could be a model, tall like you are and all. Did you ever do any modeling?"

"I posed in a swimsuit for figure-drawing class at DuVall, but not really."

"You're prettier than most of the ones in the magazines. I used to work at the drugstore so I got to read them all when they came in. You ought to get Father Leo to take some pictures of you. He's a great photographer. He's had shows of his stuff down at the bank, and at the abbey, and even at the Art Center in Little Rock."

"Does he photograph women? I mean, that's kind of weird, a priest and all."

"Well, he mostly does landscapes and stuff, but he does women, yeah. You better realize that priests are men, Cherry, in spite of those collars. But Father Leo's okay. He's my buddy."

"Cassie!" Bernadette called out from the kitchen.

"Be right there!" She stood up and stretched. She had on a loose top, and I wondered if she was a little bit pregnant. Oh, well. So what? Same song, second verse. A lot of marriages started out that way. My own dear cousin Lucille was nearly three months gone when she and her husband, Jim Floyd Hawkins, got married, and they had a great baby named Tiffany LaDawn and were really happy. If Cassie was pregnant, it was no big deal, and maybe she wasn't. It was hard to tell, since she was a big hefty girl, almost as tall as me.

"Anyhow, don't worry about finding a boyfriend. I know a few guys up here," she said. "I'll work on it."

People in love are just obsessed with trying to spread the happiness around and fix up anybody who is single.

"Cassandra Marie Culver! These dishes ain't going to wash themselves!"

"I'm coming!" She made a face and stuck out her tongue in the direction of the kitchen. "I better get back and help Bernadette, the old slave driver. Holler if you need anything. You might try that pepper sauce on the beans. It's real good."

She shined her ring on her shirt and looked at it in the light. "It does have a little fire in it, doesn't it?" Then she sauntered on into the kitchen.

5

MOST HANDSOME

It was dim in the barn, in spite of the coal-oil lantern that warmed a pocket of the dark, and when George Hardcastle pulled open the big wooden door, a swirl of white snow came in with him and made Lale squint until the door closed and shut out the light again.

"Son, what are you doing out here in the barn? Your mama's got supper about ready. You better get on in the house and get cleaned up."

Lale lay stretched out on a pile of hay with his hands behind his head. The noise of the cows chewing their cud blended with the whine of the wind, making a strange kind of music.

"I'm not real hungry, Daddy. Y'all go on and eat. I'll get something later over at the café. Cassie's girlfriends are giving her a shower tonight, and after it's over I got to go by and pick her and the presents up and take them to her house."

"You're taking your life in your hands, boy, going to a hen party. Those girls will peck you to death!" George laughed, but Lale didn't join him.

"I feel like I've already been pecked to death." His voice was gloomy in the dark. "All Cassie talks about is curtains and mixers and which dishes and glasses to pick out. I couldn't care less what kind of plates we eat off of, or if we sleep on flowered sheets or plain."

"Well, son, you didn't have to get married. Y'all could have waited awhile."

There was silence. In the dim light, George could see Lale struggling with what he had to say. George was patient. He already knew what was coming.

"Couldn't you?"

"Oh, Daddy." The words came out like a sigh, ragged and broken. "I need to tell you something, but it's so hard."

"Try me. I might be more understanding than you think I will."

"I hate like everything to do this to you and Mama, and I know it's all my fault, but we *got* to get married. Cassie's going to have a baby."

"I done figured that one out, Lale."

"Does Mama know?"

"I think she figured, too, but she likes Cassie. How far gone is she?"

"Two months, I guess, more or less. We'll have all the hoo-rah of the wedding, and won't even get settled in until it will be more showers with baby stuff. It's just all happening too fast. The truth is, I don't even want to get married, much less be a daddy. In fact, I was thinking about breaking it off with Cassie when she dropped this load on me about the baby. I just don't know what to do, Daddy. It's eating me up. My insides feel dead. It seems like my life is already over before it even starts. I don't know if I can go through with it."

George sat down on the bale of hay next to Lale, put his hand on his son's ankle. The gentleness of the touch almost made Lale cry.

"You may not believe it right now, son, but you can. I know you can. Let me tell you something, Lale, that I never was going to tell you, and you don't have to let your mother know I did. The same thing happened to your mother and me. I was a year younger than you when we got married, and maybe I felt like you do. I wanted to go to the university and play ball, wanted to see what redheaded women were like—*any* other woman, for that matter. Your mother was the only one I'd ever been with, then or now. I had it in my mind to study to be a doctor or a lawyer or even a businessman—anything besides hardscrabble farming like my daddy. But even though I was only eighteen, I was acting like a man, and I had a man's responsibilities. If you play, you got to pay. Still and all, don't get me wrong. Not for one minute did I ever regret marrying your mother and having you and your sister, and you'll feel the same way once you hold that baby in your arms. Cassie's a good, solid girl. Things will change once the wedding's over, and you'll get used to married life. It won't be so bad. You're just scared right now, and I don't blame you."

"You mean you didn't ever wonder what it would have been like if you'd gone to the university and played ball? You never looked at a bus and wondered what it would be like to just get on it and ride to the end of the road and see what was there?"

"It don't matter whether I ever wondered or not. I had a responsibility to you and your mother, and you have a responsibility to Cassie and that baby. You forget about the end of the road, son. Right here's the end of the road." George patted his leg, two short pats, as if he was dismissing him, then got up and opened the barn door. "Don't be sulking out here with the cows," he said lightly. "It'll sour their milk."

Lale tried to smile. "You go on in. I'll be there directly." As the barn door closed, the smile crumpled. He might have been acting like a man, but the boy he felt inside sobbed big greasy tears.

Unlike his father, Lale had already had other women besides Cassie. Quite a few others, including a friend of his mother's who had been his first, when he was fourteen. Sandra was a divorced blonde who had been a cheerleader with his mother, Janet, in high school. She dropped by for a visit one afternoon when Janet was out shopping with Lale's little sister, Brenda. He couldn't really say how it happened, but before she was there fifteen minutes they were up in his room with all their clothes off. He doubted many boys his age had an initiation like that one, and as much as he wanted to, he didn't dare tell his friends about it. She was the mother of one of them. They still saw each other once in a while, if the truth were told. Amazing what you could get away with if you just kept your mouth shut.

Cassie was different from most of the ones he went out with, though. She was a good Catholic girl and they had gone together over two years before he finally wore her down and she let him go all the way. It was a late-summer night, and surprisingly the aurora borealis lit up the sky. That was something rare that you almost never saw this far south. He told her it was a sign from God that it would be all right, but by that time she didn't really need much selling. Part of the problem of being a good Catholic girl, however, was that she wouldn't hear of him using a rubber, and he now saw what a fool he had been to keep on with her under those circumstances. She tried to use the rhythm method, but got pregnant after only a few months.

He winced when he remembered the night she told him. They were parked out by the bluffs, and it still made him sick at his stomach to remember it.

"I got something to tell you, darlin', and I don't know how you're going to take it," she had said in a small voice.

They were lying comfortably in the backseat of his Thunderbird, their clothes draped across the seat back in front of them. Cassie played with the thick mat of hair on his chest, running her fingers through it, which gave him goose bumps. That hairy chest had sprung out by the time he was in the eleventh grade, and the boys on the football team all kidded him about it. "Too much juice makes you hairy, Hardcastle," they'd said. "Better unload some of it." Whether they were right or not, he'd done the best he could to do just that.

"Do I really want to know?" He knew he didn't.

"That depends. But one way or the other, you'll find out, so let me just make it short and sweet. I'm pregnant."

Cold shock went through his veins. It's not like he never thought it *could* happen—it just hadn't seemed like it would. Nobody else he had been with had ever gotten pregnant, not to his knowledge anyhow. He even thought he might be sterile, since he'd had a bad case of the mumps when he was seven.

"Are you sure?"

"Oh, yeah. I'm sure. I went to the doctor in Fayetteville and there's no doubt."

"Why didn't you tell me?"

"I am telling you."

"Look, Cassie, let's think about this for a minute. Let's talk about it. You don't have to go through with it. There's ways to stop it. I know of a girl who . . ."

She interrupted him. "You're not talking about an abortion, are you, Lale Hardcastle? Because if you are, I pray that God would strike you dead right here in this car. Besides being illegal, it's murder and I am not killing this baby! If you don't want to marry me, that's fine—I'll have it by myself." She sat up and started putting on her brassiere.

"I didn't say I didn't want to marry you."

"You didn't say you did. In fact, the first thing you thought of was getting rid of it."

"Don't be like that, Cassie. It was just a shock. Of course I want to marry you."

He tried to put his arms around her, but she pushed him away. It took him ten whole minutes to get her to look at him.

"Cassie, look at me. I want to marry you. I really do. We'll go to Father Leo and start it up. It'll be all right."

He took her chin in his hand and forced her to look into his eyes. It was hard not to melt when Lale looked you in the eyes. Cassie threw her arms around him. With her face pressed into his neck, she didn't notice that he was staring out the back window, those baby-blue eyes a shade deader.

"Have you told your mother and daddy?"

"Not yet," she sniffed, pulling away from him and wiping her eyes. "I thought we'd tell them together. We don't have to tell them about the baby. Just that we're getting married. Lots of babies are born in seven or eight months."

"All right. Just give me a day or two to tell mine."

"Lale . . ."

"What?"

"Nothing."

"What?"

"You never have said 'I love you' to me. Not one time. Are you really sure you want to marry me? Because if you don't, baby or not, then I don't want to marry you."

"I love you, Cassie. I do. It's just hard for me to say. I'm not much of a talker—you know how I am." He put his arms around her. "It'll be all right."

His mouth said it, but his eyes didn't. Cassie saw it, but for now, the mouth part was enough. The eyes part would have to come later.

6

THE BEST ATTIC

Ron Bonetti wasn't kidding—he called Liz and booked me for a whole afternoon! Just having a real test booked gave me the lift I needed, so I called the woman Lana had said might have an apartment for rent, Mrs. Digby, and she said for me to come by.

The house was on West Twelfth Street, a pretty, tree-lined block in Greenwich Village. It was an old five-story red-brick walk-up with a little courtyard in the back. The first thing you saw as you entered was a flight of steep stairs centered with a strip of faded carpet that must have been a nice Oriental at one time. Mrs. Digby lived on the ground level, to the right of the stairs. The place was going toward shabby, furnished with an old green velvet couch, its down cushions a little punched out, a couple of faded chintz armchairs, and a reading lamp. Cream and rose-coral flowered wallpaper was marked with water stains, weathered over the years to a soft brown, which had become almost part of the design. It was homey.

Mrs. Digby met me at the door, shading her eyes as she looked up at me. She was about the size of Baby. Mrs. Digby had undoubtedly been taller in her youth, but she hadn't been young for several decades, and now her back was beginning to bend into a widow's hump, which made me think unkindly of a turtle poking its head out of a shell. I made a mental note to drink more milk. She smiled with a full mouthful of teeth that must have been perfect once, but were now worn to a translucent pale yellow.

"My goodness, you are a big one!" Her voice was high and crackly like a parrot's. Her hair, so thin that streaks of white scalp showed through, was dyed coal black and pulled into a tight, small knot on the top of her head. Her nose had the narrow scooped-out bridge and skinny nostrils of one of the first nose jobs ever done, and the tip had traveled off a bit to the left of center with age. Still, it was obvious she had once been pretty, and she cared enough about herself to put on, rather expertly, bright peony-pink lipstick and a dab of pale powder.

I hate it when people say the obvious about me the first time I meet them, but I didn't want to start off on the wrong foot with her.

"Yes, I guess I am big. You must be Mrs. Digby?"

"I am Mrs. Digby. Beatrice Digby. Come in, my dear, and let's chat." She poured out two cups of tea from a porcelain teapot and passed me the sugar bowl.

"You are a model?"

"Yes, ma'am. I mean, yes, I am. Trying to be one."

"First time away from home?"

"Not really. I lived at a school for a few months last spring. But this is the first time in New York."

"Oh, you'll love it here. New York is the only place for young attractive people to live. I grew up in New Jersey, near the shore, but came here when I was just a teenager—fourteen, if you want to know the truth. I had to lie, of course. I used to be on Broadway, a dancer. I was a Ziegfeld girl—can you believe it?"

I could believe it and said so. Even with her bent little back, she walked with a graceful step, like a dancer.

"I danced with Evelyn Nesbit—do you know who that was?"

"No, ma'am, I'm sorry."

"Never mind. It was a long time ago. Old history. You seem like a good girl. I can always tell. I'm a little bit psychic, you know. It helps when you have to invite people to live in your home. I have a vacancy on the top floor. It's not big, and you only have a hot plate and a small refrigerator, but you have your own bathroom. No pets. There's nothing worse than dogs and cats peeing on the carpet. You can never get the smell out, no matter what you use to clean it. I hate that. One girl sneaked a dog in here, and the nasty thing peed on the couch and I had to get it recovered. I could smell it all the way out in the hallway. I might be old, but my smeller is perfect. Of course I had to ask her to leave. It's seventy-five dollars a month, first month in advance."

It sounded high, since you could rent a three-bedroom house in Arkansas for that. I had to slow down on spending, as it looked like I wasn't going to start making money right away. If ever. I had even thought about maybe trying to find a job as a salesgirl or waitress somewhere, but would wait until I absolutely had to. I was determined not to have to ask Daddy for money. He would just say come home.

"I'd like to see it first, if that's all right."

We climbed the five flights of stairs, and I was huffing while Mrs. Digby, spry as could be, was not even breathing hard when we got to the last one. I'd always tried to stay away from exercise as much as I could, especially anything that had to do with running and balls, but I'd get into shape in spite of myself just walking around town and going up and down to my room.

We entered the apartment from the landing at the top of the stairs through a walk-in closet, which was weird but nice to have, and then we had to stoop through a door which was only five feet high, because of the slope of the roof, to go on into the room. Well, I had to stoop. Mrs. Digby had no such problem, but I cracked my head a good one on the top of the door. I actually saw stars, like in the cartoons.

"Watch out, dear," she said too late. "That is a low door."

The room had been walled off from the apartment on the other side, necessitating the odd entry through the closet, and was almost like a secret chamber in the peak of the house. It was not more than three or four hundred feet square, full of odd nooks and crannies, one of which held the small fridge with the hot plate on top. There was a bed, a Persian rug in muted colors of henna and moss green, old ivory and blue, a chest of drawers, and a small mirrored dressing table shaped like a kidney with a skirt and a stool covered in worn tapestry. A dark-red velvet easy chair and a lamp for reading were in another nook. The roof slanted on both sides, and the only place I could comfortably stand upright was the middle of the room. I would sleep with the ceiling jutting up right over my feet, and hunker down every time I went in or out through the closet. I made a mental note to put foam padding on the top of the door. I knew there were more head-bangs in my future.

The bathroom, just big enough for a claw-foot tub, toilet, and tiny sink, was built into a round corner turret with a heavy tapestry curtain instead of a door, and the ceiling was like a high peaked hat. I could stand up straight! I had always preferred baths to showers, the hotter the better. You can't soak and read and relax out the kinks in a shower. As small and quirky as it was, the apartment was like a storybook house, Rapunzel's castle. A tall window showed off a view of treetops and roofs across Greenwich Village. And it was all mine!

"This is so great, Mrs. Digby! I love it. When can I move in?"

"As soon as you want, dear."

As we started down the stairs, the door of the other apartment that mine had been walled off from opened and a man came out carrying a leather shoulder bag. A black man. A tall black man. Well, technically, he was the color of rich chocolate milk. A headband of red and orange and green African print was wrapped around his short Afro, and he was dressed in a tight red knit shirt and fringed leather vest, worn shiny in spots; bell-bottoms were molded like faded blue skin tight across his rear end. He saw me and grinned. It was like a two-hundred-watt lightbulb came on in the hallway. He had the whitest teeth I'd ever seen, perfectly lined up under a little pencil mustache. I felt like my shoes had melted and stuck to the floor.

"Hello, Mrs. D.," he said, his voice deep and smooth like suede. "Who is this?"

"It's the new girl who's taking over Leslie's apartment," Mrs. Digby chirped. "Cherry Marshall, this is Aurelius Taylor. He is a fine actor and musician. Aurelius, Cherry is going to be a big model."

"I don't doubt your word for a minute," he said, looking me over, his eyes the color of brimstone. I got a weird tingle in my lower regions that I hadn't felt since I'd first met Tripp Barlow. "Mrs. D. is psychic, you know, Cherry. Welcome to the attic. This part of the house was the old servants' quarters, when one family owned it back in the early eighteen-hundreds."

"Really? I think it has to be the best part of the house."

"Me, too. Anyhow, welcome. If you need anything, I'm right across the way. Just knock on the wall."

That was comforting. I was sure I'd think of something I needed.

He loped down the stairs, two at a time, humming a little tune. I felt like humming, too.

I packed up all my clothes and moved from the Barbizon that afternoon. It was autumn in New York, and I was in love with everything—Greenwich Village, its curving streets with names like Bleecker and Jane and Hudson, the small shops that sold antiques, pottery, jewelry, and Indian imports, the exotic smells of spices and sauces and sizzling meats that wafted out of foreign-food restaurants as you passed, the long-haired hippies and the Rastafarians who sold incense and small paintings and old clothes on tables on the streets—it was all so alive and exciting!

Most of all, I was in love with the attic on Twelfth Street, with its eccentric old ex-showgirl landlady and sexy neighbor. And I had a test booked! There was a possibility that I might become a model. A real one.

I couldn't wait for tomorrow to see what would happen next!

7

THE HEN PARTY

The parking lot of Flyin' Jack's Truck Stop was crowded with cars as Lale pulled up and parked off to the edge, under a stand of trees. He cut the engine, but left the key in to listen to the radio. He was earlier than he meant to be, but he hadn't felt like having supper with his family and facing his mother. There was no way his father wouldn't have told her the news. He ate a burger and fries at the Dairy Queen, then picked up a couple of six-packs at Chet's Quick Stop. Chet was good about letting kids get beer if he liked them. He said that if a fellow was man enough to fight in a war at eighteen, he was man enough to have a beer or two. He had fought in World War I, himself, and liked telling his war stories to the boys. There was always a new crop of boys who hadn't heard his stories and courted him to get beer.

"How're they hanging, Lale?" he said as Lale put the cans down on the counter.

"Hanging loose, Chet. What's up with you?"

"Same old, same old. Arthritis chewing on me, but that's nothing new. My back's never been the same, you know, since I took the bullet in France." He punched the numbers into the cash register. The drawer opened with a hard *ka-ching*. His hand trembled slightly as he counted out the change. His long-sleeved flannel shirt was buttoned tightly around the knobby bone of his wrist. "Don't guess you've got your calling card from the draft yet, have you?"

"Naw. You know I got a high draft number. Three hundred and ten. If I'm lucky, they won't get up to me until the dang thing's over."

"You better hope so. If Vietnam's anything like it was over in France during WW One, you better *dang* hope so. Did I ever tell you about the time me and two of my buddies got cut off from the rest of the battalion, and I lost my gas mask?"

"You might have said something about it." In fact, Lale had heard it all a few too many times. Chet sat down on the stool behind the counter, the change in his hand, getting ready to settle in for a good long visit. Business had been slow that night, and the old man got lonesome with nothing to do but read *The National Enquirer* or *Grit,* but Lale wasn't in the mood for war stories tonight. He reached out and took the bills from the old man's hand.

"I wish I could stay for a spell and shoot the breeze, Chet, but I got to go pick up Cassie, and I'm running late."

"Aw, that's all right, Lale. I'll catch you another time. When is it y'all are getting married?"

"I guess in a couple of weeks. They're giving her a shower tonight out at the café."

"She's a good little girl. You're a lucky man."

"That I am, my friend. That I am. See you, Chet. Don't do nothing I wouldn't do."

He didn't feel like a lucky man. It was all he could do to smile as he stuffed the money into his pocket and picked up the beer. He thought about trying to find one of his buddies to kill time with before he had to pick up Cassie, or driving by Sandra's to see if she was alone, but couldn't get himself up for it. He needed to get away from people and think things through. Sitting by himself in his car and waiting for the bridal shower to be over wouldn't be so bad. He'd collect his thoughts, have a few beers, and get nicely oiled before he had to face the giggling girlfriends and lug the load of presents out.

The radio was picking up WLS in Chicago, as it did sometimes on clear nights, and his favorite song, "House of the Rising Sun," blasted into the night air. It had finally stopped snowing and the stars were out. He stretched his legs across the front seat and popped the top on another can of Bud, chugged half of it down. This shower thing was taking longer than he'd thought it would. Before too many more songs had played, he'd had a pretty good start on the first six-pack, and a couple of swigs drained another can. He tossed it onto the back floorboard of the cream-colored '59 Thunderbird, where it clanked against three others. He'd clean them out sooner or later. Or more likely, Cassie would. She didn't like beer cans in the car. It would be her car, too, he realized, after they were married, and he could see her making him scrub it and wash and wax it all the time. That was one thing she went way overboard on, cleaning stuff up. He could see her nagging him about putting his clothes away and throwing his wet towels on the floor. His mother just griped and picked up after him like she always had, but he bet Cassie wouldn't after they were married. He thought about the little apartment they had already put a deposit down on. It only had a small living room, one little bedroom, and a kitchenette, and there wouldn't even be a place for his gun rack. Cassie had already said she didn't want him bringing his ten-point buck head to hang on the wall. The glass eyes creeped her out. After the baby came, there wouldn't be room for anything but baby stuff. He felt as if he were already being smothered under piles of dirty diapers and baby puke. His gloom settled in deeper.

He was on the verge of becoming a little unstarched, but he didn't care; if worse came to worst, Cassie would drive. She hated it when he drank, but he needed a little something to take the edge off, and what else was there to do while he waited? He couldn't go in and ooh and ahh over toasters and pot-scrubbers.

A few more songs played, another couple of beers went down. It seemed like those girls were going to take forever. He got out and stretched, walked into the shadows and peed behind a tree, then decided to sneak a look in the window and see how close to being done they were. He walked, a little wobbly, toward the window, his cowboy boots squeaking in the snow, took a few deep breaths to clear his head, then looked into the restaurant. Cassie was sitting in the middle of a circle of girls, opening presents. A big pile of paper was mounded up beside her, and on her head was a crown of bright-colored ribbons, rescued from the wrappings and braided together by one of her friends. She pulled a black lace nightgown out of a box, and everyone squealed as she stood up and held it in front of herself, wiggling her hips in a lewd vampy dance. They all roared with laughter. She was so happy. He had never seen the look she had on her face now as she pranced around with the black lace nightgown and the hat of ribbons. To his surprise, it made him feel sad. Maybe he just didn't know how to put that look on her face. She didn't laugh a lot around him. It was like she was always looking out of the corner of her eye to see how he would react before she said or did anything, waiting to see if he would approve of her or not. He guessed he did criticize her more than he ought to, but she should know it was for her own good; if she would just lose some weight she would be the beautiful girl she was when they first started going out in the tenth grade. In the last few years she had packed on a lot of pounds. Try as he did to get her to lay off the fries and milk shakes and go on a diet, she didn't seem to lose an ounce, and in fact she had gained quite a bit more in just the last month. She would be as big as a house before this baby was born. It seemed like she ate just to spite him. He didn't like to admit it, even to himself, but he had gotten a little ashamed of Cassie. When the two of them walked into places, people stared at them like they were wondering why someone as good-looking as him would be with a fat girl. When they were alone, though, she was sweet, and it was so good and easy to be with someone who adored you no matter what you did, who you could relax around and didn't have to put on any show for. And in the dark, Cassie was soft and warm and smelled like rich loamy earth, like bread fresh out of the oven; her skin felt like the smoothest creamy deerskin, buttery and lush. A man could fall into a woman like that and never make his way out, and it seemed like that was just what had happened to him.

Still, the one thing you can't make yourself do is fall in love, and Lale just didn't love Cassie. The old line "You deserve someone better than me" in this case was not just an old line. She did. She deserved somebody who would love her and take care of her and he knew he never would. He was cheating on her now, every chance he got, and he knew that wasn't likely to change after the wedding. Maybe he was one of those guys who just couldn't be true to one woman and would never fall in love at all. He hadn't up to now.

His stomach lurched and he felt a little sick. He thought of all his young years stretching before him, walking into places with Cassie, them getting older, her getting fatter and fatter. In his mind she was blowing up to the size of a circus freak, and he was smothering in her flesh, getting sucked into the quicksand of her swamps. He imagined them in their tiny apartment, packed together like chickens in a crate, surrounded by a dozen kids, all screaming and calling him Daddy. Cassie would never use birth control. She was too Catholic. He rubbed his eyes to clear the image. He had to get out of there. He'd drive around for a while, sober up, and maybe they'd be done with the presents when he came back.

Just as he got back into his car, a pickup pulled into the yard of Flyin' Jack's garage next to the café. Lale turned to see Snuffy Simmons park, get out, and head toward his eighteen-wheeler. He opened the back to check on the cargo, which looked to be a load of boxes of something or other, and then Bernadette appeared out the back door of the café, carrying a sack and a thermos. Lale couldn't hear what they were saying, but they stood close together and then kissed. Snuffy cupped her butt in his hand, and she snuggled up to him. Then he pulled her by the hand and they went into the garage, dark now after everyone had gone home. Bernadette's laugh rang out silver in the cold night air.

The back of the big truck was still open, and Lale went over to take a look. The boxes marked with Freyaldenheimer's wine labels were stacked high, but there was quite a bit of room left. Enough for a man to lie down fairly comfortably. He stood staring for a minute, his heart pounding. An idea was catching hold of him. He went back to his car, rummaged around, and found an old gas receipt and a stub of a pencil in the glove compartment. He was nervous and excited—his fingers felt thick as he wrote and the beer had his brain working in slow motion—but he didn't have any reason to lie to her at this point.

Dear Cassie,

I am leaving out tonight. You deserve someone much better than me. You are a good girl and I would only cause you a lot of misery. That's a fact. I know that you will be mad at me, because I am mad at myself, but in the long run you will thank me for this. You can have my car. Tell my daddy to give you the title, and tell him I'll be in touch when I find out where I will be. Think about what I said about taking care of the "problem." Bernadette will know what to do. If you decide to do it, I'll try to send some money for it when I get a job, or you can sell the car if you need to. It's not too late for either one of us now, but it will be soon. Take care of yourself, and have a good life. Try not to hate me too much. I would say I love you, but it doesn't much seem like I do, does it?

Lale

He laid the note on the seat, underneath the keys. The girls were still giggling and eating chocolate cake as he passed by the window. All he had on him was twenty-two dollars in his billfold, another six-pack, and the clothes on his back, but he couldn't go home. His daddy would know something was up if he came in and tried to pack, and by then Snuffy would be long gone. His mother would be crazy with worry, and he hated that, but he would think what to do about them later. He knew he should feel guilty, but the only thing he felt was exhilaration and a sense of relief, like a bird looking at an open cage door.

He hoisted himself into the back of the semi and settled down near the front of the cargo, where he'd be less likely to be seen, on an old piece of padding he found between the stacks of wine cases. It was cold, but not too bad in out of the wind. He didn't know where Snuffy was going, but he figured he would sneak out whenever he stopped, and hitch a ride with somebody else before Snuffy could see him and tell Bernadette and Cassie what had happened. Maybe he could make it to California. He always thought he might like to try his hand at being a surfer. Or a movie star.

It was a long way to the end of the road, but finally Lale was going to see what was there.

8

THE FIRST TEST

Ron had said for me to bring a lot of different outfits and accessories, so I just packed a big bag with whatever came to hand, not having the foggiest idea what he was going to do. I had scarves, hats, sunglasses, a long granny dress made out of white gauze that looked kind of like a nightgown, and several miniskirts and matching tights. The bag was so heavy I couldn't carry it on the subway, so I took the metaphorical rubber band off my shrinking wad and hailed a taxi. I was still a little amazed that I could stand on the street, hold out my hand, and, like magic, a taxi would pull over and stop. I remembered what Snuffy Simmons had said back at Flyin' Jack's, about all New York cabdrivers being crazy, and I always compared them to their pictures and took careful note of their names and cab numbers on the piece of paper in the window in case one of them did something weird. I had been warned about hitchhiking all my life, and to get in a car with a stranger went against my instincts, but if they had a picture of themselves right there on a license, it probably was all right. They did drive pretty fast, though, most of them, and sometimes I had to hang on to the strap to keep from falling on the floor when they went around a corner.

The studio was different from the way it was that first day—well, obviously, there were no naked men, but also Ron had hung a big piece of seamless paper from the ceiling and set lights up all around it. Over to the side was a table with a bottle of wine and glasses, a bowl of fruit, and a platter of cheese and crackers. I wondered if it was for us to eat, or leftovers from some *Good Housekeeping* picture.

"This is going to be *tremendous,*" Ron said, coming out of the back room. "Now let me tell you what we're doing. There's a new magazine called *Rouge* and the art director likes me. I think I can work for them. It's a sexy magazine for women, a little tuned toward the avant-garde artsy stuff, no nudity, well, not much; maybe they'll have a nude guy as a centerfold—just kidding, don't get nervous—but serious political articles while still being fashion-oriented. Somewhere between *Vogue* and *Cosmo*. I want to put together a presentation for them, and I want *you* to be it. Okay?"

"Okay. Wow. Sure. That's great!"

I was going to be a presentation for a magazine! I had never been photographed in a real studio in my life, and just seeing the blank seamless paper and all the lights made me a little nervous. In fact, I didn't know the backgrounds for all the pictures, like the ones Avedon did for *Vogue,* were even paper. I had practiced posing like the models in magazines in the mirror, of course, but never in front of anyone. I hoped I wouldn't embarrass myself.

"We're going to do this thing right," he enthused. "I have a terrific makeup and hair man here. He will make you gorgeous—not that you're not already gorgeous, but gorgeous-er. Sal, come on out! Cherry's here!"

A tall, slender man with short-cropped black hair came out from the dressing room. He was dressed all in black, his shirt buttoned right up to the neck, and wore big round glasses with black-and-white-checked frames and pale purple lenses, ones like Elton John, the guy from England who had just come out with a great record called "Your Song," would wear.

"Salvador de Vega, meet Cherry Marshall."

"Hi, Salvador. Nice to meet you."

"Oh, my God! Is *this* the Cherry you told me so much about! *Who* walks on water? Look at you! You are in*credible*! Ron, you didn't tell me you had something like this fabulous creature coming in! My darling, you are just to *die! To die!* That hair! Those eyes! Those *legs*! They go on for *miles*!" I had a fleeting impression of a flock of flamingos as he spoke, hands fluttering like wings.

"Hold on, Sal. Let the girl catch her breath. Do you want some coffee or tea, Cherry? I have some stuff to eat, so if you get hungry, just let me know."

"I'm okay, thanks."

I had never seen anybody remotely like Sal, who was wearing red nail polish and the biggest rhinestone bracelet I had ever seen, and it looked like he had on eyeliner. I couldn't take my eyes off him. He had a small head and a long slender neck that was a little snakelike, and he moved in a graceful dancer-ish way when he walked. He had perfect big white teeth and a way of throwing his head back and opening his eyes wide that somehow reminded me of Little Richard. And I sure had never been gushed over like that. I couldn't take it seriously. He probably said that kind of thing to all the models.

"Well, if you get hungry, we can take a break anytime," Ron said. "I have a couple of great ideas for shots, but let's see what you brought."

I opened my bag, and he went through all the stuff, picking out a long red-and-white Indian-print scarf and my gauze dress. In addition, he had a pink baseball cap, another hat with a clear plastic green visor, and a whole box of glittery costume jewelry.

"This is going to be so great. We'll start with the red-and-white scarf, Sal. Our girl from Arkansas is going to be a smash."

"Arkansas? *Arkansas!* That is so *amazing*!" Sal exclaimed. Sal exclaimed nearly everything. "I have a *boyfriend* from Arkansas! But I'm sure you wouldn't know him."

"Probably not. Arkansas is kind of a big place." Nobody *I* knew would be Sal's boyfriend. Maybe somebody from Little Rock.

"Well, never mind. He's the kind you don't bring home to Mother, anyhow. I also had a boyfriend from Nashville, which is *cheek by jowl,* as they say, to Arkansas, a country singer, but that didn't work out. I'm sure I'm not telling you anything you don't already know, but, honey, those southern boys are *big* trouble—take it from me. Unfortunately, I have always rushed toward trouble, like a moth to the proverbial *flame.* I just can't seem to stay away from bad boys. Why, just last week at Max's Kansas City, you know Max's Kansas City, I'm sure . . ."

I shook my head.

"Oh, *well,* then you'll have to come out with us one night and *play.* Max's is the most groovy fun place in New York! Or maybe we could all go to Maxwell's Plum, with all those wonderful Tiffany lights—it's the most *beautiful* fun place in New York—or to Corso's up on Eighty-sixth Street and dance! You would love it. Tito Puente plays up there, and it is the most, *most* fun, all those Latin types, dark and sexy . . ."

"Okay, gang, let's get started," Ron said, cutting him off. I had a feeling I would hear all about what happened last week at Max's Kansas City anyhow.

We all went into the dressing room, Sal hardly taking time to draw breath, giving me the list of the best places to party in New York. There was a long table surrounded by lights that was laid out with Sal's makeup box, a lot like a huge fishing-tackle box with tiers of little compartmented drawers full of all kinds of makeup and creams, brushes and combs and curling irons and different-colored wigs and hairpieces stuck to Styrofoam heads lined in a row, and tons of other beauty stuff that I'd never even dreamed of. Sal turned on the radio, blasting out a Sly and the Family Stone song. He tied a ribbon around my head to hold the hair back, then he starting dancing around to the music, at the same time getting out a huge jar of cold cream and rubbing it on my face.

"I want to thank you fallettinme be mice elf agin, uh, huh," he sang to the music. "Now let's see what's under all this goo, Miss Cherry. We have to start with a clean face, you know."

I had put on makeup before I left the apartment, because that's what I did every day when I got up, rain or shine, and nobody had told me I shouldn't. I probably wouldn't have gone on the subway without makeup even if they had told me not to wear any, though—my naked face looked like a bowl of oatmeal with two green grapes stuck in the middle, and I would never ever go out in public like that.

"Let's get those eyelashes off, sweetie, and . . . oh my goodness! Look at this! Are those *real*?" He had just wiped cream over my eyebrows, which had started to come back in white, but were splotchy, so I still brushed mascara on them.

"Yes, they're real. So is my hair."

"*It is?* That is *so amazing*. And these brows! You have such *great* eyebrows! So thick, like a white wolf! Why are they two colors? Have they been dyed?"

"Well, yes, but I'm letting the dark grow out."

"I'll take care of that, sweetie. We'll just take out what's left of that dark color, and then you'll have the best brows in New York City. Whatever were you thinking, dying these gorgeous things?"

He carefully brushed some bleach or whatever on my brows and in a few minutes they were pure snowy white.

"Fabulous! Oh my God! This is going to be *so great*! I'll just prune them a little, but we still want that wolf look . . ." Out came the tweezers and it hurt like the dickens, but they were pruned. I was a little shocked when I saw myself in the mirror, but it didn't look all that bad at all. I couldn't wait to show them to Suzan, who seemed to have an overly attentive interest in them.

It took him over an hour to get the makeup on, between dancing and posing and sips of wine, and telling me about all his boyfriends and a long list of the big stars I would meet at Max's Kansas City, like Andy Warhol and Robert Rauschenberg, Mick Jagger and Dennis Hopper, which I didn't know whether to believe or not. I did my own makeup in five minutes in the morning, but he did a lot more than I ever did. He mixed liquid makeup in his palm with lotion and rubbed and wiped and mixed and put more, then powdered, blushed my cheeks, powdered some more, outlined my lips with a pencil and then took a small brush and stroked it over several different lipstick tubes, daubing one color here, another there, until he had painted my whole mouth. You'd have thought it was the size of a truck tire, the time it took. Then he brushed on layers of eye shadow, one tiny brushstroke at a time, stood back with pursed lips and did another little stroke, taking so long that my bottom got numb and I nearly went into a coma. At last he noticed I was tilting a little.

"Need a little boost, darling?" he said, taking me by the shoulders and straightening me in the chair. "Want a sip of coffee? You'll have to be careful if you drink anything. We don't want to ruin those luscious lips."

I shook my head, and tried to wake up. I didn't want to ruin my lipstick and have to have him do it all over again, either. Sal then finished off with false eyelashes, individually placed, a hair at a time, touched up the liner some more, then brushed my hair back into a little ponytail and wrapped the big red-and-white scarf around my head and neck, like a nun's habit. All you could see was my face. Ron came in.

"How're we doing in here? Wow! Look at you, Cherry!"

I turned and looked in the mirror and didn't recognize myself. My skin and the white of the fabric were close to the same, and my lips were like the old Revlon Cherries in the Snow color my mother used to wear, but with rich deep shiny red layers of burgundy and rust and purple that glistened and made my mouth look bigger and perfect. My eyes were dramatic and black-lashed, iridescent peacock colors of green and blue on the lids, making my green eyes glow. But my eyebrows were the wildest part—stunning white, brushed up, blending so as to be almost invisible from a distance. I thought of Da Vinci and his *Mona Lisa* model who didn't have any eyebrows. I always wondered if the style back in those days was to pick them all out, or if Mona was just a girl who happened to be eyebrowless. Actually, hardly any of Da Vinci's women had eyebrows. Maybe Da Vinci just didn't like to paint them.

They led me out to the lights and put me on a stool.

"Okay, Cherry, look right into the lens of the camera. That's where you make eye contact with the viewer. When someone looks at this picture, they will be looking you right in the eye, right into your soul, and you into theirs. You will be connected, soul to soul, with the thousands of people who see this photograph. . . . That's it! Don't move!"

He did a Polaroid, which he wouldn't let me see, then adjusted the lights, did another Polaroid, adjusted again, then another one, until he liked what he saw, then he dragged over another big camera on a tripod and shot and shot and shot, taking the back off the camera each time he finished a roll, quickly putting on another back that was already loaded with film. That was handy. I had never seen a camera like that before. It must have cost a fortune. I think ol' Ron was doing a little better with his food pictures than he let on.

I was nearly paralyzed anyhow from sitting in the makeup chair so long, and now to have to sit some more without moving was torture. I was dying to get up and run around the room. I gazed into the camera's eye and tried to connect with the souls that would be seeing it, and look sexy or happy or sophisticated or whatever he told me to look like, which was hard because I felt like a mummy, all draped in the scarf like that.

Sal stood off to the side, wineglass in hand, giving me encouragement with oohs and aahs, and came over periodically to dust a little powder on my face or add a stroke of gloss to my lips.

"Okay. We got it," Ron said after ages and I don't know how many rolls of film. I was so relieved to be through. I was ready to go home and get a cheeseburger. Then he said, "Let's try another one. This time, Sal, do the makeup less dramatic. Pale lips, not red. More girl-next-door."

Back I went to the dressing room, and as Simon and Garfunkel sang "Bridge over Troubled Water," Sal took off my makeup with cold cream and started all over again.

This time, I had pearly-pink-colored lips and a pink shadow on my lids. He let me keep the lashes; my eyebrows again were au naturel. He fluffed my hair out and put on a pink-and-white-striped baseball cap, and tied a pink bandanna around my neck. All of this took another hour and a half with more wine and dancing, then he brought me back to the stool in front of the camera. Ron handed me an ice cream cone. About time. I was starving.

"No! Don't eat that! You'll ruin your lips! It's for the shot."

"Can I eat it when the shot is over?"

"Yes, when the shot is over."

I looked into the camera's eye and held the ice cream cone, strawberry, it was, while it melted and ran down my arm. When I tried to move, Ron said, "Don't move! It's perfect! Let it drip! Yes!"

It dripped until there was no ice cream left, then he took the soggy cone and tossed it into the trash while I went to the bathroom to wash, then back to the dressing room for another makeup. At this point, I was ready for a cup of coffee, but only got a couple of swigs before Sal started in again.

The next shot was me in the green cap with the plastic visor, holding a green apple. I wanted a bite of that so much my mouth watered, but it would have messed up my new coral lips. Ron took a bite out of it and put it in my hand as I sat still as a statue on the chair. By this time I had exhausted all my sexy and happy looks but he kept on shooting. More rolls of film. More orders from Ron:

"Move the little finger a hair to the right. Open the lips just a little. Too much. Look over to the right. To the left. Move the head down a bit. Up a bit. Not so much. Perfect! Don't move!"

I hated the way he talked about me *to* me like I was a guy moving some dummy in a department store or something. *The finger. The lips.* Couldn't he at least say *your* finger or lips? I was beginning to get a cramp in my arm, holding the apple in one position.

"Oh, shi . . . er, rat doodies! The apple is turning brown. Sal! Come and eat off the brown part!"

Sal dutifully took it from my hand, ate off the brown part, and washed it down with a slug of wine.

After another hour of makeup with gold-colored lips and lids, we did some of me in the gauzy dress with my hair picked out and ratted into a huge white Afro. Finally, it was over and I could move. I was totally exhausted. Who would have thought getting your picture taken was so much work? I had no idea if Ron liked what I had done or not. I went back to the dressing room, and sat in the chair. Sal packed up, kissed me good-bye, and left, saying he would call me to plan some fun dance evening, but I couldn't move. For some reason I wanted to cry. I didn't know what modeling would be like. It was hard.

Then Ron came in with a glass of white wine and handed it to me. I had never drunk a glass of wine in my life, but I didn't want him to know that, after our conversation in the coffee shop about the church. I felt far away from home and the church that preached if you had one single glass of wine or a beer it was down the chute to the flames for you, and at the wedding in Cana, Jesus changed the water into grape juice. At this point, I had a real hard time believing that God would send me to burn in hell for having a beverage, so I took a big gulp. It was like drinking a swig of tart grapes, and I couldn't help but make a sour face, which I don't think Ron saw. Then I took a smaller sip and after a few more sips it wasn't so bad, and in fact I began to relax.

"You were terrific, Cherry. I didn't tell you, but I'm going to try for a cover. Wouldn't that be wild if you got a cover from your first test?"

It would be a miracle. I was excited, but I was sure there were a lot more girls trying for that cover. Frankly, I had never heard of *Rouge* magazine. It couldn't be much of a magazine, not like the big ones. But maybe because it was new they would take a chance on somebody new. I tried not to hope too much.

"It was great, Ron." Now that it was over, it had been great. "I hope we got some good ones. Do you think we did?" At least I would have some real pictures for my book.

"Oh, yeah. We got some good ones. Lots of good ones." He put down his glass and picked up a guitar. He started strumming "Yesterday" by the Beatles, and all of a sudden I felt light and happy. Maybe it was the wine. I was still wearing the gauze dress, which brushed my ankles. I got up, stretched, and started dancing in my bare feet around two white chairs that were in front of the window. For a little while I was so lost in stretching and moving my tired arms and legs that I hardly noticed the music had stopped. Ron had picked up a smaller camera and was taking pictures of me as I danced, silhouetted against the soft afternoon light coming through the window. After a while, I realized what he was doing, but it felt so good that I didn't stop. We weren't a bossy photographer and a mannequin taking stiff posed pictures any longer. We were artists making art.

Art, I understood.

9

THE GOOD-TIME GIRL

Snuffy drove through the night, and just before sunrise, rolled into a truck stop on Interstate 70 near the Indiana border. Lale woke up, disoriented, in the pitch-black of the truck and realized the vibration of the wheels had stopped, but he had no idea when or how long he had been sleeping. He flipped on his lighter and looked at his watch. Five o'clock. He needed to pee like crazy; the beers he had drunk in the dark after the truck had started out had engorged his poor bladder until it felt as big as a watermelon. His head pounded with the alcohol, and he had a crick in his back from lying on the hard trailer floor all night. He got to his feet, stretched, and felt around until he found the lock on the inside of the back door. He opened it and stuck his head out. They were at some truck stop, with a dozen or so other trailer trucks parked around them. No sign of Snuffy. That was good luck. No telling what Snuffy would do if he caught him and realized he had run out on Cassie. Not that Snuffy was an angel himself. Lale knew he had been fooling around with Bernadette for years, even though he had a wife and four kids. Probably had had other women along the way, too. Still, it wouldn't do to have him run back and tell Cassie where he was going. Not that he knew himself. He didn't even know where he was right now. All the highways and truck stops looked pretty much the same until you read the signs. It was cold, that was for sure, even colder than it had been when he left, so he didn't figure he was anywhere near California. And it was still dark, but the sky was beginning to lighten up in the east. He pulled his leather jacket together and zipped it up, turning up the collar. He would find the men's room, and then decide whether to try to get back into Snuffy's truck, or lie low and find another ride. His head felt foggy, and his eyes were starchy. He should have had something more to eat last night instead of the second six-pack.

Lale stood in front of the urinal in the men's room, and it seemed like the stream went on for five minutes. He thought to himself there was nothing in the world as satisfying as a good pee when you needed it. The door opened and someone else came in. Lale glanced over as a pair of gorgeous legs that ended in red-lizard high-heeled shoes came and stood right next to him. He jerked his head up, and a tall willowy woman was staring at him, or at least staring at the private part of him that was exposed.

"What the heck are you doing in here! This is the men's room!"

"Don't get nervous, sugar. I'm not going to hurt you."

The woman had a soft voice, a little hoarse. Her hair was blond, hanging down over perfect breasts, which stood out like toy balloons under a bright-red-print minidress. Her brown eyes were ringed with thick false eyelashes. She reached out a delicate finger, raking a long red nail lightly over his cheek.

"You're the cutest thing I've seen all day. Granted, it's early in the morning, but I'm still working on last night. Would you like to have some fun?"

"Hold on. No. Wait a minute. What is this? Are you . . . a . . . a . . . whore?"

"That's not a nice word, is it? I prefer to call myself a good-time girl. I do like good times, don't you?" She moved closer and batted her furry eyelashes.

"It's five in the morning, for Pete's sake! What's the matter with you?"

"Five, schmive. When opportunity presents itself—and you, sweet cheeks, are a delightful opportunity—Miss Sally answers the call."

"Well, thanks, Miss Sally, or whatever your name is, but no thanks. I'm not interested."

"Are you sure? You won't get this chance again. Strangers passing on the road of life and all. Who knows where I'll be tomorrow, or where you'll be. Why not give yourself a fun little memory that will last a lifetime?"

Lale zipped his pants up and started edging toward the door as Miss Sally came close, put both her hands on his arms, and leaned in to kiss him.

"Lale Hardcastle? Is that you?"

A stunned voice made Lale's head whip around. It was Snuffy.

"What in the heck are you doing here? And what are you doing with *that*?"

"Get lost, buddy. This is none of your business." Miss Sally's voice had changed, hardened and deepened, and Lale stared at her. Now that he took a closer look, he saw a big Adam's apple, and stubble was under the heavy makeup.

"Oh, my God. You're a man!"

"Nobody's perfect, *chérie*." She shrugged.

Lale shoved Miss Sally aside, shouldered past Snuffy, and headed out into the clean morning air.

"Lale! You get yourself back here!" Snuffy had followed him outside. Lale stopped in his tracks.

"I wasn't with her. Him. She . . . he just came in while I was taking a leak and tried to start something. I didn't know she was a man."

"Forget about her. I want to know what you're doing here and how you got here."

"I guess I hitched a ride in the back of your truck."

"I guess you did. Want to tell me why?"

"I don't know."

"I think *I* know. I think it's because you are a spineless little pissant who hasn't got the guts to stand up and tell his girlfriend he doesn't want to marry her. How could you do this? What do you think Cassie feels like right now?"

"What do you think your wife feels like when you pork Bernadette?"

Lale was on the ground before he saw the punch coming. It was a solid right and it snapped his teeth together hard and threw his vision out of focus.

"You want to run away, you run away, you little turd, but you're not doing it with me." Snuffy stalked over to the truck and climbed in. Before Lale could collect himself, Snuffy threw it into gear and roared off.

"Are you all right, sugar?"

Miss Sally emerged from the bathroom and stood over him. The sun was beginning to rise and Lale squinted as it lit up the blond hair, making a halo around her head.

"I don't think my jaw is broke, but that's the good news," he said, rubbing his jaw and opening and closing his mouth.

"Funny. It's usually *me* who gets it. I've been beaten up tons of times, and I can tell by looking at you, your jaw isn't broken. You'll be sore for a couple of days, but no lasting damage. You'll live."

Lale got up on his knees, then took the hand she held out to him and pulled himself up. Miss Sally leaned against a '65 baby-blue Mustang, watching him.

"Wow. That old man can punch," Lale said, rubbing his jaw.

"You don't look so good. Some coffee might perk you right up. Are you hungry? Why don't I buy you some breakfast?"

"No offense, uh, Miss Sally, but I'd just as soon not go into the truck stop with you."

"I hear you, sugar. No offense taken. I'll tell you what—you wait for me right here. This is my car. You can sit and rest in it for a little minute and catch your breath. I'll be right back."

Lale stood, stupidly staring at the car. He tried to get his brain working to decide whether to run or fight or stay. He felt like a rabbit cornered by a yard dog. Make that cornered by a poodle.

"Oh, *really*. Puh-lease. I'm not going to bite you, although that's not the worst idea in the world. Just sit. You don't seem to have a lot of options, do you?"

She took a bag from the backseat of the car and went into the men's room. Lale opened the car door and nervously sat on the passenger side, wishing he had never laid eyes on Snuffy Simmons or his big truck.

Ten minutes later, a dark-haired man came out, freshly scrubbed, wearing jeans and a jacket. There was no sign of Miss Sally. He threw the bag into the car.

"What . . .?" Lale blinked, confused.

The man stuck out his hand. "Salvador de Vega. But you can call me Sal. Everyone does. Are you hungry?"

"I could eat. But I'll buy my own. I got money."

"Independent. I like that in a man."

They started across the parking lot to the diner. Lale tried to look at him out of the corner of his eye without being too obvious about it. Sal had a different walk in the men's clothes, somehow graceful and a little swishy, but not as much. But then it couldn't be easy to maneuver in those high heels without a swishy walk. If he hadn't seen him dressed up like a woman before, he wouldn't necessarily know he was . . . like that. Except there *was* something a little weird about his face. His eyebrows were too neat or something, like they had been plucked. Lale had never been this close to a homo before. Not one that he knew for sure. There had been a guy in school, Geordie Simms, who was a little bit sissy. He was in the band, wore socks that matched his shirts, and once had tried to take home ec to learn how to sew. Everyone teased him and gave him a hard time, but he had a mousy little girlfriend who used to sing duets with him in church, so he probably wasn't really one. Being this close to a card-carrying homosexual made Lale a little uneasy. He tried to act natural, but his jaw kept tightening up.

Oh, well, he said to himself. What the heck. Snuffy was gone. Nobody knew him at this truck stop, and it wasn't like he was going to *do* anything with the . . . guy. Girl. Whatever. They were in public, and if it came down to it, Lale figured he could take him in a fight. What could it hurt? He was hungry, and it was only breakfast. Then he would find another ride and be on his way.

10

JOE JR.'S

On the corner of Twelfth Street and Sixth Avenue was a coffee shop called Joe Jr.'s. It had great greasy hamburgers and fries and homemade soup, and best of all, it was cheap. Most of the tenants in Mrs. Digby's apartment house ate their meals there, as did a lot of actors who lived above the Thirteenth Street Repertory Company, just around the block. I have no idea who Joe Jr. was, but Tony was the owner and he would run a tab for you if he liked you. I think most people paid it sooner or later. I soon became a regular. It was too much trouble to cook on the hot plate, and frankly, I never was much of a cook anyhow. Mama never taught me—she thought it was easier to do it all herself, and so did I.

Since I had met Aurelius that first day, we hadn't managed to run into each other again. He undoubtedly slept late and I was out early. I would have known he was a musician as well as an actor, though, even if Mrs. Digby hadn't told me, because late at night I could hear him, through the walls, playing a lonesome sweet saxophone. I got to where I listened for it, and had a hard time going to sleep until he played.

I was sitting in my usual booth at Joe Jr.'s, second one from the door, when he passed by on the street. I caught his eye; he stopped and stood there looking at me through the window. He had a funny look on his face, like he was angry. Then he came into the restaurant and stood by my table.

"Are you okay? Aurelius? What's the matter?"

"Hendrix is dead."

"What? Who?"

"Jimi Hendrix. He's dead."

"You're kidding. What happened?"

"OD'd. I don't know. They say he choked on his own vomit. Stupid fool. Stupid, stupid, stupid!" His hands clenched and a vein popped out in his neck. It was a little scary.

"Wow. That's awful." I didn't know much about Jimi Hendrix. I had heard his music, of course—who hadn't?—and pretended to like it more than I really did because it was considered cool. In reality, it was too loud and jarring for me, and too repetitious. I liked songs I could sing along and dance to, music that stroked all the hairs in the same direction, like stuff by Marvin Gaye or the Beatles or the Band. It was cool and wild and crazy that Jimi Hendrix set his guitar on fire and all, but I think it was a little out of my league.

"Do you want to sit down? What happened?"

"I don't know. He was in London, on some kind of dope, too out of it to know what he was doing. Something like that." He slid down in the seat until his head rested on the back. "Seems like we just can't keep from killing ourselves. It's not enough that we've been enslaved and whipped and lynched and shot, shut out of hotels and cafés and sent to the back of the bus, but every time somebody black makes it big, we find a way to do our ownselves in. Look at Bird. Billie. Whole *string* of jazzmen. Booze. Drugs. Black man—woman, too—get a little famous and rich and first thing they do is buy a fur coat and a big car and then start shoving their bodies full of junk, like they can't deal with success with their own God-given brains, they got to jack them up on dope. We might as well all take a running jump off the Brooklyn Bridge." He sat up and leaned toward me, his eyes flaming. "What's the point of working and sweating for something, against all odds, *making it,* and then just killing yourself for no good reason? You tell me that."

"No point, I guess."

"You don't take drugs, do you?"

"No. Well . . . I smoked pot a few times."

"Pot. Hmph. That's nothing. It's the heavy drugs you have to stay away from. Uppers. Downers. Heroin. Speed. Cocaine. LSD. Like that. Those things mess up your *mind,* and your mind is all you got to get you anywhere in this life. That and your ambition. Not to mention looks. You got that, all right, and you'll have plenty of people trying to give you all those drugs, you, a big model and all. You stay away from that mess, you hear?" He leaned even closer, glaring at me. I leaned back a little farther.

"Sure. Of course I will." This was getting a little weird. I half expected him to reach across the table and grab my arm and shake it. Instead he sat back and took a long look at me.

"Cherry Marshall, right?"

"You're pretty good on the saxophone."

"You hear me?"

"Late at night."

"Didn't mean to bother you."

"You don't bother me. I like it. Do you play with a band?"

"I got a little group. We get gigs here and there, downtown in somebody's loft, mainly. I'm trying to be an actor, too, but there's a lot of us black men out there and few roles. Sidney Poitier gets to be all the doctors and lawyers and Nobel Prize winners or something, and everybody else gets to be a pimp or a mugger or somebody's black-ass Step'n Fetchit, and not many of those."

"There's parts other than those, surely."

"You try to find them."

"I'm just trying to get somebody to take my picture. That's hard enough."

"Don't give me that. Pretty white girl like you? You got it made."

"I don't think I have it made. I'm running out of money, and if I don't get a job soon, I'll have to waitress or something."

"Now, Lordy mercy, wouldn't that be awful? Why don't you just ask Daddy for more money until you make it?"

"What do you mean by that? You don't know my daddy."

"I mean you don't know what it's like to *really* be without money. Oh, I figure you're trying to make it on your own, but I'm betting you have a backup daddy who wouldn't want to see his baby starve. Isn't that true?"

"Well, of course my daddy wouldn't want me to starve, but you don't have to be so hateful about it. What's your problem?"

"My problem? You don't know nothing about problems. You sound like you're from the South. Arkansas or Tennessee. Maybe Texas?"

"Arkansas."

"Well, then you ought to know that to be black in the South is to be treated like something on the bottom of somebody's shoe."

"What do you know about the South?"

"All I need to know. I come from Alabama. I got out of there as soon as I was tall enough to turn in my cotton sack and hitchhike out. That would be something else you don't know nothing about, working in the fields."

"That just goes to show what *you* know. My grandparents were sharecroppers. My mama worked in the cotton patch when she was a girl, so I think I know a little bit about it."

"Your mama. Your grandmama. But *you* never had to do it *yourself*. I can tell. You had it easy. You never had that pearly-white skin burned by the sun until it blistered and peeled, those soft hands picked so rough you couldn't touch anything fine without tearing it to shreds."

"Okay, so I never *personally* picked cotton. I admit it." He was beginning to tick me off. "But I worked. I worked in a pickle plant and peeled onions all summer!"

"A pickle plant? A *pickle* plant? Huh. *I* spent a summer castrating pigs!" He looked at me, smug, like he was asking me to top that one. I think he had me.

"Well, I . . . I give up. You win the worst-job contest! And I'm really truly sorry Jimi Hendrix is dead, but you don't have to be black to do yourself in. White singers die all the time, too, in little planes crashing trying to fly in bad weather, like Patsy Cline and Buddy Holly and them. Hank Williams overdosed. Everybody's got to die, one way or the other, whether they're famous or not. I expect to do it myself one of these days. I bet you do, too."

He looked at me hard for a minute, then laughed.

"You're not the worst chick I ever met. Peeling onions in the pickle plant, huh? That makes me hungry. Tony! I need a cheeseburger bad, man. Extra pickles and onions."

Tony came over to the table, put down a glass of water and another place setting in front of Aurelius.

"These together?"

"Yeah, we're together. Put the girl's meal on my tab."

I looked up at him, my spoon stopped on the way to my mouth.

"I mean, since you're so bad off and might have to waitress and all, I'll buy your bowl of soup," he said. "Okay?"

"Okay. I'll let you pay. With all your savings from picking cotton."

Something was starting—you could feel it in the air between us. I was a little scared. It had never once crossed my mind to think of any of the few black guys back home as possible boyfriends. We didn't even integrate until 1962, when I was in the ninth grade, and then it was just fifteen kids in the whole school. When they first came, we were all kind of suspicious of each other, but after a while it was no big deal. They joined the football team, the choir, the honor society, and everything else; we discovered they were good athletes and singers and students, and they realized we weren't going to beat them up or make fun of them; for the most part it seemed to be okay. Our choir won a number one at the state competition for the first time ever, and the football team got into the district finals. The only thing is, I don't think we ever did totally relax around one another; we were always too aware that we might accidentally say something that might be taken the wrong way. We joked around and laughed a lot, sure, but seldom did we sit and have serious talks about anything important. I had a friend named Queen Esther McVay, who I sat with in art class, and we had fun doing art projects together, but we didn't double-date or spend the night at each other's house like I did with Baby. The black kids didn't hang out at the Freezer Fresh, where we all went. I don't remember any of them even driving up and ordering from the window. There was a barbecue place and juke joint out at Turkey Bend called Moe's that they all went to, and once in a while late at night some of us would drive by there, on our way out to the river to park, and it smelled so good that my mouth watered for barbecue, but it didn't occur to us to actually try to go in, or that it was weird that we felt like we couldn't. That's just the way it was and none of us ever thought about it.

Since I'd been in New York, I hadn't exactly had a nightlife, so I'd gotten a library card and spent most of my evenings reading. I guess partly because of meeting Aurelius, I checked out a biography, *I Know Why the Caged Bird Sings,* by Maya Angelou, who was from Arkansas, down in the Delta, and that showed me a whole different side of the situation. As I got into the book, I found out that Maya and I had a lot more in common than I would have thought. Maya's grandmother ran a store that sold to black sharecroppers, and I wasn't kidding about my grandma and grandpa being sharecroppers. At one time they'd had a nice farm and took out a mortgage to buy more land to raise cotton, but shortly after they did, the Depression came and the bottom fell out of the cotton market. They struggled for a few years, but got to the point where they couldn't make the mortgage payments and there was nobody left to borrow from, so the bank foreclosed on them, like it did on so many others. A man from town who had been a professional baseball player decided he wanted to retire back home and go into farming, so he bought their mortgage and got the whole farm for the amount of the mortgage—less than two thousand dollars—which even in the Depression was way less than it was worth. He obviously thought that price included not only the house and land, but also every single machine they had on the place, every stick of furniture, every horse and cow and dog and cat—and the sheriff did nothing to stop him. He signed the papers the day Grandma and Grandpa took their cotton crop to the gin, and as the bales came out of the baler, the new owner was waiting with a truck and took those, too. They had the clothes on their backs, and that was about all. The only thing they had left to do was pull up their socks and go to work on shares for a larger farm, leaving behind the neat white house where Grandpa had grown up and their girls had been born, to move into a four-room croppers' shack in the field they worked. They never got over it, especially Grandpa. If the man who bought their farm's name ever came into the conversation, Grandpa would spit, even though he was a Christian man and tried to see the best in everyone.

Nobody, black or white, ever got out from under picking cotton for somebody else—the landowners saw to that by always keeping the croppers in debt to them, charging them high prices for the seed and their supplies, which you could be sure always totaled out to more than their share of the profits.

Grandma and Grandpa raised two good-looking girls, though, my mother, Ivanell, and my aunt Rubynell, both of whom married young and, like Aurelius, got themselves out of the cotton patch. It's a fact that, fair or not, good looks are always a ticket to someplace better.

Aunt Rubynell's husband, Uncle Jake, owned the Esso station, and Daddy was the postmaster at the post office. Although nobody could call us wealthy, we lived in town in a two-story house and Mama had all the pretty clothes she never had when she was growing up. Even when she lived in the cotton patch she loved clothes. She was tall with a slim figure and could sew and make a hand-me-down look like an expensive store-bought dress. No matter how much money you have, you can't buy style—it's something you're born with—and Mama had it. It could be that growing up with her is why I am a little fixated on clothes myself.

The patch my grandparents had moved to was down in the river bottom, near Turkey Bend, where most of the black pickers lived, and they shared it with several other families, both black and white. Like the folks in Maya's book, they called each other Miz or Mister this or that, or Brother or Sister if they went to the same church. My grandparents called *each other* Mr. Shelton and Miz Shelton, even when they were alone, or so Grandma told me once when I asked her. He was quite a bit older than she was, and it never occurred to her to use his given name. That wouldn't have been respectful.

I never heard my grandparents say anything hateful about any of their black neighbors, but they didn't visit or talk much, even if they were picking right next to one another in the same field. Or unless one of them was in trouble, like the time my grandma was throwing the dirty dishwater out the back door and slipped and fell, landing on the jagged edge of the rocks they had piled up to use for door steps. She gashed her leg open, ankle to knee, and when Grandpa couldn't get the gaping wound closed or stop the bleeding and she turned gray and began to shake, he ran and got Miz Berry, who lived down the road, to come and help him bind it up. They got her in the truck and both of them took her to the hospital, where Miz Berry sat outside and waited for hours until they came back out with Grandma's leg sewed up and bandaged. Then Miz Berry went back to her house and cooked them a big pot of chicken and dumplings, turnip greens, and biscuits enough to last for a few days until Grandma could get up and around.

Grandma would have done as much for her, and she did when Miz Berry had a baby who couldn't thrive because her milk dried up. Grandma carried milk to her from their cow every day for months until the baby got big enough to eat. But they didn't go to see each other and drink tea and exchange recipes or whatever. Life was too hard. That was just the way it was.

That baby was a girl my same age named Reenie, and every Sunday afternoon while Mama and Daddy visited with Grandma and Grandpa we'd dig in the sand down by the river or play out in the old barn, climbing up to the loft and jumping into piles of hay. One time Reenie found a sack of pink pellets out in the barn and ate some, thinking it might be candy, but it turned out to be rat poison. She didn't swallow much, but it burned her mouth and we got scared. My mother picked Reenie up and ran down the road to her home, and then Mama and Miz Berry scrubbed out her mouth and made her throw up and then drink a big glass of fresh milk. She was all right, but it scared us so bad we stopped playing in the barn, afraid of rats, and neither of us ever again tasted anything if we didn't know what it was.

It was about this time that we were six and big enough to go to school, and when I said something to her about how much fun we would have, going to first grade together, she put her hands on her hips and told me in no uncertain terms that she had her own school to go to, that it was better than mine, and she would get to ride a big yellow bus to get to it. Her family quit the patch and moved away not too long after that, maybe to be nearer the school, which I later found out was more than an hour away on the bus. I never saw Reenie again.

I didn't know then why we couldn't go to the same school, but in the excitement of first grade I forgot about Reenie. When Little Rock High School integrated in 1957 with all the hateful mess that went with it, I was too young to really understand what was happening. It was just normal that there were no black kids at school. If I'd ever thought about it, and I didn't, I guess I would have thought, as Reenie had said, that they were happy being bused to their school and felt like it was better than ours.

A few years later, of course, I got older and the civil rights marches brought out all the ugliness of segregation onto the six o'clock news, but even then, aside from Little Rock, which seemed far away from Sweet Valley, most of the trouble was always somewhere else, in the Deep South, Alabama or Mississippi or Georgia, and didn't appear to affect us much. We didn't have protesters sitting in at the Freezer Fresh or fat sheriffs beating up people, whooshing them down with fire hoses, siccing German shepherds on them. Nobody had ever gotten lynched in Sweet Valley. We felt like we were somehow apart from it all. After I read Maya Angelou's book, I doubted the black kids felt the same way. That book made me think in ways I never had before, and made me ashamed of those white people, ashamed of being so ignorant. If you think about it, white people have done a real number on *everybody,* starting with Columbus and the explorers—first on the Indians, then on the black people they forced over here from Africa as slaves, and even right up to now on the Vietnamese, whose country we have no business being in at all and which we are destroying as hard and fast as we can.

Well, frankly, let's face it, down through history we've done a pretty good job on each other, too. Nobody knows if Cain and Abel were white or not, but I'd bet money they were.

So, sitting across from Aurelius, I was a confusion of feelings, to put it mildly. I had only had that feeling, that attraction, whatever you want to call it, like this twice in my life, and it was something I couldn't ignore. I know he felt it, too.

But what would people say if we started going out? How would my mother and daddy act when I told them I was seeing a black man? I know it was jumping the gun a little since he hadn't really asked me out at all, but would I have the courage to tell them if he did? What if they came to visit me? Well, so what if they did? I was grown, wasn't I? It wasn't any of their business who I saw! Oh, my gosh. Here I was getting mad at them already, before anything had even happened. Maybe they wouldn't care at all. They had never been prejudiced like a lot of people I knew. Daddy worked with a black man at the post office. They might like Aurelius.

Finally, though, what did it really matter what anybody else said or thought? This was New York, not the South. Nobody in Joe Jr.'s blinked an eye at us eating our lunch together in the same booth. There was nobody at all watching to frown on anything I did, no preacher telling me I would go to hell for every little thing I did or thought or said that wasn't like what the Holiness church believed, no whispering old ladies to run and tell my parents what they had seen me do. There were no Turkey Bend and Negro-only juke joints, white-only Freezer Freshes. Aurelius and I lived in the same house, right across the hall from each other.

I was starting out a whole new life, where nobody knew me and the only ties to the past were in my own mind, however strong or fragile those ties might be.

I had no idea what was going to happen between us, or even if anything would, but for right now, this moment, it felt good—it felt right—to be with Aurelius, his brimstone eyes looking at me over a bowl of soup. Everything else I would shove to the back of my mind with the rest of the confusion already piled up there, and, like Miss Scarlett, think about it another day.

11

THE TAN THUNDERBIRD

It was the end of Baby's and my first week of practice teaching in our separate schools, and the weather was warming up some. The snow had begun to melt, leaving bare patches of grass outside the parking lot of Big Bob's Burger and Beer Joint on the Buchanan strip, and there was a whiff of spring in the air. Baby and I had met at Big Bob's to have supper and compare notes. I think I was ahead in the supervising-teacher department, since Father Leo turned out to be as great as Cassie Culver had said. He had long wavy hair and a beard, and smoked cigars. He didn't care if the boys said a swear in class, and they all thought he was the coolest teacher ever. So did I. He liked my painting, said I had a great color sense, which was why he had picked me to be his student teacher. How can you keep from liking somebody who loves you for your work and not your curly hair?

On the other hand, Baby's supervising teacher, Alice Sinclair, wasn't even going to be there to help her at all, since she was eight months pregnant and big as a cow. In fact, the first day, she introduced Baby to the kids and then took off, never to be seen again. Baby was probably slightly ahead of me with the kids, though, since hers seemed to like her a lot and all of mine were boys and, for the most part, all they did was ask me to get things from the bottom shelves so they could see me bend over, the little brats. I had forgotten that high schoolers were not children. One or two who were on the basketball team were even taller than me. I would have to wear my bell-bottoms and leave all the miniskirts in the drawers or I'd never get anything across to them. But it was kind of fun, being the only woman in the whole school. I would be a liar if I said otherwise.

Baby and I got in my car, our bellies full of burgers and fries, and headed toward St. Juniper's, leaving the neon lights of Big Bob's behind us. I wanted to show her the cute guest cottage where I was staying out behind the abbey and fix her some coffee in my little kitchen. It was almost like a playhouse there, and I loved being all on my own. Baby had an apartment in Buchanan in a house owned by a cranky landlady who knocked on the door if she heard the bathwater running too long and complained if she thought Baby had eaten one of her prunes or whatever, so it was almost as bad for her as being at home.

The road was deserted this time of night, and the sky was full of stars. The only other car on the road was a few hundred yards in front of us, and we slowed down when it braked and put on its blinker to cross the train tracks that ran parallel to the highway. Only it didn't cross. It stopped right in the middle of the tracks, and the driver put out the headlights. As we came closer, we could see it was a light-colored Thunderbird.

"Good Lord, Baby! That car is sitting right in the middle of the tracks! If a train comes along, it's going to get hit!"

"Maybe the motor died."

"Then why did they turn off the lights?"

"I don't know. Do you think they might be in trouble? Maybe we should stop and see if they're sick or something."

I turned, pulled in behind the car, and honked the horn, but it didn't budge. I killed the motor, and Baby and I got out of the VW and walked up to the car.

"Hey! What are you doing? You can't sit here on the train tracks!" Baby called out as we went up to the window. I was surprised to see Cassie sitting in the driver's seat. She had the window rolled up, and I banged on it.

"Cassie! What do you think you're doing? Do you want to get run over by a train?"

She rolled down the window halfway and calmly looked down the tracks.

"Looks like it, don't it?" Her words were a little slurred. I smelled liquor on her breath. A whistle sounded, low and lonesome in the distance. I turned to look, and sure enough, way on down the track, there was a light.

She was just going to sit there and get run over.

"Cassie, this is stupid. Come on. There's a train coming."

"I know there is. I might be stupid, but I'm not ignorant. Lale run off and left me, and I'm killing myself."

She pushed down the lock on the door and started rolling up the window. I tried to get my hand in, but the window kept on coming and I had to jerk my hand back before it pinched off my fingers.

"Cassie! Roll down this window!"

"Let me alone! Just get out of the way!"

"Are you crazy? Don't do this! Baby! Help me!"

Baby ran around the Thunderbird to open the door from the other side, but Cassie was too quick and pushed down the lock before Baby could get in.

The train was coming on hard down the track, but she still had time if she would just get moving. We pounded on the doors, but Cassie put her hands over her ears and rested her head against the steering wheel.

"Let's try to push it, Cherry," Baby said, coming back around. We got behind the car and pushed with all our might, but the car didn't budge an inch. That old story about a person turning into Superman in a crisis didn't seem to be true in our case. The train was getting closer, and I was beginning to panic. I went to the window and banged on it one last time. Cassie had her head turned away, but she could hear me, I was pretty sure.

"Listen, Cassie. I know you're all upset about Lale and everything, but I can promise you that he won't even come home for your funeral if you do this. He's probably having a high old time right now with some other girl, and after you're dead and buried, he'll still be having one. Think about it. Even if you want to smash yourself into meat loaf on the front of a train, do you want to kill that baby, too? Cassie?" I had no idea if she really was pregnant, but all the signs pointed to it. She half lifted her head. At least she heard me.

"Cassie, you know suicide's a sin," Baby chimed in. "You won't go to heaven, and neither will the baby." Baby's grandmother had been Catholic and she knew which buttons to push. "You don't want to go to hell, Cassie." Baby kept on at her. "Hell is like dousing yourself with lighter fluid and sizzling and frying forever and ever."

"Yeah, you might not care for yourself," I said, taking over, "but killing a baby is the worst sin you can commit. It's an innocent little thing and it doesn't have any say in it. Let the baby live, Cassie!" I felt bad about saying those things to her with the shape she was in, but at this point I had run out of options.

"We better get out of here, Cherry," Baby said in a panic. "There's nothing we can do for her now." The train was charging on down the track, blowing its whistle like there was no tomorrow, and I suddenly realized that if it hit the car, we'd be right in the line of fire. I banged on the door again.

"The train is coming, Cassie. We're out of here. Good luck!"

We didn't have time to move the VW, so we just ran down the incline and jumped into the ditch, praying the car wouldn't land on us when the train crashed into it. As we hit the ground, I heard the T-bird's engine cough and turn over as Cassie popped the clutch, and the car lurched off the tracks, rolling down the grade on the other side just as the train roared through, so close I could see the glare from the headlight through my squeezed-shut eyelids. Tons of iron whizzed by, only feet away from us, and the noise from the whistle nearly deafened me. I imagined I saw faces in the windows with a look of horror on them, and nearly peed my pants. On the other side of the train, the taillights of the T-bird shone red between the wheels of each car as they went by, exhaust smoking out of its tailpipe.

The caboose finally passed, and Baby and I went running across the tracks.

"Are you all right? Cassie! Open this door!"

The door opened and Cassie staggered out. I grabbed and hugged her, then she slid to the ground and sat with her back to the car, crying, which made us cry, too, in relief.

"Why did you have to do that?" she said, through her tears. "Why couldn't you have let me alone?"

"Because I hate the sight of blood," I said, wiping my nose on the back of my hand. "Now come on. What's going on?"

"I told you. Lale run off and left me," she sobbed. "I don't even know where he is. He doesn't want to marry me or even see the baby."

"So there really is a baby?"

"Not yet. But you were right—there's going to be. Everyone in town will know it soon, and they'll know he didn't want us."

She staggered to her feet and lurched over to the side of the road, where she threw up.

Baby went and got a box of Kleenex out of the car and handed her a couple. "Here, take some of these," she said. "Are you all right?" Cassie shuddered at the sour bad taste of regurgitated wine in her mouth, but seemed a little more clearheaded. She nodded.

"Yeah. I'm all right. Y'all can go on."

"Oh, no. I think not. We need to get you home. Baby, you drive my car, and I'll take Cassie in the T-bird."

"It's Lale's T-bird. He gave it to me. Payment for his conscience." She laughed a hard little laugh, blew her nose, and leaned against the hood of the car. "I'm okay. Let me just sit for a minute. I don't want to go home like this. I can't face Mama."

She sat on the ground and bent her knees, resting her forehead on them. We stood around, not knowing what to do. After a few minutes, she raised her head and looked at us. I'm not sure she'd really known who we were before.

"I remember you. From the restaurant. Cherry?"

"Yeah. Sure you do. It was only a few days ago."

"Who are you?" she asked Baby.

"I'm Baby, Cherry's friend. Nice to meet you."

"Nice to meet you, too." She held out her hand and Baby shook it. "Thank y'all for saving me. I'm sorry. I'm so sorry. I don't know what got into me. I really didn't mean to do it." She began sobbing all over again.

"No, I don't think you did," I said. "No man in the world is worth killing yourself over. He might feel bad for a minute, but then he would have his whole life ahead of him, and you'd still be dead."

"You're right about that." She sniffed. Baby took a couple more Kleenex and handed them to her. She blew her nose again. "I guess my guardian angel sent you. Or maybe it was the baby's guardian angel."

"Maybe she did. But she might not send us the next time, so no fooling, I hope you won't try anything else like this. I don't think I could take it."

"I won't. Don't tell my mother. Please don't tell her."

I wasn't going to promise. I thought Annie probably needed to know about this.

"Look, Cassie, I don't think you ought to be by yourself right now. If you don't want to go home, why don't you come on with us to the cabin up at the abbey for a while? We can sit around and listen to music, I'll fix us some coffee, and you can tell us all about Lale."

"All right. That sounds good." She pushed herself up with some difficulty. "I'll follow y'all."

"I don't think so. Baby, you drive the Bug and I'll go with Cassie." I didn't want to let her out of my sight for a minute.

I got into the T-bird, turned it around, and bumped back over the railroad tracks. I shivered again at the thought of how close the train had come. Amazing. A few feet of space was the difference between life and death. Cassie got in, and we led off, Baby following. I only then noticed that the backseat was full of gifts.

"What are those presents in the backseat?"

"They're from the bridal shower. That's the night Lale run off, and I never did unload them. Need a new chip-and-dip set? I got three. Or a black lace nightgown? Take anything you want."

"Cassie, stop talking like that. Let's go over to my cabin and talk it out, all right?"

"Yeah, all right. Just please don't tell my mother."

"Wasn't Annie at the shower that night? Didn't she know Lale left?"

"Mama went home early. She saw Lale waiting out in the car and thought he would bring me on to the house, and I never told her different."

"When did you find out he had gone?"

"After the girls started to leave, I came out to see if he was waiting for me. His car was sitting there empty, and he'd left me a note. I don't even know where he went. Probably hitchhiked out. I didn't let anybody know what the note said, just said that he'd had to go do something at the last minute and I was going to take the stuff home myself. I've been going crazy for days and tonight I couldn't stand it any longer, so I took one of Bernadette's bottles of wine and just drove around to try and figure out what to do, thinking and drinking."

"Thinking and drinking don't go together too well, I guess."

"Maybe not."

"Are you feeling better now?"

"Yeah. I'm okay."

"Let's go and get you some coffee. We'll call Annie and tell her you're with us, and won't be home for a while. Okay?" She nodded her head.

I had a bad feeling it was going to be a long night.

12

ON THE ROAD

"So, what did that awful truck driver mean when he said all that about you running away from some problem? Not that it's any of my business, but, honey, we all have problems and we'd all like to just get in the car and run away from them. That's partly why I was here in this dump of a truck stop at five in the morning. I ran hard and fast from one of mine this weekend. I can't imagine *why* I followed that loser to Nashville, but that's what love does to you. It takes away every shred of judgment you possess. All your brains drain right out of your head and down into your wickie. That's what makes it hard, you know. All those brains. I should have known any western singer I met at Max's Kansas City in New York was not a real cowboy. I found out the only horse he'd ever ridden was at the five and dime, and the only affection he had for *moi* was the dough I could shell out to support him until he got his record contract. Ha! Every single waiter and car jockey in Nashville is waiting for their big record contract. He did have a lovely voice, though, really and truly. Although *lovely* isn't quite the word. More like *sexy*. That's the word, honey, pure and simple. Sexy. One of those rough, gravelly kinds of voices like Johnny Cash has. Like it was dragged out of his throat at four in the morning and beaten with a tire iron. Do you like Johnny Cash? I think he's sexy, wearing black, and all that romantic drugging and all, back before it was fashionable. I think I must be over my cowboy phase, though. Honey, it was just too, too much in the end. Literally. Not that *that* usually is a problem, but he wouldn't leave me alone for a minute! I had to make excuses to even get a few hours' rest! And a girl like me really needs her rest, don't you know? Why . . ."

"Excuse me, Sal, but would you mind not talking for a while? I got a lot on my mind right now, and I need to think."

"Oh, I'm sorry, cherub. I do tend to run on, don't I? You just sit and relax and leave the driving to Miss Sally. Yes, indeedy, you must have a lot on your mind—I can see."

They were heading north, in the baby-blue Mustang. Lale was beginning to realize, with a sinking feeling in his stomach, that his beery decision to run from his problems was probably the wrong one, but he had gone and done it and there was no way he was going to go slinking back with his tail between his legs to face the wrath of his parents and one very big angry girl. Not to mention that he would be the laughingstock of the whole town. He could just hear his friends at the wedding—"Hey, Lale," they'd yell. "She dragged you to the altar kicking and screaming, didn't she?" Not to mention what that would do to Cassie. She was probably going to kill him if she ever saw him, but she'd get over it. Heck, she was probably glad he was gone, in a part of her. Or at least she would be. She'd be all right.

He had insisted on paying for his own breakfast and broken the twenty he had in his pocket, but the rest would have to last him until he made some kind of plan. He had hated like everything to go into the truck stop with Sal, but nobody much gave them a second look. If you didn't look too close you didn't realize that Sal had plucked his eyebrows into an arch and still had the remnants of mascara on his lashes. His hair was cropped short, to make the wigs fit better, and truth be told, the truckers probably disapproved more of Lale, his blond hair growing down over his collar. Long-haired hippies were not high on truckers' lists, as Lale found out when he approached a couple about a ride, and they shook their heads.

"You might as well give it up, Lale," Sal had called from the front seat of the Mustang as he watched Lale go to the third truck, then walk away. "I'm the only ride in town for you this morning. I'll be good, I promise. I'm on my way to New York, back to civilization, and you can ride in the old blue horse as far as you want. For free."

It wasn't exactly free. Lale paid dearly by listening to the constant chatter, which nearly ran him up the wall after the first couple of hours. This last stretch of silence lasted exactly thirty seconds.

"Well, are you going to tell Aunt Sally your big secret or not? It was a girl, wasn't it? Your girlfriend? Did she catch you with another girl?"

"Nope."

"Nope what? Nope it isn't a girl, or nope she didn't catch you with another girl? Did she catch you with a boy, perhaps? Please, Lord, let him say yes!"

"Nope she didn't catch me with another girl and she especially didn't catch me with another guy. I told you I'm not like that."

"Ah, that's too bad, but we're getting warmer. So . . . there was this girlfriend you were totally true to, and you ran away from her because . . . she was stifling you?"

"Nope."

"Nope you weren't totally true to her, or nope you didn't run away from her because she was stifling you?"

"Look—I really don't want to talk about it, okay?"

"Fine. I am not one to pry. Never was one to pry. Never, never, never. I have six brothers and sisters, and they can vouch for me on that. Every one of them would come to me when they had secrets because they knew that their brother, Salvador de Vega, could keep a secret. Yes, I certainly can keep a secret. Was she pregnant? That must be it. That, of course, is the oldest reason in the world to run away. Tell me, Lale. Ooh, I bet she was pregnant. Am I right?"

Lale looked out the window at the passing trees along the highway.

"So she *was* pregnant. Hmm. Well, were you going to marry her? I would imagine she already has the cake and the dress, doesn't she? Was the wedding going to be today? My God, you didn't leave her standing at the *altar,* did you, you naughty boy? What does she look like? No, don't tell me! Let me guess. She is a cheerleader with a long blond flip. Big blue eyes, perfect teeth fresh out of their braces. Cute little buns. Wears those adorable white cotton panties called Lollipops. Am I close?"

"Nope."

"Nope. Nope to what? I've lost track here. You really have to give me something to work on. You're as bad as the lonesome cowboy I just left."

"Nope she ain't a cheerleader. She's out of school. She works at a café. And nope she ain't blond, but her teeth are pretty good. I don't think she ever needed braces. She is a tad overweight, but she's got blue eyes. Nose is a little long, but not too bad. She's a good girl."

"I see. Well, that's better at any rate. Lale, darling, you are in a mess, yes indeedy you are. You know you should be there at the wedding, but it seems that here you are instead. So. Do you have any idea of where you're going? I can let you out at the next bus stop if you want to catch a bus back home and do the right thing. I'll even float you a loan for the ticket. No one can ever say that Miss Sally doesn't rally to the cause of young love. It's your last chance. Going once . . . going twice . . ."

"That's great, thanks for the offer, but I've got to work it all through in my head first. I don't think she'd want to see me after what I done last night, running off like that in the middle of her shower and all. And my daddy would take a strap to me, and I'd have to let him. I better just keep on going for the moment, if you don't mind."

"Oh, I don't, mind, sweet cheeks. You can go all the way to New York with me if you want to. New York is absolutely *made* for boys like you. But you left in the middle of her shower, did you say? You mean you left her wet with soap in her eyes? My, what a time you picked to leave! I can't imagine."

"Let's not talk about it for a while, okay?"

"Okay. As far as I'm concerned, you never said a thing to me. My lips are sealed. And I'll never bring it up again unless you want to talk about it. I have absolutely no curiosity. You have *no* idea what kind of secrets I am holding in this brain of mine. You probably don't know it, as how could you, being buried your whole brief life in the Ozark Mountains and all, but I'm a famous makeup artist for fashion shoots and movies, and, honey, let me tell you, those stars have more dirt buried in their closets than you ever plowed back on the farm. And I guess there is something in me that just brings out the confessor in them. Or are they the confessees? Whatever. I should have been a priest. My mother, God rest her soul, wanted me to become a priest, but can you imagine! Wearing the same outfit day after day? I'd go stark, raving mad! Not that I don't like black—actually I look quite good in it, but . . ."

Lale leaned his head against the window and slept as Sal's voice continued like rain on a tin roof, lulling him into dreamland.

13

CALLING THE HOGS

After I did the test at Ron's, something must have happened, because it seemed to take the cork out of the bottle and I began to get some more tests. Ron, bless his heart, came through and gave me several 11-by-14's of all the poses, some in black and white and some in color, some in a wonderful old-fashioned sepia tone. They didn't look stiff and posed at all, like I was afraid they would. I was so thrilled that I went out and splurged on a new burgundy-red leather portfolio that zipped and had carrying handles, and Liz helped me arrange the shots. We opened up the book with a black-and-white in the baseball cap and melted ice cream cone, and then built up to some of the more dramatic ones in color. Toward the end, there were a few of me dancing in front of the window, which were my favorites. I was never much of a dancer, as my friends who had been stepped on and bumped into at dances would tell you, although I begged like crazy when I was little to take ballet like some of the other girls did, but dancing was on the sin list so I never did get a pair of those pink satin toe shoes. Still, in the picture, I *almost* looked like a dancer, arms spread out and legs silhouetted through the gauzy dress, the focus as soft and grainy as the ones Father Leo had done. Ron must not have been kidding about liking those. At the end, I put in Father Leo's. I didn't care if they weren't fashionable. They were beautiful. And I had a book! Even Suzan didn't have much negative to say about them, and grudgingly said, "These will do for a start."

Now on go-sees the photographers would at least stop and flip through my pictures, and I began to get booked for more tests. Most of the time I had to bring my own clothes and jewelry, which I was beginning to find at flea markets and the antique-clothing stores that were opening up on every corner in the Village. I got some great stuff, especially down on Canal Street, which was in a part of town called SoHo that was mostly factories and warehouses. Even though the area was a little creepy, full of big trucks and huge garbage bins, and it was sort of illegal, there were artists and people like that actually *living* there, because artists could get a whole unfinished loft in an empty factory for really cheap, as it seemed like a lot of the manufacturing was moving out of town and the owners didn't want the buildings to just sit empty for somebody to break into. While there weren't many restaurants or anything, just a few lunch places for the factory workers, like the Broome Street Bar, it was beginning to get a few stores, and there was even a small Italian grocery on West Broadway that had fourteen different kinds of olives and fresh balls of mozzarella cheese that came in little tubs of water. Because of all the artists, an art gallery had opened up on Spring Street, and you could tell more would be coming—it just had that feeling.

One of Lana's boyfriends was a painter who lived in a loft on Spring Street so she knew the neighborhood really well. She took me down there for the first time on a Saturday and we went shopping. Canal Street was the southern boundary of SoHo, and it was packed with people crowded on the sidewalks and cars all lined up, trying to get to or from the Holland Tunnel and the bridges to Brooklyn. Most of the stores along the street were supply places for the factories, but anybody could go in and buy. There was a store that just sold rubber stuff that smelled so good I just stood and breathed until I got light-headed, and one that sold nothing but plastic, sheets and shapes of every kind of plastic in every color, some that were iridescent and some that were patterned. For some strange reason I've always loved hardware stores, too, and on Canal Street there were several, with long aisles full of any kind of tool or paint or nut or bolt you would ever need. My favorite one, though, was a big store that sold art supplies called Pearl Paint. I bought a folding easel, which I set up in my little apartment, and wrote to Mama to send up my paints and brushes so I could paint when I had time. Still, I couldn't resist buying a few tubes of this great paint by a company I'd never heard of called Bloxx that was creamy smooth and had the most fantastic colors—periwinkle blue and deep Chinese red and a green the color of new willow leaves—colors so beautiful you wanted to spread them on bread and eat them. I loved living with the smell of fine oil paint and linseed oil, and I realized I really missed painting. Maybe I'd get Aurelius to sit for me. He'd make a great portrait, with his headband and all, his skin a mix of burnt sienna, raw umber, yellow ocher, and brown-pink.

Canal Street was just a few blocks from Little Italy and Chinatown, and Lana and I walked around all afternoon, looking through windows painted with red-and-gold Chinese letters, at whole ducks, braised crispy brown, hanging in rows by their necks, and small fragrant pigs roasting on spits. We ate spaghetti at an Italian place with red-and-white-checked tablecloths and candles stuck in Chianti bottles; we bought black velvet embroidered slippers for a dollar from an old Chinese woman on the street, and yellow egg-custard tarts in little fluted pastry cups from a Chinese bakery. We goggled at the live turtles and fish and squid swimming in big tubs at the outdoor Chinese market, and ducks and chickens in cages. People actually took them home live and killed them for dinner! I could imagine somebody walking a fat duck home on a leash and then whacking it with a cleaver to make Peking duck.

Just walking down the street with Lana was a trip. She was tall and dark and skinny, and if I do say so myself, we made an attention-grabbing pair. Everyone turned and looked at us, and I heard the word "models" whispered, which I can't deny gave me a thrill.

The best place to find clothes and jewelry and stuff was an outdoor flea market on Canal and Wooster where I spent every bit of a check Mama had sent to me on a brown velvet monk's cape with a hood, a black fringed Spanish shawl embroidered with red and green and yellow flowers, a turquoise Japanese kimono that was real silk, hats from the thirties and forties, old jewelry, and tons of scarves, all for really cheap. A step above flea markets were the antique clothing stores, and we found a great one called Harriet Love, where I got a black straw cartwheel hat trimmed in ostrich feathers that must have been from around 1915, and a black velvet coat lined in softest ivory satin from around the same period that was trimmed in lush black fox. My room was beginning to fill up and I hung the stuff around the walls like art. I packed away most of my Arkansas clothes, all the ones I had made, for sure, and my look started to change from mod to more . . . chic hippie, I guess, for want of a better term. I began to wear hip-hugger bell-bottom jeans with skinny turtleneck sweaters and scarves tied around my head, little rose-colored granny glasses, and big hoop earrings. I had never been so happy in my life.

Sometimes the photographers I tested with would have makeup and hair people, who were also working for free to get experience, contacts, and photos for their books, but most of the time I had to do my own and I was getting pretty good at it. I hadn't run across Sal again. He was too famous, I found out, and hardly ever did test girls unless he was paid or was a great friend of the photographer, but I always hoped I'd see him. He was fun, and was also the best at makeup I'd had, even though he took so long. In fact, most of them tended to take a long time, even on a test. On a job, they were probably being paid by the hour, like models, and liked to stretch it out. I hated what some of the other makeup artists did, though, the ones who were practicing, and sometimes I would sneak into the bathroom to fix it the best I could before the photographer started. The makeup artists didn't like it, but it was *my* face in front of the camera, not their artwork. One of them obviously had no idea what color my skin was and put on makeup that made me look like I was wearing an orange mask, and one put dark blush in the hollows of my cheeks and made me look like a skeleton. It was awful. A few of them tried to color my eyebrows darker, but it never looked good and I always made them wash it out. I was getting used to the white eyebrows. It was becoming my trademark.

Liz began to send me out for jobs, too, as I got more pictures in the book, and one of them was for pantyhose. On the go-see, the photographer did Polaroids of my legs in different colors and designs of tights, and later in the day Liz called and told me I got the job! I couldn't believe it. I was going to be making sixty dollars an hour, and they booked me for two hours! That was as much as I'd made in two weeks at the Family Hand! Of course, I had to take out for the agency's commission and taxes, and then . . . well, it was still more than I'd made in a week at the Family Hand.

Even if it was just the lower half of me, I finally was making money as a model! Mama and Daddy would be thrilled, I can tell you. Or on second thought, maybe they wouldn't. In spite of Mama slipping me a little money from time to time, Daddy had been writing and asking when I was going to make some money and said I could come home when I finally realized this wasn't going to pan out. Now they'd know for sure I was going to stay. At least for a while.

I had just gotten my daily schedule from Liz and was coming out of the lounge at the agency when Freddy cornered me. I hated it when he did that, trapping me by putting his arm against the wall and leaning in to talk like we were alone and had some secret. I know he did it to all the girls, but somehow they knew how to handle him better than I did. I always got flustered and acted like I was scared, which I think he enjoyed.

"Well, Cherry, I heard you got your first booking. Congratulations."

"Thanks, Freddy. It's just stockings, but it's a start."

"I told you you'd do well. Those legs." He smiled his little off-center wet smile. "Say, we're having a little party this weekend in the country, and Suzan and I would like you to join us. It'll just be a few of the models, some friends. I'll cook."

"Well, I don't know. I don't have any way out there."

"Lana's coming. I think she's borrowing a car. You can go with her."

Freddy and Suzan's weekend parties were legendary among the models. To be invited was a sign they thought you were going places. Lana usually went, and of course all of the more famous models, but this was the first time I had been invited. It was a big step for me, but I was a little nervous. Suzan always managed to intimidate me, even when she was trying to be friendly, and I wasn't looking forward to being in her house for the weekend. But I couldn't say no.

"All right. Thanks, Freddy. That will be nice."

Suzan and Freddy had a country house at Sneden's Landing, up on the Hudson River, forty-five minutes from New York. It was made of native stone on a quiet street, set well back from the road, with a long driveway leading up to it and a sloping back lawn that went down to the river. They had an indoor swimming pool and eight bedrooms, and every weekend there were houseguests. Suzan was a vegetarian, if she ate at all, so everyone else had to be, too. Freddy liked to say he cooked, but

I later found out it was really a woman from Ireland who made the meatless meals, which were underseasoned (certainly no salt, which made you retain water), so bland you wouldn't *want* to eat much. There was plenty of liquor, though, and cocktail hour started at lunch, with Freddy handing out bloody Marys almost the minute we came in the door. I asked for something nonalcoholic and he gave me a virgin Mary with a stick of celery in it, which was tasty, and then we had lunch. Suzan didn't appear, but the guys and several other girls gradually drifted in. Most of them were well known, and it was weird to see them without much makeup, wearing jeans and sweaters. They all looked younger than they did in pictures.

Lunch was pretty casual and we didn't formally sit at the table, just got our food from the sideboard and sat around the table or out on the patio. It hadn't gotten too cold yet, although there was a nip in the air. I sat with Lana, a little shy of talking to the others. These people were all so beautiful and famous that I felt awkward. Back home, ever since I was a kid, I had always been seen as strange-looking, too tall, too skinny, too pale. In the high-fashion world, tall and skinny and pale were good, and all of a sudden I was in a whole world with people like me, or people who thought people like me were beautiful. But old insecurities die hard and I wished I was as confident as the rest of the girls.

After lunch, we went to our room to get settled. Lana and I shared a small bedroom with twin beds and white lace curtains. A chest and ladder-back chair were the only furniture, but it had a great view of the river. I put my clothes in one of the drawers and went outside across the back patio to look at it. I had always loved the Hudson River School of painters, and wished I could paint the river and all. I'd bring my camera next time if I was invited back and try to get some good pictures, which wouldn't be the same as painting plein air, but I might try it. Lana came out and joined me and we sat watching the sun light up the orange, red, and yellow leaves and turn the river to gold.

"Beautiful, no?" she said in her cute, funny accent.

"Beautiful, yes," I said.

"Did you bring your swimsuit? The guys are already in the pool."

"Are you kidding? I'm not going to go swimming in front of five male models and have all my makeup wash off. You know what I look like without it!"

"Don't be silly. You look fine without it. You don't sleep in it, do you?"

"Of course not. I scrub it off with soap and water."

"Soap and water? But that is horrible for your face! You have to use fine cream to take it off!"

"I have some Pond's I put on sometimes." I never really thought about my skin. It was just there and I'd never had much trouble with it, not even too many pimples, thank the Lord.

"Pond's! Oh, no, no, no, no, no, my dar-ling, I'll have to take you to Saks and get you something good or you'll look like an old lady by the time you're twenty-five! The best is Elizabeth Arden eight-hour cream. You can use that for everything—your face, your elbows, your heels, even on your lips. When we get back, we'll go."

There was so much I didn't know about this beauty business. It had never once occurred to me to put cream on my elbows or heels. Probably someone had been eyeing them with distaste, thinking, "What rough ugly elbows and heels that girl has." I'd have to check it out in the mirror. One more thing to worry about. At least I didn't have to worry about my weight. With all the walking and stair-climbing, I had lost five pounds already, and this weekend's food wasn't going to put any weight on me, I could tell. For lunch we'd had boiled lentils and salad with lemon juice. That was it. I couldn't wait for dinner. Next time I was bringing a jar of peanut butter along, that's for sure.

"Sure you don't want to go for a swim?" Lana said. "Don't be by yourself. Have some fun! I brought an extra swimsuit. You can wear it."

"Thanks, Lana, but I don't think so." The idea of wearing someone else's swimsuit was about as appealing as borrowing their underwear. I guess it's an only-child thing. "I'm not much of a swimmer. You go ahead and have fun. I'll catch you later."

There was a gazebo, just like in the movies, on the long lawn, and I strolled down and sat in a cushioned chair and just drank in the beautiful scene. Fall was definitely in the air and the sun hanging low in the sky threw a soft golden glow over it all. I was a little annoyed at myself that I didn't make more of an effort to be friendly to the others. I think part of me felt like a fraud, and they were going to find out I wasn't really one of them, but just a gawky girl that somehow got taken by Suzan Hartman by mistake. Part of it, too, was that I was hesitant about talking, because of the accent. Although I didn't have the money to call the speech teacher Suzan had recommended, I practiced talking with the TV, saying "I," instead of "Ah," and trying to make one syllable out of words that we used two for—like the name Ann, we pronounced "Ayun," Jim was "Je-um." Never use one syllable when two will do just as well—that is the secret to a good southern accent. I had to think about it, though, and usually forgot.

I decided to practice the "I's" while I watched the sun go down.

"I-ee, I-ee, I-ee . . ."

"You what?" I turned around to see one of the models standing there, a guy named Paul Serrero. He was Italian, had dark curly hair, and was in the pages of *GQ* and *Esquire* all the time.

"I-ee was just practicing my I's. So people will stop asking me what part of the South I'm from."

"What part of the South *are* you from?" He plopped comfortably in the other chair. He had friendly brown eyes and a cleft chin.

"Arkansas." I said it a little defiantly. People sometimes actually laughed when I told them, like Arkansas was a big joke or something.

"Really? I know a guy from there."

"A model?"

"Yeah. Blond guy. Zack, I think his name is."

"That's a weird coincidence. I think I ran into him at Ron Bonetti's. Is he a friend of yours?"

"No, but we just did a catalog shoot together."

"Do you know how to get in touch with him?"

"Hey, baby, I'm not your local dating service. Why so interested in that guy? I'm right here!"

"I'm not interested in him, like *interested* in him. I only saw him that one time. It was just a coincidence, that's all. Not many of us Arkies up here. We might be cousins or something." I smiled and Paul laughed, which was a relief.

"Right. Tell you what—if I see him again, I'll get his number for you."

"That's okay. I don't need it."

"Good. Because I wouldn't have given it to you anyhow." He tried to look roguish, and I let him think I thought it was funny. "So," he continued, "are you seeing somebody?"

"Not really. Kind of." I wasn't, but I thought of Aurelius. I hadn't seen him since the coffee shop, but the next morning there was a red rose outside my door. He was sure taking his sweet easy time about asking me out, if that was what he intended to do. I couldn't wait around forever, no matter how tingly I got when I saw him. The nights with the library books were beginning to get long.

" 'Not really, kind of.' What does that mean?" He lifted an eyebrow. I wish I could lift my eyebrow like that. I tried to, but only succeeded in frowning.

"It means I . . . I don't know what it means. Forget it." I was flustered and changed the subject. "So how long have you been modeling, Paul?"

"Year and a half. But I really want to be an actor. I'm taking classes with Uta Hagen at HB down in the Village. This modeling stuff is just a bread job. You haven't been around long, or I'd have noticed you."

"A month."

"And you're already at the grand weekend parties? Suzan must like you. Or is it Freddy?"

"Freddy, unfortunately. I'm sort of scared of Suzan, if you want to know the truth."

"The Ice Queen? It's just her brittle shell. Underneath, she's—actually, she's brittle all the way down. Although I think Freddy gives her a hard time. Watch out for him."

"Oh, I already knew that. It stands out." Several of the other guys were running across the lawn with a football, yelling for Paul to come play.

"Hey, you guys! I'm busy here with a lady!" he yelled.

"You go on ahead and play," I said. "I'll see you later."

"Yes, you will."

He gave me a sweet smile and joined the others. Although he was good-looking, somehow he didn't ring my chimes, and it was a relief when he left.

Suzan appeared for dinner, wearing a pale-blue silk evening-pajama outfit, hair immaculate as always. Dinner was more of a formal occasion than lunch, with all twelve of us seated around the long oak dining table. There were fresh flowers in the middle, real linen napkins, three different wineglasses, and three forks. We had white wine with the first course, which was a slice of cold orange-colored rubbery vegetable soufflé, and red wine with the main course, which was vegetarian lasagna, with zucchini squash used instead of meat. The cook, whose name was Edith, had boiled the pasta until it was mushy, and I thought there was nothing bad that could ever be made out of tomato sauce, but I was wrong. Lana leaned over and whispered that Edith was from Ireland, and the Irish didn't know *what* to do but boil potatoes and meat. I watched Suzan and don't think she even had two bites, so she probably didn't notice that her cook didn't know how to cook. Or care.

We had a sweet dessert wine with some stewed figs, no sugar, of course, and then we all went to the living room, where one of the guys took out a guitar and we sang songs like "Summer Wine" and "Michael, Row the Boat Ashore." I waited for "Kumbaya," which I'd learned in church camp, but I guess that was out of their repertoire. I never have had much of a singing voice, so I just pretended to sing along, but it was cozy, with the fire going in the stone fireplace and all of us lounging around on the floor. Suzan was curled up on the couch with an after-dinner glass of wine, and a couple of the guys sat at her feet. I was getting to be more at ease with everybody, and they seemed to think I was just as entitled to be there as they were. Paul sat next to me, and on my other side was Mitch, a redhead, who turned out to be from Lubbock, Texas. It was fun talking to him, and his accent was just as thick as mine. It sounded really cute and made me feel more at home. I decided to stop worrying about it, and stop practicing with the TV. If people didn't like it, they could lump it. Paul was annoyed that I talked so much to Mitch, and moved over by a girl named Laura.

Around eleven, Suzan got up and left, and Freddy went soon after. Everyone else gradually drifted off to bed, or to whatever, and Mitch and I were the only ones left in front of the fire, still going over the last Razorback game against the University of Texas, where he had gone. Even though I didn't go to the University of Arkansas, if you lived in the state you had to be a Razorback fan, and my friends and I always went to a few of the games. I actually had seen the one he was talking about.

The conversation finally died down, along with the fire, and he looked at me with what he must have thought were sexy eyes and asked if I'd like to go out for a walk, but I said I was tired, so he just shrugged, patted me on the shoulder, and said good night. I was glad he didn't try to kiss me. He was fun but not my type. I don't really like redheaded men—I can't help but think of Howdy Doody—but I hoped he would become a friend.

I staggered when I got up and realized I'd had more wine than I thought. A little goes a long way with me, and all night they just kept pouring the glass full every time I took two sips. I really needed to find the bathroom fast, and wasn't sure if I could wait to get to my room. In fact, I wasn't really sure where my room was. Somehow in the dark the house looked different.

I started down a hallway I thought led to my room and opened a door I could have sworn was the bathroom. It wasn't. I froze in my tracks, hand on the knob. There, lying back on the bed was Freddy, stark naked, and Lana was between his legs doing . . . well, you can imagine what she was doing to him—I'm not going to spell it out. It was a pretty disgusting sight, his white legs up in the air waving around, her black hair falling in her face as her head bobbed up and down. As I started to quietly back out, Freddy lazily turned his head and looked straight at me with that creepy grin and winked. I don't think Lana even noticed I was there, as busy as she was. It really made me sick. My only friend was giving Freddy a . . . well, a you-know-what, right in the house where his wife was. Lana's own boss! I know Freddy was her boss, too, in a way, but it was the *Suzan Hartman* model agency. I felt like getting in the car and going home, but that was not an option at this late hour, especially since it wasn't my car.

I went back toward the living room, not quite knowing what to do. I couldn't just put on my jammies and go to bed and calmly read a chapter or two of *Go Tell It on the Mountain,* my new book by James Baldwin, knowing my roommate was right down the hall Hoovering away on ol' Freddy. I had no idea where anybody else was. They were probably paired up, doing the same thing, all up and down the hallways, and I kind of thought there might be a couple of guys together. The only thing I didn't want to do was open any more doors, since I could hear little moans and grunts and smacking noises coming from behind some of them, but I needed to pee worse than ever.

Finally, I remembered there was a powder room beside the swimming pool, so I went back there, found it, and did my business, then walked out to look at the pool and try to collect myself.

The stars twinkled down through the glass dome of the ceiling, and the water was alive with sparkly blue light, making the room glow like a Christmas bulb. I didn't think anybody would be out there, but I was wrong. Suzan was curled up on a wicker chaise, still wearing the silk evening pajamas and looking for all the world like the Blue Fairy who had flown down hunting for Pinocchio and lit beside a magic pond. I stood in the door for a minute, and then turned to leave, hoping she hadn't seen me. But she had.

"You might as well come on out," she said. "Sit with me for a while."

I sat in the chair next to her. She took a long swallow of wine from the glass she still held, then poured more.

"Want a glass of Chardonnay?"

"No, thanks. I had too much already. I'm not really used to it."

"Baptist?"

"Holiness."

"Just as bad. Maybe worse. I was Baptist." She dragged out the word. Baaabtist. Her impeccable accent was slipping. It was the wine, but maybe it was also being around me. Accents are contagious. "You know, I've been in New York longer than I lived in Arkansas," she mused, more to herself than to me. "Funny. Just when you think you've managed to get far away from the past, it comes back to haunt you. Like you, walking right into my office, bringing it all in with you." She didn't have that sharp tone in her voice she usually did, or the ice in her eyes. She was softer. Almost wistful. I think she was pretty drunk.

"You didn't remember me, did you? From the fair that time?" I said, after an awkward pause.

"Of course I remembered you. You're memorable. My mother even talked about you years ago when you were in her class. 'Susan,' she said—she never calls me Su*zan,* which irritates the life out of me, as Freddy well knows—'I have a little white-haired girl in my class who just might be a model one day. You'll have to see her if you ever come home.' So I knew about you. I just never expected you to show up on my doorstep. Not many girls from Sweet Valley have the ambition or the guts to go after what they want."

"You did."

"Well *I* was from Little Rock, after all. That's a *big* difference." She laughed, like she was making fun of herself. "Yeah, I had guts then. When you're young and beautiful, all you need is a lot of guts and a few brains, and as you get older you realize that what you need is just the opposite. At this point I don't think I have much of either one left." She took another long drink of wine. Her hand trembled as she balanced the glass on the edge of the chaise, holding it by the rim. "Who was it?"

"Who was what?"

"Who was with Freddy?"

"I . . . don't know what you mean."

"Sure you do. It must have been quite a shock. Let me guess—you needed the bathroom, got lost, and walked in on Freddy and . . . Tricia? Laura? Lana? Give me a clue."

"I'm sorry, but I really don't know what you mean. I didn't see anybody with Freddy."

"It doesn't matter. He's been with them all. And half my girlfriends. Probably *all* my girlfriends. He had a quickie with one of my bridesmaids before we left on our honeymoon. Then she wiped herself off, came out, and caught the bouquet. I hate women. I really, really hate them. Even more than I hate men."

How casually she said it. Like she'd had all the emotion drained out of her, and was just reciting a fact. I was a little shocked. More than a little.

"Your bridesmaid!" I said after a minute. "That's horrible! Was she a close friend?"

"Is there such a thing?"

"Sure there is. I have friends I'd trust with my life." I could never in my wildest dreams imagine Baby sleeping with anybody I even half liked. Even Cassie, I knew, would never betray my trust like that. Lana, however, I'd keep my eye on.

"Good for you. I hope they never fall for somebody you're in love with. And you better hope you never fall for somebody one of *them* is in love with. You'll find out that friendship takes a backseat to love every time."

"Do you . . . I mean . . . are you still in love with Freddy?"

"Was I ever in love with Freddy? I wonder," she mused. "I must have been. Nothing else explains it. But now . . . now, I *loathe* Freddy."

"Then why . . ."

"He has controlling interest in the agency. He made sure of that. He didn't put a nickel into it—his *experience* and his *expertise* were his contributions—but I was stupid enough to sign a contract without reading it because I loved and trusted him. Large payment for a lesson well learned. Always read your contracts. Always."

"Not to put too fine a point on it, but if you hate all women and don't trust them, why are you telling *me* all this?"

"I'm drunk, or you can bet I wouldn't be talking to you at all." She paused, considering, looking at me through narrowed eyes. "No, that's not true. I could tell the first time I saw you. You're more *noble* than me." I couldn't tell if she was being sarcastic or not. "Nobility was never one of my virtues, I'm afraid. *You* believe you would have hot slivers shoved under your fingernails before you would betray a friend, don't you?"

"I don't know about hot slivers, but I know I would never sleep with a friend's boyfriend. Ever."

"Not even if you were *insanely* crazy about him? Madly, deeply in love with him?"

"I would never be in love with a friend's boyfriend."

She leaned back, a satisfied look on her face.

"That shows me how young you are, in spite of reaching the advanced age of twenty-two, Cherry Marshall. I can tell you've had a sex life, but not an extensive one. Am I right? One boyfriend? Two?" Maybe she *could* read my mind. I shifted on the cushion, not really wanting to tell her about Tripp and Faye, or anything else.

"I've had one guy. Who is with somebody else now. But she wasn't my friend, and I sure wasn't hers. I didn't even know about her when I met him." It was a lie, sort of. I'd actually had another little sexual encounter, when I found out Tripp was married, but I didn't feel like going into my lone sorry scuffle at midnight in the potato patch with Ricky Don Sweet. It was just closing the door on our high school romance, and as far as I was concerned, it didn't count.

"Cheers to old boyfriends. May they never come back to haunt us." She smiled and lifted her glass to me. "Sure you won't have a little nightcap?" I shook my head. My eyelids felt sandy. She poured herself another glass, draining the bottle. "Yes, I do have to admit I've been on both sides of the cheating fence. It's worse to be the one cheated on, I can tell you. But noble or not so noble, under it all we are just two little girls from Little Rock, aren't we?"

"Sweet Valley."

"Right. Two sweet little girls from Sweet Valley." She laughed. "Come sit by me, Cherry. Just for a minute."

I felt a little funny about it, but she scooted over and made room for me on the chaise, patting the cushion. She put her arm around me and I could smell her perfume, Youth-Dew, which was what my mother wore. It was weird, like she was a twisted twin of my mother, and I felt like any minute Rod Serling would step out from behind the potted plant and say, "Here's Cherry Marshall, a good Christian girl who thinks she can come to New York to become a model, and still be the same old person she always was. In reality, she has entered . . . the Twilight Zone."

"I heard you and Mitch talking about the Razorbacks. Did you go to many games?" Suzan asked. Her breath smelled like wine, but mine probably did, too. Between her breath and the Youth-Dew and the wine in my stomach, I felt a little fuzzy, like I was there but at the same time was standing off to the side, watching myself.

"I've been to a few."

"I had a boyfriend at the university when I was sixteen. Randy Reed. Raaandy Randy. I lied to my parents and went on the bus to visit him once for a weekend up in Fayetteville. He sneaked me into the dorm and we literally screwed the mattress off the bed for two whole days, not even going out for food. Lived on Cheetos and Hershey bars and Cokes from the machine. He nearly got thrown off the football team when somebody discovered us, but he was one of their best half-backs, so all they did was send me packing back to Little Rock like the little wench I was and told him not to see me again. Which of course he did." She sighed. "He was so *beautiful*. *I* was so beautiful. We were so heartbreakingly young. Everything was *brand new* and we fit together like a key in a lock. I swear, I nearly went into a coma, the orgasms were so powerful. He was maaad about me. When I left for New York without telling him, he quit school and joined the marines. He never once tried to get in contact with me, but I heard he came back to Arkansas after he got out and became a bad drunk. One winter night when he was sloshed to the gills, he stopped to take a leak on the side of an icy road, slipped down the embankment, and crashed through some brush. A stick punched out his eye. Then he was a one-eyed drunk. Good old Raaaandy. Never heard about him again. He might even be dead now, for all I know."

I could swear there was a tear on her cheek.

"Do you know how to call the Hogs?" she said, her face changing, lighting up. "Like they do at the football games?"

"Sure."

"WOOOOOOO, PIG! SOOOOOOIE, RAZORBACKS!" she whooped at ear-splitting volume, and I jumped half out of my skin. She saw my face and doubled over with laughter. "Look at you! What kind of Arkie are you anyhow? Are you *chicken*? C'mon. Do it with me, Cherry! Let's do it together!"

Well, how could I pass up a challenge like that?

"WOOOOOOOOO, *PIG*, SOOOOOOOOIE! RAZORBACKS!" The two of us called the Hogs, over and over, and the loud, high-pitched squeals rang against the glass walls of the pool room, echoing like we were a whole stadium full of fans. I started to laugh, too, and we hugged. Then Suzan kissed me gently, on the lips. Not a sexy kiss, but like a sweet sister would.

"What in the devil is going on, Suzan?" Freddy appeared at the door.

"I could hear you all over the house. It sounded like you were being shoved into a wood chipper!" His hair was standing out in all directions.

"We were just talking about the Razorback football team and decided to call the Hogs," I said.

"And then here *you* appear!" Suzan said, relapsing into hysterical laughter. I felt almost as drunk as she was, and had to laugh, too. We laughed until we collapsed on the chaise, hugging each other.

"I'm going to bed. Try not to wake up the rest of the house or someone will be calling the police." Disgusted, Freddy turned and left.

"Calling the Hogs! And then here *you* appear! That was so funny!" We wiped our eyes and Suzan fished another bottle of Chardonnay out of a cabinet.

"I had a scholarship to the university. Academic, believe it or not. No dummy, this girl. Never actually got there, though. I was in the Miss Little Rock pageant and one of the judges was a scout from Eileen Ford. I only got first runner-up, the winner having knockers the size of bowling balls, but two days later I was on a bus for New York. I was barely seventeen. Left before high school graduation, which didn't set well with the folks, I can tell you, but if you don't walk through the door of opportunity when it opens, baby, it slams in your face. Moved in with Eileen. Boy, she's a tough old buzzard. The girls who lived in her house had to do the housework, babysit her kids. She watched us like a hawk, and I couldn't wait to make enough money to get out from under her scrutiny. Did you know I was on the cover of *Seventeen* before I had been in town three months? I'm sure my mother showed you all my covers. For a girl like me, it was like being shot out of a cannon. You can't imagine the men that came out of the woodwork. Everyone from photographers to the guy who runs the newsstand propositioned me. At least I'd had a little experience with good ol' Randy. I heard a booker tell one of the girls who was a virgin to go out and get laid. Really. She said that her eyes were blank and she could never make love to the camera until she made love to a man. I had no such problem. I started sleeping with the photographers right from the start. My eyes got worldly pretty quick, and I got covers. But you, now, you still have some innocence in your eyes." She said it with a little half-smile, mocking me, but maybe mocking herself more.

"I don't think I can sleep with men to get jobs, if that's what you're trying to say. I just don't think I can do it."

"You don't have any *idea* what you can do. Beauty is a powerful tool, if you know how to use it. It is the key to all the doors there are. If I've learned one thing in my life, it's never say never. Those are cold words to choke on."

"Can't you make it without all that? Don't you think I have any chance at all?"

"If I didn't think you had a chance, I never would have taken you on. Like I said, I'm in this for the money. And I think you'll make money for me. But there are no guarantees." She shrugged. "I really don't know." There was a little quiet moment while she went someplace else in her mind.

I wanted to make money, too, but more than that, I wanted . . . I don't know how to put in words what I wanted. To be more than I was, I guess. To be more than just a gawky girl from Sweet Valley who works at some job and goes to church and gets married to somebody who works at some job and then has kids and always has to buy the cheapest detergent and cans of dark tuna instead of white and gets the family's clothes at Wal-Mart or yard sales and pinches pennies enough to maybe take the kids on vacation once in their lives to Six Flags Over Texas or Disneyland. But probably not.

"What would you do if you had all the money you wanted?" I asked Suzan. "Like if the guy from the TV show *The Millionaire* came to your door and gave you a million dollars? What would you do with it?" I leaned back against the cushions, just a little out of her reach.

"Hmm. I would hire someone to kill Freddy, and then I'd move to Paris and live on the Left Bank, near Notre Dame. I'd eat in small cafés, drink kir, and have a young lover who didn't speak English who would come when I called and leave me the hell alone the rest of the time. I would read all the books I never read in college, like *Madame Bovary* and *Sister Carrie* and take long walks and haunt the Louvre. I'd walk every day along the Seine wearing a long hooded cloak, like Cathy in *Wuthering Heights*." She got misty-eyed at this image, her voice trailing away.

"You could do all that now, I bet. Except for the killing part. Why don't you leave him?"

"Give him the business?"

"Start a new one . . ."

She paused a long minute, squinting up through the skylight at the stars. I felt like I'd said the wrong thing. Something in the air had changed. Underneath the wine I felt the ice creep back in.

"I'm not here to be your best friend," she said in her normal voice, the Arkansas accent gone. "I'm here to guide your career, help you become a model, if that's what you decide you want to do. And finally, you may not. So let's think of tonight as a little interlude. A little down-home interlude. And tomorrow, we're models again. Professionals. Just objects that make pretty pictures to sell products for big companies."

She got up and unsteadily walked toward her bedroom, where I presumed Freddy had gone to bed. She was muttering something about Merle Oberon having a big, strange bumpy forehead, and how much better Linda Darnell would have been as Cathy.

I looked up at the Big Dipper through the roof and waited a minute to make sure she was gone, then found my little room, where Lana was sleeping soundly, wearing a white T-shirt, a big smile on her face like she didn't have a worry in the world. I found the bathroom, brushed my teeth, and got between the soft sheets.

14

THE END OF THE ROAD

As the Mustang eased into the fluorescent light of the Lincoln Tunnel, the sun was rising over Manhattan, washing the skyscrapers in gold and red. Sal was at the wheel, Lale asleep in the passenger seat, his head lolling against the window. They had driven the last part of the night in silence ever since they had stopped at a motel in western Pennsylvania and the night clerk had taken one look at Sal and decided there were no rooms at the inn. The clerk was one of those fat macho guys Sal hated the most—the kind who sits and watches TV all night at the desk, sleeps most of the day, then sacks out in the recliner with a can of beer in front of the TV at home while his wife works two jobs and cooks his dinner; the kind of tough guy who thinks the only good queer is one beaten up and lying bloody in the gutter. All it took for the rooms to be fully occupied was a look out the window at the baby-blue Mustang with the good-looking blond guy sitting in the front seat. If there was one thing the night clerk wasn't going to abide, it was a couple of queers having their perverted sex right next to the room where he was sitting. His palms itched to hit Sal, just looking at his cropped hair and prissy walk, like he had a corncob up his butt.

"Hit the road, buddy, you and your girlfriend out there. There ain't no rooms available."

"Look, friend, that's not my *boy*friend. We've been driving for hours and just want to get some sleep. You'll have no trouble, I promise."

"Yeah, sure. Blondie there is your brother, right? The two of you look just alike. But it don't matter. Like I said, we got no rooms."

Lale watched through the car window and shifted uncomfortably in his seat when the night clerk stared out at him. Sal shrugged and started toward the door. Then he turned back.

"By the way, junior—give my regards to your wife. We're old pals. She used to give me a blow job every Saturday, through the bars of her cage at the monkey house in the Bronx Zoo."

Before the clerk could get off the stool and maneuver his belly around the counter, Sal had scooted out the door and slid in behind the wheel, laughing like a maniac. The Mustang skidded and slung gravel as the clerk lumbered onto the driveway. All he could do was grind his teeth and give a rude hand gesture to the rapidly receding taillights.

"So what was that all about, man?" Lale asked, a little scared. "You'd of thought you were trying to rob him or something. You weren't, were you?"

"I *should* have robbed his fat tushy. But no, it seems he smelled a gay man and was afraid to let us near him. Mark my words—anytime you find a gay basher, right under the skin is a closet queen. The opposite of love isn't hate, you know. It's indifference. If there's hate, there's love, too. Or at least lust."

"Yeah. Right. So he thought you and me were . . . boyfriends? Well, did you tell him we weren't?"

"What for? I'm not ashamed of you."

"All right. Fine. Just keep driving. When we get to New York, I'm out of here. I promise I'll pay you back for the meals and the gas when I get a job. But I'm not ever going to be your boyfriend, no matter how nice you are to me. Got it?"

"You've made yourself clear, darling. Still, never say never. One never knows, does one?"

"In this case, yeah. One knows."

After emerging from the tunnel on the west side of Manhattan, Sal made a turn down Eleventh Avenue.

"Wake up, sleeping beauty," Sal said. "We're home. New York City."

Lale stretched, rubbed his eyes, and looked around. "Is this it? Where's the skyscrapers?"

"Look out the window, in the upward direction, sweet cheeks. You can't see the skyscrapers for the buildings, baby. Let's pull in and have a little breakfast. I could use a cup of coffee."

They parked the car on the street in front of the Sunrise Diner. Morning traffic was already heavy on the West Side Highway. Near the tunnel exit, several streetwalkers, still dressed in their evening finery of cheek-peeking skirts and midriff-baring tops worn under cheap leather coats with tatty fake-fur collars, eyed the drivers, searching for a flicker of interest. Cold and tired, their makeup the worse for wear, they bravely marched up and down the sidewalk in their painfully high heels to keep warm, waiting for the morning rush of guys who wanted a quick blow job before heading to work.

Lale got out of the car and stretched, then stared in disbelief as one of the streetwalkers, wearing a purple wig-hat, came over to him. Her legs were muscular, covered in black fishnet stockings. Her white patent-leather high heels were scuffed with black streaks.

"What're you doing with this guy, gorgeous?" she said, coming too close to him. "Why don't you let a real woman show you what it's all about? On the house."

"Get lost, sugar," Sally snarled. "He's mine."

"Wait a minute, Sal. I'm not yours," Lale interrupted. "You have to stop saying that to people."

"You're not?" The woman reached out to touch Lale's hair. "So there's a chance, hmm?"

"No!" He jumped back. "No chance! I mean, I'm not interested, ma'am, but thanks just the same. I just meant that me and Sal here are not together, that's all. I just met him and he offered me a ride. That's all."

"Uh-huh. Way to go, Sal. If you find any more like this, send them my way. See you around, gorgeous. Look me up if you can ditch this guy. I can usually be found right here. Ask for Yolanda. Everybody knows me."

"What kind of a place is New York, anyhow?" Lale said as the woman sauntered away. "You didn't tell me it would be like this."

"I haven't told you much of anything, have I? So much to tell, so little time. This is just the normal morning crowd here." Sal laughed. "Don't get so uptight. There are a million different kinds of people in this city, and you'll meet them all, top to bottom. Now that you've started somewhere near the bottom, come on in and let's have some breakfast. I really need that coffee."

"I don't think so. This here is where we part company. Thanks for the ride and all, but I don't think I care for New York all that much. I'll try to get another ride out of here as fast as I can."

"Really? And go where, may I ask? Home? I would doubt there are many New Yorkers heading to Arkansas. Maybe you can find your truck-driver friend—Smitty, did you call him?"

"Snuffy."

"Right. Snuffy. Maybe by chance he's in New York? Assuming he would give you a ride back home after the punch he threw at you. I had the feeling you weren't at the top of his hit parade."

Lale looked at the ground, then up the long avenue with its endless row of grimy buildings; nothing but brick and concrete and traffic as far as he could see. He was so tired and cold.

"Or maybe you have bus fare hidden in your boot there?" Sal went on, raising one eyebrow.

"No. I told you. I have ten dollars in my pocket. That's it." His voice broke, and he looked back at the ground.

Sal put his hand on Lale's shoulder and forced him to look him in the eyes.

"Don't be silly, Lale," he said, in a kinder voice. "I'm not going to jump on you, although the thought did cross my mind while you were sleeping so soundly with your pretty little rosebud mouth open and that delicate strand of saliva dribbling down your chin. Let me treat you to breakfast, then you can decide what you want to do. I'll help you. Whatever you want to do. No strings attached."

Lale hesitated. The street was piled with garbage waiting the morning pickup, and cars were going by, their drivers either studiously ignoring or ogling the women still defiantly strutting and shivering in the cold like a small flock of bright birds. Well, he was here now. He was at the end of the road, for better or worse. Lale shook his head and pushed his hands into his pockets. He had stupidly spent half the money in his wallet treating Sal to supper last night when they stopped at a steakhouse on the road, and he knew the rest wouldn't get him far.

"All right. Thanks, Sal. I'll pay you back when I can get a job. I mean it."

"I'm keeping a tab."

The Sunrise was warm and lively, full of freshly scrubbed people, their hair still damp from the shower, going to work, and others, exhausted, dressed in club clothes, coming back from a night of partying. It was a long narrow diner with a counter down the length of the room and red booths that matched the Coca-Cola signs. Hand-lettered blackboards above the counter announced the specials of the day. Sal and Lale found an empty booth, and a waitress wearing a tight green uniform and silver eye shadow came over to their table.

"Hey, Sal, when did you get back in town?"

"Five minutes ago, Freda, and it's *so* great to be back in civilization! I'm simply *not* cut out for the country life. But I brought back a souvenir. Meet Lale. If you can believe it, until two days ago he'd never been out of *Arkansas*."

She eyed Lale with a practiced once-over.

"Arkansas, huh? How did you luck into meeting Sally here?"

"Um, I needed a ride, and he had one. We're just friends. That's all."

"Oh, don't worry, sugar. I can tell you're straight. Anybody can see that written all over you. I have never been wrong about that. I have built-in radar."

"I can think of a time or two you were wrong, Freda."

"That was a *choice,* Sal. Of course I knew the score. I was just curious."

"Right. Freda here has built-in radar, darling. Or should I say *gay*-dar?"

"Ha. That's a good one. Anyhow, welcome to New York, Lale. What'll you have?"

"I'll have eggs, over easy, yellows not too runny, sausage, and biscuits."

"Sorry, no biscuits. No grits, either. How about a bagel?"

"What's that?"

"Bread. You'll like it, I promise."

Sal seemed to know quite a lot of the people in the diner. He waved to them as they came in the door, and blew kisses to a few. A tall, well-built man came in carrying a big flat leather portfolio, sat at the counter, and ordered coffee. He glanced around the room and zeroed in on Lale, who met his eyes, then looked away.

"Who's that guy at the counter? The one with the big black satchel," he asked Sal in a low voice.

Sally turned around and looked. Then he smiled and waved.

"That's Michel Denon. He's a fashion photographer. One of the *biggest.* He shoots the cover for *Vogue* every month. I work for him a lot. Has his eye on you, does he?"

"No offense, Sal, but I think I told you once or twice—I like girls and it makes me nervous to have so many guys giving me the once-over. Is everybody in New York, uh, like you are?"

"A little too many for some people's taste. Not quite enough for mine. But not Michel. He likes girls. Boy, does he like girls! Maybe he's had the odd guy or two—who can know, really—but basically he's straight. Ooh. He's coming over."

"Good morning, Sal. Who is your friend?" Michel had a French accent that went well with his long dark hair and expensive, butter-soft leather jacket.

"Hello, Michel. This is Lale Hardcastle. Lale, meet Michel Denon, fashion photographer extraordinaire."

"Lale. What a charming name. Who are you with?"

Lale looked at him with surprise.

"Well, I'm with Sal, here. I thought you knew him."

Michel laughed. "Of course I know Sal. No, I mean who is your agent?"

"Agent for what?"

"He's fresh from the farm, Michel. That is no lie."

"How marvelous! You have such a healthy, all-American look. You have to let me shoot you."

"Shoot me? What do you mean?"

"No, no, no, my darling, not with a gun! I mean with my camera! How delicious!" Michel laughed as if Lale had said something particularly funny. Lale's face turned red.

"Here, let me give you my card. I am legitimate. Our friend Sal here can vouch for me. I'll take some pictures of you and send you up to Ford

Models. They are the best in town. You will be in the pages of *GQ* before you can pick the hay out of your ears. Call me. I am serious."

"If you're serious, Michel, how about this afternoon? I can get the boy in shape and be there by three."

Michel raised an eyebrow. "Three? Are you sure? All right. See you at three, farm boy." He went back to the counter, still chuckling.

"Way to go, sweet cheeks. In town fifteen minutes and already you have been offered a freebee from a tough street girl who doesn't do *anything* for nothing, and now you're given the chance to become a star model!"

Lale had had enough. He felt like he was going to explode, but tried to keep his voice low and not yell and cause himself more embarrassment.

"What are you doing, telling him I'll be up at his place this afternoon? Wouldn't it be nice if you talked it over with me first? What if I don't *want* to get my picture taken and be a model? It sounds awful sissy to me. And why does everybody have to call me names, like 'sweet cheeks' and 'farm boy'? I hate that! I'm not an idiot! Everybody from Arkansas is not stupid! I could have gone to college if I wanted to. I still could! I made all A's my senior year!"

"Oh, my dear—I mean Lale—I'm sorry! Don't get your jockeys in a wad! It's just my way of speaking. I don't mean anything by it, and I'm sure Michel didn't either. I promise to stop. I know you're not an idiot. In fact, *I'm* the idiot! *I am!* I admit it! But you should be *happy* I leaped right in to set up this shoot. Do you have any idea how many men and women in this town would shove their grandmothers in front of a *truck* for a chance to shoot with Michel Denon? I know it's sudden, but when doors open, you have to run right through because they close just as fast. Don't you believe in fate? Like, for instance, ask yourself, Why was Miss Sally put right in my path, just when I needed her most? Think about it. Your guardian angel had to do *overtime* to set this whole thing up: arranging to have me meet that hunky singer from Nashville at Max's Kansas City—I could just as easily have gone to another club that night—and then fall for him and actually *go* to Nashville with him, against my better judgment, I want you to know, have him *dump* me—yes, I confess it was he who asked me to leave and not the other way around—in the middle of a party, no less, so that I packed my things and, crying and hurt, absolutely *ruining* my makeup, drove my little

Mustang up Highway 70, of all the roads I could have chosen, through the night, all in order to be at *that* particular truck stop at five in the morning when Mr. Lale Hardcastle was shot like a bean in a flip from the back end of an eighteen-wheeler! It *had* to have been your guardian angel doing it all! Consider the *odds* of that happening! Astronomical! Besides, what are your options? I mean, really, Lale. Let's be serious for a minute. Do you think you are going to leave me in this diner and go get a job driving a tractor in Manhattan? What else are you qualified for? Thank *God* you have that face and body! Not to mention the *hair.* And eyes. Don't make me go through it all piece by piece! You would be *crazy* not to go to Michel. If nothing else, it might be a way for you to get enough money to pay off my tab, which is now hovering around twenty-five dollars, and buy a Greyhound ticket back to the Ozarks and that poor lovely little thing you left at the altar, if that's what you still want to do."

"Don't talk about Cassie. I mean it, Sal."

"Sorry. No bad memories, right? My lips are sealed."

Sal made a motion of zipping his lips, leaned back, and looked at Lale, not speaking, which was definitely an effort for him. The silence finally got uncomfortable, and Lale took a sip of his coffee, then cleared his throat.

"What would I have to do, if I decided to go get . . . shot by this guy?"

"Just let someone, well, frankly, me, scrub you and dress you up and then you simply stand and get your picture taken. Nothing to it. You don't have to have a college degree. Just the God-given face you are wearing on top of that body."

"What does it pay?"

"Top models get seventy-five an hour. Assuming Ford takes you, and I can't imagine they wouldn't, since they are blonde-obsessed. You would probably start out at sixty."

"Sixty? Hmm."

"What's wrong?"

"That don't sound like a whole lot."

"Really? How much are you used to making?"

"I think minimum is a dollar forty-five, isn't it? At least it is in Arkansas."

It was all Sal could do to keep a straight face, but he made a mighty effort.

"I didn't mean sixty cents, Lale. I meant sixty dollars."

"Dollars?"

"Dollars."

"An *hour*?"

"Yes, my dear. Sixty dollars. An *hour*."

Lale was dumbstruck. The most he had ever made was fifty dollars a week. He knew for a fact that the richest man in town, a lawyer, made twenty-five thousand a year, because he talked about it all the time. Twenty-five thousand a year was . . . well . . . less than seventy-five or even sixty dollars an hour. A whole lot less.

Freda brought the food, and Lale bit into his bagel, lightly toasted with melted butter dripping off the side. It wasn't biscuits, but it wasn't bad.

15

GHOST IN SUNLIGHT

Rouge magazine came out. I saw it on the newsstand on the corner near my apartment. I couldn't miss it—on the cover was a face wrapped in *my* red-and-white Indian-print scarf with a makeup job that had all the finger marks of one Salvador de Vega. But it wasn't my face. It was somebody I had never seen before in my life, somebody who had the same big red lips and green-and-blue eye shadow, only her eyes were blue and her eyebrows were black, and she looked cheap, like some off-duty hooker. I was in such shock I couldn't move. Normally I would have cried, but I was not the girl I was when I first came to New York. A red curtain of rage fell down in front of my eyes. I thought Ron really liked me. I trusted him! I felt so betrayed, like he had cheated on me with some other woman. Before I could even think, I marched over to 830 Broadway and barged into his studio, waving the magazine.

Ron was in the middle of a shoot, and the girl must have thought I was nuts. I didn't care.

"Ron Bonetti, how could you have used me like this? All you had to do was tell me you were trying out lights for another girl for the cover and it would have been all right. I knew it was just a test. But *noooo,* you said you were going to do a cover try, and wouldn't it be great if I got a cover on my first test, and . . ."

"Hold on. Hold on, Cherry. Wait a minute. Let me explain."

"Yeah, right, explain! How many times have I seen you since we did that shot? Three. And you knew all the time, didn't you, that it wasn't going to be me! You could have at least warned me! I saw this on the *newsstand,* for Pete's sake!"

"Calm down. I was going to tell you. I was. I just didn't find the right moment. The art director loved the pictures. He really did. It was just that the girl on the cover was his girlfriend and he made me do the exact same picture with her, same makeup, same everything. Same scarf, and I am really sorry about that. I had it cleaned for you."

It was so raw and painful. My scarf. Sal, using the same lipstick brush on those big hooker-y lips that he had used on mine.

"Excuuuse me, Ron, but I can't wait here all day. I have another booking at three," the girl standing on the seamless paper said in a whiny voice. I glared at her. Here he was, cheating on me with her, too. I wished he'd go back to food pictures.

"Take a break, Rhonda. I'll be right back," Ron said. The model stomped out to the dressing room, giving me a filthy look. It was all just too much and I started to cry then. I couldn't help it. I went to the window, taking big gulps of air, so Ron, or God forbid, Rhonda, wouldn't see the tears, but it wasn't something I could hide. Ron came up behind me and put his hand on my shoulder. Then he tried to give me a hug, but it was a little awkward, since he only came up to my chin.

"I know it's a big disappointment, and I'm really sorry I didn't tell you, but didn't you see the other picture?"

"What other picture?" I sniffed. I always seemed to be crying around him and never had a Kleenex. I wiped my nose on the back of my hand.

"In the back. The last picture in the magazine. They call it 'Fini Rouge.' "

He held out the magazine, and on the last page, there was me, dancing in front of the window with the two white chairs, pale light outlining my body through the white gauze dress. You couldn't really see my face too well, since it was a soft shot, but you could tell it was lit by a big smile. Underneath was a little poem:

How strange it seems
To think this little photograph
On common paper lightly cast
May look into your face and laugh
When I myself have wholly past
. . . When I myself am a Ghost in Sunlight

—ANONYMOUS

There I was, in the pages of a magazine. It wasn't the cover, but my goodness, I had never seen myself in print before. I had a tear sheet to put in my book! I started to cry all over again.

"Don't cry, Cherry. It's a beautiful picture. The 'Fini Rouge' page is noticed. You'll get a lot of attention."

"I know it's a beautiful picture. I was just crying because . . . because . . . it is so beautiful."

"Yeah, well. Look," he said, clearing his throat while still patting me clumsily on the shoulder, "I wasn't kidding that you were going to be a big star. I'll tell you what. I have a little job to do for *Vogue*. It's shoes. But you can do it, and that'll give you a foothold in *Vogue,* so to speak. Will you do it for me?" I sniffed again and he fumbled in his pocket, this time producing a handkerchief.

"I can't do shoes. I wear size eleven."

"Oh. Well, I'm also doing socks and stockings for the same layout. I know you can do those. Okay?"

"Okay. Call Liz and book it." I blew my nose. I had already gotten several more jobs doing pantyhose for various ads, like the little cardboard things they fold around the hose in Kmart. I had tested for a few lingerie ads, too, and was booked for a Vanity Fair nightgown one, with a great photographer named Neal Barr. I was fast becoming the queen of underwear, it seemed, which was fine with me. We got paid more for lingerie. Still, I'd like to have my face in a picture. The Vanity Fair layouts always had the girl's face turned in shadow, her hand in front of it or something.

"And I'll tell you what else. How about you go out to dinner with me?"

"You mean like a date or something?"

"No, no, nothing like that. Just friends. There's a great Italian restaurant on Hester Street called Puglia's. Authentic. Just like Mama used to make. It'll cheer you up."

"You're just trying to bribe me. I'll never get over seeing that ugly girl in my outfit on the cover of *Rouge,* you know, bribes or not. She wasn't even classy—she has rusty elbows, I bet."

"Okay. Be that way. I'm sure Rhonda wouldn't mind going with me to Puglia's."

I looked over at the dressing room, where Rhonda was staring at us.

"All right. Fine. I'll go."

"Great. I'll pick you up at eight tomorrow night."

I think I had a date, whether he called it that or not. He was most certainly not my type, but then I wasn't too sure what my type was, or even if I had one. But he was able to give me work, and that I desperately needed. I'd have to tell him right up front, though, that I wasn't going to sleep with him. And the dinner might be fun. I'd liked Little Italy that time Lana and I went there. It seemed like Aurelius wasn't going to make a move anytime soon, although the day we found out Janis Joplin had died he had left me a copy of "Piece of My Heart" and a note: "I guess white singers can be hell on themselves, too. XX A." But he hadn't tried to ask me out or anything. Maybe I'd read it all wrong and he just wasn't attracted to me. He may even have had a girlfriend or three, for all I knew, although I never saw any girls coming out of his place. I certainly would have heard them if he had anybody sleep over, the walls were so thin. But as far as that went, I didn't know if Ron was single or not. He'd never said. Well, it would be a night out. A nice change of pace from writing letters or reading. I had gotten pretty far in James Baldwin's *Go Tell It on the Mountain,* which I could relate to, since it was about a preacher and a boy who had a conversion experience that totally equaled St. Paul's wrestling with the angel on the road to Damascus. Lordy, that Baldwin could write! There was one long passage where he was fighting for his soul that hit you like hard rain falling until you could barely breathe, and you couldn't get yourself out of it. It was so familiar to me, and made me feel guilty for not even trying to go to church. Just not quite guilty enough to go and find one.

I had no idea if Aurelius was a reader or not, but if he was, Baldwin was somebody he most certainly would have read, and if he did ask me out, I wanted to be able to talk to him about black literature. It was a whole new world for me, but then every day in New York seemed to be the start of a new adventure, and although I missed home a little, so little I was ashamed of it, I was thrilled when I woke up every morning in my little bed under the eaves in the attic on Twelfth Street and felt such gratitude just to be able breathe that electric New York air.

16

CASSIE'S PLEA

Dear Cherry,

Baby gave me your address—I hope you didn't care. I guess you have been too busy to write, but she keeps me up on you. We all saw your picture in *Rouge*. Eileen down at the drugstore found it, and Father Leo has it up on the wall in the art room. Mama says to tell you you're the prettiest one in the magazine, and she thinks you are going to be bigger than Twiggy. We all miss you.

I'm doing all right, still working at Flyin' Jack's, although I'm as big as an elephant and Bernadette has to do a lot of the work. It's hard for me to even reach the sink to do the dishes. She says every day she is going to fire my butt, but she won't. The doctor says it could come any day now, and my feet are so swollen I can't wear anything but house shoes. You wouldn't even recognize me, I'm so puffy. I hate how I look. As soon as the baby is born I'm going on a diet. I'm almost glad Lale isn't here to see me. Almost. Ha.

Snuffy has been to New York on a Freyaldenheimer's run a time or two since you left, but he would never look you up—he's too shy. I asked him to keep an eye out for Lale, and he said he would, but he won't. It would be a miracle if he saw him walking down the street anyhow, and he wouldn't tell me even if he did see him. Snuffy and Bernadette and everyone else think I am better off without Lale, except for me. You haven't run across him by any chance, have you? I hated to ask you to look, but you are in the best place to find him. I saw him again in *Playboy,* one that Chet saved for me. This time it was him all right, no doubt, full face. It was an ad for L&M cigarettes, and he was standing close beside a skinny blond girl with her hair done up in curls and a lot of false eyelashes and makeup on. Underneath, it said, "A cigarette for the two of you." His hair is shorter now, brushed over to the side. It is so thick! He always had the thickest hair. The picture is in color and his blue eyes just shine.

Oh, Cherry, I hate myself for writing you when you haven't even written me one time, but I'm desperate. I need to talk to Lale. I need to talk to him so much that it's making me sick. Everyone in town is gossiping about me and it's just hard to hold my head up and go to work every day knowing that they're all whispering behind my back and feeling sorry for me. It is especially hard on Mama. She is at St. Juniper's every morning at six for mass before she goes to work, and she has cried a tub of tears and lit a huge box of candles. I don't think God is listening to her.

Lale's mother and daddy won't talk to me, like it was my fault Lale ran off, and outside of Bernadette, my friends act funny, like they don't know what to say, and none of them ever calls for me to go to the movies or out to eat with them anymore. Baby is the only one who acts normal around me, but she is pretty busy at school and I don't see her much. I don't know why I had to be so stupid. I have prayed to God for forgiveness and confessed to Father Leo, but forgiven or not, there is still this baby inside me, rolling around, part of Lale that will forever be part of me.

You're my only hope to find him, Cherry. I know it's a lot to ask, but if you could somehow check with some other models or something I know you could find him and talk to him for me. Tell him I don't expect him to come home, but if he would just call me it would mean so much. Then I might be able to hate him and go on with my life, but as it is I can't even hate him. There is just a big gaping hole where he pulled my heart out.

Please don't forget about me. I am begging you.

Love,
Cassie

17

SOHO

"Welcome to SoHo, sweetie. That's short for 'South of Houston.' "

"You mean *Huse*ton, don't you? Like in Texas? Ain't that how it's spelled on the sign?"

"No, darling, I mean *House*ton. Don't ask why it's pronounced differently. It just isn't much like Texas, I guess."

After breakfast, Sal didn't have to twist Lale's arm to go on to his apartment. There was no place else to go, and they had to get ready for the meeting with Michel at three. Lale had crossed a bridge, and whatever happened he was going along for the ride. Sixty dollars an hour was a powerful influence on Lale's good intentions, and he was kind of getting used to Sal. In for a penny, in for a pound.

They drove down the west side of Manhattan, the Hudson River on the right and a row of seedy-looking buildings on the left. As they went farther south, the buildings got seedier, some of them meat-packing places with big burly men in bloody coveralls hauling huge sides of beef and pork and legs of lamb out of refrigerated trucks.

They made a left turn on Canal Street, and then another left up Greene Street.

"At one time, the early eighteen-hundreds and beyond, this part of town was the main drag of New York, theaters and exclusive shops down here on lower Broadway, where all the rich women came to their dressmakers. No off-the-rack in those days, honey. Every stitch was made to order. This part we're in now, only a couple of blocks west of Broadway, was the back door, so to speak, of the biggest red-light district in New York. Right on this block, Greene Street, there were *fifty-two* whorehouses! Can you imagine? Then, of course, when all the immigrants started crowding in down here, the ritzy businesses moved uptown, as they would tend to, since that was where the land was, most of it farms, can you believe? Chicken coops on Fifth Avenue! The theaters and expensive stores went to what is now midtown Broadway, and the fancy madams and their pleasure parlors went right with them, leaving this part of town to the dressmakers, who had *finally* discovered ready-to-wear, and who had tons of cheap labor in the immigrants. All these wonderful old cast-iron buildings were built as *factories* in the later part of the century. The place I live used to be a blouse factory. Wait until you see it. It's absolutely to *die*. You'll love it."

In his worst nightmares, Lale couldn't have imagined a place as bad as this to live. Big trucks blocked most of the dim, narrow cobblestone streets, boxes of garbage were piled high on the sidewalks, and Lale saw more than a few fat rats rummaging around. The buildings were high and dark, some of them with loading docks right off the street where trucks could back in. Noise from the trucks and machinery made a din that echoed in the cavernous street and everything seemed to have a coat of black soot on it.

"You don't mean you *live* down here, do you?"

"Yes, isn't it *amazing*! Don't worry about the streets—they're really quite safe. They're much quieter at night. And you will *love* the loft. Here we are. Home sweet home."

Sal neatly pulled the Mustang around a truck that was parked half on the sidewalk, got out, and shoved up a rolling door in the wall that opened to a good-size room. Then he got into the car, drove into the room, got out, rolled the door back down, and pulled on a rope. The room started to rise, and Lale jumped when he realized it was an elevator. The elevator stopped on the fourth floor, Sal opened a set of double doors with a key, then drove the Mustang right into his apartment. Lale sat for a minute in disbelief, then got out.

"I told you, you wouldn't believe it! Isn't this just the *best*?"

The room was three hundred feet long and thirty feet wide. A row of iron columns painted creamy green ran down the center, but there were no walls to divide the space. Tall windows, grimy with New York dirt, let in pale light, and the noise of the factories and the stream of cars and trucks plowing down Broadway, two blocks away, made a muted roar in the background, like the ocean. The floors were concrete, splattered with various colors of paint, strewn with Oriental rugs, and a red velvet curtain hung across part of the back wall, tied by a gold tasseled rope. A large bed covered in a gold-and-red satin coverlet and throw pillows could be seen behind it. The walls were partially plastered in crumbling layers, colors of yellow and green and blue, the brick showing through in places, as though someone had started to tear it down and quit in the middle. There were two red velvet couches and a leather chair set in a conversation arrangement around a low coffee table, and farther down, a wooden counter divided the kitchen area from the rest of the space.

In the front part of the loft, near the door where the car was parked, enormous canvasses were stretched directly onto the walls, and a long rough table was loaded with twisted paint tubes and brushes. A glass palette made from an old window was smeared with rows of oil colors. Several bold abstracts were in various stages of completion. Heavy with paint so thick it threatened to fall off the canvas onto the floor, all the paintings, like Edvard Munch's, seemed to scream.

In another part of the open space was a lighted makeup table lined with rows of wigs and hairpieces in varying colors pinned to Styrofoam heads. Cases that looked designed to hold fishing tackle overflowed with makeup.

Lale stood rooted to the spot, trying to take it all in, not sure what to do, where to go.

"Come on in, darling. Don't stand there like a tourist. I swear, it is like pushing a Cadillac up a hill to get you to do *anything*. Just sit over there at the table, and I'll make a nice pot of tea. Since you are light on luggage, we'll have to figure out something for you to wear for your test. Not to be rude, but that shirt and jeans are getting a little whiffy. It is clear you didn't pack your Arrid. And we have to do something with that amazing head of hair. As gorgeous as you are, you could stand a little pruning and polishing."

"Okay. Okay. You don't have to carry on. I'll sit. This is all just a little new for me, all this living in warehouses that were old whorehouses or shirt factories or whatever. I never had a car in my living room before, but I can see where it might be handy. I also don't see anyplace for me to sleep, and I ain't going to sleep in that fancy bed you have over there. No way."

"Will you stop it? Of course you aren't going to. That's *my* bed. Although since I've been gone, I'm sure Preston has given it a workout. The sheets are undoubtedly *not* fresh. You can sleep on the couch. Preston is my roommate, although I think he must be a teensy bit annoyed with me right now. I neglected to mention to him I was taking off for Nashville. Heat of the moment and all. He is the painter, which is how we got this place. You have to be an artist to get to rent these, and Preston is a *wonderful* painter, don't you think? I consider myself an artist, too, as does anybody who has worked with me, but somehow the powers that be who pass out these spaces think it has to be on a canvas or a pedestal to be art, not on a human face, which is *my* canvas. Nevertheless, the rent is right—one hundred a month—which we split. You can just be a guest for a while until you get on your feet, and then if you want to find another place, that is up to you. I'm sure Preston will never know you're here. He has his head in his work night and day. He never even talks, which frankly I don't mind, as he rarely has anything interesting to say beyond 'Cool, man.' Leaves *me* more space to talk, which I love to do. If you didn't notice. In the meantime, let's get you out of those clothes and into the shower."

The bathroom—a shower and toilet—was behind another curtain near the kitchen, which had a blue wooden table and four chairs, a sink, a hot plate, and small fridge. Open shelves held dishes and glasses and an old tin pie cupboard served as a pantry. But there were fresh flowers on the counter and the cupboard was painted Spanish Gold, with red-and-turquoise knobs. To his surprise, Lale kind of liked it.

Lale stood in the shower for as long as the hot water lasted, letting the last few days wash out of his system. It dawned on him that he hadn't thought much about Cassie or his folks since he'd landed in New York, and that bothered him. What was wrong with him, that he could so easily leave them behind? It seemed like Buchanan was as far away as the moon, and instead of two days, it had been years since he lived there. He was afraid of what the future held and part of him was deeply ashamed of what he'd done, but most of him just felt alive and happy and free.

He came out wrapped in a towel, and saw that Sal had laid out some pants and a shirt for him on the bed, and a clean pair of boxer shorts, something that looked like red paisley silk.

"What the heck are these things? They look like bloomers. Don't you have any Jockeys?"

"Afraid not. You really have no choice. While you were in the shower, I put your things in to soak. Industrial-strength detergent. Here, put these on and get dressed, and I'll give that lion's mane a trim. I'm quite good with hair, although makeup is my forte."

The shirt was some kind of shiny black nylon material, and the pants were bell-bottomed hip-huggers, too tight to button.

"I can't wear these. They're too little. Are they yours?"

"Oh, no. *Mine* would be much smaller than those. Those are Preston's. The only ones I could find that weren't covered in paint. He would be in a rage if he knew I lent them to you, but he seems to be elsewhere. Probably buying out the oil department at Pearl Paint. He spends every dime he gets on the stuff. Little excessive for my taste, if you want to know the truth. Slathers it on like cream cheese. He does sell occasionally, though. At least the buyers get a lot for their money! I like watercolors myself. Light, simple, tasteful. We used to be lovers, you know, Preston and I, but that went by the by *ages* ago. Except for the odd occasion, like ships bumping into each other in the night kind of thing. But he'll have no problems with you here, I'm sure, once he finds out you're straight and I'm not sleeping with you. Although you would be surprised to find out how many straight men like a little diversion from time to time. Especially young married men. It's not cheating, they think, if it's with another man. I know *several* of those, and in fact . . ."

"Okay, okay. I hear you. How much of my hair are you going to cut off? I suffered for this hair. Coach nearly didn't let me play my senior year, but I was the quarterback, and he didn't have much choice."

"I'll just shape it a bit. My, what thick hair it is! You really *will* have to start using some hair products. Long might be hippie-chic, but the suits paying for the ads still want a reasonable length. It's the moms and dads that have the money, and the readers of *Esquire* and *Playboy aren't* hippies. Oh, you are going to be the find of the year, Lale Hardcastle! And it was all *my* doing! If I do say so myself, I am a *genius*."

Sal clipped happily away as the sandy-blond hair fell on the floor in fluffy piles. Lale looked at himself in the mirror and saw with cold eyes a stranger emerging.

18

LALEA

Dear Cherry,

I hate to write you about this, but it is so hard to get you on the phone. Cassie had her baby, and it was a little girl. She had a hard time and lost a lot of blood, and is still in the hospital. The worst part is that the baby is, well, she's harelipped, I guess is the only way to put it. But it's really a bad one. Her little mouth is just gaped open, split from top to bottom, and her nose is all over her face. Her eyes are kind of on the sides of her head. Everyone is in a state of shock. Annie is just killed. The little thing is so deformed that she can't really suck, and if she does manage to get some milk down she throws it up. I was in there when Cassie begged them to let her try to breast-feed, and she tried and tried, but just couldn't. Every time she looks at the baby she cries, so much that her milk dried up. I guess they are trying to feed her with a bottle with some kind of special nipple, but that isn't much more successful than the breast was, and I think they are going to put a feeding tube down her poor little nose. Cassie won't eat, either. She is so pale she's green, and weak from all the blood she lost. I'm so worried about her. She just stares at the wall. Lale's mama and daddy have only been to see the baby one time, and I heard Janet told somebody they don't think the baby was Lale's, or else why would he have left like he did? It is horrible. If I ever get my hands on Lale Hardcastle, I will chop off his balls and boil them in vinegar. I guess you haven't found him yet, or you would have told me.

Besides all that (as in, Aside from *that,* Mrs. Lincoln, how was the play?), things are going all right here. Cassie's little brother, Barry, got in trouble for making clay pipes in my class, and I got in trouble for letting him. They were great pipes, though—the bowls were little faces with tiny glasses, headbands, and funny beards, long hippie hair making the stem. The principal, ol' Roamin' Hands Bachman, was hanging out in my class, like he likes to do, saw them, and confiscated them right out of the kiln. He didn't buy for a minute that they were for tobacco, and said Barry was too young to smoke tobacco in any case. The next day, Barry and some of his buddies brought six goats to school and let them out in the halls during assembly, and while Mr. Bachman was trying to handle the pandemonium, Barry sneaked into his office and stole the pipes back. It was crazy. They had to let school out for the rest of the day until they could round up the goats and scrub the floors. Nobody can prove for sure it was Barry who did it, but everybody knows. I think part of the reason he did it is that he was so upset about Cassie that he just had to let off some steam. He is just angry at the world, and I don't blame him. Father Leo has been visiting Cassie, but I don't think he is doing her much good. There's not a lot he can say, and thank goodness he's not one to talk about God's will and all. I don't think God would do something like that to someone who is already hurting like Cassie was. She named the baby Lalea, by the way.

Speaking of Father Leo, I've been up to the abbey a few times to see him. He is building a raku kiln out in the field near the bluff that he'll let my class share. I wish you were here to help us. It's not the same since you left. I think Leo misses you, too. He has that big painting you did, the *Virgin Mary on the Rocks*, hanging in his office. (The one where she is sitting on the ice cubes in a martini glass, not the other one on the cliff. I think he hung it to shock Father Bennett, but it really is good.) Leo has the most amazing gray eyes, doesn't he? Like clear water. He gave me a pot he made on the wheel, a perfect red one, that has the Philippine Tagalog word for love on one side and happiness on the other. It is a crying shame he is a priest. Ah, well.

How is your romance with Aurelius going? Have you done it yet? If you were down here, you would be tarred and feathered by the Ku Klux Klan just for having lunch with him. If you didn't already know, they have a chapter here in Buchanan, even though there is only one black person living in town that I know of. His name is Scipio Jones and he works making pots up at Lost Acre Hollow, which is where I met him. He built himself a cob house out in the woods, dug the clay and mixed it with straw all by himself. Pretty impressive. He's going to let me bring my class out to see it and we'll do a project making little cob houses. He's pretty cute, too, so I might just follow your lead and see what it's like. The Klan knows he's there, but it doesn't look like they're going to do much about it. Can't burn down a cob house. I heard that the Klan had started a little movement to get the name of Buchanan changed to No Niggers, Arkansas, but then Scipio moved in and it would be stupid to have a town called One Nigger, Arkansas, so they had to give it up. Some of the Kluxer kids are in my class. They don't know what to make of me. I am not white, but I'm not exactly black, either, and frankly they like me, so they are confused. I love it.

Remember that article in *Cosmo* we read about how the new hot thing was white women going out with black men? Let me know if it's true what they say, you know, about the size.

Much love,
Baby

19

ITALIANS

When I read Cassie's letter, I felt like a dog. It was true that I hadn't written to Cassie even one time since I'd come to New York, but I hadn't known what to say. I didn't want to tell her about the Zack business until I knew for sure he was Lale, and frankly, it hadn't been at the top of my agenda to find out. In truth of fact, I dreaded like everything finding Lale and having to give him a tongue-lashing for running out on Cassie. He would ask me what business of mine it was and I'd have to say it wasn't any really, but he was a jerk anyhow, and then where would that go? I mean, was he going to say, "Oh, thanks for pointing that out to me. I'll run and get on the bus and go right back to her"? I hate confrontations. I sort of knew already that Zack was Lale, but when I saw the old *Playboy* Cassie mentioned at one of the photographers' studios and looked at his picture in the L&M cigarette ad, I knew for sure.

I was still putting off answering her letter, trying to decide what to do, when I got Baby's letter a few days later, and then I was *really* sick to my stomach. I was going to have to do something, but I didn't know what. Poor Cassie. I thought it couldn't get any worse, but it had. How could Janet and George Hardcastle not believe it was Lale's baby, knowing Cassie like they did? They used to like her. But on the other hand, I could see how they wouldn't want to believe it of him. He was their son. I don't know if he had even written or called them, but surely he must have. How could you go off and not tell your parents where you were? But then if he had, why hadn't they told Cassie where he was or given her his address? The whole thing was just a mess that I had somehow gotten sucked into, even though it was totally none of my business. I had to write to Cassie, so with a heavy heart, I did:

Dear Cassie,

I'm so sorry I haven't written to you, but I've been really, really busy. Baby wrote me about you having the baby and all, and I want you to know that I am so sorry, I can't tell you how sorry, that it turned out like this. But they can probably fix little Lalea's mouth, can't they? I'm sure she will be beautiful after a few operations.

I wadded up the letter and threw it away. From the way Baby talked, little Lalea looked like a leaf-nosed bat, and I doubt that it would be comforting to have me tell her it was going to be all right when I hadn't even laid eyes on her. It wasn't going to be all right. And if you tell somebody you are too busy to write to them, it just means to them that they are on the bottom of your list of things to do. I got out another sheet of stationery and tried again.

Dear Cassie,

Please forgive me for not writing and not being there for you. I've just been caught up in my new life—no excuses. I wish I could help you, I really do. I'm glad you have your mom and Bernadette, though, and Baby. There is no better friend than Baby. The only thing I can say is that I am going to really try to find Lale. He is lower than a snake's belly, but he needs to know what is going on, and I promise you, I'll make it up to you and do something, if I can at all. I don't have a phone in my room, but I'll try to call you as soon as I find out anything. Hang in. You're a good, strong girl and you'll get through this. A lot of people love you, including me, as bad a friend as I have been.

Love,
Cherry

I stared at the letter, and couldn't think of anything else to say. I thought that after that night when Cassie had tried to let the train run over her she had pulled it together. Baby and I hung out with her a lot last spring, and the two of them came up to St. Juniper's and we all made pots on the wheel with Father Leo every weekend. Baby and I even spent the night at Cassie's house a few times and we rode her horses bareback across the pastures and ate homemade rolls and sweet grape jelly Annie had made from their own grapes at breakfast. My practice teaching was over in May, and I went back to Sweet Valley, but over the summer we wrote once in a while, and in her letters she seemed to be fine. Lale's parents kind of ignored her, she said, but his sister, Brenda, was friendly to her. I guess the baby being born harelipped like that just sent everybody over the edge.

But Cassie was not in my world anymore, and while I really felt bad for her, the ugly side of me wished she hadn't made me promise to find Lale. Now, with this letter, I really had to try, or I'd be as low as him. I decided I would call up a few of the agencies tomorrow and ask them if they had anybody named Zack. It wasn't the most common name. Then I'd . . . I'd . . . well, I'd figure it out, a step at a time.

For right now, I had to get ready to go out to eat with Ron Bonetti. I figured the chances of him running into Aurelius were slim, but frankly I didn't care if Aurelius saw me going out with somebody else. In spite of all that electricity bouncing between us, he hadn't tried even once to talk to me since the day at Joe Jr.'s when Hendrix died, and except for the Janis Joplin record and note under the door, there had been nothing. He still played the sax late at night, though, and that was comforting, and there was the rose that was left by my door the day after we talked, but it might not have even been him that left it, although I couldn't imagine who else it would be. There were several more kids living in Mrs. Digby's house, and while we spoke to one another as we passed on the stairs or something, I didn't make friends with any of them. We were all too busy trying to get somewhere in some career.

There were a couple of actors and a dancer and one quiet girl who was writing a novel and worked in a jewelry shop on Greenwich Street, but none of them would leave me flowers.

I splurged on a new outfit—a pair of mustard suede hot pants trimmed in burnt orange, and I wore them with a matching turtleneck sweater, dark-orange wool tights, brown granny boots that laced up to the knee, and a long coat of mustard-and-burnt-orange chenille with brown fake-fur trim. I had a scarf tied around my head and big Monet chandelier earrings like the ones Maud Adams had on in that month's *Vogue,* and the whole effect was pretty high-fashion. The hot pants were a little on the short side, but the coat covered everything, which didn't make it feel so bare. It was getting colder and soon I'd have to look for a heavy coat. New York winters were bound to be a lot colder than the ones I was used to. I could probably find a good one in an antique store down in the Village. Maybe real sheepskin. That would be warm.

I made a lot of noise locking my door, but didn't hear a sound from Aurelius's apartment. He never was there, except late at night or in the mornings, when he was asleep. There was no way he would be downstairs when Ron came by, but you never knew.

Mrs. Digby was sitting in her parlor with the door open when I walked by.

"My, my, don't you look spiffy! Hot date?"

"Not really, Mrs. Digby. Just a friend. He's taking me out to some Italian place in Little Italy."

"I'm glad you're getting out. I was beginning to worry, a pretty girl like you staying home every night. Come in and have a little cup of tea. I just made it. How is the modeling going?"

"Not too bad," I said, dropping into the chair nearest the door so I'd be sure to hear the bell. "I'm going to do a big ad for Vanity Fair nightgowns, and I've started a class learning how to walk down a runway and be in fashion shows. They usually use special girls who just do shows, but they're starting to use more of the photographic models now. I don't know how I'll do. I'm pretty spastic when it comes to walking."

It was unhappily true. The man they had running the class, Gerald le Forge, was about ready to give up on me. You had to walk like you were on a straight line, one foot in front of the other, with your shoulders sort of slumped and your hips thrust forward. You walked slowly and had a bored look on your face, and weren't supposed to react to whoever was in the audience, like you wouldn't notice even if Jim Morrison was sitting there in the front row in his black leather pants with his weenie out. And we had to learn how to pivot, up on our toes, looking graceful, in the highest heels you can imagine, in order to turn around at the end of the runway. I had already twisted my ankle, which was horrible, since I had to do so much walking making the rounds of go-sees. Fortunately, it wasn't sprained, but it made looking bored harder. Still, Gerald promised he'd try to book me at one of the smaller shows to practice. We got the same hourly rate as for photography, so that was good.

"Oh, I'm sure you're going to be swell at it," Mrs. Digby said. She was a hip chick, ol' Mrs. D. "I thought I couldn't dance a step when I first started with Flo Zeigfeld, but before I knew it I was kicking up just as high as the rest of them."

"I wish I could have seen you in the shows."

"Nothing like them around anymore. People think of burlesque as a strip show on Forty-second Street, but it used to be real classy entertainment. High-toned men and women came, dressed to the nines. Everyone dolled up to go out in those days, even if it was just shopping, hats and gloves and walking sticks and spats for the men. And after the shows, the sharpshooters were always waiting around the stage door, flowers in hand, to see which one of us they could take out for a late supper. I was one of the most popular, if I do say so myself, and had scads of boyfriends. I met my first husband that way. He was a real gentleman, that Reggie. I knew he was husband material when he didn't make a pass on our first date. Didn't even try to hold my hand or kiss me! And he wore expensive shoes. You can always judge a man by his shoes, remember that. Reggie wooed me properly, I can tell you. Flowers, candy, little gifts of jewelry sent to the dressing room every night—not too expensive, but tasteful. Of course I knew not to sleep with him until he proposed and I had a rock on my finger! He thought I was an angel and my feet didn't touch the earth when I walked. After we were engaged for a few months and had the date picked out and the invitations sent, I finally did go to bed with him, but I wouldn't give him head until after the actual wedding ceremony. I suppose you know what that means?"

"Yes, ma'am, I do." I was good and shocked, but tried to keep my face expressionless, like I had to do for the runway.

"I knew no nice girl would do *that* until the *wedding* ring was on the finger. I suppose times have changed, though."

"Yes, ma'am, I think they have."

"Anyhow, at the same time I was seeing my first husband—Reggie Digby, his name was. I may have said that already; isn't that a nice name? I never changed my name again although I did change husbands a few times—my real name was Bernice Schwartz, and that was no name for a Ziegfeld girl. Beatrice Digby was so much classier. So, as I was saying, all the while I was letting Reggie woo me, on the side I was also seeing another boyfriend who was in the mob. You know about the mob, I imagine?"

"Kind of." I had to work harder at keeping my face expressionless.

"Well, he was the most attractive man you ever wanted to meet. Dark. Dangerous. All women love dangerous men, don't they? I know I used to. This one was named Al Paris, although I don't think Paris was his real last name. Probably something long and Italian. Is the young man you are going out with tonight Italian, by any chance?"

"Uh, well, as a matter of fact, he is."

"I knew it. I'm quite psychic, you know. Every woman should have an Italian in her life. Anyhow, Al Paris loved, loved, *loved* to have me give him head. It was his favorite thing in all the world, and to tell you the truth, in my day I was quite proficient at it—in fact a lot of the gentlemen said I was the *best* there was, and . . ."

"Mrs. Digby, I don't mean to interrupt you, but this is kind of a lot of information. Maybe I shouldn't know all this."

"Oh, piddle. You young people these days are so straitlaced. Fine. I won't tell you the end of the story." She picked up her teacup and took a sip, her mouth in a little moue. I hated to make her unhappy.

"Well, okay," I said. "So you would . . . do you-know-what to Al Paris, but not to Mr. Digby. But why didn't you marry Al Paris if you liked him more?"

She set her cup down a little harder than she meant to, sloshing out some of the tea, and looked at me in amazement. "Are you serious? An Italian? One who said he was in the *mob*? What kind of husband would that make? I would never get a moment's peace when he was out of the house, and the very *minute* an Italian man marries a woman she becomes the *wife* and they start having mistresses! No, it's better to be the mistress with men like that, and marry men like Mr. Digby, who was the owner of a furniture manufacturing firm, and who, as I said, I saved the big surprise for until the wedding night."

"So what happened? Was it a huge success? So to speak."

"No, actually he didn't really like it. Only man I ever knew who didn't. I worked and worked and worked on him, but it never got past half-mast, and he never let me try again. I think he was embarrassed. What a disappointment, to find out too late, after the wedding, that you weren't allowed to do one of the things you do best in life! Forget any chance of him reciprocating, if you know what I mean. That would have been much too embarrassing for him to try. We stayed together for a year, but it never really worked. Although I do have fond memories of Mr. Digby, even today. He bought me this house, bless him, and of course all the furniture, which came from his factory. A gentleman all the way. If I have one lesson to pass on to you, Cherry, it's to get real estate out of them, and have it put in your own name."

"I'll remember that. What happened to Al Paris?"

"I don't know. He disappeared a few months after my wedding. He used to say his secret mob name was the Ghost, because he was always there but nobody could see him. I think he was some kind of collector or hit man or something and had to do a lot of waiting around."

"I guess somebody saw him."

"Most likely. Anyway, dear, have fun with your Italian man tonight. Is he married?"

"He never said."

"He's married."

As if on cue the doorbell rang and Ron was standing there with his yellow aviator glasses and neatly cropped beard, holding a biker's helmet.

"Hi, Ron. What's with the helmet?"

"We're going on the bike tonight. I thought I'd surprise you. By the way, you look fabulous. I always wanted to walk into a restaurant with an Amazon in suede hot pants."

"Is it too much?"

"Too much is never enough. You're perfect."

Mrs. Digby followed me into the foyer, her ever-present smile lighting up at Ron.

"Mrs. Digby, this is my friend, Ron Bonetti. Ron, this is my landlady, Beatrice Digby."

"Charmed to make your acquaintance, Mrs. Digby." He actually took her hand and kissed it. She simpered like a young girl. If you only knew, Ron, I thought, that you are kissing the hand that has launched a thousand guys.

"Cherry didn't say you were such a charming young man, Mr. Bonetti. You're not in the mob by any chance, are you?" She actually fluttered her eyelashes at him.

"No, ma'am. I'm a photographer."

"That's lovely. Well, have a nice time, children. If Aurelius comes in, Cherry, should I tell him you're out?"

"I don't think Aurelius will ask, Mrs. Digby. Good night."

"Who's Aurelius?"

"Nobody," I said, and walked out the door.

My head was whirling from the conversation with Mrs. Digby, and I almost ran into the motorcycle parked on the curb.

"Wow. This thing is huge! Is it a Harley?"

"Is there anything else?"

"I've never ridden on a motorcycle before. I mean, you're right out there, aren't you? With no roof or sides or anything to protect you." I guess I sounded a little scared. I was.

"Don't worry. Here's a helmet. You'll be as safe as you would be in a Cadillac convertible."

Right. I hated the helmet squashing my hair down, and the strap got tangled up in my earrings so I had to take them off. I worried that the tail of my coat was going to get caught in the spokes and drag me off onto the pavement under the wheels of a car, or break my neck like Isadora Duncan, but I didn't want Ron to think I was a baby, so I climbed on behind him.

"Put your arms around my waist. Hold on and don't wiggle around too much."

I jumped when he stomped down on the starter, and I grabbed on to him, winding my fingers into the leather of his jacket, and off we went. It was pretty wild, zooming east across town and then down Broadway, zigzagging between the cars. Everyone stared at us, but after a few blocks I sort of got my seat and didn't feel like I was going to fall off. The tail of my coat flapped behind the bike, and the cold wind whipped my legs. It was impossible to talk. I just hung on for dear life and watched the buildings whiz by like lights on a carousel.

Puglia's on Hester Street had been open for business since 1919. The smell of good garlic permeated the walls and floors, and the red-and-white-checked tablecloths were soft from scores of washings. The maître d' greeted Ron like an old friend, and gave me his arm as he guided us to the table right in the window, where everyone on the street could look in and see us.

"Maybe we could sit in the back?" I asked. I wasn't too keen on a couple of guys who were staring in at the window, pretending to read the menu.

"No, no, no, signorina! This is *best* table in house! Only the best for the beautiful signorina!" So we sat down and I ignored the guys peering in until they finally sauntered off.

The waiter came right over with menus and water, and Ron ordered a bottle of Chianti. His eyes were a little bright, and it seemed like he might have already gotten a head start on the drinks, but for a guy who had vodka for breakfast, it was normal. Ron drank more than anybody I ever knew, but you could hardly tell at all.

"Do you ever get drunk?" I asked.

"No. There's a trick to getting drunk that I haven't mastered. In fact I wish I *could* get drunk."

"Why do you want to get drunk?"

"To get someplace else besides my head, I guess."

"Is your head such a bad place to be?"

"Tonight, Cherry *chérie,* I wouldn't trade heads with anybody."

I didn't quite know how to answer that, and he smiled like he was joking, so I just didn't respond. I never knew with him if he was kidding or not. He always wore yellow glasses, which made it hard to see his eyes.

"Why do you always wear those glasses, Ron?"

"It makes the world always look sunny."

"Even at night?"

"Especially at night. Besides, I'm nearsighted and need them to see."

"Can you take them off, just for a little bit?"

He took them off, and he wasn't really that bad-looking. His eyes might have been a little small, but they were a nice brown. He grinned, then put the glasses back on.

"Sorry. I would rather be able to see you, but I'll try to wear regular glasses if it bothers you."

"Oh, it doesn't bother me." But it did.

The waiter brought the wine, which was a little on the sour side, but I sipped it without making a face, and was proud of how sophisticated I was.

"So," I said, turning my glass so the candlelight caught red glints in the wine, "this is not a date, right?"

"Right."

"Then what is it?"

"It's dinner. Everybody has to eat dinner," he said with a little smile. I put my glass down and looked him in the eyes, as best I could.

"Are you married, Ron? I need to know that right off."

"Married. What makes you think I'm married?"

"Stop stalling. Are you married?"

"Well, if you put it that way, yes. I am. Kind of. To my high school sweetheart, Becky. Rebecca. No kids."

" 'Kind of.' What does that mean?"

"Well, we're sort of having a trial separation."

"Sort of? You moved out or what?"

"Not exactly. We're still living in the same house, but we're not sharing a room. Well, actually, we *are* sharing the room, but not . . ."

"So she doesn't care if you go out with models?"

"That could be part of the problem. But she's got her own life. She likes to bowl. Out in Jersey. I told you I lived in Jersey. She hates coming to the city. That's another one of the problems. You marry a cute cheerleader from high school, she turns into a bowler who hates New York, and you turn into a photographer who is in love with the city. But I don't want to talk about all that tonight. Can't we just have a nice dinner?"

"Oh, Ron, I wish you had told me that before. I just got burned by a guy I didn't know was married, and now here I am out with you!"

What was it about me, that married men thought I would go out with them? I vowed to start asking every man I met if he was married long before we got to the dinner part. And I had my doubts that Becky thought they were having a trial separation.

"You're not getting burned. We're having a meal. That's all. We're colleagues. There's nothing in the marriage contract that says you can't be friends with other people, especially people you work with. Becky has large amounts of male friends. She's part of a mixed bowling league that goes out every single week, and I'm not jealous."

Well, sure. Of course not, I thought. They weren't male models. Straight male models, that is.

"All right. Fine. You're having a trial separation and we're colleagues, but we're just going to be friends. That's it."

"Of course. I'm not like a lot of the photographers who hit on the girls, you know. Have I ever made a pass at you? Have I? You're insulting me."

"I'm sorry." He acted like he really was insulted. And no, he had never made any kind of pass. I was confused. If I was married I would not like it in the least if my husband was taking models out for dinner, and even if he and Becky really were having a trial separation I'm sure she didn't, either. But then, when you think about it, did marriage mean you had to put a lock on yourself for the rest of your life and never see anybody but your husband or wife? I couldn't imagine my mother or daddy just going out to dinner with somebody of the opposite sex like that, but this was New York and the rules weren't the same, it seemed like. I felt so far from marriage that I couldn't even think about it. Then I had another thought.

Maybe he didn't find me attractive.

"Not that I don't think you're attractive," he said, reading my mind, "but you're not my type."

"Well, that's a relief. You're not my type, either. Glad we got that cleared up." I took another sip of the sour wine. I meant it, that he wasn't my type. Not that I don't like short men, but for some reason, even though he was cute, Ron didn't light my fire, and apparently I didn't light his. In fact, there weren't many men that did light my fire. Only two so far, one who was far away in my past and one right next door who apparently was playing hard to get or something.

So, good. Even though there was something weird about it, I decided to ignore the questions and try to relax and have a nice evening, since we were here already and all.

The menu was in Italian, and I had no idea what anything was. I never took a foreign language at school because it didn't occur to me that I would ever go to a foreign country. Like New York.

"I can't read any of this, Ron. Do they have spaghetti?"

"Spaghetti? Well, of course they have spaghetti. But you can get spaghetti in any joint in the U.S.A.! You can get it in *cans* made by Chef

Boyardee, for Pete's sake! But you don't want to order spaghetti here. This restaurant is the genuine thing. The chef is from Sicily. They ship the olive oil and the spices and the tomato sauce from Tuscany. They make their own pasta right here by hand from grains grown in Sicily and ground into flour in mills that are hundreds of years old. There are dishes in this restaurant you can't get any other place in New York. Why don't you let me order for you? I'll surprise you. You'll love it. You wait."

Ron signaled the waiter, who quickly came over and rattled off a list of specials in a language that may have been English, but I couldn't understand a word he said. I just looked mutely at Ron, who picked up the menu and scanned the list.

"We'll have the . . ." Ron pointed to the menu and rolled off a name in Italian. If it had tomato sauce on it, I thought, it would be good. Even cardboard with the sauce I smelled at Puglia's would be good.

We drank the wine, his glass emptying much faster than mine, even though I kind of got used to it after a few sips. I didn't know why people were so crazy about wine.

"I want to thank you, Ron, for letting me do the stocking shoot for *Vogue*. I called my mother and told her I was going to be in *Vogue* and she told everybody she knew, neglecting, of course, to say it was just legs. They'll all go crazy trying to find me and think she's a liar. I wish I could do something where you could see my face for once. Even the Vanity Fair nightgown shot I'm doing, you won't see my face." It was the style of the ad, but I had seen the pictures Neal Barr did for the test, and they had dramatic lighting that made my hair look like a halo, my body long and lean, but my hand was over my face. The worst thing about that shoot was that they would have to put fake fingernails on me, because I always clip them short, and I dreaded it. I'd had to have them for another leg shot I did, where my hands were pulling on the stockings, and it just took forever. They had to put forms on the ends of my fingers, mix up some kind of paste, paint it on, let it dry, and then shape them into points and polish them. The long nails did make my hands look a lot better, though, almost graceful, but they were torture to try to wear. When you're not used to long nails, you can't push an elevator button or dial the phone or even button up your blouse. Forget picking your nose. I nearly mutilated my sinuses once without thinking. I left them on for about a day after the shoot was over and then cut them off. The part attached to my actual nails was on there pretty good and I had to gnaw them, taking a layer of fingernail with it and practically destroying my fingertips. I would have to be paid pretty well before I let them do it again.

"You'll have that mug in print yet. I've got a shoot for *Glamour* coming up, and I'm going to try to use you for it. It's a small editorial on scarves, but you look good in them. I like the way you tie them around your head."

I did love scarves, because my hair was so wild. I tied them around my waist for belts, too, and knotted them like necklaces around my neck. The thought of being in a *Glamour* editorial warmed me up, even though we didn't get paid as much for editorial work as we did for ads, the day rate being the same as our usual hourly rate, but the bonus was that everybody wanted the editorial models for their ads so you got more work from it. I smiled, all rosy, and Ron added a splash of Chianti to my glass.

The waiter brought over a covered dish and put it in the middle of the table. Then, with a flourish, he lifted the silver lid.

I screamed.

In the middle of the platter was the head of a . . . sheep, I think, cut in half, the eyeball and tongue and teeth all in place, the ear still there, roasted and crispy. It was the most horrifying thing I had ever seen in my life. The waiter jumped and dropped the lid, which clattered around the floor, and everyone in the restaurant turned to look at me. Ron was shocked.

"I didn't order this!" he shouted at the waiter. "I ordered a veal dish!"

The waiter was totally confused, and people from across the restaurant were standing up to see what was going on.

"*Sì,* this is what you ordered!" the waiter said in his heavy accent, grabbing a menu and pointing at an entry. "See—right here." He read the name of the dish, which kind of sounded like what Ron had said, but I couldn't tell. "This is what you said! Capuzella! It is delicacy in Sicily!" He looked like he was going to either cry or punch Ron in the nose. The eyeball in the poor half a sheep's head stared up off the plate at me, white and blank. My stomach started to rebel.

"Cover it back up! I can't stand looking at it! Do people really eat this? An eyeball! Teeth! Oh, Ron, I think I'm going to be sick!" My stomach started to roll and I yawped a little.

Ron, a slight shade of green himself, draped his napkin over the offending half a sheep's head and tried to look like he didn't know me.

The maître d' was making his way toward our table, pushing aside several other customers who were getting up to see what had happened.

I grabbed my purse and ran out the door, then stood by the street and gulped several breaths of fresh air, and thankfully didn't throw up, which would really have been embarrassing.

Ron threw some money on the table, and as he ran out after me, announced to the room, "Does anybody want a half a sheep's head? It hasn't been touched!"

We drove to a playground several blocks away and sat on a bench until I started to feel better.

"I'm really embarrassed. Now you can't go back to that place ever again."

"No, it's all my fault. I didn't really know what I was ordering. I have a confession. I don't speak Italian at all. My grandfather was from there, but I never learned any of the language, outside of penne alla vodka and spaghetti al dente. I was trying to impress you."

"I'm impressed. I'll never forget it as long as I live. Do you go there a lot? They seemed to know you."

"Not really. A couple of times. But they never gave me a good table like they did tonight. The head waiter was showing off for you, not me. That was the real reason I invited you, if you want to know the truth—I knew they'd give me a good table if I walked in with you. Especially in that outfit."

He was half grinning and I couldn't tell if he was kidding or not. I figured he was half kidding.

"Well, they'll remember you the next time, that's for sure. And I better never show my face in there again, so you'll have to bring somebody else."

"That's all right. They probably get their sauce from the same supplier in Brooklyn as everybody else anyhow. I made up that stuff about tomatoes grown in Tuscany and all. Are you hungry?"

"Starving."

"Are you still up for Italian?"

Across the street was a pizza joint called Famous Ray's, and we got a couple of slices and a Coke and sat on the bench watching some kids play basketball on a concrete court behind a chain-link fence. There seemed to be a lot of Ray's pizzas in New York: Famous Ray's, Original Famous Ray's, The REAL Famous Ray's, just plain Ray's, and there was even one called Not Famous Ray's—Ray was a busy guy, and I didn't know if Ray was even an Italian name. Ron said that there was no such dish as pizza in Italy. Not like the ones we have here; it was more like tomato sauce on a cracker. But I didn't care if this was authentic Italian or not. It was thick with pepperoni, melted cheese, and red sauce on a goopy crust that wilted until the oil ran down my wrist.

"Hey, look!" Ron said, as we scrubbed the grease off ourselves with a wad of napkins and threw away the paper plates and cups. "There's the Duck Guy!"

"Where? What Duck Guy?"

"Coming down the street—the Duck Guy! He's a legend! He sells ducks. Wait right here." Ron ran down the street, leaving me to stare after him. Sure enough, right in the middle of the street there was a guy pushing a big cart loaded down with huge yellow stuffed ducks.

It was dark and there weren't all that many people out in the neighborhood at this time of night, so I couldn't figure out why the Duck Guy was still out trying to sell ducks. Although there was Ron buying one, so I guess he did the business. The streetlights cast a yellow glow on the playground, where only two or three boys were still jumping and shooting hoops. New York streetlights were different from the ones we had in Arkansas. Ours were whiter or something, but I liked the yellow light. It made everything feel a little eerie, like in old detective movies, where dangerous, exciting things were waiting to happen.

Ron sprinted up to the Duck Guy, gave him some money, and picked out one of the ducks. It was nearly as big as Ron. I couldn't believe it.

"Here," he said. "That's to make up for the sheep's head."

It was at least four feet tall and looked like the prizes my boyfriends used to win for me at the county fair. My bed had been loaded down with them back home, purple dogs, white teddy bears, red teddy bears. This duck was bigger than any of them. It would take up half my apartment.

"Oh, Ron! It's just the cutest thing!" I lied, in a gushy girl-voice. "I can't believe you would do that for *me*." What I couldn't believe was that I had to ride on the back of a motorcycle holding a huge fuzzy stuffed duck with orange felt feet and beak and a green ribbon around its neck. Well, I guess he meant well. And the Duck Guy *was* a legend. Whatever that meant.

"You really like it?"

"I *love* it." No sense in hurting his feelings. I don't know if he expected me to give him a kiss or something, but I just clutched the duck and he patted me on the shoulder.

Even if he was married, Ron was all right. No reason we couldn't be friends. I vowed I would never sleep with him, or even kiss him, but I guess I had to take his duck and be nice about it. I'd figure out what to do with it later. He was, after all, going to use me in a *Glamour* editorial!

I could hear Suzan in the back of my head, though. Was taking a duck the first step in sleeping your way to the top?

20

MONKEYS, SCHMONKEYS

"Did you use my hairbrush? There are definitely blond hairs in this brush."

Sal was furiously cleaning the hairbrushes, putting them into tall jars filled with blue Barbasol antiseptic. Lale lounged on the couch, strumming a guitar and watching.

"No, I didn't use your hairbrush. Why would I do that?" he said. "I have my own hairbrush. Maybe Preston used it."

"You know Preston doesn't brush his hair. I am serious, Lale, you are *not* to use my *personal* things! There are a *zillion* hairbrushes on the makeup table, and you have to pick out the *one* that is my *personal* one. Are you trying to make me crazy?"

"You were crazy the day I met you."

"*That,* my darling, is the one true thing you have said all day. I am *crazy* to keep up this charade that you are the boarder hêre, when clearly you have *taken over* this place! Just look at it—your stuff is everywhere! Your boots, your clothes, your hair products! A guitar on which you have learned to play exactly *one* song. If I *never* hear "Wipe Out" again it will be too soon!" Lale stopped playing, put the guitar aside, his face impassive.

"Not to mention the phone calls you get at all hours of the day and night," Sal continued, shoving the brushes into the jars, hard. "You hand out *my* private number to every woman you happen to ogle on the street, not to mention your growing fan base of lovesick females. You are going to have to get your own phone line if you stay here. Even Preston is fed up with it. He has threatened to move out, and if he does then we will undoubtedly lose the space unless one of us can convince the powers that be that we are artists. *Why* they think that someone who slops paint on a canvas is entitled to space and another artist who carefully applies makeup to faces is *not,* is beyond me. I just hope the inspector can't see your masses of stuff and realize you do no work here."

Sal meticulously started going through his makeup case, tidying it and wiping off any makeup that had smeared on the containers. "But frankly, I wouldn't be unhappy to have Preston out of the picture. His personal hygiene always left a lot to be desired. Some people actually are *into* rancid body smells and all that, but not *moi.* I was always a bath *and* shower man myself, and frankly the smell of skin freshly washed in Irish Spring soap is the biggest turn-on of all. I could just take bites out of a bar of Irish Spring!"

Lale started playing again, this time a softer, slower version of "Wipe Out."

"What were we fighting about?" Sal asked finally.

"The hairbrush. I think."

"Oh, yes. Did you use my hairbrush or not? Tell the truth."

"Okay, I might have! What's the big deal? They all look alike to me anyhow. And since you have turned me into an Irish Spring bath *and* shower man, you should be happy. It was clean hair. If me and my stuff bother you, and Preston is whining about me, I could always find another place and Preston can stay. I could afford it. I'm making a lot of money."

"Which you would do well to try to save. Models don't go on forever, you know. Pretty faces are lined up from Malibu to Montauk waiting to take your place."

"I'm scared," Lale said sarcastically.

"So go look for another place," Sal went on. "You'll never find an apartment for thirty-three dollars and thirty-three cents a month like this one. And besides, what would you do for entertainment? You'd miss me. Tell the truth—I've grown on you."

"Yeah. Like a wart. Nah. I wouldn't miss you at all. The only reason I stick around is to see what weird thing you're going to do next."

But Lale smiled when he said it. Sal *had* grown on him, and every time he thought about finding his own place somehow he put it off, not quite ready to leave the loft and be on his own. He told himself he stayed because Sal was indeed as famous as he said he was, and had a lot of contacts in the business, like Michel Denon, who had been right-on about him being a successful model the minute he saw him in the coffee shop, but it was more than that. Sal was action. He knew the ropes in a world of which Lale was totally ignorant. There was nothing about New York Sal didn't know, and he was generous with his knowledge. Lale was using Sal, but he figured Sal knew the score. Sal was using Lale, too, and the fact that he was straight didn't seem to bother Sal at all. He simply liked having the beautiful maleness around, all that lovely testosterone coloring the air. And as Sal always said, one eyebrow cocked, *you never know.*

The pictures they took with Michel that first afternoon in New York got him in to see Eileen Ford, who, with great delight, signed him on the spot and suggested he change his name to something else. He picked Zack Carpenter, not unhappy to give Lale Hardcastle a little anonymity. He was working practically the next day, landing a job on his first go-see, an underwear shoot for the Sears, Roebuck catalog. In one of the shots, to everyone's horror, the end of his penis had been peeking out of the leg of the boxers, and somehow it had gone unnoticed by the photo editors and the shot appeared in the catalog, full-color. Sears received a spate of angry letters, but a bigger flood of letters wanted to know who the model was. Some women included pictures of themselves to pass on. The photo editor nearly got fired, until they discovered that plaid cotton boxers, item #A-16, had been the best seller in the history of boxer shorts. Although Eileen Ford seemed upset and told him to watch himself in the future, her mouth twitched when he said that he guessed he was just too big for his britches. And she put him up a notch, to the seventy-five-an-hour board.

Lale had been busy ever since. Too busy to really think much about finding another place to live. He slept on the couch until he got his first paycheck, and then got himself a futon from a place on Broome Street, and set it up in the corner on the farthest side of the loft from Sal's, near the Mustang's parking spot. He hung an Indian-print bedspread to separate it from the rest of the space, added a full-length mirror, shelves, and a big rack for the rapidly increasing wardrobe he was collecting. He had never had so many clothes in his life. It had never crossed his mind to want any. A couple pairs of jeans and a few shirts were all he needed back home. That and his leather jacket; a new pair of boots every few years and sneakers from time to time; some sweats. He hadn't even owned a tie. But now, clothes were his bread and butter. He got a lot of catalog jobs, which weren't the glamorous bookings, and the Sears, Roebuck people watched him like a hawk to make sure his "package" was completely covered, but it was steady and paid the bills, and it was giving him experience in front of the camera, which loved him from every angle. Occasionally some smitten stylist would give him clothes that he modeled, some he got as gifts from new designers who wanted their clothes to be seen around town on handsome young men, and a few he bought himself, with help from Sal. He was still a little ashamed of telling people he was a model, but the glamour jobs had started to come, and after a few major ads, like the L&M one in *Playboy,* and the checks that came with them, it got to be easier. People noticed him on the street, looking twice, thinking they recognized him, like he was a movie star or something. And he decided one day he might try that, too—acting. Several people had said he looked a little like James Dean, who was no sissy, that's for sure, and the more he looked at himself, the more he thought so, too. Secretly he thought he was even better-looking—Dean's eyes were a little too close together. He even read a book about Dean that said he got his start at the Actors Studio on West Forty-fourth Street. Not only Dean, but Marlon Brando and Marilyn Monroe studied there, too, and he passed by it a few times, watching the actors hanging around outside, looking cool and smoking during the scene break, thinking he might stop in one day and see what that method thing was all about.

On a shoot for an MG sportscar ad, on Coney Island, with a cute blonde in a bikini and ponytails, he met Axel Rodriguez, an assistant to the photographer. Axel was trying to break into filmmaking and asked Lale if he wanted to be in a movie. Flattered, Lale said yes before he even knew what kind of film it was. It turned out to be a student film, since Axel was taking classes at the NYU film school, so there was no money involved, but Lale was invited to the class for the screening and critique—which turned out to be quite favorable—and was shocked when he saw himself up on the big screen, larger than life.

He couldn't take his eyes off of himself. It was a moody black-and-white short called *Ace in the Hole,* only ten minutes long, of four guys playing poker on a long drunken night, a lot of loving close-ups of his eyes and mouth with a cigarette dangling from his full lips. At the end of the night, after fights and accusations and a case of beer, one of the players kills another one. It took all night to shoot in Ron Bonetti's studio, and since they were drinking real beer, it *really* got more drunken and wilder as the night ground on. In the big murder scene, Lale playing the unfortunate victim, they used Hershey's syrup for blood, and the actor playing the murderer went a little over the top and smeared it not only all over Lale's body but the walls as well. Axel loved it, but was a little put out since Bonetti had told them he wanted them to leave the place just like they'd found it, and it took them forever to get it cleaned. They were so wiped out they showered and just dropped to the floor naked, getting an hour's sleep, when some model who sounded like she was from Arkansas, or parts close by, wandered in looking like a large, scared white rabbit and woke them all up.

Lale had thought about her more than a few times since that morning and finally, when he was waiting in some studio on a go-see, he saw her in a magazine. At least he thought it might be her—the photo was a little grainy—with Bonetti's byline. So she was getting some work. Good for her. He'd ask Bonetti about her if he ever saw him again. He realized he didn't even know her name.

Not that he had much time to think about strange women. There were enough women in his life, and frankly part of the reason he hadn't moved out from the SoHo loft was that he wasn't crazy about letting people know where he lived. You never knew when somebody might just show up at the wrong time, and he would never bring anybody to the loft. Sal was definite about that. He would much rather go to their places anyhow. Then he could leave when he got good and ready, not having to worry about making breakfast or having them all over him in the morning when he needed to get showered and out to work.

In fact, he hadn't given out his address to anybody, not his friends back home or even his parents. He had forced himself, or rather Sal had forced him, to call his mother and father a few days after he hit New York, just so his mother wouldn't worry any more than she had to, but he hadn't told them much about what he was doing. Just that he was going to be working as a model, like in the catalogs and magazines, making good money, and was staying with a new friend until he found a place to live. There had been a long silence on the other end of the phone.

"Mom? Are you there? Mom?"

"I don't know what to say, Lale." There were tears in her voice, but she was trying to keep them back. "You've had all of us worried sick, I hope you know that."

"I didn't mean to make y'all worry. I wasn't thinking about y'all at the time, and I'm sorry. I just had to get out. I couldn't take it, Mom. I just couldn't. I would have died. I really would have smothered and died."

"I don't guess there's anything I can say to make you come home and do what's right, is there?"

"I don't guess."

"We didn't raise you like that, Lale. What am I going to tell your daddy? I don't think he would understand. I sure don't understand. What about Cassie? And the baby?"

"I'm going to send some money for you to give her when I get some. I can't talk to her yet. She'd probably like to kill me, and there's nothing I can say to her to fix things. She'll be all right. She's a good strong girl. I ain't coming home, Mom." There was a long pause.

"What is this all about, Lale? Really? Is there something you're not telling me? Is it the baby? Are you sure that baby's yours? Is that why you left like you did?"

Now that she said it, it did seem like a good reason for him to have run off. Of course he was sure the baby was his. Cassie would never cheat on him—he'd stake his life on it. But really, didn't every man have just a little doubt? He didn't want to lie, but he didn't mind leaving a doubt in her mind, either. The real reason was just too ugly to admit to his mother.

"Is any man ever really sure?" he said in a quiet, unsure voice.

"Your daddy was sure."

"Well, I ain't my daddy, and as much as I'd like to be like him, I have to be me, Mom. Don't worry about me. I'll write to you. I'm staying with a friend right now, but you can send me mail care of General Delivery, the Canal Street Post Office, Three-fifty Canal Street, New York, New York. And I'd appreciate it if you didn't give out that address to anybody else."

"You mean Cassie?"

"I mean anybody."

Lale had, of course, thought about Cassie a lot since then, mostly feeling guilty, sometimes missing her. The girls he went out with were invariably skinny models, or skinny girls who wanted to be models, and to his surprise he missed the comfort of Cassie's soft body. At times, though, he would realize that he hadn't thought about her at all for days, and that bothered him. When he got his first big paycheck, he sent two hundred dollars to his mother to give to her, and one other time, he sent three hundred. That should cover the hospital costs and buy some diapers, he figured. But he never wrote to her, and the more time went by, the less he wanted to write. He just didn't know what to say, and anything he wrote would be phony. He wasn't about to go back to Buchanan, and there was nothing else to tell her. She would find somebody else, and the less she heard from him the better off she would be. "Least said, soonest mended," as his dad used to say.

Sal finished tidying up the makeup table and sat down to apply makeup to his own face. He was obviously taking Miss Sally out tonight. It had gotten easier for Lale to live with Miss Sally. The modeling world was so populated with gay men that it was almost abnormal to be straight. He had no trouble with them, though, always making it clear up front that he liked women. Not many people knew he lived with Sal. And Sal seemed content to just let him be. He didn't ask questions when Lale was out all night, and Lale didn't ask him any. Sometimes they would go to clubs together, but usually they would arrive separately, and act like they'd just happened to bump into each other. Sal knew everybody in town, and he was always part of some big group, so it wasn't unusual for Lale to join them. Lale had met a lot of famous photographers through Sal, and consequently got more work. In fact, he had just been booked for a new national perfume campaign, Diamonds & Ermine, that was being shot by Milton Greene, one of the biggest in the business, who at one time took a lot of pictures of Marilyn Monroe and even produced a movie with her, *The Prince and the Showgirl.* That would be a nice chunk of change, and maybe a TV commercial down the road. That's where the big money was, commercials, and Lale was a natural for them. If he didn't have to speak. He still hadn't managed to get rid of his accent, and that held him back. Maybe they would do a voice-over. He really had to find the time to take speech lessons. Or acting classes. It would be less embarrassing to say he was an actor instead of a model.

As Sal began the tedious process of doing his eye makeup, Lale put aside the guitar and started opening a stack of letters he had picked up at the post office on his way home. The third letter in the stack had a familiar handwriting on pink stationery. He sniffed it, and thought he could smell the perfume his mother always wore, Ma Griffe. It gave him a little pang of homesickness.

Dear Lale,

Well, you've got a daughter, or at least that's what everybody in town thinks. I know it couldn't be yours, and if that girl was honest she would name the daddy, but maybe she doesn't even know herself. It's just as well you were not here to see it and be saddled with it—it is deformed, a harelip. A bad one. It is never going to be normal-looking, even if they do surgery on it. They have it in an incubator at the Children's Hospital in Little Rock, and I don't think it's going to get to come home from the hospital anytime soon. She named it Lalea, and I wish she hadn't, but there was nothing I could do about it. At least she didn't try to call it Hardcastle. Your daddy is just sick over the whole thing, and believes her that it is yours. We've had fights about it. I don't have to tell you he still won't think about writing to you. But you're my baby, and I love you, no matter what. I've told everyone the baby is not yours, but you know how this little town is. I would love to see you, but I think you should probably stay in New York for a while, in case you are thinking of coming back. People are mostly on her side.

I saw you in that magazine *Esquire,* in an ad for Haggar pants. You looked so handsome. I have started a scrapbook with all your pictures. I even went to Fort Smith to a drugstore where nobody knows me and bought *Playboy,* blushing the whole time, after somebody told me you were in it. The girl at the counter looked at me like I had two heads, and I had to hide it from your daddy. I never dreamed you would be doing so well, sweetheart. Please write to me, or call me. I wish you would at least give me your phone number, in case of emergency. I miss you so, and Brenda misses you, too. She wanted to move into your room, but I wouldn't let her. All your stuff is still there, just like it was when you left. I wish you hadn't given Cassie the car, but I know you felt like you had to.

I just hate to see her driving around in it. Your daddy gave her the title, against my will, saying it was the least he could do. I hate it that he feels that way, and it's tearing us up, but that's not for you to worry about. We'll get through it. He just loves you and misses you, like I do.

Please write me soon.

I love you so much,
Mom

Lale read the letter, and sat staring at the wall for a long time. He couldn't imagine what a harelipped baby would look like, but it sounded bad. He felt like he was two inches high, swinging his legs off the edge of a deep chasm. But it was too late to do anything. Too late. Was it his fault the baby was deformed? Was it something in his sperm? Was Cassie so hurt by him leaving her that the wound went all the way into the baby? Whatever it was, it was his fault, he knew, but it was too late. Like a fire that had already burned down the house, what was done was done, and if he went back it would just make everything worse. His mother was right. He could never go home again. For a moment, he thought of his daddy, the talk they had in the barn, how his daddy had been in the same boat as him at one time but was more of a man. He took responsibility, and here Lale was pretending to his mother that the baby wasn't even his. No wonder his daddy wouldn't write to him. On top of it all, he was the cause of them fighting, and they had never fought before. He had never disliked himself so much in his life.

He would send his mother some money for herself, he decided, to buy something nice. And some more to give Cassie. It sounded like Cassie would probably have a bigger hospital bill, with the incubator and all. He would send her another five hundred. Maybe a thousand. That would go a long way to salving his conscience. Heck, maybe he would send her more than that. It was only a day or two's work for him, but to them it was a lot. His daddy didn't make five hundred dollars a month. He wished his daddy would be proud of him, but he knew he never would be, even if he made a million dollars.

"You're awfully quiet," Sal said, blotting his red lipstick and putting on the blond wig. "Anything wrong?"

"Are you going out tonight?" Lale asked, putting the letter aside as

Sal slipped into his girdle and padded bra, put on a blue sequined miniskirt, chiffon top, and high red heels.

"No, I'm wearing this outfit to cook pasta in! Of course I'm going out! I'm taking Miss Sally to Max's Kansas City. Want to come along? You look like you need a little outing to cheer up. Was it something in that letter you just read?"

"Cassie had the baby."

"Congratulations! You're a daddy!"

"It was a girl."

"Well, how sweet. Are you going to go back, do you think?" Sal tried to be casual, but his voice was a tiny bit tight.

"No. I won't be going back."

"Well, I'm sure she'll be fine. You've been sending money?"

"Yes. I'll send some more."

"Good boy. So don't look so sad! You're a good daddy, paying child support. Better than a lot of guys, believe me. Come out with me. We'll celebrate."

"Maybe I'll come over later."

"Seeing some girl?"

"No, no girl. If I come, I'll be by myself. But don't look for me. If I come, I'll find you."

"Suit yourself. I'll be at the usual table." Sal took a shaggy black fur coat from a garment bag and put it on, preening in front of the mirror.

"What in the world is *that* mess you're wearing? It looks like something a truck run over and left on the highway."

"It's monkey fur. I found it at the flea market. Isn't it *divine*?"

"*Monkey* fur? You're wearing the skin of your closest cousin? Why don't you just skin Preston and make a coat out of him! All that paint he has on him would make a pretty-colored coat."

"That's disgusting," Sal said, putting on a wide-brimmed red felt hat with a huge rhinestone spider on the band.

"So is monkey fur."

"Oh, monkeys, schmonkeys. I look *great* in it! Try to come to Max's. Please. You'll feel better if you do. See you later." And Miss Sally swept out the door, monkey fur trailing in the dust.

21

ON THE WAY TO MAX'S

The cabdriver slammed on the brakes, swerved, and stopped near the curb to pick up the beautiful blonde. She was a classy-looking dame. Black fur coat, big hat. Probably one of those Upper East Side socialites slumming downtown. He wouldn't mind a fare uptown. As she got into the car, though, he saw in the mirror that she wasn't quite as classy as he had thought. She might even be one of those high-class hookers, wearing a lot of makeup, fake jewels.

"Max's Kansas City, Seventeenth and Park Avenue South."

"Oh, boy," the driver muttered as he heard the voice that was soft but not quite female, "I got a live one." He looked again, hard, in the mirror and confirmed it was one of those men that aren't really men, but like to dress up like women. He would have put her out, but the meter was running, so he just shrugged and set off across Broome, turning right up Sixth Avenue. It takes all kinds, and he had definitely had all kinds in his cab. He could write a book, and would one of these days, if he ever got the time. Working twelve-hour shifts didn't leave much time for anything else.

"Why are we going this way?" Miss Sally said, leaning forward to talk through the hole in the scratched-up bulletproof plastic window. "We should have gone east. This is out of our way."

"It's faster, lady. Keep your hat on. I'll get you there." Sheesh. This guy was as pushy as a real dame.

As they threaded through the traffic, an old red Chevy with New Jersey plates and fuzzy dice hanging from the rearview mirror pulled up beside them. Three guys with fifties-style crew cuts were hanging out the windows, hooting and hollering, drunk as skunks.

"Look at the blonde, guys! Woo woo! Hey, sweetheart! Give me a kiss!"

"That's all I need," the driver mumbled. "Yahoos from Jersey out for some fun in the big city and me with *this* thing in the car." He tried to change lanes and lose them, but the traffic was too heavy and they pulled closer to him.

"Hey, sweetheart! Blondie! Look here! Don't be bashful!"

Sal put his head down and tried not to look at them. What was wrong with people? Why couldn't they just mind their own business? It seemed like after the riot last year at the Stonewall bar on Christopher Street, a lot of antigay creeps had come out of the woodwork. Gay bars had always had to pay off the police just to exist, since it was illegal to have homosexual sex or even *dance* with another man, but sometimes the police would pull a fun little raid anyhow, just for laughs, or maybe because the payoff money was late that month. For whatever reason, on the night of the Stonewall riot, things got out of hand. When nine cops came in and started putting people in paddy wagons, the gays fought back—something unheard of. Usually they just covered their faces, paid a fine, and went quietly back to the bar the next night. But it was 1969. Nobody wanted to cover their faces anymore. They were tired of being arrested and beaten up just for being who they were; like blacks in a white world, except there was not even a "separate but equal" place for gays. They had to find their own places the best way they could. Sal hadn't been there that night, but some of his friends were. When the cops started putting people in the wagon they got a little rough and somebody in the crowd threw a lipstick, then somebody else bounced a beer can off a policeman's head, then it started raining anything they could get their hands on. As more things were thrown, the cops ran inside and barricaded themselves in the bar, smashing up all the mirrors and furniture and the cash register in a rage. People outside uprooted a parking meter and rammed it into the door. Guns were pulled, reinforcements were called in, and still the crowd didn't disperse. Men in high heels had discovered they were quite the equal of men with macho.

The riot raged over three days. Miraculously no one was seriously hurt, but things were starting to change; organizations were formed. No more back of the bus, Ma. We're queer and we're here! Still, it hadn't all changed in a year. Not by a long shot. Max's Kansas City was one of the few places, if not the only place, in New York that embraced everyone, from straight Wall Street types to artists and writers to rock stars and transvestites who wore feather boas and mascara. It was mecca for Sal and his friends, but right now, getting there seemed to be the problem. Sal was as strong as the next guy, but in a situation of one high-heeled queen against three drunk bigots, it was wiser to try to avoid trouble.

"Can't you go any faster, driver? Let's get off of Sixth. Make a right here."

"I can't fly over two lanes of traffic, lady. I'm doing the best I can."

"Hey, blondie! Look here! Want a beer?"

In spite of himself, Sal looked out the window at the crew cuts, who were holding out cans of beer and were weaving closer, close enough that one reached out and touched the cab. Sal's glance met his small piggy eyes. Even through his drunken haze, he saw Sal was not the gorgeous girl he thought she was.

"Well, take a look at that, guys! That ain't no lady! Hey, faggot! Suck my dick!" He hurled the beer can at the window, but it was nearly empty and bounced off.

The cabdriver had managed to get over to the right lane, but the Jersey car was glued to him, then pulled slightly ahead, nosing the cab into the curb. As the taxi was forced to stop, the red car blocked its escape, and all three of the guys jumped out and ran for the cab. The driver locked the doors, but the men started rocking the car and smashing at the windows. The driver, a big guy himself, who was—not for nothing—from Carroll Gardens in Brooklyn, grabbed a sawed-off baseball bat from under the seat and flung open the door, whacking one of the guys on the shoulder as he got out. He managed to bloody another one's nose while two piled on top of him. In the melee, Sal opened the back door and ran. He was sorry he had worn his highest platform shoes and a tight sequined skirt. People on the street stopped and stared as Sal awkwardly scurried down the sidewalk holding on to his hat, which threatened to fly away and take the wig with it.

"Hey! She's getting away!" The two guys got off the cabbie and took off after her, mercifully leaving the driver to deal with the other one, who was holding his bleeding nose and wanted no more of the bat. He ran after his friends, all of them nursing bruises and itching to take their rage out on somebody weaker.

The cabbie jumped into his car, backed onto the sidewalk, and drove away, cursing his lost fare and wiping blood from his scraped knuckles.

"That's the last time I'm stopping for somebody because of their legs," he grumbled.

The first two thugs reached Sal and one grabbed his hat, pulling it off along with the wig.

"Whoo-ee! I scalped me one, Bobby!" They laughed as Bobby put the wig on his own head.

"Give me that wig, you filthy beast!" Sal was scared, but that wig was human hair and cost a fortune.

The two men started throwing the wig back and forth, like children, with Sal in the middle, trying to grab it and screaming, "Somebody call the police!"

A couple walking down the street ran across to the other side and stood watching as the third guy came running up to join the fun.

He grabbed Sal's coat and threw him down to the sidewalk, getting his nose blood on the fur, which hurt Sal more than the fall to the pavement.

"Nooooo! Not the monkey fur!"

Then he forgot the fur and realized there was no way he was going to get out of this one alive.

In a flash, he wondered if Lale would be sorry.

22

RESCUING MISS SALLY

We were cruising up Sixth Avenue on our way home, since I'd told Ron I had to get up early in the morning. He really wanted to go somewhere for a drink, but I'd had enough drinks for one evening, and said frankly I thought he ought to get home to his wife, and he couldn't do anything but agree with me. I didn't want him to think I was preaching to him or anything, but there was no sense in aiding and abetting him when he was sort of cheating on her, friend and colleague or not. I sure wouldn't like it if my husband came dragging in at two in the morning after being out with someone like me, no matter what he said.

The wind had gotten a lot colder and, let me tell you, it was a job trying to hold on to that stupid duck and his jacket, too, and I wanted more than anything to get someplace warm, like my bed. I was going to have to get a heavier coat and soon. Or wear longer pants.

As we got near West Fourth Street, some kind of commotion was going on.

"Look, Ron! Those guys are mugging that woman! Oh my gosh!

They pulled off her . . . wig! Wait a minute. Isn't that . . . it looks a lot like . . . ?"

"Oh, my God. It's *Sal*! Hang on, Cherry!"

Ron revved the motor and came roaring down on the guys, who had just thrown Sal to the street. One of them jumped out of the way as the Harley bumped up on the sidewalk, and two women who were coming out of a store screamed and ran back inside.

"Ron! Cherry! Help!" Sal struggled to get up, which wasn't all that easy with the tight skirt and platforms he was wearing.

A few more people came out from adjoining stores to see what the ruckus was about, one of them yelled, "Call the cops!" and the guys, seeing they were in trouble, decided to split and ran back down the street to their car.

Sal was shaking, looking kind of weird and sad in the smeared makeup without his wig, which was lying in a heap on the sidewalk. He retrieved the crumpled red hat, which had been stomped. A rhinestone spider on the band was all bent up. I leaned down and picked up Sal's wig, handed it to him, and Ron said, "Get on behind Cherry, Sal! Let's get out of here!"

Sal hiked up his skirt and jumped on and we roared back out onto the street with me hanging on for dear life to Ron and that stupid duck, Sal hanging on to me with one hand and putting his wig back on with the other. My coat was bunched up and twisted around my neck and I thought I would choke, but off we went, up Sixth Avenue, just as a police siren started wailing.

"Go to Max's!" Sal yelled in my ear, and I yelled it on to Ron. We made a right on Fourteenth and headed to the East Side. I guess, for better or worse, I was finally going to Max's Kansas City.

23

WAITING IT OUT

As soon as Lalea was born, they knew they couldn't do anything for her in the hospital in Fort Smith, so they sent her by ambulance, siren blaring, to Arkansas Children's Hospital, which was one of the best in the country. Cassie had to stay in the hospital for another several days, she was so weak from blood loss and grief, but as soon as she was allowed to go home, she drove the Thunderbird to Little Rock, over her mother's and everyone else's protests. Since she'd gotten there, she hadn't come back home even once, and nothing anybody could say or do would make her leave the baby.

The neonatal ward of the Arkansas Children's Hospital was decorated in that trying-to-be-upbeat, cheery way children's hospital wards are, with fall pumpkins and funny scarecrows painted on the window that separated it from the waiting room. Murals with giraffes and elephants and monkeys ran around the soft blue walls, and balloons festooned the cribs. The nurses wore smocks printed with bright fish or animals. It takes a special kind of person to take care of sick babies every day, and all these women were special. There were seventy-two beds in all, separated into pods, eight incubators in each pod, the dividing walls laden with beeping monitors. Six of the incubators in Lalea's pod had babies in them, most of them preemies. Lalea was seven pounds, a giant next to some of the other babies, and they had put her off to herself in the corner, to give her privacy, they said, but really, Cassie knew, it was to keep people from staring at her and freaking out.

The parents were allowed to go into the ward and see the babies only after scrubbing their hands with antiseptic and putting on a mask and a bright-yellow sterile gown over their clothes. Cassie's hands were chapped from all the harsh scrubbing, since she did it several times a day, and lotion didn't seem to help much. The nurses were great about letting her sit beside Lalea, but she couldn't stay at the incubator all the time, so, like several other women had done, she made herself a camp out in the waiting room. Each of the mothers had their areas staked out and the others knew not to encroach on anyone else's space. Some had brought coffeemakers and pillows and blankets from home, and most passed the time knitting or reading or doing crossword puzzles. One woman worked on a king-size quilt that took up a whole sofa, so no one else could sit there. The sofas were in high demand, since you could actually sleep stretched out on them, and the ones who had been there the longest jumped on them just as soon as they became available. Cassie slept in a recliner, with her canvas bag containing a can of deodorant, toothbrush, bar of soap, and couple of changes of underwear on the floor beside it. At night, the nurses handed out pillows and blankets and collected them in the morning. Cassie used her purse for a pillow, afraid someone would steal it while she slept, although that wasn't too likely since she slept only in catnaps and startled awake with every sound. She had dark circles under her eyes from lack of sleep. Too, the old chair tended to fold up with her if she relaxed, so she had to lie rigid to keep it open.

In a hospital, there was little difference between night and day. In the middle of the night there was always activity, people going in and out, the nurses working on their tiny patients, talking, laughing, making small noises, their rubber-soled shoes swishing on the polished floor, the smells of their midnight lunches wafting in the air. Even if she'd had the money for a motel, which she didn't, Cassie didn't want to leave the baby for even a night. Something might happen, and she wouldn't be there. She was all the poor little scrap of life had in the world, and she wouldn't abandon her now. Her mother, Annie, came when she could, but she had to work at St. Juniper's all week, and it was a hard three-hour drive through the mountains to Little Rock. None of her friends had even come once, except for Baby and Bernadette, and she didn't expect to hear from George and Janet Hardcastle after the way Janet had acted. She suspected George might have come, but he was the kind of man who tried to keep the peace, and Janet probably wouldn't let him, old henpecker that she was. So screw them. She didn't need any of the Hardcastles.

Lalea's doctor, Charles Fulton, was the head of the pediatric department, a wonderful white-haired man with kind blue eyes that radiated love and confidence. But even Charles Fulton wasn't God Almighty and couldn't promise her a miracle. When she first got there, after he had examined the baby, he took Cassie to a special private room set aside for just that purpose and talked to her for a long time.

"Cassie, I don't have to tell you, this little girl has got a lot of problems. Besides the obvious one, which is one of the worst cleft palates I've ever seen, she has a problem with her heart. A lot of babies with cleft palates do. Somehow, in the womb, when the palate is developing, the heart develops at the same time and something went wrong with it, too. The great vessels in the heart are transposed. It more than likely will cause renal failure, which in real language means the heart just stops working."

Cassie knew the news would be bad, but hearing it said out loud made it real. Her face went pale, and he took her hand.

"Was it something I did that caused this?" she finally asked. "One night when I was first pregnant, I got drunk. I drank nearly a whole bottle of wine. But I never had another drink after that. Not a single one."

"I don't think that would have done it," he said. "It's not good, but there's a lot of women who drink a whole lot more than a bottle of wine when they're pregnant and their babies are fine. You can't blame yourself for this. It just happens sometimes. Nobody knows why but God."

"I do blame myself. God is punishing me for what I did. I wasn't married to her daddy. I'm willing to be punished, but why does He have to punish that baby, too?" She broke down then, and the doctor put his arm around her shoulders and she sobbed into his white coat while he held her.

"I don't believe that's true, Cassie," he said gently. "God doesn't go around punishing girls for being in love and having babies. What kind of a God would that be? He created us to love each other and have babies. God didn't make it a sin. Preachers did that. I don't know why Lalea is like this, but I believe with all my heart that it isn't something you drank, anything you ate, or something you did. It just happens sometimes."

"Isn't there *anything* you can do for her? Can't you operate and fix her a little bit or something?" She looked up at him, tears in her clear blue eyes. He was silent. "She's going to die, isn't she?"

This was the part of his job he hated the most. "No operation is going to make her into a normal baby, Cassie. And I'd be less than honest if I didn't tell you that most babies like her don't live long."

"How long?"

"Nobody knows that, my dear, but God. A few weeks at most, I think."

Cassie straightened up and wiped her eyes. The life had drained out of her and she was empty. She felt old, like she would never laugh again. In spite of what the doctor said, she knew in her gut that the night she drank the bottle of wine and tried to kill herself was the moment it all went wrong. That was the night the great vessels in the heart transposed and the palate didn't close. She should have just let the train take them, but she didn't, and now she had to face the consequences of what she had done.

"Are you all right, Cassie?" he asked. "Do you want me to call the chaplain to be with you?"

"No. I just want to sit here by myself for a while. Thank you for all you've done for us, Dr. Fulton."

"I'll check back with you a little later, then."

He left her, his step heavy. He envied doctors who could be case-hardened and not hurt for their patients. He'd never been able to do that, and it took its toll.

At least they would take Lalea out of the incubator once in a while and let Cassie hold her. The preemies' mothers weren't allowed to even touch them, their skin was so delicate and tender, translucent to the point that you could see the blue veins, almost watch the blood as it ran through their tiny bodies. Most of them were under three pounds. There was one baby boy who weighed just one pound, and would have fit in the palm of her hand. But nobody could hold him. All the parents of the preemies could do was watch them, talk to them, and maybe once in a while gently touch the bottoms of their little feet. It was a quiet group, those other six mothers. They all had husbands who came with them, at least part of the time, men who took turns watching the babies, and they all learned soon enough that Cassie had no husband. They didn't ask questions and she didn't offer answers, but her cheeks burned when she caught them looking at her, pity on their faces.

Her mother brought her fresh clothing once a week, and Baby sometimes came on the weekends and brought magazines, which Cassie pored over, searching for pictures of Lale. Bernadette came when she could leave the restaurant, always bringing food.

"Honey, I wish you'd try to eat something," Bernadette said, handing her a bag. "I never thought I'd say it, but you're getting down to skin and bones and you need to keep up your strength. Won't you at least have a little of this good tomato soup? It's still hot here in this thermos. I brought you a pimento cheese to go with it. Lots of mayo, like you like it, and sweet pickles. Don't that sound good?"

"Thanks, Bernadette. That sounds real good. You can leave it and I'll eat it later. I am eating. I really am. It just seems like nothing sticks."

It wasn't true. Cassie hadn't had a real meal since the night she gave birth to Lalea. Food stuck in her throat and she gagged when she smelled it cooking in the cafeteria, so she didn't go down there. She drank Tab, and once in a while bought a package of peanuts or cheese crackers from the vending machines. Still, she burned with nervous energy and walked the halls as fast as she could in an endless circle. The nurses had gotten used to her and paid her no mind when she passed their station over and over. The weight had melted off. She was hardly aware of it until the day she pulled up her pants in the toilet and they fell back down to the floor. She had to ask the nurse for a safety pin to keep them up. She stared at herself in the women's room mirror, hardly recognizing the face looking at her. For the first time she remembered, she could see her cheekbones and hip bones. Her engagement ring got too big, and after the third time it fell off her finger, she put it away in its green velvet box, afraid she would lose it. It was almost a relief. After

Lale had left, she'd worn it for a long time, hoping that one day he would come walking in through the door, but after she saw him in the L&M ad in *Playboy* magazine with that cute curly-haired blonde, she knew he wasn't coming back. She didn't blame him. What was there for him with her in Buchanan, Arkansas? Just a hard life of being poor, farming, and living with a girl he didn't love and a deformed baby. She had cried so many tears there were none left. Now her eyes just felt dry, sandy, and hot.

Dr. Fulton had sent Dr. Nick Barker, a plastic surgeon, to examine Lalea, even though he knew surgery was something that would probably never happen. Dr. Barker told Cassie he couldn't operate on the baby until she was a year and a half old, and then she would be in for a life of operations. Painful operations.

"She would look better and be able to eat, but I have to be honest, Cassie, if she lives, she's never going to look normal."

If she lives. And if she lived, all those surgeries would be expensive. They didn't have any insurance. None of them had ever been sick, except for her grandfather, and he had Medicare—thank God President Johnson did that good thing, at least. Her father had died way too young of a heart attack in front of the TV set when she was in the eighth grade, and never spent any time in the hospital.

"Well, I guess it's a good thing Lalea's daddy's not here to see her," Cassie said, almost to herself.

"If you don't mind me asking, where is her daddy?" Dr. Barker said carefully.

"Oh, he's in New York City. He's a big model in the magazines. Isn't that funny? He was the handsomest boy in Buchanan, and now he makes his living with his looks. It seems almost like somebody played a trick on him, making his baby like this, don't it? If she'd looked like him, she would have been so beautiful."

"I think she would have been a beauty from your side, too, Cassie."

"Me? Are you kidding? I don't think so. I have this big old nose, and I'm fat." He stared at her in disbelief. "I mean . . . I used to be fat." She still couldn't get used to her new body.

"I'll keep in touch with Dr. Fulton. Here's my card. Call me if I can help you in any way."

She knew Dr. Barker wasn't expecting to operate on Lalea, and if he did, there was no way to pay for it. Bernadette had been good about her taking time off from work, but Cassie knew she was going to have to hire somebody else soon. The restaurant was just too much work for one person, and Cassie felt bad about that.

"Did you ever find anybody to work for me?" she asked Bernadette now.

"Well, I've been meaning to talk to you about that. Yes, I hired Melanie Johnston, but she knows when you get ready to come back, the job's still yours. Oh, honey, I wish you would at least go home for a night or two and get some sleep. Lalea will be just fine. These nurses here know what they're doing. Won't you let me take you home, just for one night?"

"I'll be all right. Don't worry about me."

"I worry. Can't help it. We all worry. Nobody will ever recognize you, you're so skinny."

"Yeah. I guess I am. That's something I never thought I'd say."

"Well, no black cloud without some small silver lining, right?" Bernadette tried to smile, but she didn't think it was such a silver lining.

Bernadette scrubbed up, put on the yellow suit, and leaned over the incubator. Even though she had seen the baby several times, it was always a shock. Lalea had a feeding tube down her gaping nose, held in place by tape, and there were I.V. tubes in her heel. Cassie joined her and smiled.

"Look at her ears. Don't she have the prettiest ears? Just like rosy little seashells. And look at her hands. She has Lale's hands. You can always tell the daddy because the little fingers are alike. I have my daddy's little finger." She looked at her hands. Bernadette looked at her own hands.

"Well, I'll be. I guess you could say my little finger looks like my daddy's, too. He had big old rough coal miner's hands, and mine ain't much better from all the dishwater and burns. Seems like I just can't keep from burning myself." Hot tears scalded her eyes, but she knew it would just set Cassie off again if she cried, so she held them back.

"Well, I'll run on, darlin'," she said after taking a deep breath. "It's a long drive. If you want me to come and get you, just call me collect from the pay phone, anytime, and I'll be here. Think about just going home for one night. Annie can come sit with Lalea."

"I might. Thanks, Bernadette, for the soup and the pimento cheese. You're the best."

Bernadette left, and Cassie settled down in her recliner and took out the latest issue of *Playboy.* On page twenty-six was a big picture of Lale, sitting on the back of an MG convertible, a girl with blond ponytails beside him. Cassie ran her finger over the page, then put it into her bag and tried to sleep.

24

MAX'S KANSAS CITY

There was a long line of people waiting behind a red velvet rope to get into Max's Kansas City when we pulled up on the Harley. They all turned and looked at us, and I guess we did look a little like a traveling road show.

"So here we are, Sal," Ron said. "I think I'll stick with the plan to go on home. Cherry, want me to drop you off at your apartment?"

"NOOO! Cherry has to go with me! *Please* come with me, Cherry. It is *so* much fun, and I need somebody to be with me until my nerves, which have been jerked out by the very *roots,* calm down. Please. Please, please, please."

The excitement had woken me up and I wasn't as tired as I thought I was. Plus, I was curious about Max's, which Sal had talked so much about, so I got off the bike with him.

"I'll stay with Sal for a while, Ron. You go on ahead."

"Okay, if you're sure. I'll give you a call tomorrow." He gave me a little peck on the cheek, then turned to Sal. "Sal, I'm trusting you to take good care of this girl. See that she gets home safe and sound."

"I'm a big girl, Ron. I can get myself home. All you have to do in this town is stick out your hand and a yellow car stops."

"They all stop for you—that's true." He smiled, then roared up Park Avenue South into the traffic and out of sight.

As we walked up to the door, I got a better look at the people behind the rope. They were mostly clean-cut types with short hair and suits, the women wearing nice dresses and heels, tasteful jewelry. A small black woman with thick glasses sat on a stool by the door, admitting people, but it seemed like the ones she was picking to go in were ones who looked most likely to be kept out. Some were dressed in outlandish hippie outfits, ratty old fur coats, dirty jeans, with long scraggly hair and chipped nail polish. A few were like Sal, men wearing women's party outfits, sequins and feathers and bright makeup. It was a shock when I first saw Sal as Miss Sally, but he did look pretty good as a woman. Better than most of them.

The woman on the stool acted like she owned the place, and I could tell at one glance that she was one tough lady. As people in the nicely dressed line came up, she'd look them over and say things like, "Sorry, you can't come in with no jacket," Or, "Sorry, you can't come in—it's couples only," or if they were a couple and had a jacket on, she'd say, "Sorry, you can't come in—you have on brown shoes." There was no rhyme or reason to it. People's shoulders sagged and some of them walked away, their faces red with embarrassment or anger, while others just waited around to see if she would let them in anyhow. Sometimes she did, if they waited long enough. I was a little scared of her and hung back, but Sal grabbed my hand and we went right past the people in the line, all of whom glowered at us, and he gave her a big hug.

"Dorothy! You're looking *marvelous*!"

"Hey, Sally. You look a little wilted, if you don't mind me saying so."

"I *am* wilted, Dorothy! You have no idea what just happened to me *tonight* right here on the streets of New York City! If it weren't for my friends rescuing me, I would be *dead, dead, dead*! Beaten to a bloody pulp by a screaming mob of gay-bashing New Jersey rednecks!"

"Well, that's awful, Sal, but here you are safe and sound and all's well that ends, and all that." She pulled on a cigarette and narrowed her eyes up at me, squinting through her cat's-eye glasses. "Who's your friend? I haven't seen this one before."

I guess I fit in with the freaks, considering my outfit, windblown hair standing straight up, and the fact I was carrying a big yellow . . . well, you know what.

"Dorothy Dean, this is Cherry Marshall. Cherry, Dorothy. She's going to be a big, *big* model."

"She's a big one already. When you look like her, it's either become a model or join the circus. Hey, Cherry. Nice outfit. Nice duck. So go on in and have a drink. Unwind. Comb out your nerves."

I smiled at her, but couldn't think of anything to say to that. I wasn't sure if I should be offended or not, so I decided not to be. We walked through the door into a long room of tables with a bar over on the left wall. I did a double take when I recognized a few people who were sitting on the stools and at the tables there. Then I did a triple take.

"Is that who I think it is, Sal?"

I pointed discreetly behind my hand so the person couldn't see it.

"If you think it's Robert Rauschenberg it is. He's here *all* the time. Hi, Bob!" he called out, waving, and Bob waved back, like they were old buddies or something. Bob smiled a pearly smile at me while I smiled back at him and kept on walking behind Sal. I couldn't believe it. It really *was* Robert Rauschenberg and he was sitting with a group of people, most of whose pictures I had seen in *ARTnews* magazine. I think the skinny guy who looked like a big bird was Roy Lichtenstein, the one who did those pop-art cartoon things, like panels from lurid women's romance comic books. Some of the others I had seen before but couldn't remember their names. One might have been Larry Rivers. But I thought all of them were famous painters, and I noticed then that the walls were full of their paintings! It was unbelievable. Like a museum with food.

Louise Nevelson was at the bar wearing her trademark head scarf, heavy blue eye shadow, and three-inch-long false eyelashes. Louise, unlike the Duck Guy, was a *real* legend. We had studied her in art class at DuVall University and made Nevelson-like sculptures out of wood scraps we got from the lumberyard. I tried to be cool and not stare as I stood close enough to reach out and touch her, waiting for Sal while he popped into the bathroom to fix his wig and makeup. He made his way back to me, stopping at nearly every table to tell his almost-getting-killed story again. He was still a little hysterical, waving his arms around dramatically. Of course, Sal was always a little hysterical, so it was hard to tell if he was really traumatized or just enjoying acting out the story.

I was having a good time gaping at all the art and had just spotted one of Louise's sculptures on the other side of the room when a creepy guy with a terminal case of dandruff pushed by me and walked right up to Louise Nevelson and put his hand on her shoulder. She turned, gave him a look that would have withered an undertaker, and with two fingers moved his hand away like it was a dead fish.

"Louise!" he said, not for a minute giving up as he tried to wedge in beside her. "You look wonderful! How are you?"

"Do I know you?" Louise said, frost heavy in her voice.

"Louise! Of course you do! I just saw you at your opening at the Whitney! Don't you remember? I've seen you at every one of your shows! We've had long talks. We know each other well!"

"Did I ever f*** you?"

I was shocked that someone like her would say that word right out loud. The man cleared his throat, a little red-faced.

"Well, no, Louise. I'm afraid I never had that pleasure."

"Then I couldn't have known you *that* well."

Sal caught up with me and nudged me on through the crowd. A guy with long greasy hair was sitting by the cigarette machine picking his nose. A big nose. I was disgusted and was about to ask how that one had managed to get in, when Sal waved to him.

"Hey, Mickey!" He blew a kiss and Mickey smiled a big white smile, a silver tooth sparking the light.

"That's Mickey, the owner. He's amazing. You'll love him. He'll love *you,* no question." Mickey was surrounded and it was too hard to get across the room, so we continued on. I was glad. I didn't want to shake his hand, seeing where it had just been.

"The painters and the writers hang out in here in the front room," he said, like a tour guide, "but we're going to the *back* room, which is a *lot* more fun. Come on. You're in for a surprise!"

Sal waved and blew kisses to more people as we passed, and I felt like every eye was on us. There was a weird red light beam, like an electric current, shooting across the restaurant, and it continued far into the back room, lighting up a doorway that glowed like the gates of hell. I felt a little apprehensive, like the room would be full of Hieronymus Bosch characters or something.

"What is this room? Why is it red like that? Where is that beam coming from?"

"It's a laser beam. A friend of Mickey's who lives across the street let him put the machine in his apartment and shoot it across right through the front window into the back room. Cool, huh?"

"Yeah. Cool." But it made me nervous. It was only light but I could imagine it would burn a hole in you if you reached up and touched it. As we passed the coffee machines and neared the door, I had a feeling of vertigo, like I was on a high board, about to dive into a pool full of blood.

We walked in and Sal again stopped at nearly every table to say hello, giving the people air kisses while I stood back holding the duck and feeling stupid. The room made everyone look red, and it took me a minute to get used to it. I felt like Dorothy Gale, who had wandered into the *Ruby* City of Oz by mistake. The tablecloths were deep red and a big inflamed fluorescent sculpture in the corner added more thick crimson to the atmosphere. In this light, everyone was beautiful, or at least interesting-looking. If they had any zits you couldn't see them. Right beside where I was standing sat an extremely tall, handsome blond guy who could have been a male model in *GQ* and an exotic girl with wild blackberry hair and an armful of silver bangle bracelets. Her thick eyebrows went up at the ends like ravens' wings and I thought of painted gypsy caravans with her dancing in full skirts in front of a roaring fire, him in a Brooks Brothers suit watching her. I didn't want them to see me staring, so I glanced down to my other side and realized I was right in front of Jane Fonda and her husband Roger Vadim. She had her hair cut in a perfect shag and he did, too, his with a little pointed curl on his forehead that made him look devilish. They were smoking and drinking and talking, just like they weren't movie stars. I always thought people like that would have bodyguards or something, but here everyone was just sitting around like normal people, relaxed and having a good time.

Except for me. There were at least two other women in the room who had white hair like mine, one of them also had white eyebrows, and all of a sudden I didn't feel so special. I didn't belong here. I wanted to turn and go home, and if Sal hadn't finally come back just at that moment, taken me by the arm, and pulled me on toward a table, I would have.

Over in the corner, crowded together in a big round black vinyl booth, was a group of weird-looking characters and, believe it or not, the guy in the middle looked just like Andy Warhol. It *was* Andy Warhol. Nobody else would look like that on purpose. He had on round, dark sunglasses with transparent rose-colored rims and a black leather coat. In the light his skin was the color of bubble gum and his white wig looked pink. Frankly, I'd never been a huge Andy Warhol pop-art fan. His Campbell's soup cans and big multiple portraits were clever ideas, but it all seemed too easy, somehow, the blowing up the black-and-white photos and just smearing some paint on them. I'm not even sure he did it himself. I read he had a factory and a lot of people worked making his art. My favorite painters had always been Alice Neel and Edward Hopper, and my style was kind of a cross between theirs, people in bright sunlight, moody like Hopper, but a little looser, like Neel. I liked to put paint on a canvas and create a person, not just color one in like the Warhol photo ones.

I would never be famous like these people, but I missed painting a lot and decided with even more resolve that I was going to try to make the time to get back to it.

We were only a couple of tables away from the Warhol group, and I gratefully sat down, stashing the duck under the table, while of course Sal went over to speak to them and air-kiss some more. He stood there for a minute telling them one more time how near he had come to death, when Andy leaned over and said something to him in a low voice, and Sal looked back at me, then motioned for me to come over.

"Cherry, Andy wants to meet you. Andy, this is Cherry."

"You can't be Cherry," Andy said. "We already have a Cherry. Cherry Vanilla."

"Well, nice to meet you, too, Mr. Warhol, but I'm not a Cherry Vanilla, I'm Cherry Marshall."

They all laughed like I had said something really funny. I didn't know if they were making fun of me or laughing at what I had said, which wasn't particularly funny. One of the women had pretty blue eyes and wild, curly light-brown hair. She stuck out her hand and I shook it.

"I'm Viva," she said, "and Andy meant we already know somebody named Cherry Vanilla—in fact there she is, over in the corner." I looked, and there was a kind of ordinary brown-haired girl sitting in a group next to a guy with long red hair and a green baggy sweatshirt who was standing up on the chair proclaiming something loudly in a foreign language, like he was giving a speech.

"Is that her with that guy standing up on the chair? What language is he speaking?"

They all roared with laughter again. I was beginning to be a little confused, and my smile was stiff.

"That's Andrew! He's reciting from *Finnegans Wake*. He can recite seventeen pages of it!"

"*Finnegans Wake*? You mean like James Joyce?"

"Exactly! You're a smart girl," one of the women said.

"Yeah, well, I went to college." Even in Arkansas we had heard of James Joyce, although I didn't necessarily want to tell them I had tried to read some of *Finnegans Wake* one time but didn't get even seventeen pages into it. It did seem like a foreign language to me. I couldn't imagine memorizing *any* of it. I wondered if the people at the Warhol table had read it. Somehow I didn't think so. Most of them looked fuzzy-eyed, like they were stoned, and most could have used a good bath. In the chair next to Andy, there was a skinny girl with short white hair and black eye shadow wearing a silver tissue minidress, her head on the table, passed out cold. A little pool of drool had formed under her mouth. Nobody seemed to think it was weird. They just ignored her.

"So if you can't be Cherry, what can we call you?" Andy Warhol said.

"How about Blizzard? That would be a good name for her," a woman with blue-black hair and purple eye shadow said as she drew in a lungful of cigarette smoke. She was wearing what looked like a black patent-leather bodysuit. I bet she was sweating in it. The room was stifling.

"Oh, Ultra Violet, that's no good. Too much like a Dairy Queen drink," a guy with long shaggy hair said in a slurred voice. "How about Electra? I like Electra. Her hair looks like she stuck her finger in an outlet." Everyone thought that was hilarious, too, except me.

Ultra Violet. Cherry Vanilla. Viva. Didn't anybody have a normal name, like Linda or Mary?

"Great. I like Electra," Andy said.

"Well, thanks, guys, but I kind of like Cherry, since I'm already used to it. Sorry about that other girl. She'll have to change her name. Maybe she could be Fudgsicle."

That really made them roar. I nodded to them and went back to the table with Sal. "Well—you really made a hit with Andy!" Sal gushed. "He *never* gets that enthused. Maybe he'll ask you to be in one of his movies."

"I don't think I want to be in one of his movies. I'm not much of an actress."

Although I had never seen a whole one, I had read about his movies and seen clips in art class. Most of them were either weird and boring, like a close-up of somebody's eye that went on for hours, or everybody was naked and stoned.

"Do you think any of *them* are actors? You don't have to act to be a superstar. You just have to have—IT. And you have IT, my sugarplum, in spades."

I wasn't so sure I wanted to have IT, and I wasn't so sure any of the people at Andy's table had IT, either. In fact, looking around the room, most of the people seemed like they were on some kind of drugs or drunk or something. People were making out at tables, and some of them were going a little too far. At one of the tables a woman had her top pulled up and you could see her bare breasts. The room swam in red light. It was getting really hot in there. I didn't know where to look, so I tried to read the menu.

"Are you going to eat dinner, Sal? I already had pizza with Ron, but I'll have a Coke or something."

"Pizza? Oh, my darling, you have to have something besides that. Pick anything off the menu and it's on *me*. Mickey lets me run a tab. In fact, he lets most people run a tab. Once in a while somebody even pays it."

A pretty blond waitress who was chewing gum came over.

"So, what'll it be, guys? We got steaks, chops, lobster, you know the drill."

"Hi, Debbie. I think we'll have the lobster tails tonight."

"Going for broke, huh, Sal? What'd you do, rob a bank? Lobster tails it is. For both of you?"

"Uh, I don't know," I said, looking at the price list. "Maybe I'll just have the fried shrimp." The lobster tails were $8.95 and the shrimp was $3.50. I didn't want Sal spending all that money on me, and frankly I had never eaten lobster and didn't know if I'd like it.

"No, no, *no*. You *have* to have the lobster. Two lobsters, Debbie. And bring on the salad."

"Be right out."

"I made *her* night," he said. "Most people in here usually just get the salad, share it, and eat the rolls. Poor Debbie Harry is the only waitress who will work the back room. She wants to be a singer and likes hanging out with all the singers back here—over there is David Bowie, the one in the blue feather boa, and Lou Reed, the one wearing silver sequins. Lou's band, the Velvet Underground, plays here. The place is just *crawling* with singers! The front-room crowd are the bigger tippers, though. And Siberia, the upstairs where the bridge-and-tunnel crowd is shoved—you saw them standing in line—tips the biggest of all. They think they'll get elevated to the downstairs or something, I guess, poor clueless things."

"Don't these people back here have any money?" I was sure Jane Fonda and Andy Warhol had enough money for lobster if they wanted it.

"Some do. Though if most of the regulars get a few bucks, they spend it on drugs. A lot of them would be dead if it weren't for Mickey's credit and the chickpeas. He's a saint."

I thought of him picking his nose, but that didn't necessarily make him not a saint. I guess even saints have boogers.

The menu said STEAKS, SEAFOOD, CHICKPEAS. There was a bowl of them on the table, like peanuts. I ate one, and it was hard and salty.

"Don't eat those. They're dreadful. Save your teeth for the lobster."

A beautiful blond girl in a form-fitting blue satin dress came over and gave Sal a big hug.

"Candy! Don't you look *wonderful*! Cherry, I'd like you to meet Candy Darling. She's the prettiest girl in the room, don't you think?"

She was. I said so. She had pale creamy skin and a cute little nose. Her makeup was perfect.

"Aren't you sweet?" she said in a soft voice. "You're pretty yourself." They giggled, and Sal whispered in my ear that Candy was like him—a chick with a dick. It was hard to believe. Even at close range, she looked exactly like a woman. This evening was getting crazier and crazier. Three more queens came and joined us, Holly Woodlawn, Wayne County, and Jackie Curtis. We talked about the best places to get big-size shoes, which I certainly appreciated, and makeup and hair tricks. I liked them all a lot, and nearly forgot they were men. They would be great girlfriends.

Then Debbie brought out the lobster. I made a couple of attempts to cut it open, but my knife kept sliding off the shell. Sal noticed me struggling, took pity, and showed me how to tear off the little flippers and shove the meat out with a fork in one chunk. It tasted sweet and came with a small dish of salty butter. It was a little rubbery but not at all fishy. I tried to concentrate on chewing the lobster and not notice what all else was going on in the room, but it was impossible. A woman they called Andrea Whips got up on a table and yelled, "It's showtime!" then proceeded to take off her clothes while doing a drunk little dance. I thought she was going to fall off the table and land right on top of us, but she caught herself at the last minute every time she started to go over. Everyone was clapping and cheering, and then another girl with long black hair got up on a table right in front of Andy's group and said, "Hey, Andy! Andy! Look at me! Look at me, you coldhearted bastard! Can I be in one of your movies *now*?" She had a fork in her hand and started sticking herself in the legs with it, hard. Blood trickled down in four thin rivulets. She kept screaming at him to look at her, all the while jabbing herself harder and harder, but Andy didn't even look up one time, just kept on talking like nothing was going on. A couple of guys grabbed her and pulled her off the table kicking and screaming. Sal and the others didn't seem overly concerned with her, or Andrea Whips, either. I guess they were used to stuff like that. But I sure wasn't. What was I doing there? I couldn't help but think of my mother and daddy and what they would say if they could see me now. Our preacher, Brother Wilkins, would drag me out by the hair of the head and make me kneel all night on my knees on a rough stone floor and pray for forgiveness for even being in such a place. I started thinking about how to gracefully get up and go home and not hurt Sal's feelings.

Before I could say anything, a girl in a minidress made out of a flag came by our table with a plate of brownies and held it out to me. "Go ahead," she said. "Take one. They're great." I took one. Then the girl said, "Only eat half."

Well, that was weird. I certainly wasn't fat, and who was she to tell me to only eat half? I hate it when people who don't even know you tell you what to do, like what to eat or not eat. A lot of people just assume if you're a model, you don't eat anything, and frankly a lot of the girls don't. They live on coffee and cigarettes and a salad once in a while. But I like food. I bit into the brownie and although it wasn't the best one I ever ate, it was pretty good. Brownies were my favorite. I guessed the restaurant just passed out dessert after a meal for free, like the free chickpeas. I ate the whole thing, washing it down with the rest of my Coke. I noticed Sal didn't take a brownie. Candy did, and some of the others, but they didn't eat the whole thing. After a while, it began to really get hot in there, and I started to sweat. The lobster must have made me sick. My head was beginning to swim and it was hard to draw breath.

"I have to go to the bathroom, Sal. Be right back."

In the hallway, there was a phone booth, and I blinked to clear my eyes as I saw a naked butt pressed against the glass side. The phone booth rocked back and forth, and the windows were all steamed up. I went on past, trying not to look because I was really getting sick and woozy-headed by this time, and pulled open the bathroom door. There was a couple in *there,* as well, going at it hard and heavy against the sink. They hardly even looked at me. The guy's pants were down around his ankles and his belt buckle was banging against the floor. I began to panic. What kind of a place was this? I opened the door to run out of the bathroom and slammed right into a man, nearly knocking him over. He grabbed me by the arms, pushing me back inside, and I screamed.

It was Lale Hardcastle.

"Hold on, honey! Where's the fire?" Then he got a good look at me. "Wait a minute! I know you! You're the girl that was in Bonetti's studio that day!"

"You were one of the naked guys," I finally said, almost in a whisper. How could we be having this conversation right in the women's bathroom with two people who were doing what they were doing not six feet away from us? My stomach was feeling worse and I was really having a hard time keeping my head together. Far from being able to smack Lale Hardcastle across the face, all I wanted was to get out of there and breathe some fresh air.

"I was. Sorry about that. I can explain. By the way, my name is Zack Carpenter."

"Right. Zack Carpenter. Of course. I have to go." I tried to push past him, but he still had his hands on my arms. The girl by the sink moaned. The slap-slap of flesh and the clanking of the belt buckle on the floor became faster.

"Don't be in such a hurry. What's your name? Where are you from? I've been thinking about you ever since that day. I saw your picture in *Rouge.*"

He was talking but the words coming out of his mouth sounded like a swarm of bumblebees. I was getting frantic. I felt like if I didn't get out of there that instant I would start screaming.

He pulled me close to him and kissed me on the mouth, sticking his tongue down my throat. I couldn't believe it. I jerked away from him, wiped my mouth with an "Ugh!" and ran out of the room, slamming the door in his face. Then I raced out through the restaurant, past all the famous painters, past Louise Nevelson, who was still holding court at the bar, past Mickey, past Dorothy Dean, past the line of people in suits and nice dresses and out into the night. I ignored the voices that were calling after me. If I didn't run home right this minute, a red-horned demon was going to grab me and take me straight down to hell.

I didn't even look at the lights—I just ran without stopping. Crossing Park Avenue South, I nearly got hit by a car. The driver slammed on the brakes and started yelling at me. Horns were honking like crazy, but I didn't care. I got to Fifth Avenue and ran down to Twelfth Street, not stopping once, hardly drawing breath. I think Lale had come out of Max's after me, but I didn't know for sure. I had never been much of a runner, but right then, there was nobody, nobody, nobody who could catch me. Just as I got to the safety of my block, out of nowhere, somebody jumped out and grabbed me, and then I did start screaming. He put his hand over my mouth and pulled me into the shadows.

"Cherry. Hush, baby. It's me. It's Aurelius. Stop screaming, Cherry. You going to rouse the cops."

"Aurelius?" He held me in his arms and I was so scared that I was shaking like a trailer house in a tornado.

"What happened, baby? What's after you?"

"I don't know. A boy. A man. The devil. I don't know."

"What are you on?"

"I don't know. What do you mean?"

"I mean drugs. What kind of drugs did you take?"

"Nothing. I didn't take any drugs. I ate some lobster. I ate a brownie. I drank a Coke. I don't know. I feel sick. I'm scared. I don't know what's happening to me."

"A brownie? Where did you get it?"

"Somebody at Max's Kansas City gave it to me. Some girl dressed in a flag. I don't know."

"It was probably a pot brownie. Those things can be lethal. Can you throw up?"

"I don't know." He took me to the curb and stuck his finger down my throat. For the second time that night, I gagged, and this time I threw up a river of chocolate with green specks and white lumps of lobster in it. It was disgusting. But he didn't seem disgusted. He pulled out his handkerchief and wiped my mouth. Then we sat on the nearest stoop for a few minutes.

"Are you any better?"

"I don't know. Yes. I think so."

"We're nearly home. Let's try to go on."

We got to our house and he opened the door and we started up the stairs. Mrs. Digby had her eye to the crack of her door as we passed.

"Good evening, Mrs. Digby," he said, like we had just been out for a stroll. "I hope you had a lovely one."

The door closed and we went on up to our floor, him half carrying me up the steep stairs. Aurelius got the key out of my bag.

"Ouch!" he said as he banged his head on the little door leading into my room. "I forgot about that thing. I lived in this apartment when I first came here. You and me, we're too big for rooms like this."

He went into the bathroom and started running hot water into the tub. I didn't feel like the demon was after me anymore, and was shaking a little less, but I still felt awful. A pot brownie. Maybe *that's* why the flag girl had said to just eat half.

"Come on. Let's get you in the tub. That'll relax you. Come on. It'll be all right. Trust me."

My arms and legs felt too heavy to move, and I was in a floaty place where I didn't really care what I did, so I let him undress me and put me in the tub. It didn't even feel strange. I sank down in the warm water up to my neck while he sat on the toilet top beside me and talked and sang to me, stories about him growing up in the cotton patch, funny old songs by Hank Williams or Bob Wills and the Texas Playboys. "Hey, good-lookin'! What'cha got cookin'? How's about cookin' somethin' up with me?" He had a great voice. I slowly began to relax and finally, when the water got cold, he handed me a towel.

"Where's your nightgown?"

"I sleep in a T-shirt. It's in the top drawer of the dresser." My voice sounded like it was coming from far away, from somebody else's mouth. It was so weird, I didn't even care that he saw me naked. In fact, I felt like I was wafting away on a pink cloud. The sounds of the cars on Sixth Avenue might have been horns some angel was playing on the cloud next door.

Aurelius helped me into my T-shirt, then he turned back the covers and put me in bed.

"Will you be all right?" he asked.

"Stay. Stay with me." I was feeling so warm and cozy, and reached up for him. He hesitated, but lay down on my small bed, on top of the covers, kind of stiffly, and put his arms around me. I melted into him and it seemed so natural. I reached over and kissed him, the biggest, softest lips I had ever kissed. He kissed me back, and it was hard to get my breath.

"Get under the covers with me. Please?"

He hesitated, pulled back, and looked me in the eyes.

"I don't think so, baby. You still a little stoned. I don't want to take advantage of you."

"I don't care. Take advantage of me."

"You don't mean it. You're a good girl. I know bad girls, and you ain't one."

It had been so long since I had even kissed a man—apart from the slurpy ambush by Lale. I felt like a big overripe peach, dripping and ready to fall from the tree. It was so unlike me. Maybe I *was* stoned.

"I don't have a whole lot of experience, but I'm no virgin. I want you to. You can't tell me you don't want to. I know better." I put my face up to be kissed again.

"Look," he said, taking my arms from around his neck, "I never wanted anybody as bad as I did you that day in Joe Jr's. I wanted to throw that table over and grab you and take you right on the floor in front of Tony and the dishwashers and everybody, but you know that would be nothing but trouble for you and me."

"It would have been something new for Tony and the dishwashers." I started to giggle. I couldn't stop. He rolled over and sat on the edge of the bed. I managed to quiet down.

"You're white."

"Right."

"And I'm black."

"I know."

"If we were in Alabama, how long do you think we'd last? They've hung men for doing less than I done tonight."

"They don't hang people anymore. Not even in Alabama."

"Maybe they do and maybe they don't. Maybe they just make it look like an accident these days. But one thing is sure—they make it hard for them to live."

"Nobody cares here. Nobody knows you're here with me tonight. It's just you and me. And Mrs. Digby." I giggled again. "And she's cool. You have no idea how *cooool* Mrs. Digby is."

I put my arms around him and he leaned down and kissed me again. I thought he was going to give in, but he stood up and tucked the covers over me.

"I can't. Not like this."

"Are you scared of me?"

"Yes. And that's the God's truth."

"Okay. Good night." I turned my back on him and didn't move as he let himself out. I was hurt and felt like crying.

In a few minutes, I could hear the wail of the saxophone through the wall. Maybe he was right. I don't know how I would tell Mama and Daddy I was dating a black man anyhow. Maybe his parents felt the same way about white girls. I knew so little about him, I didn't even know if he had parents or brothers or sisters. I felt like a bad girl. He was much better than I was. That saxophone sure made me feel lonesome.

I fell asleep thinking about my daddy, and how when I was a little girl and had a nightmare I would call out to him and he would come and put his arms around me and I would drift back off to sleep, believing that there was nothing in the world that could ever hurt me. I missed him so much.

25

THE BIG YELLOW DUCK

I woke up the next morning with a headache, and the whole night seemed like some kind of bad dream. Was there really a girl up on a table sticking herself in the legs with a fork in front of Andy Warhol? Had I really thrown myself at Aurelius and been turned down? I had a taste in my mouth like I'd chewed on an old inner tube, and went and scrubbed my teeth and washed my hair, which made me feel a lot better. After putting on my makeup, considering everything, I looked fairly okay, which was lucky since Mrs. Digby had slipped a note under the door saying Suzan had called early and left a message saying she needed to see me and to please come in today by ten. It was a little scary. She had never left a message for me before. What could she want? It was too early for spring-cleaning, that dreaded time I had been told about when the girls who hadn't produced enough income were weeded out—and I had been working a fair amount. The Vanity Fair shoot with Neal Barr was coming up in a couple of days, and the ad was going to be in all the big magazines. I had seen the contact sheet from the test we did, and while you couldn't see my face because that was the way they did all the ads, the setup was really pretty, a long white satin slip that clung to my legs, and I looked as graceful as a dancer. My hair stood out like a halo, backlit, and the Vanity Fair people apparently were happy with it or they wouldn't have given me the job. I felt like I might get more work from Neal, who was really nice and did a lot of big stuff. Then there was the promise from Ron about the *Glamour* editorial scarf thing. They'd have to see my face in that! I took a couple of Bayers to chase the dregs of the headache away and vowed I would never go near a brownie or cookie or anything that was being served by a girl wearing a flag again.

I dressed in a pair of embroidered jeans tucked into my knee-high lace-up boots and a poor-boy orange sweater and the chenille coat. I'd go look for a heavier coat today if I had the time.

Before I left, I listened at Aurelius's door, but he was probably still asleep. I didn't know what I would do when I saw him again, but I'd worry about that later. It was probably just as well.

It was so funny. Well, not ha-ha funny, but weird funny. My big romance with Tripp Barlow had started out when I had unknowingly drunk Hawaiian punch that had been mixed with cherry moonshine and I got sick and passed out. He took me back to his place and put me to bed, too, and the romance started the next morning. I was a virgin, and maybe I'd needed to get a little drunk to get the ball rolling, so to speak. I felt a little pang, thinking about it. Tripp was my first love, and I missed it all—the romance, the companionship, the fun of being with a guy. Not to mention the sex. Tripp had been *great* at that, and I hadn't been with anyone since him. It had been nearly a year. I tried not to think about it, but those old human urges do have a way of springing up from time to time.

The Cherry I was then, Tripp Barlow, and Arkansas seemed a million miles away—another lifetime. Now that I thought about it all again, from this perspective, I was actually glad his wife, Faye, had come after him and we hadn't gotten together. I sure wouldn't be in New York now. Who knows what would have happened? We might have gotten married and had a baby, like Tripp and Faye had, and I would be teaching school somewhere near Sweet Valley. Not the worst fate, but not for me. Sometimes the bread lands jelly-side up. Maybe it was for the best that Aurelius and I didn't get together last night. Or maybe we still would.

I opened the front door and almost fell over my big yellow duck. I had totally forgotten about that thing. Then Lale Hardcastle stepped up, and smiled. Oh, Lord. He was the last person I wanted to see.

"You forgot your duck."

"How did you know it was my duck? How did you know where I live?"

"Sal told me. He was worried about you and asked me to check on you this morning. Where did you go in such a hurry last night?"

"Tell Sal I'm all right. Tell him I'll call him later. You didn't need to check on me, but thanks for bringing the duck. I have to go. I have an appointment." I stuck the duck inside behind the door and started down the steps.

"Wait a minute. You can't just run off like that again."

"Sure I can. Watch me." I didn't have time to have a fight with Lale Hardcastle right then, and I hadn't been so foggy last night that I forgot him kissing me in the bathroom. He really was a jerk, and sooner or later I would tell him just what I knew about him, but now was not the time.

I was walking fast, but he wouldn't let me go. He walked fast right beside me.

"I know you're at Suzan Hartman. Are you going to a booking?"

"Sal tell you that, too?"

"Well, Sal's a friend."

"Apparently. Sal seems to have a lot of friends."

"Including you."

"Including me. But that doesn't mean *you're* my friend."

"Oh, come on. Why are you so mad at me?"

"I'm not mad at you. I don't even know you. I am just late for an appointment."

"Well, can I see you again?"

"I don't think so. I have a boyfriend."

"Really? Who?"

"That's none of your business."

"Is it Bonetti? You were out with him last night."

"Sal tells you a lot, doesn't he? Tell Sal that what I do is none of his business, either. And no, it's not Bonetti. We're just friends."

A taxi with its for-hire light on came by and I leaped into the street and flagged it down. As the door slammed practically in his face, Lale put his hand on the window, fingers splayed, hoping to stop it or something, I guess. I ignored him and he had to back up so the cab wouldn't run over his feet. He stood in the street watching after the car as I glanced back and smiled to myself. I'd bet a dollar against a doughnut hole that not many women had ever treated him like that. I had never been that rude to anybody in my life, but there are some people who deserve it.

26

DIAMONDS & ERMINE

Suzan's office smelled like a dirty ashtray. I hardly ever went into her office if I could help it, and frankly, she hadn't invited me in too many times, either. Once was when she decided that I finally had enough pictures for a composition card, and she had gone through my book and picked out five. On the back of the card were four smaller pictures, the one from "Fini Rouge" of me in the gauzy dress, then a hard-edged one in tight jeans and a black turtleneck sweater with my hair picked out wild and a lot of bad-girl black eye makeup on. The third one was on the street with me in a chic suit and briefcase, my hair slicked back in a bun like I was going to work, and in the last one I was wearing a silk camisole and stockings, to show off my legs. It was a pretty good array of my different looks. On the front of the card was a big one in the red-and-white scarf that should have been on the cover of *Rouge*. At least it was somewhere. There was a list of my height and sizes, with a small asterisk that noted GOOD LEGS. It was so great to be able to hand out a card when I went on a go-see instead of just having to apologize and hope they would remember me. I mailed some to my mother and Daddy and to Baby, and Mama handed them out to all her friends and the family. She said that Daddy wasn't too happy with the stockings one or the sexy one, but he put it up on his dresser, so I think he was proud of me. He didn't write much himself, but always put a sweet little note at the end of Mama's letters. Once I got a letter from him that was just one line—"Have I told you lately that I love you?" It made me cry. It would be hard spending the holidays by myself, but it was too expensive for them to come to New York, and truth be told, I didn't really want to leave because of work. It was too soon to go back home—almost as if I was afraid I would be sucked into that other life again and not be able to come back.

Suzan was wearing her uniform of black turtleneck sweater and black slacks, her hair in a French twist, and, if it was possible, she looked even skinnier than usual. Her shoulder blades stuck out like wings and there was a tightness around her mouth as she dredged the smoke out of the cigarette. She was going to get those lines around her lips soon, I suspected. You could almost see them already. Despite the heavy makeup she was wearing, I could tell there were dark circles under her eyes, and they looked a little puffy. Almost bruised.

"Hi, Suzan. Did you want to see me?"

"Yes, sit for a minute. Did you bring your book?"

"I always do."

"I got a call this morning from Nancy Marks at BYD and O. Apparently somebody mentioned you to her and she wanted to meet you for a new national campaign they're doing for a perfume called Diamonds & Ermine. I think it is too soon, your book is by no means ready, but you might as well go over and see. Don't count on anything."

She leaned over to get a piece of paper to write the address down, and couldn't help wincing. She had to steady herself with her hand on the edge of the desk.

"Are you all right, Suzan?"

"I'm fine."

"No, you're not. What's wrong?"

"It's just my rib. I fell last night. Slipped on the bathroom floor."

"Don't you want to go see the doctor? It might be broken. I'll go with you."

She almost smiled, but not quite.

"Thanks, but no. They wouldn't do anything anyhow. You can't put a broken rib in a cast. It'll be all right. I just have to remember not to stretch and not to breathe too deeply. I've had these before."

"You have?"

I was being nosy, but she obviously was in pain. I'd never had a broken rib, but once I got hit in the ribs by a football when I was playing with my cousins and it knocked the wind out of me. I woke up in the middle of the night in such agony I couldn't draw a deep breath. Mama and Daddy had to take me to the emergency room to get an X-ray. The doctor said it was just cracked, and this seemed like it was much worse. I wondered if Suzan had gotten drunk and fallen down.

"Oh, once Freddy was horsing around and accidentally kicked me. It was nothing. He was just playing. Men don't know their own strength."

The idea that maybe Freddy wasn't just horsing around but did it on purpose occurred to me, too. She wrote down the address for BYD&O.

"Call after your meeting and let me know how it goes. I'm sure Nancy will call herself if it's good news."

"Great. Okay. Wish me luck?"

She smiled then, a ghost of a smile, and there for a minute she was the Suzan that I had been with the night we called the Hogs.

The offices of BYD&O were on the top floor of the building, and glass double doors opened into a waiting room that was all gray and steel and glass. The receptionist took my name and I sat in a row of chairs with several other girls who also wanted the job as badly as I did. We all smiled, secretly sizing one another up. I could tell that one girl had on patty nails because her real nails were too wide and you could see the edges. They were also polished an ugly shade of frosted pink that looked cheap. I hated this part of it, the waiting, them looking at me, maybe thinking that I looked cheap, too, because of my hair or something. I felt pretty good about my new look, though, and had given away all my pastel miniskirts and matching tights that screamed *mod.* Fashion was so much fun now. It seemed like everyone was wearing a costume every day. Almost anything went—midis were definitely in now in a big way, as well as gaucho pants and fringed leather vests, big floppy suede hats, tweed knickers, Indian- and Persian-print long granny dresses, short jackets with long gathered skirts, and boots, boots, boots with everything. It almost didn't matter what was in style; it was what looked good on you. Aside from scarves, belts were my new fun thing, and I scoured the flea markets for them. I found a real silver concha belt at a flea market on Canal Street for seven dollars that was crammed in the bottom of a box of junk, nearly black, until I got it home, shined it up, and saw the heavy STERLING mark on the back. I discovered you could put on a pair of tight jeans, a turtleneck, a good pair of boots, and a great belt and go anywhere. I also started collecting jackets. I got an old Eisenhower jacket at the army surplus store that went great with a pair of tweed knickers; a black velvet jacket that had a map of Korea embroidered on the back in silk thread; and finally I found my long sheepskin coat, which was so warm even the New York City wind couldn't get through it. I was in heaven in the antique-clothing shops and went with Lana every chance we got. My little closet was jammed. But neatly jammed. I sent boxes of stuff to Baby and Mama, which they loved. There were so many wonderful things to buy that I had to be careful to save out the rent money, especially now that I was making a little more. You never knew when it would all dry up, Daddy said, although I think he was surprised at how much I was making in such a short time. So was I.

A middle-aged woman in a navy-blue suit came out and looked right at me. "Cherry?"

The other girls glanced at me, trying to act cool and hide the fact they were miffed. Most of them had been there before I was.

"Are you Nancy?" She was tiny and tilted her head up as I rose, trying not to show how shocked she was at my size.

"I am indeed. Come with me." We went down a long carpeted hallway past cubicles with secretaries typing away, to her office, another small, gray and glass and metal room. She ushered me into a black leather chair and took my book, flipped through it pretty fast. Too fast.

"How long have you been modeling?"

I inwardly sighed. Same old question. They all somehow could tell I was new. "I started back in early September. But I have some new bookings coming up—one for Vanity Fair lingerie, and one for Clairol. I'm going to be Platinum Babe Number Twenty-one." Clairol seemed really happy to have somebody whose hair didn't have to be bleached out, and I felt like I would get more work from them.

"Well, we're doing a national campaign for Diamonds & Ermine perfume—maybe you've heard of it?"

"Of course. I love Diamonds & Ermine!" In fact, I had never used it at all, as I tended to not like many perfumes. But perfume was a big part of New York advertising, so once in a while I would go to Saks Fifth Avenue and hang out at the perfume counter, trying out all the ones I saw in the ads. I bought some Emeraude, which smelled good for a minute, but it was too sweet, like White Gardenia, which gave me a headache. Patchouli was beginning to be the big one now, mostly in an oil that got all over everything and smelled for days. I bought some from a guy on the street with Rasta hair and sticks of incense laid out on a table, and although it made me feel like a real cool hippie, people in elevators practically passed out from the fumes. Even after a bath, I could still smell it. I had no idea what Diamonds & Ermine smelled like, but I was sure I was going to like it.

"The concept is going to be all white—a blond man in a dinner jacket and a woman in a white ermine coat and diamonds. We have the man already, but hadn't found the perfect woman until I saw your picture in a makeup artist's book."

Sal. It had to be him. I needed to give him a call, even if I was kind of mad at him for telling Lale where I lived. I'm sure Sal didn't know what Lale was really like, or that he was even named Lale.

"Was it Salvador de Vega?"

"Actually, it was. Loved some of the shots of you he had. Okay. Let me introduce you to the people from Parvu, who are here from France, and we'll go from there."

I followed her down some more hallways to a room filled up with a huge conference table, where two men and a very chic French woman were sitting in deep leather chairs, looking at stacks of pictures. Their eyes widened a little when they saw me. Nancy introduced me, and the men got up and came around the table. The woman just nodded and smiled from her seat. One of the men kissed the air a fraction of an inch above my hand, and the other one gave me two pecks, one on each cheek that just about touched the skin, but not quite. The hand kisser had a bottle of perfume and asked if he could spray it on my wrist.

"Mmm! Wow! That smells so good!" I practically swooned over it, although it seemed kind of too heavy for my taste and went all the way up into my sinuses. Well, that would be a bonus if anybody had a cold. They all beamed at my reaction, so I spread it on a little thicker. "I'd buy that in a minute! Where can I get some?"

"Please," the air kisser said, handing me the bottle and tenderly wrapping my fingers around it with his own. "Take this one. It is for you."

"Thank you so much!" I clutched it like it was a newborn kitten.

"Where are you from?" the woman said in a cute French voice. "That is an unusual accent."

"Arkansas."

"Ah. Yes. The South." It sounded like she said, "Ze Souse." They all looked at one another, one of the men raised his eyebrow, and I began to get a little uneasy. I wanted to ask if there was something wrong with being from the South, but was afraid to. What difference did it make what kind of accent I had for a picture in a magazine? And why was a French accent so great while an Arkansas accent raised eyebrows anyhow? I just hate that. People are so . . . provincial. They looked at me some more, then gathered around and went through the pictures in my book, studying each one while I stood there, caressing the perfume bottle. The woman whispered something to one of the men. He shrugged and I thought I heard him say something about dubbing, like the other one. Then they stood up again, and the first man grasped my hand and air-kissed it again.

"*Enchanté,* Cherry. Thank you for coming."

Nancy handed me my book and walked me out. I had a feeling the perfume was my consolation prize.

"Not to be nosy, but what was all that whispering about?"

"There will be a lot of copy with the ad, and it will have to be read in the commercial. The accent might be a problem. Do you think you can work on it? Not that you are guaranteed to get the commercial, even if you should happen to do the print."

"A TV commercial? Wow. Well, I'll sure try. I mean, if I'm lucky enough to get it."

A TV commercial! That was a *ton* of money. Every model in New York would give their right arm to be in a TV commercial. Well, obviously they wouldn't be able to do a commercial with just one arm, but they would give a lot.

But they hadn't said for sure I had it. In fact, I probably didn't. Still, I couldn't help but hope. I thanked Nancy and walked out, feeling her eyes on my back as I walked. I tried to be as graceful as they taught me in runway class. A TV commercial! If only I could stop talking like a hick. I was already trying to say words like *ice* clearly. I-eece. Three people at least had told me an ugly joke about a southern girl who pronounced it "ass." You've heard it, I'm sure.

A week later, I wrote Baby.

Dear Baby,

You won't believe this, but I'm going to be the new Diamonds & Ermine girl!!! It is a series of print ads in all the big magazines, and I'm going to be in the TV commercial, too! I might not get to use my own voice, though—they might have to dub me because of the way I talk, but I don't care. Suzan told me from the start that I should take speech lessons, so I called this one guy who she recommended but we got into a huge fight the first lesson and I walked out. The lesson was on breathing. He kept wanting me to breathe in and down my back and up my chest and around my abdomen or something. How stupid is that? You just breathe in and out with your lungs—your back has nothing to do with anything. I tried to do what he said, but I did it wrong and he just kept telling me to breathe down my back and finally he yelled at me so I got my stuff and left. I'm not letting anybody yell at me, commercial or not. I'll just keep practicing with the TV and maybe some of it will rub off. I don't want to be an actress anyhow, and if they don't like my voice they can just dub it.

Now comes the weird part, and don't get mad at me until I tell you all of it. I did the first shoot yesterday, and the photographer is this really famous guy, Milton Greene, who does a lot of work for *Bazaar* and all. He has a big studio on the East Side in a tall skinny townhouse. The house is only about as wide as a trailer house, but has five floors stacked up, with beautiful furniture and chandeliers on every floor. I was really nervous, since it was such a big deal, and I had never met the man. He turned out to be a great guy, funny and easy and so nice to work with, and his wife, Amy, who is a doll, was there. She used to be a model, too, but is tiny. Models have gotten taller over the years, and now you have to be at least five feet seven to join an agency, but you could have definitely been a model in the old days.

I'm just beating around the bush. The main thing I have to tell you is that there is a male model in the shots with me and it turned out to be—you won't believe this—Lale Hardcastle. I haven't told you that I ran into him, literally, at a restaurant here, and the reason I haven't written you, or part of the reason, is that I haven't had the courage to confront him about Cassie. In fact, I haven't written to her to tell her I saw him. I can hear you yelling at me, and I'm sorry. I know I ought to, and I'm going to, but if you will wait and let me do it, that would be better than you telling her, because she would wonder why I didn't tell her sooner. Oh, Baby. It is just all too complicated. He is a jerk—we know that for a fact—and I don't like him the least little bit, but it isn't so easy to tell a complete stranger that you know all about him running off and leaving his girlfriend and all the rest of it about his deformed baby and all. I will tell Cassie. I swear I will, but this Diamonds & Ermine thing makes it harder. I have to act like I like him, at least in the pictures, and if we are fighting I don't think it would work. There is a lot riding on this for me. So please don't think badly of me. I'll do the right thing, I swear it. Just not right now.

On another note, I finally got to do a fashion show. It was for a group of Italian designers who are trying to get into the New York market but are not famous, so I guess Gerald le Forge, the dictator who teaches the runway classes and is head of the bookings for it, thought nobody would notice if I messed up.

You wouldn't believe how chaotic those shows are backstage. Each one of us has a person who is our dresser, and we all sit and get our hair and makeup done, then jump into the clothes the dressers hand us and they shove us out onto the runway one by one when the music starts. It is really hard to do, like a choreographed dance or something, and you have to walk on an invisible straight line, one foot right in front of the other, which isn't that easy. You go out when the girl ahead of you gets to a certain place, then you have to pass each other as she comes back, you go on to the end of the runway and do your pivots, trying to look bored and sexy and slinky and chic, and by then the next girl comes out and you have to pass by her and go off, run like crazy when you get out of sight of the audience to the dresser who throws another outfit on you, the makeup artist touches up your hair and makeup, and they grab you and throw you back out there, where you have to look bored and slinky again, although you are really nervous and sweating and hoping it doesn't show on the underarms.

You know how clumsy I am, how I used to step on people's feet on the dance floor? This is ten times worse. The shoes were really high heels, and all I could think of was trying to walk and not look too gawky. I worked and worked on it all, trying to be more graceful, but I can see why Gerald just about gave up on me. Still, at this show I did really well at first. I even got a hand of applause for a great outfit with an embroidered cape and crushed patent-leather knee boots. But when I came out in a chiffon evening dress, I had too much confidence and tried to do a big double swirl so the dress would sweep around, and I turned my ankle and nearly fell off the runway. The crowd gasped. I didn't actually hit the ground, just stepped on the hem of the dress and staggered, but it was so embarrassing. Everyone said not to worry about it, but Gerald was not happy, I can tell you. I doubt he gives me another show in a hurry.

So what's going on in Buchanan? When do you get out for Christmas? Have you seen Father Leo much? I still haven't gone to bed with Aurelius. Since that night at Max's, when he was so sweet to me, he has not tried to ask me out at all. I just don't know what to make of him. We don't really see each other all that much, since we have such different hours, but I just knew he really liked me. And I really like him. I don't know what I'm doing wrong. And please, please, please, don't say anything to Cassie about Lale. I PROMISE I will tell her.

Love you lots,
Cherry

27

SUZAN AND FREDDY

The pool room was quiet, no beautiful young things frolicking, leaving wet towels and glasses everywhere. Suzan loved it when she was all alone in the house at Sneden's Landing, when Freddy was in the city and all the models had gone home. She didn't have to pretend to be the den mother, didn't have to pretend that Freddy wasn't humping some new girl in his bedroom as she drank and the kids felt sorry for her. Her ribs still hurt from the last beating Freddy had given her. When she was working in front of the camera, he at least would never hit her in the face. She might have to miss a job. But now it didn't matter, really, and he once had popped her between the eyes, blackening both of them. Thank goodness she was a pro with makeup. She used a special coverup designed for port-wine birthmarks that would cover any bruise. The swelling was a bit of a problem, but Arnica gel and ice usually took that down within a day or so. She almost didn't care anymore. Had she really once loved this man? He disgusted her, his bad breath and thinning hair and pale flabby belly, the way his tongue quivered when he laughed. Everything about him irritated her, and she supposed he could say the same about her. He hadn't had a real hard-on in years. Not with her, at any rate. She stared into the blue water and thought about the night she and Cherry had called the Hogs. Freddy looked so funny, it was worth the beating he'd given her afterward. What a pig he was! No, that was unfair to pigs. Pigs are honest in their greed. Freddy had never been honest with her about anything. Not two hours ago, she had discovered he was siphoning off a great deal of money from the agency and putting it into a secret account. It wasn't enough that he had the lion's share of the business; he wanted it all. But he was getting sloppy, leaving his desk unlocked. He must have been too drunk to lock it. She had been looking for a contract and almost idly tried the locked drawer in his desk. There were a lot of things in there she hadn't expected, including the secret bank statement. Love letters, of course, some from women dating back to their early days together. He kept in touch with most of them, it seemed. There were little gifts they sent, nude photographs, poems. One note said, "If you'll give me a thousand dollars, I will love you." She was shocked he was still attractive to women, even for money; surprised that they would give him those things. Well, he was the owner of a famous model agency. Why should she be surprised? Suzan tried to remember, like opening a dusty old trunk, when she had been the new young girl he loved. To a seventeen-year-old from Little Rock, he was worldly and suave, the man who wore suits and ties every day, could order a good wine in a restaurant, and had a car and driver. He knew how to make love in ways good ol' Randy had never dreamed about, took his delight in satisfying her to the point that she cried. He surprised her with little gifts, funny things like a stuffed dog or expensive things, such as a garnet bracelet. The first year they were together a bouquet of pink roses arrived every morning with the newspaper. She thought it was sweet at first, but her apartment began to smell like a funeral parlor. After a few weeks, she hated roses. Roses took over your life. You had to smell them, you had to deal with them, watch them wilt, decide when they were over the top and then throw them out, crushing their petals under coffee grounds. She found herself sad all the time, constantly watching the flowers die. Finally, she begged him to stop sending them. She had begun to break out in hives from all the flowers. Maybe he was trying to kill her even then. Death by roses.

They had literally met on the street. She'd signed with the Fords a few weeks earlier and was walking down Forty-sixth Street carrying a heavy suitcase after a test. She was hot and tired, and he stepped out of a limousine and offered to carry her bag. He was handsome, older, dressed in an expensive suit and nice shoes, handmade of soft Italian leather and new. Even then Suzan knew quality. Charm wafted off him like fine cologne. What would it hurt to have a handsome stranger carry her bag for a block or two to give her arm a rest? The car followed them and waited when they stopped in front of a coffee shop and Freddy offered to buy her a cup of coffee. Well, why not? It was broad daylight. Coffee turned into a burger, and they sat for three hours talking. He was a producer on the TV show *Ted Mack's Original Amateur Hour,* which she watched faithfully. He was the one who found the contestants. He showed her his card with the show's logo printed on it, so she knew he was legitimate, but she didn't doubt it. He was so sincere. He looked at her with an honesty as clear as his transparent gray eyes. He seemed delighted with everything she said, her accent, her stories about sneaking off to the university to see her boyfriend in Arkansas. Riding home in the limo felt familiar, like she belonged in one. It was the swankiest feeling in the world. He called her the next morning, early. He wanted his voice to be the first thing she heard that day. Of course she accepted his dinner invitation. Soon they were seeing a lot of each other. But she was seventeen and a rising young model. Other men were pursuing her, too, photographers, male models, executives—any man who had a heart that pumped red blood was after her; everyone wanted a piece of the new hot beautiful blonde. But Freddy was quietly persistent. He bided his time, becoming the shoulder she cried on, the older man with the love and understanding. By the time she was twenty, he gave her an emerald-cut diamond and they married at Christmas, her twenty-first birthday. By this time she was one of the top money earners in the agency, raking in six figures a year. She had been on twelve *Vogue* covers, scores of others. She worked constantly, was always on trips, up and out early, working late at night. She never knew Freddy kept a head sheet of the agency's girls in his desk like it was his own personal catalog to fill in the time while she was gone. He had his pick. Suzan, after a couple of years, was tired of it all and wanted to take a break and have a baby, but Freddy was adamantly against it. She would ruin her career, he said. They'll forget you and move on to the next new girl. You have to work while you are hot.

She got pregnant on purpose, and for the first time, Freddy hit her. He forced her to have an illegal abortion. In a garage on the West Side, Hell's Kitchen, far from clean. There was no sink, even, for the woman to wash her hands. She paid the woman two hundred dollars, cash, and while Freddy waited out in the car, the woman butchered her. She got an infection, spent three weeks in the hospital, and it took months to get her strength back. The doctor told her she would never again be able to have children. Freddy felt horrible about it. He sat by her bedside and cried. He almost made her believe he was sorry, but she had taken a step away from him in her heart, and although he convinced her not to leave him, she never took that step back. She would never again be so close that he could hurt her that badly. Which, perversely, only made him want to hurt her more. She threw herself into her work, and they maintained a life together.

Then Suzan hit her late twenties. Work got slower. When she occasionally ran into old clients, they told her they had been trying to get her, but her booker told them she was unavailable. Her booker said she had done no such thing. The fashion world gets bored easily and always wants a new face, a new look, a newer model. They never tell you you're too old. They just stop calling, like a boyfriend who wants to break up but doesn't have the guts for a confrontation.

Though she was slowing down, she was still a star at the peak of her beauty, and she was angry. It was Freddy's idea to quit his job and start the agency. At first it was an adventure, just the two of them and Gina, her booker, from Ford. Freddy did the bookkeeping. Suzan was the only model for a while, and she worked night and day to keep the agency going. She took any job she could, no matter how small or demeaning, no matter how tired she got. She would accept a booking of an hour, was always on time, always a pro. Gradually, other girls joined the agency, and finally Suzan quit modeling altogether.

As they got more successful, Freddy got more dissolute and the abuse got worse. She actually tried to leave him a few times, but he tracked her down. Once she went to Paris, the best two weeks of her life, but he appeared in a little café where she was having a kir and steak frites, slid into the booth next to her, and calmly picked a potato off her plate. His fists convinced her that no matter where she went he would always find her, and next time would be worse. He had spies everywhere. He had control of the company, and he had control of her.

She knew he meant it. She was scared of him. And she was stuck.

28

THE FORTUNE

It was night in the I.C.U. at Children's Hospital. In the waiting room, the lights had been dimmed and the pillows and blankets passed around. Cassie stretched out on the couch, luxuriating in lying down without having to stiffly hold the old chair to keep it from folding up on her. She almost relaxed. By default, Cassie had moved up to the biggest couch in the waiting room, as she had been there the longest. Every few days, another one of the mothers left with her baby wrapped in a blanket, her husband carrying her bags, both of them beaming as they said good-bye, ecstatic to be leaving, but sad for the ones left behind. The other mothers would say good-bye in return, each trying to be happy for them, each hoping it would be her turn next. Once in a while, a mother would leave without her baby, which terrified them all as they hugged her and offered what comfort they could, secretly relieved it wasn't them, praying that their baby would be one of the lucky ones. And then they reshuffled their seats, making room for the new ones who came to join the colony.

By now, Cassie had acquired stacks of crossword puzzle books, paperback novels, and bags tucked neatly beside her couch. But she didn't talk much to the other women, and caught them sneaking looks at her from time to time. They thought she was strange. Maybe she was. Her clothes were so big that they were tied up by string, and even though her mother brought fresh ones every week, nothing she had fit anymore. After begging and threatening Cassie to get out and get herself some new clothes, Annie had finally taken the bull by the horns. She brought Bernadette.

"You haven't breathed fresh air in weeks," Annie said after they visited for a little while with Lalea. "And you look like a refugee from some war or something. I'll sit right here with this baby and you go shopping. Bernadette, you carry her to that elevator if you have to. Lalea will be here when you get back. I promise you that." She handed Cassie some folded money.

Bernadette was quite a bit stronger than Cassie at this point, and just as hardheaded, so rather than throw a fit and embarrass herself, Cassie went. The light outside hit her full in the face, as if she had been down in a coal mine for ages, and she had to put her hand over her eyes to shut out the pain. The cold air filled her lungs and almost hurt. She coughed. It had been warm when she went into the hospital. How had that happened?

"Girl, you are the color of a fish belly," Bernadette said, taking a good look at her in the sunlight. "Just listen to you cough. You haven't had one good meal since you gave birth to that child. If you want to kill yourself, you're doing a right good job of it."

"I'm not trying to kill myself. I tried to do that once, and now God's making me pay for it."

"Well, that's the silliest thing I ever heard. Anybody who thinks they know what God is up to just hasn't got good sense, is what I think. Anytime I hear those preachers saying, 'God wants you to do this,' and 'God wants you to do that,' it makes me want to reach for my pistol. Of course, it's usually God wanting you to give them money. No better than thieves. At least thieves aren't talking you to death while they rob you."

Cassie just let her run on. No sense in trying to change her mind. She knew what she knew.

The noise and the color in the mall almost made her panic, she had been in the quiet of the hospital for so long. She passed by a ragged, skinny girl and almost said, "Excuse me," to her, and then saw that the girl was with someone who looked just like Bernadette. It was a mirror. She walked up to it and stared at the face with big eyes looking back at her. She ran her hands through her hair, which she had to shampoo in the tiny restroom sink with one hand while holding the water faucet on, so it never quite got clean. It had been so long since she'd had a real shower.

"Didn't you even recognize yourself, Cassie? See what I mean? We have to at least get you some clothes that fit, and maybe stop off in the beauty shop and get your hair trimmed. The ends are so split they look like hay."

"I don't know," she said, turning away from the mirror. "I don't want to be away too long."

But she did get her hair trimmed, and nothing felt as good as the girl washing her hair. She really knew how to do it, digging deep and rubbing and massaging until Cassie moaned. Then they went to Casual Corner and got a couple pairs of jeans, a few sweaters, and a coat. Even her coat had gotten so big it was like wearing a tent. She first tried on a ten, then an eight, until finally size six fit. Unbelievable. She used to have to squeeze into a sixteen. She stared at herself in the mirror, like it was somebody else. The dressing-room light was horrible. She didn't know how they ever sold a stitch of clothes in that awful fluorescent light. It made her skin look green and the circles under her eyes mud-colored.

Bernadette shoved an armful of dresses in the door at her.

"Here, sweetie, pick you out one of these. You can't wear jeans all the time."

"You do."

"Yeah, but that's me. You need at least one dress, in case you need to get fixed up to go someplace."

Like a funeral, Cassie thought, looking at a black knit dress. She added it to the pile without trying it on, pulled on her clothes, and got her stuff together.

"Let's get out of here. I've been gone too long as it is."

Cassie couldn't rest on the comfy couch. She tossed and turned for an hour or so, then got up and scrubbed to go into the nursery, where she put on the yellow suit and sat holding Lalea. She hated the feeding tube snaking down her throat. It had irritated her poor little nose until it was raw. She smeared a dab of Vaseline on it. Lalea was still the biggest baby in the pod, but she hadn't gained weight like she should have. Her tiny fingernails were blue, and her feet were a shade of purple, laced with dark veins. No amount of rubbing seemed to warm them up.

Cassie kissed her head, rocked her back and forth, and sang a lively little song to her.

"Pony girl, pony girl, won't you be my pony girl? Don't say no, here we go, riding 'cross the plains. Marry me, carry me, far across the plains! Giddy up, giddy up, giddy up, let's go! Ooooh, my pony girl!"

She caught movement at the nursery window and looked up to see George Hardcastle standing there. He stared at her as if he didn't recognize her, then went to the door and spoke to the nurse. Cassie kept singing as he came over, wearing the yellow protective suit.

"Cassie? Is that you?"

She looked up at him and he recognized the cornflower eyes. She was so thin and fragile, not at all the robust girl he had last seen a few months before. He wanted to hug her but hesitated, afraid she would push him away. He wouldn't blame her if she did.

"Hi, Mr. Hardcastle. What brings you here?"

"Can we go someplace and talk?"

"We can talk right here. Does your wife know where you are?"

Her heart was pounding, but she couldn't let him know. He looked so much like Lale, but without the cockiness Lale had. George was weathered by sun and wind and rain, callused from the fields, beaten down by hard work and a dissatisfied wife. He was a nicer person than his son. You could see the kindness in his eyes, but Cassie wasn't going to be taken in by that. She had gone through too much at the hands of the Hardcastles.

"She knows," he said, with a bitter edge. "I don't blame you if you don't want to talk to me, Cassie, but I have some things I need to tell you."

"Don't you want to see your granddaughter first?" She pulled back the blanket and George stepped up and looked down at the baby. Tears filled his eyes. Cassie pulled the baby closer to her.

"Well. I'm sorry, Cassie. I'm real sorry."

"Yeah. Me, too."

She wasn't going to ask him about Lale. She would cut out her tongue first.

"I want to apologize to you for the way Janet and I have treated you.

I don't expect you to understand Janet—God knows I don't understand her myself, and I've always found it easier to go along with her than fight her, but this time she's gone too far."

"I'm listening."

"I know the baby is Lale's. There was never any question in my mind about that. And Janet knows it, too. She just doesn't want to admit it, because then she would have to admit her son did a stupid, bad thing, and that she won't do. Lale hung the moon for Janet."

"Yeah. I know the feeling. So you've come to apologize for Janet? Why didn't she come herself?"

"She won't do that. But it doesn't much matter. I had to come when I found these."

George pulled out a stack of letters.

"These are from Lale. They don't say much, but in every one of them is a money order, made out to you."

"What do you mean? Lale sent me money?"

"Yeah. A lot of money. There must be over five thousand dollars in here."

"Why did he send it to Janet and not to me?"

"You can answer that as well as I can. He was ashamed to face you, I guess, but in his way he wanted to do something for you and the baby. Why she never gave it to you is a different story. One she's going to have to account for."

"I don't want his money. Give it back to Janet."

"Don't be hardheaded about this, Cassie. You're going to need money for this hospital and a lot of other things. Lale ought to pay you. He can afford it." He handed her the stack of envelopes. She looked at the familiar handwriting, and the return address: General Delivery, 350 Canal St., New York, NY. The stack was thick in her hand.

"Here. Let me hold her a minute and you can go put that money up."

George reached for Lalea, and after a moment, Cassie gave her to him.

"Watch her little neck. She can't hold up her head. Be careful of that tube. She has one in her leg, too."

She was lighter than he expected. He looked at her, searching for something he recognized, but he didn't need to search. His heart recognized her, even as her little finger and her hair color and the shape of her ears were familiar to him.

Cassie put the stack of envelopes in her purse and turned back to look at them, even as the alarm started beeping on the monitors. She knew which baby had set it off. George's startled eyes met hers in panic, and the nurse came running up and took her from his arms. Cassie started to grab at her, but another nurse held her back as a doctor materialized and they put Lalea down in her bed and started working on her.

"Get the mother out of here! Now!"

"My baby my baby my baby my baby my baby my baby my baby. . . ." Cassie half screamed until it became a moan.

George carried her out of the ward and tried to get her out to the hallway, but Cassie fought him, ran back, and put her hands on the nursery glass, trying to see what they were doing to her baby in the middle of the circle of doctors and nurses. After a while, she knew Lalea was gone. She could feel it. She pounded on the glass, trying to get their attention.

"Open the window! Open the window!"

"You're going to break that glass, girl!" George said, trying to pull her away.

"Tell them to open the window. She can't get out and go to heaven with the window shut!"

She looked up at George, and his heart broke.

29

ROOMMATES

"You ought to be in Diamonds & Ermine."

"I agree. Are you giving me a present?"

"The best present." (He hands her a bottle of perfume.)

"Perfume?"

"Not simply perfume. An extraordinary elixir. Immensely complex. Like you, love."

"Really? Complex how?"

"There are more elements in Diamonds & Ermine than in any other fragrance on earth. One hundred and twenty-three."

"One hundred and twenty-three? How do a hundred and twenty-three elements blend together? It might be too many."

"Just enough. They take the finest hints of jasmine blossoms, rose petals, heliotrope . . ."

"That's three."

". . . and add the merest whiff of lavender, rosemary, nutmeg; a hint of bitter almond . . ."

"It does sound like me. What else do Diamonds & Ermine and I share?"

"Oils of pomegranate, twigs of patchouli, cedars of Lebanon, gums of myrrh."

"Gums of myrrh? Hm. Beautiful words, but what does it smell like?"

"Poetry. Endlessly fascinating. You could wear it for a thousand nights and never tire of it."

"I like that."

"It only needs one more ingredient to attain perfection."

"And that is?"

"You, love."

"I can't say this crap!" Lale threw down the script. "I can't even pronounce half the words, much less look like James Bond while I'm saying it! Why can't they just do a voice-over and not make us have to say it? They're going to get somebody else's voices anyhow. We're too country for these highfalutin French folks."

"Speak for yourself. I've been practicing. Which you ought to do, too, if you want to be an actor like you say you do. They might do a voice-over, but we have to say the words anyhow, so somebody else can time their voices to us. You know that. It's not that hard. It's just stupid dialogue."

"You can say that again."

We were down at the SoHo loft, with Sal's baby-blue Mustang parked by the door. The ad had already been shot, and while it wouldn't be out in magazines for a while, they decided they liked the way we looked together and were going to take a chance on us in the TV commercial. It would be more money than any of our parents had ever seen at one time, and it was a little scary. I had trouble at first, thinking of Lale as Zack, and almost called him Lale a time or two, but now was not the time to let him know I knew who he was. In spite of the fact I knew he was a no-good snake, I had to pretend, at least for the camera, that I was in love with him. It wasn't hard to see how Cassie had fallen for him and why he had been voted best-looking every year in high school. He was the prettiest boy I had ever seen, like a blond Warren Beatty. Sleepy, blue, bedroom eyes, pouty mouth, strong straight nose. I wondered if Warren looked at himself in the mirror as much as Lale did. I had to stop myself from laughing at him sometimes, the way he'd stare at himself, make faces, and touch up a twig of hair that kept falling over his forehead. I guess in all fairness, I spent some time looking at myself, too. But it was our job, so we had an excuse. In front of the camera, though, we really did have something together—they all said we did. It wasn't love for each other, so it must have been a connection to our own images reflected in the lens, a love for the idea of the two of us together that was greater than either of us alone. I can't say it any better than that. We were kind of like actors in a movie who have to be in love, but turn it off when the cameras stop rolling. With all that pretend love, it was hard to keep on being cranky with him. I never could be mad at somebody for too long. I had to make myself keep remembering Cassie, and him running off on her like that. Then, I could be frosty. He never knew how I was going to treat him, cool or warm, which kept him on his toes.

Sal, of course, was doing the makeup, and it wasn't hard to tell that Sal was really in love with him, even if Lale seemed to have no clue.

"Zack, your skin is just *gushing* oil in front of these lights," he'd say, making an excuse to lovingly wipe a little powder on Lale's cheeks.

"What about me, Sal?" I pretended to be miffed. "My face could be shining like a gasoline slick and you'd never even notice."

"Oh, *you.* You don't even have *pores,* Miss Cherry. You're perfect, and you know it!" But he'd roll his eyes and pat a little on my face, to humor me. Then Milton Greene strolled in for the first shot, told us to stare in each other's eyes, and started working. He did a few Polaroids, changed the lights a bit, shot a few rolls of film, did two or three different setups, and before we even got warmed up, Milton said he had it, and that was the end. It was so fast and simple. That's a real artist for you. The makeup took way longer than the pictures did. I guess Mr. Greene was pretty sure of himself, which he had a right to be. He had photographed every big celebrity in the world, and he was probably bored to death with us, although he treated us like we were hot dogs on a stick or something. He made us feel like we would be as famous as any of them. After all, as he said, Sophia Loren and Marilyn Monroe were just pretty young girls when they started out.

After the shoot, Lale and Sal and I went over for dinner to Elaine's, a place on Second Avenue near Eighty-eighth that Sal said had the most celebrities in New York, although the food was not so great. The lighting was warm and golden and the walls were dark wood paneling. It was run by a big friendly woman wearing white glasses. Her name was Elaine—what else—and she came and gave Sal and Lale a hug and shook my hand with a smile when they introduced me, but I noticed she kind of ignored a lot of the regular people, like the bridge-and-tunnel crowd I'd seen at Max's, who were standing three deep at the bar waiting for a table. The B&Ts didn't seem to get a break anywhere. But she gave us one of the best front tables against the wall, next to the bar. Restaurants love having pretty people right where they're the most visible, even if they aren't famous. It was getting to the point that I kind of expected to be treated like I was famous, and was disappointed when I wasn't. I knew I was getting the big head, but the voice whispering in my ear telling me to be modest had gotten drowned out by the bigger voice yelling, *Model!* People were just crazy about models, like they were about movie stars, and there was no reason to pretend I didn't like it. We ordered a bottle of wine to celebrate. I was getting used to having a glass of wine after a day's work, and looked forward to it. That was another way I was slipping away from my raising. Soon I'd probably have two, and then I'd be a drunk. Ah, well. One day I'd deal with it all, but not now. Sal ordered fried calamari to start, which I liked a lot until he told me it was squid. I'd never even heard of eating squid, which I pictured as octopus, thrashing around under the sea in some horror movie. It was so exotic. At least it was fried. All we had in Sweet Valley was hamburger joints and home-style catfish buffets loaded down with deep-fat-fried everything. Even the rolls were deep-fat-fried. No wonder Arkansas had the most overweight people of anyplace in the U.S.A. But truth be told, I missed it. Actually, I think pasteboard would taste good if it was battered and fried, and I ate most of the calamari.

"So, Cherry, didn't you say you were a painter?" Sal asked. "With an art degree? And you've had shows?"

I had just stuffed a big piece of veal chop into my mouth. It was kind of dry.

"Hmm." I chewed fast, trying to get it down so I could answer. It took a few minutes. "Yes, I have a B.A. and had shows at school. One at the bank. No, I haven't been painting, but I would love to. I just don't have the room for it in my apartment."

"Oh, *really*? That's interesting," Sal went on, "because I have a *huge* loft down in SoHo, and my roommate, who is a painter, just moved out. Would you be interested in maybe setting up an easel and painting down there? There's *loads* of room. Zack wouldn't mind, would you, Zack?"

Lale looked surprised. Not as much as I was.

"Why would Zack mind?"

"Well, he lives there, too." Sal smiled at Zack with a loving glint in his eyes. Zack sawed away on his steak, not looking at either one of us.

"You do? I didn't know that! You guys *live* together?"

Well, this was weird. If they were living together, then why did he try to put the moves on me? Were they boyfriends? What about Cassie? Now that I thought about it, I remembered that Sal had once said he had a boyfriend from Arkansas. What was going on?

"Come on, Sal. We're roommates, Cherry. Just roommates. That's *all.*" Lale seemed a little red-faced, but Sal went on, as if he didn't notice.

"Right. We're *just* roommates, and since our painter roommate moved out we are in danger of having to give up our great loft, as only artists can rent them. So what do you say? The rent's right—thirty-three dollars and thirty-three cents a month for each of us. Thirty-four cents for me—I'll throw in the extra penny. You'd be able to come and paint as much as you want, or not at all if you don't want to. But you'd be the artist of record on the lease. What do you say?"

"Wow. Well . . . sure. That's great. I would love to."

Even sight unseen, it seemed like a pretty good deal to me. I'd just have to keep an eye on Lale, although he had been a perfect gentleman ever since that night at Max's. I think he was too smart to try that again. Or maybe he really was, down deep, gay.

So that's how I got a studio. And why I started hanging out with Lale and Sal in SoHo and painting again. And why I still couldn't bring up Cassie. Not yet. At least not until the commercial was done, which we were scheduled to shoot in a few days. After that was over, I was really going to have to sit down and talk to him and write to Cassie, even if he got mad and made me move my painting stuff out. I had to, before the ad appeared, or she would see it and my rear end would be grass.

Milton Greene let us see the contact sheets for the ad, and they were pretty great, I had to admit. They were in color, the two of us looking at each other like we were madly in love. I wore a white ermine coat and a necklace and earrings of huge, real diamonds, Tiffany, no less—they had a guard bring them who hung around until the shooting was over—and Lale was duded up in an expensive tuxedo and white tie. Up on Milton's wall was a picture he had done back in the fifties of Marilyn in white fur, and the ones he did of us were a little reminiscent of her. Not that she and I look much alike, but the lighting or makeup or something was similar. The French people were really happy with them, and popped the cork on a bottle of Dom Pérignon to toast us. That's all that mattered. Suzan was happy, too. She actually smiled at me when I went into the agency now, and I had to hide in the bathroom whenever I saw Freddy coming because he was sure to corner me and get in my personal space, like they say up here, with his boozy breath. The other models were beginning to be friendlier, too, famous ones I didn't even know—like Lois Chiles—said, "Hi, Cherry," when I saw them at go-sees, like they knew me, as if I had passed some test or something and was one of them now. It had all happened so fast. It wasn't even Christmas yet. When the commercial came out, it would really be a big deal, but until then I was going out on as many go-sees as I could, trying to get more work and keep it all together. I even got a job doing catalog, which is the bread and butter of models, for JCPenney. The clothes were awful and the work was hard, changing one outfit right after another all day long as fast as we could, not much in the way of styling, but it was great because Suzan had told me I was too exotic for catalog work. They put a short blond wig on me and darkened my eyebrows, but I didn't care. It was good money.

Wearing those catalog clothes, I realized how much I had changed. Not even a year ago I shopped at JCPenney in Sweet Valley and thought the clothes were pretty good. I had a charge account there and Daddy let me charge up to a hundred dollars, which I paid out fifteen or twenty dollars a month, then I could charge another hundred. Now, after wearing all these designer things, I knew the difference between clothes and fashion. The girl who shopped at Penney's seemed like somebody else now. A pitiful relation with uneven hems, poor thing.

"So let's go over it again," I said, picking up the script Lale had thrown on the floor. "You can do it. Just pretend you're an actor in a bad soap opera. Have you ever watched those things?"

"Don't make fun of soaps. They pay a lot of money. Lots of actors get their starts in them. I'm going to start going to the Actors Studio, too, one of these days, and sit in on the lessons with Lee Strasberg. He's a famous teacher. James Dean and Marlon Brando used to study with him. I'm not going to just be a pretty boy my whole life with somebody else saying the words for me. This modeling thing is just the beginning. In fact, I've already been in movies."

"I remember. The naked one. You have to show it to me one of these days."

"I wasn't naked in the movie. It was an NYU student film. I've done three of them, and Axel thinks I'm pretty good. I'll take you to a screening over there of the next one."

"Sure. I'd love to see it. Why don't you get Sal to introduce you to Andy Warhol? I'm sure he'd put you in one of his movies."

"Nah. Those superstars don't go nowhere except showing off at places like Max's."

" 'Anywhere,' " I interrupted.

"Anywhere. They never get in the big movies, just those stupid home movies Andy makes. I hung out over there at the factory a time or two and all they did was sit around and get stoned and take each other's picture. It was boring."

"You're not into getting stoned?"

"I never said I didn't smoke a little pot, but those guys are zonked out all the time. I like to be in charge of my brain."

"Yeah, we saw one of his films in art class once. Or at least part of it. The whole thing was six hours long and it was of a guy sleeping. For forty-five minutes, all that was on the screen was his stomach, going up and down as he breathed. I was never so glad to get out of an art class in my life." I changed the subject. "Did you take art in school? You never did say where you were from in Arkansas."

"No, I didn't take art. Not many of the football guys did. I'm from Buchanan. Little place up in the Ozarks."

"Right. Buchanan. Isn't that where St. Juniper's is?"

"Yeah. You know that place?"

"I heard of it. You still have family up there?"

"Mother and Daddy, little sister, Brenda."

"What did they say when you came to New York to model? My daddy wasn't crazy about it at all."

"Oh, they didn't say much. I didn't come up here to model—I just kind of fell into it accidentally. Photographer saw me and wanted to take some pictures and all, so that's how it happened."

"Yeah, I can see that. Photographers are always stopping me on the street, too, wanting to know who I'm with. That's their pickup line. I've gotten work out of it, though. Most of them are legit, but you have to be careful. I always make them go through my booker. Who was your photographer?"

"Guy named Michel Denon."

"Oh, he's one of the French photographers! He's famous. A lot of the girls go to France their first year to get some experience. Suzan said something to me about it, but I don't think I'm ready to leave New York yet. I feel like I just got here."

"Me, too. It's been good to me—don't get me wrong—but I still think I'll move on one of these days. There's something a little bit, I don't know, sissy, about it all."

"Yeah, I guess a fair number of the guys in the business are gay." I glanced at him to see if he would react to that. He shrugged.

"Makes no difference to me. Me and them get along. I let them know right up front that I'm not like that and they leave me alone."

"Do you have a girlfriend?"

"No."

"None at all?"

"Nobody special."

"I bet you go out with a lot of girls. Don't you?"

"I guess you could say that."

"Did you have a girlfriend back in Buchanan?"

"Why are you so interested in my girlfriends all of a sudden?"

"I'm not. I couldn't care less. I'm just trying to get to know you, since we're working together, and I'm kind of your new roommate."

"I think you're more interested than you let on." He leaned back, narrowed his eyes at me. I got chilly again.

"I think not. I have a boyfriend, and he's not the kind of guy who sticks his tongue down some strange girl's throat the first time he meets her."

"Are you still mad about that? Is that what this is all about?"

"I'm not mad. It just didn't thrill me, that's all."

"Do you want one pint of blood or two?" He held out his arm and started rolling up his shirtsleeve.

"Forget it. Let's just read this copy. And try not to be such a hick when you talk. There's not much call for hicks in the movies."

"What about *The Beverly Hillbillies,* Miss Smartypants?"

"Right. Forget what I said. You'd be perfect as Jethro's twin brother."

"Thanks. I think. Okay. Here we go . . . You ought to be in Diamonds & Ermine . . ."

30

FATHER LEO

Dear Cherry,

There's no way to ease into this, so I'll just out with it. Little Lalea passed away. It was so awful, I can't tell you. I thought Cassie was going to hang on to the coffin at the funeral and not let them bury her. It took two men to drag her away so they could take it to the graveyard, and as they lowered it into the ground she hyperventilated and nearly passed out. They had to find a paper sack and make her breathe into it. I've never seen anybody as overwrought as she was. Annie was right there with her, of course, and her brother, Barry, me and Bernadette and Snuffy, but there wasn't a big crowd. Janet and Brenda didn't come, of course, but George did, and he sat right beside her and held her hand. That gave the old biddies in town something to talk about, that's for sure. Somebody ought to take a peach-tree switch to Janet. She's got a mouth on her sharp as a yellowjacket stinger, still telling everybody who will listen it wasn't Lale's baby and it was a blessing it died. She totally blames Cassie for running Lale off and taking him away from her, and nothing is going to change that. Frankly, I think Lale was ready to run off in any case, but there's no doubt this kicked it into high gear. Has he said anything about Cassie or anything? I have kept my promise not to say anything to her, but I wish you would write her. She's going to find out when that ad comes out, and it will be harder on her than if you tell her yourself. I really worry for her. She did try to kill herself on the railroad tracks that time. But I'm not going to butt in anymore about it. You do what you need to do.

On this front, things are pretty much the same, with a few new wrinkles. We did giant papier-mâché animals in class, and the whole art room was crammed with elephants, giraffes, and dinosaurs. They're pretty incredible, though, and the show we had was great. After it was over, we hauled them down to the Children's Hospital in Little Rock, as a memorial to little Lalea, and the kids were so thrilled to get them. But the trip down there was mind-blowing, I can tell you. I borrowed a Ford Ranchero to carry one of the elephants, but it wasn't tied down too well and it flew up like Dumbo and bounced down the highway! Some state troopers thought it was a foreign car rolling over and over and they nearly had a heart attack, roaring down on us with their sirens blaring. But when they saw it was just me and a girl (a cute blonde) from my class chasing it down the road, they helped us tie it back down and didn't even give us a ticket. Fortunately there were no wrecks because of it. It was skinned up pretty good, but you can always fix papier-mâché with a little paste and paint.

Oh, one more little thing happened. I slept with Father Leo. Well, not exactly slept . . . I can hear you screaming now, so calm down and I'll tell you all about it.

You know I've been hanging around a lot up there at the abbey. Father Leo was teaching me to use the pottery wheel and I was getting pretty good at it. Then he told me he'd had an offer of a grinding stone at an old abandoned gristmill that sits down by Bad Luck Creek. The owner said he could have it to make a kick wheel out of, and Leo said he would give me his old one for my class. The only thing we had to do was go out and get it. That was Saturday morning. When I got there, bright and early, it was just him and me. The other two guys he had asked to come and help didn't show up. That's sort of fishy, isn't it? I thought so at the time, too, but couldn't be sure. He didn't have on his priest suit, either, just a flannel shirt, and he looked so cute, with his long hair and beard that has some red glints in the sunshine.

I had no idea how we were going to get that thing into the truck—you know I'm not much good for back-breaking work—but off we went. It was the first time we had been out together alone like that, and it was a little tense, to say the least. It must have been obvious I've had a crush on him for a long time, but then I figured he must be used to that. Everyone has a crush on their priest. To make conversation, I asked him how Bad Luck Creek got its name.

"Well," he said, in his teacher's voice, "that's debatable. A lot of settlers had plenty of bad luck back when they first started up here, but I think it goes back to this old mill we're going to, which rumor says has a secret room that used to be part of the Underground Railway long before the Civil War started."

Remember when we used to play Nancy Drew and looked in old houses for secret rooms? I waited for Father Leo to tell me more. The man does love to teach.

"The miller got word that a man with his wife and four kids had escaped and were coming up from Louisiana. Their owner had the slave catchers all up the line on the lookout for them—six slaves were a valuable commodity. I can't imagine how they did it, but they made it to the mill, all still together. Unfortunately, not long after they arrived, one of the miller's children came down with diphtheria, and the whole family got it and died. The runaway family took care of them until they buried the last one, but then they came down with it, too, and all of them died, except for one of the kids. The doctor who had been treating them was a sympathizer, but his wife wasn't, and apparently she blew the whistle.

"The child who was left, a girl about twelve, came out carrying her little bag, clearly set for travel, when the catchers came whooping down and gave chase, shooting their guns. She got scared and jumped into the creek, right out there by the wheel, and drowned."

Just as he said that, we pulled into the yard of the mill. It was really creepy. The creek ran right next to it, dark and deep. An old wheel with the slats rotted out sat still in the water, a grave marker. The windows were broken out like blind eyes. Cherry, I swear I thought I saw a little black girl peek out of one of them. I asked him if it was haunted.

"Oh, absolutely," he said, laughing. He was enjoying the whole thing just a little too much for my taste. He said he thought he'd heard voices coming from someplace, maybe underground, like a swarm of bees buzzing down there. Inside the building, he said, even in the summer, there are unearthly cold spots that made the hair stand up on your arms.

I asked him if he'd ever been in the secret room. He said he hadn't, and why don't we go look for it? You know, Cherry, how you and I never liked tight places, and the last thing I wanted to do was look for an underground room where a bunch of people had died. What if they were still down there, like in a big grave? But I didn't want him to think I was a wuss, so we went inside.

Well, the *Reader's Digest* version is that after a lot of trying, we found the trap door. It was just a dusty little room under the floor, no bodies, but there was still a platform they used for a bed and some pots and things. The hair did stand up on my arms, as promised, when we heard a noise, although it was probably just a mouse or something, but it scared me so much I grabbed Leo and the next thing I knew we were kissing and he had his pants down, or maybe I pulled them down. It happened so fast I can't say positively he even got all the way in, so I'm not sure it really counts. It was his first time with a woman in fifteen years, so I don't blame him for being quick on the trigger. We never did get the grinding wheel into the truck—we just went back to the abbey, both of us kind of in shock. I haven't talked to him since, and that has been a couple of days ago. I'll let you know what goes on. I think I am in love with him, and it is all so awful.

Please reconsider about writing to Cassie. I love you and miss you so much. Do you think I'm awful?

Your bad-girl friend,
Baby

31

SIN

This was horrible. I'd sort of had a crush on Father Leo, too, when I was his student teacher, but I never thought he would actually do anything with any woman, he was such a dedicated priest and he was a cool teacher, too. It was sure different from the Holiness church I belonged to, which had a long list of sins, swearing being right at the top.

"Don't take this the wrong way, Father Leo," I remember saying to him after I had gotten to know him better, "but I have to tell you my parents were pretty nervous about me coming up here. I think they believe all Catholics are going to hell."

"Why do they think that?"

"Well, y'all drink, and that's a big sin. Y'all pray to Mary, and we don't believe in that. There's a lot of things they think will send you to hell that Catholics don't seem to think twice about, like dancing and playing cards. Our pastor, Brother Wilkins, is always saying that if you have one single sin on your soul when you die, it's down to hell with you because only the totally pure will go to heaven."

"Do you believe that?"

"It's pretty harsh to think God would send people to torment forever for going fishing on Sunday or drinking a beer. And I can't make myself believe all the Buddhists and Jews and African natives and everyone else in the world are going to hell and just a few Christians who haven't gone fishing on Sunday will be in heaven."

"Heaven's a big place. They won't have a lot of people to talk to, will they?"

"No, and half of them won't be speaking to each other anyhow, if it is like it is in church. Somebody is always mad at somebody else for taking over the Sunday-school Christmas pageant and not putting their kid into it or something."

He laughed.

"Your church doesn't have a patch on us. I've seen Catholics get into fistfights over bake sales. But there might not be any hell at all. Or what if the atheists are right and it's just lights out when you die? Then it won't matter anyhow, will it?"

"I guess it won't. But I don't like to think that."

"No, I don't, either. I believe the teachings of the Church, or I wouldn't be in this job, but I also believe in Karma—what goes around comes around—and I believe in reincarnation."

"You really think we've lived before?"

"And will live again. It's the only thing that makes sense. Isn't birth itself a miracle? That tiny egg and sperm uniting to make a whole human being. Why is it more of a miracle to be born more than once? Is a baby who dies at birth never given another chance? Is that all the life they get? I like to think we live over and over—like a driver getting out of an old car into a new car—and we learn lessons from each life until we finally get our degrees, so to speak, and can go to heaven."

"Do all Catholics believe in that?"

He laughed. "Are you kidding me? For them it's heaven, hell, and purgatory. It's better to keep my beliefs to myself and toe the traditional line in this outfit. So you can't blow the whistle on me."

"Father Leo, there's one big thing about the Catholics I don't understand. Why can't priests get married? Preachers in every other religion can."

"Ah, that's a hard question. And a good one." He took out one of his Cuban cigars and put it in his mouth but didn't light it, for which I was grateful. "They could at one time—did you know that? Saint Peter, who was the first pope, had a family. Saint Paul encouraged bishops to be faithful to their wives."

"So what happened?"

"It's hard to say it was one single thing. Before Christ came along, the Goddess was the supreme being. Woman was revered for being able to give birth, and sex was sacred. Then the male God began to dominate, and in the early church, A.D. three or four hundred, a few men like Saint Jerome and Saint Augustine came to believe that women were poison, à la Eve, who got cozy with the devil and seduced poor Adam, innocent doofus that he was, and the outcome was wicked sexual intercourse. Guys like Old Jerome and Augustine saw the body as evil, the spirit as good; a war was constantly being waged between the two, and the body had to be conquered if the spirit wanted to go to heaven."

"That's crazy. The human race would die off if everybody was celibate!"

"Oh, I think they knew that not everyone could hack celibacy and there would always be plenty of humans. They both, by the way, came to this philosophy late in life, after having, by all reports, a robust and wicked sex life when they were young. So much easier to be celibate when you're old and can't cut the mustard anymore, you know.

"So the two of them helped put the celibacy issue on the table and it rocked on for centuries, debated pro and con. Finally, what decided it, I think, was not morality but good old greed.

"Grateful parishioners would give land or money or livestock or whatever to their bishops in payment for favors, or in the hope of greasing their way to heaven, and the bishops were getting rich. Since priests and bishops were still marrying and having families, they would naturally leave their properties and money, as well as their titles, to their offspring, but by making a mandatory celibacy rule—voilà—no offspring, so the goods and land went directly to church coffers.

"In 1139, all clerical marriages were pronounced invalid, and the children declared bastards, who couldn't by law inherit anything. Anybody who didn't like it was excommunicated, which was the same as sending them to hell. The Church got enormously rich, and celibacy for the clergy has been the rule ever since. End of story."

"But that was such a long time ago. You'd think they would change it now."

"To the contrary, my dear. At Vatican Two, just five years ago, it was reaffirmed. I have it memorized. 'Let them'—the seminarians—'be warned of the very severe dangers with which their chastity will be confronted in present-day society . . . may they learn so to integrate the renunciation of marriage into their life and activity that these will not suffer any detriment from celibacy.' "

"Did you ever have a girlfriend, Father Leo?" He lit the cigar. I realized I'd overstepped.

"Let's just leave it that the celibacy rule is not why I became a priest. It was in spite of it. If you want to play for the New York Yankees, you don't go trying to change the rules of baseball. And I do want to play."

Did he still want to play? If so, what was going to happen with him and Baby?

32

GIRLFRIENDS AND GENTLEMEN

The commercial was in the can, as they say. It had been three days of hard work, in fur, under bright lights. Sal had to keep repairing my makeup for real. I'm afraid I do have pores. It was so weird to have all those people hovering over us like we were movie stars. I could see getting used to it. First, there was the director, who talked to us about our motivation and had us say the lines over and over, told us when to look at each other and how to look, when to smile, how to move, when to simper, when to flirt—although I instinctively kind of knew that anyhow, which he was really happy about. There were script girls and cameramen and a girl who just polished my earrings and kept my clothes from bunching up. If we wanted coffee, there was somebody to run and hand us a cup with sugar and milk, just like we wanted. There were several just looking, and I never really knew what they did. It was pretty crowded. We had to be there by seven in the morning for hair and makeup, and a lot of the day was spent waiting around for them to get the lights set and everything ready. By the end of the day I was exhausted and the only thing I wanted was to go home and get in a hot tub. Anybody who thinks this stuff is fun and games ought to hang out on a set for a day.

I knew they were going to dub us, and they did. As much as I practiced with the TV girls, I still sounded southern, and Lale didn't even try. But they did a great job of matching the movement of our lips to the words, which was so weird to see. Lale had an English accent, like James Bond, and I sounded kind of Swedish. I guess it was because of my coloring. Most of the real blondes we had in the agency were from Sweden, and Gunilla Knutson had made such a big splash with her "Take it off, take it all off" Noxema shaving commercial that Swedes were hot. Well, let's face it, blondes of any kind were always hot. So it was French perfume with a Swedish/British accent done by Arkansas rednecks, what the heck. The Parvu people had a little dinner for us after the screening, at a fancy French restaurant on Fifty-second Street near Fifth Avenue called La Grenouille, which means "The Frog," although I didn't see frog legs on the menu, and then they took us in a limousine to a nightclub called Le Club that had fireplaces and deer heads with huge antlers on the walls, which was kind of weird in New York City, and we danced until after midnight. Although a lot of my model friends went all the time to the clubs, it was the first time I had been, and you would have thought I was a Karo nut pie out on a picnic table and the men were flies. Guys kept asking me to dance and cutting in when I danced with Lale, which he did *not* like at all. Finally he just sat and glared at me while I danced with a guy who was a rich stockbroker or something like that, probably old enough to be my father. It was pathetic. But I'd never been the belle of the ball before and I loved it.

"Dance with somebody else, Zack," I said when I got a break. "There's tons of women checking you out."

"Don't tell me what to do, Cherry. I'll dance when I get ready to."

"Excuuuse me, Mr. Gripey Gut." But I felt kind of sorry for him, and when "Let It Be" by the Beatles started up, I held out my hand to him, we went back out onto the dance floor, and he held me tight. He smelled so good, like Tribute, which I'd always loved. It was the same cologne Tripp used to wear, and it woke up some little part of me that had been shut down all these months. I slumped and snuggled into his neck, forgetting for a minute that he was off-limits, and he gave me a little kiss on the ear. What was the matter with me? I had to stop this. The print ads would be coming out any minute, for the Christmas rush, and I still hadn't written Cassie. I made up my mind to do that when I got home, and not wait a minute longer. It was already probably too late and she would hate me. She must be still depressed over losing Lalea. That image shattered any romance beginning to bud, and I broke away from him. I could hear Suzan's voice saying, "You'll find out that friendship takes a backseat to love every time." Not this time.

"I have to go, Zack. I'll try to come over to the loft in a couple of days and work on the painting. See you." I practically ran off the dance floor. He just stood there and shook his head. He never knew what to make of me. Which was probably why he was interested.

Mrs. Digby was still up. As usual, she peeked out to see who was coming up the stairs that late.

"Hi, Mrs. D. Can't sleep?"

"I was just checking to see if my door was locked."

"I'm glad it wasn't. Can I come in for a minute?"

She was still dressed, so I figured it would be all right.

"Would you like some tea, dear? Some cookies and milk? I just made some chocolate-chip tonight."

"That would be great, Mrs. Digby. Thanks so much." She made the best chocolate-chip cookies, with little niblets of toffee in them. I dug in as she got me a glass of milk.

"You're all spiffed up. Hot date?"

I had on this great long dress of Quiana nylon in a wild electric-blue, burgundy, and brown print, that had an empire waist, long pirate sleeves, and a tobacco suede short fringed vest over it. I loved Quiana—it flowed and felt great and was practically indestructible.

"Not really a date. They took us out to celebrate finishing the commercial."

"I can see you had a good time. There are stars in your eyes. But I also feel there is something bothering you."

You can't fool somebody who is a little bit psychic.

"You've had a lot of boyfriends, right, Mrs. Digby?"

"My, yes. I tried to count them one time, but kept forgetting their names. Isn't that awful, when you can't even remember your beaus' names? I should have kept a diary all those years, but frankly, if you're taking the time to write it down, you aren't living it."

"I think so, too."

"Are you having man problems?"

"Kind of."

"Aurelius?"

"For one. I can't figure him out. Why doesn't he like me?"

"He does like you. He's just afraid you'll reject him, dear. Don't you know that men like Aurelius are rejected all the time? The one place they are in control is with women, and he just won't take a chance that he'll fall in love with you and you won't return it. He's not used to women like you."

"Ah. Well, that's one way to look at it, I guess."

"You said 'for one.' Is there another young man in your life?"

"Not exactly. But there's this guy model I'm doing the Diamonds & Ermine job with. I know he likes me but it's complicated. He used to go out with an old friend of mine, but he doesn't know that I know her. *She* doesn't know I'm working with him. Plus, he treated her pretty badly. I mean, for one example, they were engaged and he got her the cheapest ring the jewelry store had. True, he didn't have much money at the time, but this was ridiculous. You could hardly see the diamond with a magnifying glass."

"That's a bad sign. Most gentlemen, if they had to, would take out a discreet loan to get their girlfriend a diamond. I've never trusted a parsimonious man."

"You'd be right. He left her practically at the altar when she was pregnant."

"Oh, my. I assume he's attractive?"

"Extremely. Unfortunately."

"That *is* a problem. Back in my day, if an interesting man came along, the friendship between girls came in second, and we all understood that was just the way it was."

"So you would go for the guy in spite of the friendship?"

"Well, that would depend on whether she was in love with him and how good a friend she was. And how much you were willing to hurt her."

There was always a catch to everything decent.

"In that case, he's off-limits. So back to Aurelius. What would you do with Aurelius?"

"I'd knock on his door and make the first move. If you are successful with Aurelius, you won't want to be with this model fellow, will you?"

Mrs. Digby was a wise old bird, but I wasn't sure I wanted so many gentlemen friends that I couldn't remember all their names. There were words for girls like that back in Arkansas. Although what I was about to do had words to go with it, too. I'd stuff that into the crowded closet in the back of my mind to worry about later.

By the time I got to the top of the stairs, I heard the saxophone. I stopped off at my apartment, brushed my teeth, freshened up my makeup, took a deep breath, then went right up to Aurelius's door and knocked. The music stopped. He opened the door. It was dark and I couldn't read the look on his face, but it was too late to turn back.

"Can I borrow a cup of sugar?" He stepped back and I went in. His place was bigger than mine, but it felt like home. One small lamp glowed on a table in the corner.

"This is a nice surprise. Can I get you a glass of wine? Or would you prefer sugar?"

"Wine's fine."

I'd had a couple of glasses of wine earlier, but was cold sober now. He already had a bottle open. He took a crystal goblet out of a cabinet and poured it full of garnet-colored wine and handed it to me. His hand touched mine. On purpose. I took a big swallow.

"What's that you were playing?"

" 'Autumn in New York.' "

"It's beautiful. Go ahead and play some more. I just wanted to watch you for once." I sank into the chair next to the bed and he picked up the sax and played while I drank. I didn't know much about jazz, but the sound was mellow and lonesome, and with the wine, I began to relax. He played until my glass was empty. I didn't know what to do next. I'd made the first move but didn't have a second one.

"Come here." He laid the horn aside, held out his hand, and pulled me down beside him on the bed. He stared at me for a long minute, like he was trying to read my mind, then gently put his lips on mine, melting me into a puddle.

"I won't reject you, Aurelius, I promise I won't," I said as we came up for air.

"You don't know anything about me."

"Let me learn. You said you wanted me. You said you wanted to throw the table over at Joe Jr.'s and take me on the floor. Well, now there's no table. . . ."

I started unbuttoning his shirt. I didn't care. It had been more than a year since I had been with Tripp, and it all had built up.

"Wait right here. Don't go anywhere."

He went to the bathroom and I heard water running. He was taking a shower. I lay back on the pillows and wondered what to do. Maybe I should slip next door and take a bath, too. I'd worked up a sweat with all that dancing. But he had said to wait right there. In a few minutes, the door opened and he came out all damp and steamy, wrapped in a towel. Then he took off the towel and stood there lit by the lamp, a long stretch of beautiful brown muscles. His penis was darker than the rest of him, so black it was almost purple. It was certainly a good size, but not huge like I had heard. I let him unzip my dress, unlace my suede boots, and pull off my tights. I wiggled my toes against his belly and liked the way they looked there, their nails painted black-cherry red. He seemed as amazed at me as I was at him.

"You're the whitest white girl I ever saw. You glow in the dark, woman."

He lifted his sax carefully off the bed and onto the chair. Then he stretched out beside me, touching me like a blind person would read Braille. My nipples stood straight out of my flat breasts, and he kissed them. His tongue was as pink as they were and his mustache tickled. I waited for the kisses to go on down my belly into the thick white patch of bush, like Tripp used to do, which made me go wild, but he didn't. I started to worry. Maybe I should have taken a bath when I had the chance, although it never bothered Tripp. In fact, he would call me up before a date and tell me to be sure and not bathe. He loved my "woman smell." Guys are sure different. I wanted to get a whiff of my armpit, but it was too hard without being obvious. Aurelius kissed my mouth again and rolled on top of me, spread my legs, and slid inside. I wasn't quite ready for that little maneuver, and it was tight, practically creaking with rust from disuse, but after a minute it got better. Just as I started to enjoy it and feel that tingle begin, the insanely delicious one that starts from a mile away and gradually gets closer until it feels like a bomb explodes, he got stiff; he moaned and then stopped cold. I couldn't believe it. Was that it? I tried a small movement, to see if I could get the engine going again.

"Don't move."

I stopped and stayed motionless, and so did he. In fact, he gradually relaxed until I felt the full load of him settle.

"Aurelius?"

He was asleep, I swear.

"Aurelius." I shook him a little. "Are you awake?"

"Mm-hmm."

But he wasn't.

He was dead weight on top of me. Gradually, I inched out and leaned up on my elbow, looking at him. He was so gorgeous in his sleep. His little mustache wiggled as he breathed, greedily gulping deep lungfuls of night with every breath. It was beautiful to watch. The air had gone out of my balloon, though. I'd never had anybody go to sleep on me before. I guess playing music is more tiring than I knew. Plus, the wine bottle had already been half empty when I got there. It might have been a mistake to come over uninvited like that. I got my clothes together and tiptoed to my room. I ran a tub of hot water and did, one more time, what I had been doing all these months to relieve the tension, all by myself. I didn't know any more about Aurelius than I had before, except that he probably wasn't worried about me rejecting him.

33

PAINTING IN THE LOFT

Dear Cassie,

I hate to start off by saying I'm sorry I haven't written you, but I am. After what all you've been through, a simple sorry just isn't enough. I can't imagine it and pray I never have to. You will probably have more babies, but none of them will ever replace Lalea, and the only thing I can say is that I know she is waiting for you in heaven. Father Leo thinks we are reborn again, so maybe she will come back to you as another baby. I would like to think that.

I found Lale. It's a long story, but I have to tell you that we did a modeling job together and it is going to be in the magazines soon. I haven't told him I know you—I just didn't know what to say about it all and I felt like it wasn't any of my business and I would mess it all up if I said anything. He is with the Ford modeling agency in New York, going by the name of Zack Carpenter. Their phone number is 212–555–6500. They might be able to get you his number and address. I know they could get a message to him. He is really successful in this business. The ad is going to be for a perfume called Diamonds & Ermine. You might be upset when you see it, but please remember it is just a job, like an acting job. There is *nothing* between us, nothing at all. That's what these jobs are—you pretend to like somebody for the picture, then when the camera stops you sometimes don't even remember their names.

I wish, though, that you could manage to forget about Lale and move on. He did something really bad to you, but I doubt he will ever settle down to just one woman. Too many women chase after pretty boys like him, and they are all too weak to resist the attention. You have so much to offer a man, Cassie, and I'm sure there are a lot of guys back home who have just been waiting for you and would appreciate you and love you.

I wouldn't blame you for being mad at me and not writing again. I haven't been a good friend to you since I left, I know, but life takes turns we never expected, and no matter what happens, you will always be a special girl to me.

Love always,
Cherry

I let out a sigh of relief. It was out of my hands now. I didn't exactly lie to Cassie, but there was no point in telling her the whole thing, either. I figured she would just find another boyfriend and go on with her life. That's what you do—you just go on. I also wrote a letter to Baby.

Dear Baby,

Well, that was quite a letter you wrote me last. I'll try to call when I get the chance so you can tell me what is going on with you and Father Leo. Letters are too slow. This might all be for the best, you know. If Father Leo isn't really that dedicated to being a priest, he should drop it and get on with something else. He can join the Episcopalians if he really wants to keep on in the church thing. They're as close to Catholic as you can be, and they can get married. I can't really see you as a preacher's wife, but who knows? You might love it. You'd have to clean up your act, though, and learn how to play the piano. HA! But I'm jumping the gun. I have you guys married already, and you only had that one little episode in the haunted cellar. Which hardly counts, in my book. So don't feel so guilty.

Speaking of episodes, I finally had one, too, last night with

Aurelius. It wasn't quite as short as yours was, but nearly. What is it with these guys? Are we so hot that they can't control themselves? I think Tripp spoiled me. I had no idea—I thought every man would be like that! Anyhow, Aurelius is so beautiful I could just sit and look at him all night. I hate to tell you, but what they say about black men is not true. I mean, he's certainly normal, but not huge like we heard they all are. And he's a sweetheart in spite of not being able to last more than a minute and not doing you-know-what to me. In fact, there was hardly any foreplay at all—he didn't even give me time to do anything to *him,* just zipped right in and *boom.* And then he fell asleep on top of me. Have you ever had anybody fall asleep on you? I thought I was going to have to stay that way all night but I managed to wiggle out. He's a heavy guy. But he slipped a note under my door and we met this morning for breakfast at Joe Jr.'s. He was happy as a clam, acted like it was the greatest experience of his life, and is taking me to hear him play with his group tonight, at somebody's loft down in SoHo. He's terrific on the saxophone, so it should be fun. I'll let you know how it goes. It has to get better. I think he was just nervous.

I wrote to Cassie, just told her that Lale's name was Zack Carpenter, that he was with the Fords, not much else. If she wants to track him down, she can, although I think it would be a big waste of time. He is not about to go back to Arkansas for any reason. It's awful, Baby, but I don't want to go back, either. It would be great to see you and Mama and Daddy and all, but I can't leave right now. The ad is coming out and the commercial will be out about the same time, so I need to be here. Suzan thinks I'll get a lot of work out of it. Oh, Baby, it doesn't seem real—so much has happened to me in such a short time. Gina, the head of the bookers at Suzan Hartman, said it happens that way sometimes, that a girl will go out and get a big job on her first go-see. Some girls take a long time to get work, but it seems like things are really happening fast for me. I just wish you were here to be with me. I feel so far away from you. Please give Father Leo my love. If it comes handy, tell him I think he's doing the right thing, whatever it might be. He explained that celibacy rule to me, but I never really understood why they've clung to it. I think they should have changed it a long time ago.

I'll end on a funny story. I did a hair show for the buyers at Saks Fifth Avenue last week. It was wigs, mostly, falls and hairpieces. I had to be there at five-thirty in the morning to get ready, because they did it before the store opened, and my hair really took a beating, all that brushing and teasing and spraying, hot curling irons to smooth it out, crimpers to put the curl back in. My head was sore. Anyhow, we finished after the store opened up, and I was standing by the elevators, staring out into space with my hand on my hip, not thinking about anything except getting a cup of coffee, when the doors opened and I went to get on. The woman standing next to me screamed bloody murder. "You moved!" she yelled. She thought I was a mannequin standing there and had come to life!

Love,
Cherry

After I dropped the letters into the mailbox, I strolled up Fifth Avenue and looked at all the window decorations. Christmas is the best time everywhere, but especially in New York. The streets are full and everyone is happy, shopping like crazy, carrying armloads of pretty packages, rushing in the cold to get presents for their loved ones. It felt so good to think I would have a real date with Aurelius that night, and I wondered what I should get him for Christmas. I looked at a display of Scottish sweaters in the window of an expensive men's store. Maybe I'd get him a cashmere sweater. A red one. That was kind of boring, though, not really his style, and it might be too expensive for a first present. He might not get me anything and I didn't want to embarrass him. Still, they were so beautiful, all the colors fanned out like a rainbow. I wanted one of each hue, just to put on the wall and look at. I went in and picked out a Holbein violet-gray V-neck for my daddy. He has blue eyes and would look great in it.

Right next door to the men's store was an African shop. Aurelius wore a lot of stuff like that, woven headbands and dashikis and beads. There were some great silver-and-leather bracelets for men. I picked out one in case he got me something. If the romance wasn't going anywhere, I'd send it to my cousin G Dub, who was living up in Canada, where he'd moved when he got his draft papers. Oh, what the heck. I'd get one for G Dub anyhow. I hadn't seen him in over a year, and all of a sudden tears came into my eyes. I missed my family so much. We wrote all the time, but it wasn't the same. At least I knew I was able to see everyone else, but G Dub couldn't come back to the U.S.A. because he'd get arrested. Maybe I'd go visit him one of these days. He'd moved to Toronto from Vancouver, and that wasn't far at all from New York.

I chose a pair of chandelier earrings with those little white shells and lime-green African beads for Mama, blue and red ones for my aunts Rubynell and Juanita, black for Baby, and I got my cousin Lucille a pair in orange, since there weren't any pink ones. In fact, there wasn't anything pink in the store at all. Diana Vreeland, the editor of *Vogue,* once said that pink was the navy-blue of India, but it sure wasn't in Africa. Lucille loved pink, and her poor little baby, Tiffany LaDawn, who was a year and a half now, had to wear those awful frilly pig-snout-pink dresses all the time. I tried to get her cute little T-shirts and things, but Lucille would never let her wear them so it was a total waste of money. I'd get her a Betsy Wetsy doll or something. On the spur of the moment, I got a leather-and-silver necklace for Lale and a length of batik fabric for Sal that he could throw over a chair or tie around himself like a sarong. I was sure they would get me something. If they didn't, no big deal. I'd keep it for myself. If Lale did get me something, it would be interesting to see how much he spent on it. He kept trying to find out who my boyfriend was, but I would never tell him, mostly because Aurelius wasn't really my boyfriend. Until last night. Now he was, I guess. It was all so new, I didn't really know what to think. But it was fun to shop in the African store, and I was glad I'd read James Baldwin and Maya Angelou. I had a lot to learn about black culture, but it all made me feel closer to Aurelius.

Bopping on down the street, I couldn't pass up a shoe store that had the cutest granny boots in the window. I already had some nearly like them in brown, but a hunter-green pair called out to me, "*Cherrrry, get in here, girl, and buy us!*" One of my favorite things was shopping for shoes, even if finding my size was hard. One of the models I did a lot of leg stuff with, Laura White, and I loved to go to the Saks shoe department and try on shoes when we had a free hour. All the salesmen were shoe fetishists, she told me. You could see their eyes light up when we walked in, and three or four of them would fight for our attention, bringing out the sexiest high heels for us to try, lovingly getting down on their knees to buckle them around our ankles, their hands sometimes shaking. Then we'd parade around, like we were on the runway, pretending to decide whether we wanted them or not, while the guys' tongues practically hung out. We always bought something, so they had the double pleasure of making the sale while getting the thrill. The salesman who showed me the green boots insisted on personally lacing them up for me. I think it was true, about the shoe thing. Of course I had to buy them.

Loaded with packages, I walked on down to SoHo, to the loft, even though it had started to snow. The air was cold and fine and I was used to walking now. I probably did at least a couple or three miles a day on rounds, sometimes more. The walking and the stairs were good for my legs, and they were my main source of income, so I didn't mind it. In fact, I felt stronger than I ever had before, with all the exercise. I planned to paint for a few hours and then meet Aurelius, who would be playing nearby on Prince Street. I had stretched a new canvas and was going to start a painting today. It was working out pretty well, the arrangement we had. Lale and Sal were hardly ever there, and if I had a free afternoon to paint, I had the place all to myself. There was a lot of light, plenty of space. I didn't take up near the room Preston had, with his huge canvases and that crazy paint table with the window glass he used for a palette. Sal said he missed the smell of oil paint after Preston moved out, and I knew what he meant. It felt so good to get my hands back in paint again. Mama sent all my paints and brushes up, and like riding a bike or typing, I fell right back into it. My subject matter was changing, though, partly due to this new style of painting called photorealism. Although I didn't project my photograph onto the canvas and copy it like the photorealists did, I always carried a little camera around with me on the streets and snapped pictures, which I was using as reference for a series of portraits of street people. I had some great ones of homeless people, Rastas selling incense, hippies smoking on doorsteps, or stoops, as they call them up here, old ladies gossiping on a bench in the park, kids with nannies on the Upper East Side, the other models behind the scenes at the shows—I had a ton to choose from. Today I was going to start a portrait of Sal, as Miss Sally, as a surprise for him. I had photographed him in a great sequined gown with red lizard high heels and a tiara, no less. We wore the same size shoe, and I gave him several pairs of high heels a client had given me on a job. As a rule, I don't like to wear ones that are too high. It's bad enough being five feet thirteen. I don't want to get into Frankenstein territory.

At first, SoHo had seemed creepy. The streets were full of big trucks and garbage, most of the buildings used for manufacture of some kind. Walking down the street was like running a gauntlet, with the workmen yelling and whistling, but a lot of them had gotten used to seeing me and were pretty friendly. They didn't mean anything by it—to them it was a compliment. At night, the neighborhood was deserted until early in the morning, when they loaded up the trucks for the day's deliveries. Right across from the loft was a pie factory, which wafted out the smell of baking and always made me hungry. Big trucks backed up to the doors in the wee hours, guys yelling and singing and carrying on as they loaded in the pies, not caring that they'd wake anybody up. People weren't really supposed to be living down there, since the spaces were rented out to artists just to work, but of course a lot of them did. The city inspected once in a while but it was hard to catch people. Sal slid in through the back door, so to speak, when he moved in with Preston, and when Preston moved out after going into a snit about Lale living there, they'd had to get another painter in, or move out themselves. Artists had to be accredited with the Department of Cultural Affairs in order to get a lease, but Sal had a friend they turned down, a twenty-two-year-old girl, even though she'd had several shows, because they said she was too young to be a "serious artist," so instead he took me to meet with a weird guy they called a fixer. The first thing he did was show us a newspaper clipping with a list, complete with pictures, of the one hundred most evil people in New York City, and he was on it. That was supposed to make us feel better, I guess, like if evil is on your side it's all right. Well, even if it was kind of shady, I showed him slides of my work and some programs from my painting shows, so the certificate-of-occupancy papers came through. I still didn't really understand it, which is probably for the best. I guess in theory, the space was mine and I could make Lale and Sal move out, but they knew I would never do that. I loved my attic on Twelfth Street too much. Still, I was beginning to like SoHo a lot. I could see why Sal and Lale, even though they could afford to move, stayed.

I walked down West Broadway to OK Harris, the gallery that showed the photorealists, and stopped in to see a show by a man named Ralph Goings. Most of the paintings were of pickup trucks. I got as close as I could to them and could hardly see the brushstrokes. He was amazing. Even if I used an opaque projector I would never be able to make my stuff look that real, although, as I said, my own work leaned more toward the realists, with their crisp shadows and hot-sun-on-metal feel.

I loved the idea of capturing a moment in time on canvas, like a photograph, but better. The mundane subject matter was fresh and important, too. It was the ketchup bottles and pickup trucks and diners that made up the fabric of our days, and to glorify them in a painting was to glorify the small moments of our lives. More galleries were coming to the neighborhood, or at least that was the rumor. It was convenient for the artists to have galleries in the neighborhood, not that most of them would ever have a show there, but some did, and it was inspiring to go look at other people's work. It always made me want to run to the studio and paint.

On the way into the loft, I had to dodge out of the way of a guy carrying a big painting, which was a common occurrence and horrific, as you can imagine, in a big wind. I pictured him taking off like the Flying Nun, soaring down to the Battery and on out to sea. There were a couple of other painters in our building, and three sculptors. It was almost like a big family, the neighborhood, and although there weren't any supermarkets or dry cleaners or drugstores nearby, there were some new things coming in, like the Wooster Street Performing Garage, where they put on plays. Unfortunately you had to stand up for the shows. Maybe they would be able to afford chairs soon. At 99 Wooster Street there was a place called the GAA Firehouse, which Sal loved, since it was one of the few gay dance halls in town. It seemed like wherever there was a big concentration of artists, there were a lot of gay men. Well, why not? They were the most creative, and the most fun. Nearly all the hairdressers, makeup people, and stylists were gay, plus a large percentage of the male models. I didn't know of any gay women in the business, although I'm sure there must have been a few. Sal once said, "Don't you know, my darling, that gay men have the *best* qualities of women and lesbians have the *worst* qualities of men? I mean, think about it—none of them have the *slightest* interest in decorating, clothes, or makeup and hair. They go to barbershops, wear flannel shirts, drink beer out of the can, and watch sports on TV, for Pete's sake!" Maybe he was right. I'd never met a gay woman. Not that I knew of.

I pulled on the rope in the elevator, let myself in, and went over to my easel. The heat was never that great, so I kept my sweater on. I had an old pair of gloves I'd cut the fingers out of to paint in when it got too cold, but today wasn't all that bad. There were electric heaters scattered around, but not near my work area, so I went looking for one. As a rule, I never went into Lale's and Sal's private spaces, but I figured there must be a heater behind Lale's curtained-off room, so I stuck my head in—and screamed. Lale was lying on his bed.

"What are you doing here? You scared me to death. Why didn't you say anything?"

"I didn't feel like talking." His eyes were red and he looked awful.

"Are you sick or something? What's the matter?"

"Nothing." He sounded like he had been crying.

"Zack? What's going on?" I sat down on his futon and put my hand on his shoulder. He was gritting his teeth, holding back the tears.

"I don't want to talk about it."

"Okay. You don't have to." I waited. I knew he did want to talk. "Do you want me to leave?"

"No. It's just that . . . oh, Cherry. I did something bad, and now it's turned out awful for everyone. I hate myself. I'm nothing but a stupid selfish *model*." He said it like it was a dirty word.

"Come on. Don't say that. So you're a model. Big deal. That's nothing to be ashamed of. I mean, how many guys your age back home make as much money as you do? None of them, I can tell you right now. They're sacking groceries at the Kroger's and you're in the magazines they put out on the newsstand." I patted his arm, rubbed my hand up and down it, warming him up. "Now. What did you do that was so awful?"

"Don't try to make me feel better. There's nothing you can do about it. Go ahead and paint, I'll just lay here for a while."

"I don't like to see you hurting like this. I care about you. I really do." Surprisingly, I found it was true.

That seemed to loosen up something in him. He turned over and wrapped his arms around my legs, put his head in my lap, and sobbed. I stroked his hair and talked like I would to a baby.

"Just let it out, sweetie. Let it go, Lale. There's nothing you can do about it now. You can't turn back time and you wouldn't even if you could."

Shoot. *Lale.* I knew I'd make that mistake sooner or later. Maybe he wouldn't notice.

He clung to my leg as I brushed his hair with my fingers. It was thick and wheat-colored, like Tripp's was, but curlier. I wiped his cheeks and rocked him. Finally he pulled himself together, realized what I had said.

"Did you call me Lale?"

"Did I?" He'd noticed.

"How do you know that name?" He sat up on the side of the futon. "Cherry? What's going on?"

"Zack . . . Lale . . . I know who you are. I know Cassie. I know about the baby. I know all of it." He had a look on his face like I'd just hit him over the head with a frying pan. "I came to Buchanan just after you left. I practice taught with Father Leo up at St. Juniper's. Cassie was my friend, and I was supposed to find you for her up here in New York and talk to you, but I never could get up my nerve to do it. That's why I was so weird and cold to you. I'm sorry."

He got up and went into the other room, and I heard him pacing back and forth. He slammed down something that sounded like books. Then he threw something big like a chair. A few more things crashed around. I was afraid to move or say anything. Just when I was trying to figure the best way to sneak out, he pushed the curtain back and came in. He was still agitated but had worked off some of the anger.

"I wish you had said something about all this sooner. I feel pretty stupid right about now."

"I know I should have. But how was I going to casually bring it up? You have to admit it was a pretty awful thing you did to her."

"I guess I wasn't thinking about her when I did it."

"I guess not."

"And then it seemed like it was too late." He sat beside me on the futon. I inched away a little bit. "But you're right about one thing," he went on, in a quieter voice. "If I had it to do over, I'd still leave." He turned and looked at me, right in the eyes. "Tell the truth—would you go back to Arkansas now and teach school or whatever it was you did?"

"No. No, I wouldn't. I understand. But that doesn't make what you did right."

"No, but that's the way it is." Neither one of us said anything for a minute.

There was no good way to ask this. . . . "Do you know the baby . . . died?"

"I just found out. Mama wrote me. Did you know my mama?"

I shook my head.

"You might as well read it. You know it all anyhow. It's all my fault, not hers. I didn't lie outright about it, but I let her believe the baby might not be mine, all the time knowing it was. But that I can fix. I'll write her and tell her the truth."

I bit my tongue on that one. At least that would help the situation some. He picked up a pink letter and handed it to me. Her handwriting was round, like a girl's. I felt like I shouldn't read it, but I couldn't stop myself.

Dear Lale,

Well, that harelipped baby died. I'm glad it's over with. Now maybe things will get back to normal. Your daddy has been just awful to live with ever since that girl had that baby. It was in the hospital in Little Rock and over my objections he went up there the very day it died. Then, to add to the insult, he went to the funeral and sat with her like she was family. Everybody in town is talking about it and making me out to be the bad guy for not taking her to my bosom, but they just don't know the truth. Your daddy gave her all the money you sent. I was saving it for you, knowing you would need it one of these days when you get back home, and there was no need for you to send her so much. But your daddy wouldn't have it any other way, so she has it. She made out pretty good, I would say. I tried to get him to write to you, but he is being stubborn. He said he feels like he doesn't have a son. No matter what, though, you will always be my baby. Don't feel bad about any of it. You paid your dues and then some, even if they weren't yours to pay. That girl's still got your car, and this morning she took off, and as far as I know she didn't tell anybody where she was going. I say it's good riddance.

I wish you could come back for Christmas, but I understand if you don't want to right now. In time, it will be all forgotten and you can come home again.

I love you so much,
Mom

Baby had said Janet was a cold woman, but it sounded like she had dropped a marble or two. To be bitter might be natural, but she took it to a point way past natural. The thing that scared me, though, was the part about Cassie leaving. She wouldn't get my letter. I handed him back the letter and sighed.

"Well? What do you think I should do?"

"I don't know. Have you had anything to eat?" I had to take one thing at a time. Right now, I needed to get Lale up and moving, and then we could talk about what to do. If anything.

"Not since breakfast."

"Get your coat on and let's go to the Broome Street Bar and get a burger. It'll make you feel better."

The Broome Street Bar, a workers' lunch place, wasn't the fanciest joint in town, but it had good burgers. We ordered two with tomatoes, pickles, and onions, thick fries on the side.

"Do you think Cassie might come up here?" he said through a mouthful. "I don't think I could face her." That thought had been on my mind, too.

"No, I doubt if she'd do that. She's got her pride. She probably just needed to get away by herself for a little while and think everything through. If she calls or writes me, I'll let you know. She's still my friend, you know."

But I didn't know if I would still be her friend when she saw the ad.

34

DR. NICK

Cassie stopped off at the diner to tell Bernadette she was going to Hot Springs or Little Rock or someplace to get away for a few days and think.

"Sweetheart, do you think that's wise, to go off all by yourself like that? Why don't you stay with us and let us take care of you? You'll be back to your old self before long. I know it sounds corny, but time really will make it better."

"Y'all don't worry about me. I think I'll maybe go down to Bathhouse Row in Hot Springs and get me one of those massages and sit in a pool of hot water. Wouldn't that be something? I just really need to be by myself for a few days, okay? I promise I'll call y'all. Don't worry."

"Well, you can't tell me not to worry. It's nearly Christmas. Will you be back by then? I really need you at the diner. That Melanie Johnston is just plumb lazy. I'm having to do way too much of the work."

"Of course I'll be back for Christmas. Then we'll fire Melanie's butt and you can take it easy again. But I gotta get out of here, Bernadette, just for a while, to get my head back on straight. And at least *try* not to worry. You're worse than Mama."

In the end, Bernadette couldn't stop her any more than her mother could. She had three thousand dollars in her purse, the other two spent on the hospital and doctors and the funeral for Lalea. At least Lale had done that much, and she appreciated it. Maybe he did still love her, at least a little bit. And while she hated to lie to Annie and Bernadette, she had to go find him and see for herself if there was even one little shred left. Not that she believed there was, but until she heard it from his mouth, she didn't think she could go on with her life. She needed closure, as they say in the funeral business.

She waved as she put the Thunderbird in gear and set out, not even looking back at Bernadette standing in front of the diner, waving until she was out of sight. Never in her life had she been on a trip where she didn't have a schedule—nobody to call, nobody waiting for her to get there on time for school or work. She was free. Maybe that's what Lale felt like when he left out that night in the back of Snuffy's truck.

She drove down through the mountains, stopping at a luncheonette/gas station that had a big sign saying BLUE BIRD DINER—EAT AND GET GAS. The menu was heavy on chili with peppers, fried onions, hot dogs, and sauerkraut, and Cassie realized she should pay attention to what the sign said, so she ordered a tuna melt. There was a gift shop attached full of blue glass birds called the Blue Bird of Happiness. She bought one, feeling kind of silly, but she could use some happiness. It was cheerful, sitting on the dashboard with the sun shining through it, splashing blue light on the seat.

Going down the twisting road, her mind was a tangle of what had happened, what she might have done differently, what might have been, what might be. Before she headed toward New York, though, she had a stop to make in Little Rock. The T-bird seemed to go by itself to Children's Hospital, like it knew the way. She pulled into the parking lot, took a deep breath, and got out of the car and stretched. It was already late afternoon. Where had the hours gone? Well, she was here. She needed to go back one more time, to see if any part of Lalea was still there. And she wanted to see where they'd put the papier-mâché animals Baby's class had donated. Baby had told her they put up a little plaque saying the animals were there in the memory of Lalea Culver. She'd take a picture of it to add to the pitifully small stack she had of the baby. That would make her feel better, to know that even though nobody knew who Lalea Culver was, they would see her name and wonder. It would show she had at one time existed. Maybe some of the other mothers she knew would still be there and she'd check to see how they were doing.

The waiting room looked the same. There were still piles of books and knitting, anxious mothers putting on yellow scrub suits. Only the faces had changed. She went past the glass window to the activity room and admired the big giraffe, elephant, and dinosaur Baby's class had made. They were sturdy enough for the children to sit on, and there were little bald kids with big smiles in hospital johnnies and I.V.s dangling from their arms clinging to the animals. It was harder than she had thought it would be. She took a couple of Polaroids of the plaque.

"Hey, big guy," she said to a little boy sitting on the elephant. "What's your horse's name?"

"This isn't a horse!" The boy giggled.

"No? Then what is it?"

"It's an elephant."

"Oh, right. It has that big ol' nose. What's his name?"

"Peanut."

"Peanut. Because he likes to eat peanuts?"

"Yeah. And because he's not as big as a big elephant. If he was big, I'd call him Jumbo."

She ran her hand over his little bald head, smooth as a peeled egg, tears in her eyes.

"Ride 'em, cowboy!" she said, and walked out of the room.

She went back to the preemie ward. She didn't see any of the mothers she had known there. They had all gone, one way or the other. One of the nurses behind the glass spotted her and came out and gave her a big hug. That started the tears flowing for sure.

"How're you holding up, Cassie?" The nurse held her at arm's length and looked kindly into her face.

"I'm okay. I'm really okay. I wanted to see the animals. A friend of mine did them. I guess I just needed to come by one more time."

"I'm glad to see you," she said gently, "but if I were you I'd make it my last visit. You can get lost here. One of the mothers started coming around after her daughter died, and it didn't go so well. She began volunteering and was here every day. She got obsessed with the place and couldn't get back to her real life."

"Oh, I'm not doing that. In fact, I have to run right now. I have someplace I need to be."

"Well, you take care. You're a special girl to all of us." The nurse hugged her again and left.

She stood for another minute and the place seemed at once familiar and strange to her. Some other baby was in the crib that had belonged to Lalea. Lalea was gone. She was really gone from this earth. Cassie walked out, relieved that she didn't have to come back to this place again. Ever.

As the elevator went down a couple of floors, it stopped and Dr. Nick Barker stepped in. He glanced at her, then looked again, as if trying to place her.

"Cassie? How are you doing? I thought . . ."

"I just came by for a visit. No, Lalea died. She's not here anymore." She raised her chin when she said it.

"I'm sorry."

"Yeah, me, too." There was an awkward silence. Cassie kept her eyes on the numbers as the elevator descended. Dr. Nick kept glancing at her. The doors opened and they walked out. Cassie kept moving. She wasn't going to say good-bye. What was the point? But Dr. Nick called after her.

"Cassie? Say . . . I was just on my way to get some dinner. Want to join me? I know the cafeteria's not the greatest food, but it's cheap and fast."

Dr. Barker was not handsome, but not ugly, either; starting to bald, he was old but not too old, probably mid- to late thirties. He couldn't be interested in her that way. He probably just felt bad for her and wanted to find out what happened with Lalea. Well, why not eat with him? She had to eat. She'd find a hotel later and then decide what she was going to do. She didn't have a timetable to get to New York. The idea of being on the road alone was not as appealing now as it had been early in the morning.

"Sure. I'd like that."

It was the dinner-hour rush, and a mass of visitors, as well as technicians, doctors, and nurses wearing scrubs, some in hair and shoe coverings from the O.R., grabbed plate lunches or sandwiches, wolfed them down like it was their last meal. It was strange for Cassie to see them out of their normal element, joking and laughing. They seemed to all be having a great time. How could that be, when they worked with sick and dying people every day? She'd be a wreck if she had to work in a hospital.

"The barbecued pork's pretty good," Dr. Nick said as they finally got their turn at the steam table that was loaded down with fried and fatty dishes. "The best of a bad lot. They tried some low-fat dishes, but everybody wanted their chicken-fried steak and mashed potatoes with gravy."

"I guess you can't change Arkansawyers. They grew up on that stuff."

"Yeah. And secretly, I think the hospital figured it's good for business. We fill 'em full of grease down here and take it out of their arteries upstairs." Cassie smiled, not sure if he was kidding. It sounded plausible to her.

They filled their trays and when Cassie started to pull out her wallet, Dr. Barker wouldn't let her pay.

"Doctors get a discount. You're with me."

They went to the corner table just vacated by a gang of nurses and Cassie wiped it off with a napkin.

"Sorry. It's the waitress in me. You'd think nurses would be neater, somehow, wouldn't you?"

"Let's hope they're neater in the operating room."

"How do y'all surgeons do it, Dr. Barker? How can you bring yourself to cut open somebody and rearrange their face or take out their cancers and then come down here and eat like you'd just spent the day baking a cake or something?" Dr. Barker squeezed lemon into his tea and added three packets of sugar, shaking them and then ripping them open all at once.

"You get used to it. It's hard at first, especially if you work with children. But you wouldn't last long if you let yourself go around in tears all the time. Sometimes some of the nurses, especially the ones who work with the sickest kids, get burned out, and they have to rotate to another job for a while. It takes a special person to come in to work day after day and not know if somebody they've gotten attached to will be there or not. And we can't help but get attached to our patients, no matter how hard we try not to."

"Do you work on a lot of kids?"

"Quite a few. Cleft palates, mostly, like your baby. Though my main business is cosmetic surgery."

"That seems a little . . . not to hurt your feelings . . . shallow or something. I mean, to go through all that when you don't need to, just for vanity."

"I don't look at it like that. I believe the way we feel about ourselves has everything to do with how happy and healthy we are. It's good to think you have the power to change someone's life by making them beautiful. Or even just making them look a little more normal."

"Must be kind of like playing God."

"I suppose you could say that. But then God gave man the brains to do it, so maybe He intended for it to happen, if we try to do some good. Like the old church song goes, 'God has no hands but our hands.' "

"I missed that old song, I guess. I'm Catholic."

Cassie picked up her fork and started to eat. She felt a little self-conscious. Dr. Barker kept staring at her. Her cheeks got hot.

"What? Do I have something on my face?"

"I'm sorry. No. You have a lovely face. I can't help it, being a plastic surgeon." He laughed. "I'm like a dentist friend of mine who always, in his mind, fixes everyone's teeth he meets. He married a girl who had a cute little overbite that made her look pouty and sexy, and I think the chief reason he did was so he could straighten her teeth. Right after the honeymoon, he put her in braces. She wore them for three years and when they came off, she wasn't cute and sexy anymore. Her lip had fallen in and her whole face was different. She hated the way she looked and so did he, so he put braces back on her to make them the way they were to begin with." He took a big bite of his barbecue. Cassie waited.

"What happened to her?"

"Oh. When the braces came off two years later, she divorced him. How's that barbecue?"

Cassie laughed. A small laugh, but it was the first one in a long time.

"I get it. You're thinking you want to fix my nose, don't you?"

"You have such a beautiful bone structure. If you had that bump taken out of the middle of your nose and just the tiniest little bob on the end, you'd be perfect."

Cassie laughed again.

"Are you going to marry me so you can fix it?"

"That might not be the worst idea in the world." He said it like he wasn't kidding.

Cassie looked at him and took a bite of her sandwich. He was crazy, but he did have nice eyes.

35

THE TRIO

Lale felt better after we ate, and I got some painting done before Sal got home, at least the preliminary sketch and the background colors laid in. The photograph I was working from didn't have a lot of detail, though, so he would have to sit for me at least a time or two so I could get things like hands and ears and nostrils a little clearer. It couldn't be a surprise anyway, so I just let him see it.

"Oh, my *God*! It is *me* already! You are amazing, Miss Cherry. I can't believe you are doing my portrait. I'm so *honored*!"

"It was going to be a surprise, but you'll have to sit. So sit." I got my sketchbook out and did some pencil sketches of the various ears and things I needed. He was pretty patient, up to a point, and then had to get up and move around.

"Sorry, sweetness. I was just not *made* to sit in one spot too long. Let me change and we'll take you out to dinner. Want to go to Fanelli's?"

"Well, if it's just for a quick bite. I have to meet a friend on Prince Street at ten."

"Do tell—who is it?"

"Just a friend. He's in a jazz trio and they're playing at a loft over there."

"Really? Can we go? It sounds groovy."

"Uh, I don't know. It's one of those invitation-only things. I didn't know you were into jazz."

"I'm into *life,* baby-o! It sounds like a blast. I'm sure you could get us in. As gorgeous as we are, how could they turn us away? Zack, what do you think? Want to meet Cherry's beau?"

Great. I had to open my big mouth. Now they would go with me and meet Aurelius. What would he think about me walking in with a handsome model and a guy in a dress?

"I didn't say he was my beau. I said he was a friend. You won't take Miss Sally, will you, Sal? I mean, not that she's not wonderful, but you know . . ."

"Who do you think you're talking to? Miss Sally only goes where she knows in advance she'll be loved and appreciated."

"I think I'll just stay here, Cherry. I'm kind of tired."

"Don't be *silly,* Zack! It'll do you good to get out and about. You look a little peaked."

"So this guy you're meeting, is he the boyfriend you talked about?" Zack did look a little worn out from the afternoon, but who could blame him?

"Kind of."

"Well, in that case, sure. I'll go."

Fanelli's was the other workers' bar in SoHo, framed pictures of boxers hanging on the dark, wood-paneled walls. It was what they call a beer-and-shot place. A guy who unloads trucks all day would come in and, without even asking, the bartender would set a shot glass of whiskey and a mug of beer out on the bar. The guy would down the shot, then drink the beer without drawing breath. The bartender would also pour you a nice cold Chardonnay if you asked, thank goodness, which was about all I could handle, and they had pretty good pasta e fagioli. While I wasn't too comfortable going there by myself, with the guys it was okay.

By the time we finished dinner, it was nearly ten and had started to rain. The snow from earlier hadn't really stuck, and the rain was turning what was left to mush. I was glad I'd worn my rubber boots and not the new green suede ones. The streets were nearly deserted as we found the loft on the corner of Prince and West Broadway. A guy standing downstairs with his coat collar turned up asked us who we were invited by and let us in when I showed them the invitation Aurelius had given me. We had to climb four flights of rickety stairs. It didn't seem like these places were ever swept, or if they were you couldn't tell it. They for sure hadn't been painted since the first coat was put on—that I'd bet money on. The dented metal door opened up to a dark space that somehow seemed cavernous and intimate at the same time, floors painted black, brick walls, with a lot of people hanging around at little tables, candles everywhere. Balloons tied with long ribbons were thick on the ceiling. At one end of the room was a rigged-up spotlight, focused on three musicians, Aurelius with his saxophone, a black guy named Justin de Mar on drums, and a skinny white man, Arturo Furness, playing bass. I caught Aurelius's eye and waved. He nodded in my direction. Lale turned and stared at me.

"Is *that* the guy?"

"Yep. That's him."

I could kick myself for bringing him. What was I thinking?

36

JAZZ

Dear Baby,

Last night was not the best night I've ever had, understatement of the year. First of all, Lale and I finally talked about Cassie and the whole thing, and instead of bawling him out, I really felt sorry for him. He's not a bad guy, just young and not ready to settle down, and not terribly concerned with anybody but himself—big revelation. But, get this, he was the one who let Janet think the baby was not his, and he is miserable about the whole thing. I think he really feels bad for what he did and how it turned out, and he is going to at least set his mother straight, so that is something.

I had a date with Aurelius later, but hated to leave Lale like that, so I took him and Sal with me to hear Aurelius play at this loft not far from them. It didn't occur to me to tell Lale that Aurelius was black, or, more the truth, maybe I just didn't want to tell him, but we walked in while Aurelius was playing and Lale was dumbstruck. I had forgotten how people back home can be. It never crossed my mind Lale would be so shocked that I'd be with a black man—he's pretty cool about gays, but I don't know why I was so surprised. As you pointed out, Buchanan is the home of the grand dragon of the Ku Klux Klan, and Lale grew up there. The grand dragon might be his grandpa, for all I know. Janet seems like she might have a little dragon in her. Just kidding. Kind of.

Sal was great, though. He's Puerto Rican, and has been kicked around a little in his life, too. He invented himself from nothing, a poor family of seven kids, the little queer one who all the kids in school picked on, so he learned how to make them laugh and they wound up being his friends. He didn't tell me all this head on, just dropped hints, but I could read between the lines. You have to meet him one of these days, when you come up here. You'll love him. He never meets a stranger.

Anyhow, the trio was great, in spite of Lale's remarks about how the music was horrible and didn't even have a tune, etc. If I didn't know better I'd think he was jealous. Ha. I tried to ignore him for the most part, but I was boiling inside. I was so proud of Aurelius. He looked great, wearing a white shirt that was open down the front, African beads, and chamois pants that clung to his muscled butt and legs like velvet skin. He's a real professional and was clearly the star of the trio, although the others were good, too. At the break Aurelius came over to where we were and sat down, put his arm around me, and gave me a little kiss. I made it a bigger one. I could see Lale holding it in, wanting to hit him or something, but there was nothing he could do without being a total A-H, since I was clearly with him. Sal told Aurelius how much he dug the music and the two of them got into a discussion about jazz, people I'd never heard of, like Thelonious Monk, John Coltrane, Sonny Stitt, and Miles Davis, fusion—which I didn't quite grasp—and I don't know what all. It seems like Sal knows a lot about everything, and he has actually met Miles Davis a time or two. He said Miles did a concert where he played the whole thing with his back to the room, and then when he finally turned around, the crowd went wild. I'm going to have to learn a whole new culture, I can see. It's nothing like the blues music they have out at Turkey Bend.

Lale finally got tired of Aurelius getting all our attention, saw a girl across the room he knew, and wandered over to talk to her, giving her a big wet smack on the lips. He looked back to see if I was watching and I pretended not to see him. He is the most irritating man I know. Thank goodness he left with the girl, some trashy hippie chick who looked like a wannabe model, making sure they went right by our table, of course, and didn't cause any more trouble. Sal drifted off to sit with some guys who were gay, a couple of them actually in drag. I guess it's looser down here than I thought. I moved up to a table close to the trio and watched Aurelius play the rest of the night.

I hate to agree with Lale, even a little bit, but the sweet saxophone Aurelius plays at night by himself at the apartment didn't sound at all like the jazz he was playing at the loft, and I'm not really sure if I like it or not. You can't dance to it, there's no real beat, it's more just for listening, and even though some people were bobbing their heads, frankly some of it was off-key. But then once in a while, one of them would have a solo and go off on a riff, where he would play by himself, work to get something going, like he was straining to find the notes that kept eluding him, chasing, chasing after the melody, as ragged as it was, and we sat on the edge of our chairs, not sure at all it was going to happen, whether he would find it or it would fizzle out into a toneless chaos; then all at once, he found it, and like an orgasm, the notes came, strong and loud and soul-saving, and everyone went crazy. The drummer went on for about twenty minutes by himself, and got into some kind of hypnotized state where he was pounding the drums in such a frenzy that he took us all with him, transported us to the jungles of Africa, and in our minds Justin de Mar was wearing face paint and feathers, beating on big skin drums with sticks, but it had a tough city edge to it, too, like he was drumming out all the pain, the betrayal, the enslavement, the lynching and knifing and whipping, the denial of the most basic, decent things in life; all the horrible things the blacks have been subjected to down through the ages came out in that drumming somehow, along with a possibility of salvation. It's definitely music that can change your life. Gosh. I guess I liked it more than I thought.

We left around two, back to Aurelius's apartment, and went to bed. It's weird—I am so hot for him when he's up on the stage, and he is so sexy and the best kisser I ever kissed, but, Baby, he is just not great in bed. He still won't do anything to me—you know what I mean—and it's so frustrating. He did let me do it to him this time, which was a step, and he was really into it, but when I gently suggested he return the favor, he just came right out and said, "I can't, baby. I'm sorry. I just never could do that." I asked him if it was something about me, thinking maybe I should wash (again) or put on perfume or something, and he said, "No, it's not you, it's me. I just never could bring myself to do it to anybody." Oh. Well. I guess that's that. It was also really fast again, but at least he didn't fall asleep on me. I think he felt bad and held me afterward, which was sweet, but I sneaked out and went to my own bed. I hope it gets better. I've never had this problem before. What am I going to do?

On a totally different note, I had a weird experience on the subway a couple of days ago. There were no seats and I was standing, holding on to the handstrap, when one of those Jewish religious guys, Hasidim, they call them, got on. You might have seen pictures of them on the news about Israel. They wear black suits and hats with brims and have long curls dangling by their ears, although the rest of their hair is short. They're kind of like priests or something, but they don't have to be celibate. I had never seen one in person before I came here, but there are a lot of them in New York, especially in the diamond district, for some reason, which is in the Forties. My booker, Liz, is Jewish, and she has taught me a lot of funny words in Yiddish, like *schlemiel,* which is a nerd, *schlong,* which is a weenie (not the hot-dog kind!), *meshugana,* which means crazy, and *shiksa,* which is a white girl who isn't Jewish, like me. Anyhow, this chubby Hasid came and stood right beside me, hanging on to the next handstrap, our elbows practically touching. I was riding along, like I always do on the subway, reading the ads above the seats, not thinking about anything in particular, when I felt a hand on my thigh. I looked down and the hand was attached to the Hasid's arm. I thought, "This can't be what I think it is. He's a religious guy. It must be some kind of mistake." So I moved down a couple of straps. The Hasid moved with me. There was the hand on the thigh again. "Noooo," I thought to myself. "He really *is* doing what I think he's doing." So I turned to him and said, "Shiksas will cause you nothing but trouble." I don't even know why I said that, but I did, and he bugged his eyes, stared at me with an open mouth, and turned white as a sheet. Just then the train stopped, the doors opened, and he ran out as fast as his legs would carry him, holding on to his hat, curls bobbing, like some incubus or something was after him. It was so funny! When I told Liz about it later, after she quit laughing, she said that they believe God speaks through the mouths of dumb animals (like blondes, I guess), and he thought it was God talking to him. I can't dispute it. I don't know why I said that to him, so it could very well have been the Lord talking to him through my mouth! Liz told me about a book called *Tales of the Hasidim* by Martin Buber, which I checked out of the library, and it has some good stuff in it, just like what happened to me. Well, not really, but similar. I recommend it if you can find it.

Speaking of priests, WHAT IS GOING ON!? I'm dying to know. Write me soon.

Love,
Cherry

37

THE CHRISTMAS PARTY

I stood in line at the post office for what seemed like an hour holding a huge heavy box I was sending to Mama and Daddy. I got them so many things, it was ridiculous, but it was the first time I'd had the money to really get everyone nice presents, so I went all out. Mama would love all the stuff I sent, mostly clothes and jewelry I'd gotten at the flea markets and antique stores, but Daddy wouldn't like any of it. He wanted me to save my money. He still thought this modeling thing was just a phase I was going through and I would be back soon to live next door to them in Sweet Valley. I hoped he would at least wear the pretty cashmere sweater. I didn't think he'd ever had real cashmere before. I hadn't until now. I thought genuine lambs' wool was the best.

Finally I made it up to the head of the line, my arms practically falling off, and hoisted the box over the counter to a girl with blue eye shadow, home-bleached hair, and a bad attitude. Not full of Christmas cheer, that one, although I couldn't blame her. Being a postal clerk at Christmas would not be my dream job. Daddy was the postmaster in

Sweet Valley, and I hung around there sometimes. Those people were under a lot of pressure, especially at Christmastime.

It would be the first Christmas I wouldn't be there with the family, and that was sad, but I just couldn't make myself stop grinning. People were glancing at me and whispering to one another like they thought I was somebody important, but they couldn't quite figure out who. It was because the Diamonds & Ermine ad and commercial had come out! Everybody back home, of course, went crazy. Mama bought all the copies of *Vogue* they had at the Kroger store and drove around to every place that sold magazines within twenty-five miles to find more. Lucille wrote and wanted to know who the cute guy with me was, and if I was sleeping with him. They kept the TV on day and night, just in case the commercial ran. If it did, they stopped whatever they were doing and watched. Of course, the thing went over big in Buchanan, as well, I can tell you. Baby wrote me about it.

Dear Cherry,

You're always a big star with me, but you got nothing on Lale—he's *the* star of Buchanan. That's all anybody is talking about. Nobody knows what to think about the two of you together, and of course they all think you're engaged or something. I keep telling everyone that it's just a job and there is nothing between the two of you, but of course they don't believe it. You're both pretty good actors—you guys did look like you were in love, and if I didn't know better, I'd think so myself. What is up with those voices, though? It's hilarious to hear those accents coming out of your mouths. People really think the two of you have changed your voices. I can't believe how ignorant these hillbillies are. I bet your life is changing already, big time. I had no idea you would be so successful this soon! I'm sad that I'm not there with you. I miss you so much. I don't know if Cassie has seen the commercial or not. I haven't heard a word from her. She took a little trip to Little Rock and never came back, but she called Bernadette and said she was okay, just spending a few days with a friend. At least she's moving on, thank goodness.

But I have my own news. Leo and I have really started something and it is *so incredible,* but so hard at the same time. We have to keep it a total secret, of course. We meet out at the old mill, in our hidden cellar room. It's not so creepy now. We fixed it up with a mattress, candles, and quilts. It's not that cold down there, and there is even a little fireplace. Oh, Cherry, I love him so much. And he loves me. I hate to tell you, since Aurelius is like he is and all, but Leo does *everything* to me, and he is amazing—a quick learner, given that he hasn't had all that much experience. Most of all, even more than the actual sex, I love to hear him talk. He is so smart and knows everything about the history of the Church, and photography and music and art—I never get tired of listening to him. I don't know what he is going to do about the priesthood. It was his whole life. I'm only the second woman he has ever been with, and that's a little scary, too. We talk about it endlessly. I know he agonizes over it, but when we're together, it doesn't matter. There is no Church and no black robes in the mill cellar. There is just us, doing what God designed us to do. I don't feel guilty at all about it—I think celibacy is a stupid rule and sooner or later they are going to run out of guys who want to be priests. I hope. Maybe then they will change it.

Hang in with Aurelius. Be patient. Maybe he'll get better. You aren't tempted to go with Lale, are you? He *is* pretty cute. And I bet he knows a thing or two about pleasing a woman. Oops. Forget I said that. I don't want to be disloyal to Cassie, and I'm sure you don't either.

Love,
Baby

The agency had their big Christmas party at Elaine's. All Suzan's models were there, plus photographers, bookers, magazine editors, designers, stylists, hair and makeup people, everyone who was anybody in the fashion business. The place was so crowded the waiters had to pass drinks overhead. A hand would appear, take one off the tray, and disappear back into the mass of people. I had brought Aurelius, who was cool as always, but seemed a little uncomfortable. Maybe because he was one of the few black men there. I hadn't realized before how it must feel to always be in the minority everywhere you go. Suzan only had three black women and two black men models in the whole agency. There has never been a black girl on the cover of *Vogue,* although after Martin Luther King was assassinated in '68, *Glamour* put Katiti Kironde on the cover, just that once. Naomi Sims has been on the cover of *The New York Times*'s *Fashions of the Times* magazine, and Diana Vreeland has used her in a *Vogue* layout, but not on the cover. Still, it seems like things are changing for them. An all-black agency called Black Beauties opened a couple of years ago, and even the blonde-obsessed Fords have a few.

But I didn't have time to worry about Aurelius. It seemed like I was one of the big girls now, because everyone was coming up to tell me how great the commercial was, how beautiful the ad, to touch me, and give me their cards, which I stuck in my purse until there was a fat stack of them. The photographers all said they wanted to work with me, and I smiled and said yes to everything. In all the confusion and my neglect, Aurelius wandered away, although he was easy to find because he was tall and his Afro stuck up above the crowd. I spotted him talking to one of the black models and got a pang of jealousy. He had never said how many girlfriends he'd had, or anything about other women at all. In fact, I realized I knew precious little about him at all. I'm sure he must have had quite a few, he was so good-looking. A lot of girls were checking him out. I felt like I'd brought a T-bone steak to a pit-bull party. Well, if he was going to be attracted to other girls, then so be it. I'd give him a lot of rope, because, like Rod McKuen, or somebody like that, said, "If you love someone, let them go. If they don't come back, they were never yours." Or words to that effect. It sounded good in the poem, but not so good in practice. *Did* I love him? Did he love me? Mama always said if you have to ask yourself, you don't. But I sure didn't want him to go off with anybody else, especially one of the beautiful black girls.

Sal wriggled up to me. He was wearing a red velvet Santa cap with white fur trim.

"Oh, my *God*! I'm *dying*. How can we breathe in here? You are so lucky, Miss Cherry, to be taller than most people because at least the air is fresher up there. I'm about to *expire* from the heat!"

"Well, take off that stupid fur hat. Here, I'll put it in my bag for you." I got the hat off his head and wiped the sweat with my napkin. It came back brown from the makeup.

"Oops, I smeared your makeup. You'll have to go fix it."

"I'll never get near the bathroom. There's a line out the door. Nobody will notice." We edged our way to the back of the room, which wasn't so crowded. At least we could stand and talk without bumping our drinks on each other's faces.

"So *you're* the belle of the ball. Got any offers from Hollywood yet?"

"No, don't be silly, but Suzan thinks I'll get a lot of work out of it. Apparently there was a big surge in the perfume sales right after it came out."

"Wonderful! Oh, my *God*! There's *Diana Vreeland* coming in the door! You have to meet her. This is the time—I can feel it in my bones."

She was tiny, but her personality took up a lot of room. I had heard her name forever, since she was the editor in chief of *Vogue,* but I had never really seen a good picture of her. She was shockingly ugly, a dark little woman with a wad of coal-black hair poofed up like a goiter on top of her head and the rest chopped blunt under her ears. She had beady black eyes and the biggest nose I had ever seen on a human being. She wore a fire-engine-red knit dress to match her lipstick and rouge, and her skinny little arms were heavy with ivory bangles. An ivory necklace shaped like the tooth of some prehistoric tiger dangled from a gold chain thick enough to tether a ship. I couldn't take my eyes off her. The crowd parted like Moses was directing the band, and she immediately was surrounded by people taking her coat, handing her a drink, and acting like they would kneel and kiss her feet if they only had the room. I didn't want to be another one trying to get her to notice me, so I just hung back sipping my glass of white wine, chatting with Sal. After several minutes, I heard a voice like a well-smoked foghorn.

"You!"

I turned and there she stood, a pint-size samurai, pointing a cadmium-vermilion-lacquered fingernail at me.

"Me?"

"Yes, you." She came toward me and I bent down to be able to hear her above the howl of the party.

"The Diamonds & Ermine girl. Marvelous! I had no idea you were this tall! *Divine!*"

"Thank you, Mrs. Vreeland. Coming from you, that means a lot."

"What else have you done? Do you have a book? Who are you with?"

"Yes, ma'am, I mean, yes, I have a book. I'm with Suzan Hartman, and I've done legs for *Vogue* and hair for Clairol and several other things."

"Marvelous. Are you wearing Diamonds & Ermine right now?" She sniffed and frowned.

"Um, not really. Although I do like it."

"You should always wear scent. Scent is as important to a well-turned-out woman as her makeup, her nail varnish, her pearls."

"Do you like Diamonds & Ermine, Mrs. Vreeland? Is it something you wear?"

"No, but that doesn't matter. Any scent is preferable to none. Chanel No. 5, to me, is the ideal scent for a woman. She can wear it anywhere, anytime, and everybody—husbands, beaus, taxi drivers—*everybody* loves it. Elaine, here at the restaurant, wears it. *No one* has gone beyond Chanel No. 5." I remembered Elaine smelling particularly good when she hugged me. I'd graduated from a handshake to a hug, a big deal in these circles.

"I like that one, too. Remember what Marilyn Monroe said about it . . ."

" 'What do you sleep in, Miss Monroe?' "

" 'Chanel No. 5'!" we said together, then laughed. Her whole face crinkled when she laughed and she didn't seem ugly anymore.

"Chanel was the first couturier who added scent to the wardrobe of the woman—did you know that? No designer had ever thought of such a thing. Chanel No. 5 is a totally marvelous product—best bottle, stopper, box—and of course, still one of the *great* scents. Do you know the story of why it's called No. 5?" Mrs. Vreeland pulled out a long cigarette holder and inserted a pink cigarette. Sal whipped out a lighter and lit it for her. She took a puff, settled back, and looked at me. I was so mesmerized by her I forgot to speak. It didn't matter.

"Chanel wanted to put out a new scent, but didn't yet know which one or what to name it. A number of scents to choose from had arrived at the rue Cambon. Coco called up one of her great Russian friends—a very aristocratic, superior man—and asked him. 'Help me to choose. I have a migraine. My head is in quarters. You've *got* to do this. Come over instantly.'

"He arrived and was taken to the bedroom, where Coco was lying on the bed, barely able to *speak,* she was in such pain.

" 'Over there is a stack of ten handkerchieves,' she said. 'Place them along the mantelpiece. Put a sample of scent on each handkerchief, and when the alcohol's blown off, let me know.'

"He did this, and she pulled herself off the bed to go over to the mantel. She picked each one up in turn. First one: *'C'est impossible!'* Second, *'Horrible!'* The third, *'Pas encore.'* The fourth, *'Non.'* Then, suddenly, *'Ça va, ça va!'* It was the *fifth* handkerchief! With those great instincts, she was correct even when she was *practically* unconscious.

"As for men, the two best men's scents in the world were both made by Rigaud. One was called L'Eau Merveilleux and the other was called Cananga. These were *strong* scents. They reminded me of marvelous

Edwardian gentlemen in Paris early in this century. When my sister and I were children, we used to be brought in to curtsy to our parents' friends and to kiss them good night, and it was a *pleasure*. Many of the men had whiskers and rather longish hair—this wasn't an American stockbroking group—and they all smelled the same. It had bay rum in it, Florida water . . . it was clean. It was a healthy smell—good for the skin, good for the soul . . . and *strong*. There's a whole school now that says the scent must be faint. *This is ridiculous*. I'm speaking from the experience of a *lifetime*.

"Chanel always used to say, keep a bottle in your bag and *refresh* yourself with it continuously. I always carry purse scent—that way I'm never without it. Do you notice any scent on me now?" I leaned down to sniff. "Don't come any closer—if you have to *sniff* like a *hound* it's not enough!" I straightened up immediately. She took a little vial of Chanel No. 5 out of her purse, spritzed her neck and wrists, then continued.

"You should never put scent on immediately after your bath. That's the biggest mistake going—there's nothing for it to *cling* to. Napoleon never bathed in water, you know. His valet, I'm told, every morning, took literally a *whole* bottle of scent, L'Eau Imperiale—one of those divine Napoleonic flacons with bees all over it—and poured it *right* down the emperor's body. *One* bottle! Now whether it was a pint bottle or a two-pint bottle . . . don't ask me. But this is something I understand *totally*." She paused to take a puff on her cigarette. I felt like I should contribute something, but didn't know what.

"That seems like a lot of perfume to buy every day. But then I guess Napoleon didn't have to pinch his pennies."

"Perfume *is* an extravagance. But it's odd that Americans, who God knows are an extravagant people, have never used scents properly. They buy *bottles*, but they don't splash it on."

She paused again and took a long swallow of her drink. Chanel No. 5 wafted off of her. It, or the sheer overwhelming weight of her personality, was making me light-headed.

"Come to my office Monday afternoon at two."

Then she turned on her heel and walked away, the waves of people parting as she moved. I shut my mouth, which I had found hanging open.

"What was *that*?" I asked Sal, who was grinning at me.

"I think that was the sound of your career being made, Miss Cherry, darlin'."

38

FOX IN THE HENHOUSE

The light from the TV flickered across the room. Cassie sat crosslegged on the floor with a bowl of popcorn in her lap, crunched the little half-opened ones in her teeth, licked salt from her fingers. The show was some made-for-TV movie and she didn't even know the plot, her mind flitting from one thought to another like a hummingbird. She was waiting for the commercial.

Then it came on. She scooted closer to the set, like a three-year-old, and mouthed the words she had memorized along with the two on the screen.

"You ought to be in Diamonds & Ermine," he says, in a British accent. A good tight close-up of his face, eyes looking down at someone, small smile playing on his lips. The camera pans back to include *her,* ringlets of platinum hair fluffed out, her small nose tilted up in profile.

"I agree, are you giving me a present?"

She raises her pale eyebrow teasingly at the man, who wears a tuxedo and a white bow tie. He delicately runs a finger along her bare shoulder, just above a white ermine coat collar.

"The best present." He hands her a bottle of Diamonds & Ermine.

She snuggles into the ermine, turns her head slightly away, as if she is totally uninterested.

"Perfume?"

He gets down on one knee, takes her chin in his hand, forcing her to look into his eyes.

"Not simply perfume. An extraordinary elixir. Immensely complex. Like you, love." She lifts her chin, moistens her glossy lips with a pink tongue.

"Really? Complex how?"

On it goes, coy touches, scorching looks. The words were meaningless. It was the seduction she could see so clearly. No matter how many times Cassie watched, it always ended the same way, with Cherry and Lale looking longingly into each other's eyes, like they couldn't wait until the camera was turned off and they could leap into bed, practically panting as they said the final exchange:

"It needs only one more ingredient to attain perfection."

"And that is . . . ?"

"You, love."

You, love. You, love. You, love. It echoed in her head.

It didn't matter that the voices weren't theirs. The eyes were. She knew it wasn't acting. No wonder Cherry had never written her that she'd found him. What had she been thinking? She had sent a fox into the henhouse to find her rooster.

After the months of staring at him on the pages of magazines, seeing him in motion was a shock. He had changed so much from the shaggy-haired boy in the worn Levi's, but he still had those intense blue eyes, the lashes so thick they looked false. Through some trick of nature, he had a double row of eyelashes, like she'd read Elizabeth Taylor had. Cassie used to covet those eyelashes. She'd hoped the baby would have them, but she hadn't. Not that it mattered now.

Cassie turned off the TV and washed the bowl, put it back in the cabinet. As she brushed her teeth and got ready for bed, she looked at her profile in the mirror. No doubt about it—she had a big nose. It had a bony hump in the middle, thin nostrils like little wings on either side. They had studied a picture by John Singer Sargent called *Madame X* in art class and Lale said it looked like her. He meant it as a compliment, but Cassie knew she had even more of a bump, while Madame X's nose was elegant and beautiful. Still, it must be said, Madame had quite a beak.

Nick Barker didn't make any bones about it. He wanted her to let him take out the bump and make her beautiful. She was tempted. Maybe she should. Would Lale love her if she had a perfect nose? It was almost like the hand of God had driven her to the hospital that day and arranged for her to run into Nick. After the cafeteria dinner, he surprised himself by asking her to go for a drink at a nice place near the hospital, reluctant to let her get away. He found himself opening up to her, which was unusual. He gave her the basic information, where he grew up, where he went to school. His father was a doctor and he had been expected to be one, too. He'd had a boring life, he said, all school, then all work, and not much play. He'd been married once, when he was a resident, but was divorced, no kids. He lived in a big house with a swimming pool, in a neighborhood she knew was a ritzy part of town. But it was a waste, he said. He used it only to sleep, since he was at the hospital by six and didn't come home sometimes until midnight or later. In fact, this was the first time he had taken even this much time off in months. He should be making his rounds right now, he said, but still he sat and talked to her.

"Where are you staying tonight, Cassie? It's too late to drive back to Buchanan."

"Oh, I'll find a motel somewhere. I'm free as a bird. I'm on an adventure."

"Why don't you come back to the hospital and wait for me? I'll make rounds and then you can come and sleep in my guest room."

"I don't think so, but thanks, Dr. Barker."

"Please call me Nick. No strings attached. I promise. No one is ever there, and I have five bedrooms. You'll be doing me a favor. Bring some life to the poor house."

It was a little weird, but he seemed like a nice guy and he had a big reputation as one of the best doctors in Little Rock. She finally said yes, something that she would normally not even think of doing, but by the end of a couple of glasses of wine, he felt like an old friend.

She sat in the doctors' lounge reading magazines while he made rounds, getting curious looks from the other doctors and nurses, and she ignored the whispers as they wondered who she was.

"Can I help you?" a dark-haired nurse wearing O.R. scrubs that couldn't hide her big bosoms said when she came in for the third time and Cassie was still there.

"No, thanks. I'm waiting for Dr. Barker."

"Ohhh," the nurse said, the word full of meaning. "Would you like some coffee?"

"No, thank you."

"I guess it wouldn't be as good as what Dr. Nick makes, would it?"

"I wouldn't know."

The nurse took a cup for herself and left, not speaking again. The air behind her was frosty.

He carried her suitcase in, showed her around, and then left her alone. By the time she got up the next morning, he was gone. She was already in bed when he came home that night, and she thought he might have forgotten she was there. She didn't know what to do, how to get in touch with him. He'd neglected to give her his phone number. She knew she should leave, but it would have been rude not to say good-bye, and the indoor pool was so beautiful she decided to take a swim. Then she shopped for food, there being nothing in the fancy state-of-the-art fridge but a bottle of white wine and a dried-out chunk of cheese. She'd make him a nice dinner to thank him, if he ever got home. He did come home, early, and was so grateful for the dinner that she laughed.

"How long has it been since anybody cooked you dinner?"

"I can't even remember. Usually dinner is whatever the cafeteria throws together. Sometimes it's a piece of chocolate from some patient's bedside table, or a doughnut and coffee in the lounge."

"How do you keep on running like you do?"

"Adrenaline."

After dinner, she did the dishes and he said he had to run back to the hospital to check on a recent surgery. He told her not to wait up for him. She locked her bedroom door when she went to bed, but there was no need. She never heard when he came in, and by the time she got up, he was already gone.

She made dinner again that night and left it warming for him. In the morning, he left a thank-you note. The following night, he came home early with a tub of Kentucky Fried Chicken and they shared it at the kitchen table and talked. She showed him pictures of Lale and he said over and over the man was a fool for leaving her.

It was hard to believe he was being this nice to her for nothing. It couldn't be that he was so anxious to operate on her nose, could it? He mentioned it often, sometimes kiddingly, sometimes seriously. He said he would do it for free. She told him she liked her nose like it was, thank you, but the more she looked at it, the more he talked, the bigger it got. The weight loss had, if anything, made it look even bigger, with less face to surround it. Still, it was weird. What was in it for him?

She tried to find clues about him when she was all alone in the house, which had obviously been decorated by a professional. There wasn't any of him in it, no homey things, no pictures sitting on the tables, no souvenirs from vacations. The shiny new kitchen appeared as though it had never been used, and his room was the only one that looked lived in at all. He did like fast fancy cars; there were three she'd never heard of in the big garage—he had to tell her what they were—a 1956 silver Jaguar XK140, a black 1955 Gullwing Mercedes 300SL with doors that opened up like . . . well, a bird's wings, and the one he used for every day, a new 1970 red Aston Martin with buttery leather seats, like the one James Bond drove.

There were several books about antique cars around and lots of medical books, but nothing much else to read. No novels at all. A few magazines about men's fashion and cars. He did have an amazing wardrobe—she could tell how expensive the suits were. They were made of good wool and had labels from someplace in London. His shirts were soft cotton or linen or silk, folded in cardboard, lined up on a stack of shirt-size shelves, one to a shelf, and his initials were on all of them in the same color thread so you could hardly notice it. It all said money. Like him, everything had a faint odor of a cologne called Pub, which came in a heavy cask-shaped bottle with a cork top.

Under his bed she found a basket with magazines of naked women, not simple ones like *Playboy;* these were much worse. Some of the women were having sex with men, some with each other. The pictures were unlike anything she had ever seen before, and she spent an hour looking at them with amazement and not a small amount of arousal. Nick didn't have much of a love life—that was obvious, since she was living there and hadn't seen hide nor hair of a woman—but at least this proved he did like the opposite sex, which was somehow a relief.

Then, poking in his underwear drawer, she found a small album with photographs of a younger Nick with more hair and a thin, pretty honey-blonde in a polka-dot bikini on the beach somewhere. They were smiling and had their arms around each other. Her hair was done in the teased-up style of the early sixties, like the girls in the beach-party movies. On one picture she had written, *To one Nicky from another, Love always, Nicole*. This must be the ex. The woman's nose was big in some of the shots. But there were other pictures of her, some in the snow in winter, others with a group, more on the beach. In these photos, her nose was not the same at all, even though the hair and everything else was the same. It was small. Cassie stared at the pictures. Maybe he had fixed her nose and she didn't like it and left him, like his dentist friend's wife. Well, she obviously left him for some reason.

She put the album back, tried to arrange the underwear exactly as it was before. She felt guilty, like an intruder. She also felt a little sorry for Nick. But she couldn't be another Nicole for him, if that was what he thought she would eventually be.

She drove to the drugstore and flipped through all the magazines, as she did every month, to find pictures of Lale. She wasn't disappointed. He was in a lot of them this time, each with a different beautiful woman. There was one layout that had a story. It pretended he and a dark-haired girl with a long high ponytail were on their honeymoon. Every picture was them in some romantic pose wearing beautiful outfits—on the rocks by the sea, on the terrace of a hotel room—they were laughing, kissing, so in love. It was torture, but she couldn't stop herself from looking. She went over all the things that could happen when she got to New York, all the conversations that might occur. None of them was good. In her mind, she was sweet to him; pleading with him; angry at him; indifferent to him. All the scenarios ended badly, with him telling her he didn't want to see her and walking out.

It hadn't been real, her actually going to New York to find him. She had been living in a bubble in Nick's house, putting it off. Until she saw the ad for Diamonds & Ermine, and then the TV commercial. After that, she decided that no matter how it turned out, she had to go.

39

NANA'S

Suzan invited me to lunch, which was something I never thought she'd do. We went to a restaurant right across the street from the agency called Nana's, an old-timey lunch place with little-old-lady waitresses who must have started working there when they were young girls and who, fifty years later, still served food like meatloaf and mashed potatoes and tapioca pudding. They made great doughnuts and sugared crullers, which I'd never seen before, and there was a long counter with stools where you could sit and drink a cup of coffee and take a load off between go-sees. We sat at one of the tables by the window. Both of us ordered the meatloaf, which surprised me a little. I thought Suzan was a vegetarian.

"Oh, not really. It's just the lowest-calorie food around. You're the only one in this town who would understand, but the thing I miss most about Arkansas is the food. Nobody up here knows what okra is, much less that you're supposed to fry it. The tomatoes taste like cardboard, they boil the squash into a bland pulp. When I first got here, I asked for fried catfish and hush puppies and they didn't have a clue what I was talking about. I realized soon enough, though, that I had to give up anything that tasted good, which translates to fried. I can just think about fattening food and my hips get bigger."

"Well, I guess I'm lucky then. I never seem to gain, no matter what I eat, and with all the exercise I've been getting, I think I've lost a couple of pounds."

"When I was modeling, I used to eat twice a week. Sunday and Thursday. I mean, eat a real meal, meat and vegetables. Though never any sugar. The rest of the time I'd have a boiled egg or a salad with lemon-juice dressing for dinner. Vats of coffee the rest of the day. And cigarettes, of course." She had one going during the meal and paused between bites to take a puff. "Be glad you aren't hooked on these things. Most of the girls have to smoke to stay thin. It works, but it's a deal with the devil. All it asks is that you give it your health, and I seem to be feeding it just fine. I'd like to quit at this point. The spirit is willing, but the body is weak."

"I have a friend who's a priest, and he once said the church believed the spirit and body were at war with each other, and the spirit had to defeat the body to get to heaven."

"Or to get in the magazines. Not so different, are they, heaven and success?"

"Not in this business. By the way, how are your ribs?"

"Mended."

I wanted to ask her more, but she said it in a way that let me know not to pursue that train of thought. I still didn't know why she had invited me for lunch, so I didn't push it.

"You're probably wondering why I invited you for lunch."

"Um, kind of."

"No special reason. I just wanted to big-sister you a little bit, I guess. You're about to be shot out of a cannon and I don't know if you're ready for it."

"Were you? You made it big pretty fast."

"Of course I wasn't. Who's ever ready for it? One minute you're seventeen, scuffling to make the rent, and the next they're running to get your coffee and you're calling the shots. No young girl is able to make that transition without losing herself. I would just hate for you to make the same mistakes I did and do anything stupid."

"Like what?"

"Like, get involved with the wrong man . . . or let anybody talk you into changing agencies. That's the first thing the others will do, try to get you to go with them because they're bigger and they'll say they can do more for you, but that's not true."

"Oh. I'd never leave you, Suzan. You took a chance on me and I appreciate it." She took a bite of meatloaf. I thought she looked a little relieved. "As far as the wrong man goes, who would that be?"

"A Freddy."

I was totally shocked. I had never, never gone near him and had to keep myself from cringing when he came around me. He literally made my skin crawl.

"Suzan, I would *never* sleep with Freddy! Frankly, I hate to say it, but he creeps me out. I have a great boyfriend, a jazz musician named Aurelius Taylor, so please don't worry about that. Ever."

"Oh, I don't think you would sleep with *Freddy.* Not that he wouldn't try. He's stuffing half the girls in the agency. Maybe most of the girls in the agency, fools that they are. But there are a lot of Freddys out there, and you should be on the lookout for them. They're charming when they want to be, but they'll never love any woman more than they love themselves. They have no conscience and think women exist to support and please them. Like a pimp, only with better manners in public."

"I understand. Don't worry. I promise I won't get taken in by a good-looking pimp. Of any kind."

She laughed. "They don't usually have PIMP stamped on their foreheads. Kind of silly advice, isn't it?"

"Not at all. I'll be alert. And don't worry about me going to another agency, either. We're Arkansas girls. We have to stick together."

"Yes, we do. There's not many of us up here." She shook out another cigarette, lit it. "So you'll be meeting with Mrs. Vreeland on Monday. She's a terror on the surface, but kind underneath. Eccentric to the point of nuttiness. She polishes the bottoms of her shoes. I wouldn't call her a liar, but she exaggerates everything. She likes to think she discovers the girls, so let her think that. Dress outrageously. Have fun with it. I know I haven't been the nicest to you, and I'm sorry. Maybe I saw myself and was trying to run you off to save you—who knows? But it looks like you're going to make it in spite of me. My time in the spotlight is over. I've made a mess of my personal life and got screwed out of more than half the agency, but I know a lot about the business. I hope you'll come to me for advice from time to time."

"Of course I will. And forgive me for saying this, but I don't understand why you think your life is over and you have to stay with Freddy. You're not even forty. Why don't you leave him and start over? You could call the new agency something else. Everyone would go with you—nobody would stay with him."

"I wish it were that easy." She looked wistful for a minute. "Have a merry Christmas, Cherry."

40

CHRISTMAS

I woke up to bright sunshine coming through Aurelius's window. It was the first time I had slept in his bed all night long, which was kind of a shock. I guess I was more tired the previous night than I thought. We'd gone to a little theater down the street, Cinema Village, that showed older movies, and saw *True Grit* with John Wayne, who I never particularly liked, but it was set in Dardanelle, Arkansas, near where I grew up. We laughed all the way through. It was so stupid. They had the actress Kim Darby talking in this weird stilted way that was supposed to be an Arkansas accent—Arkansas by way of Hollywood. I just hate phony southern accents. Nobody can do them right. John Wayne didn't even try for an accent, thank goodness. He was playing John Wayne like he always does, except older and drunker with an eye patch, and he swore a lot. My daddy saw it last year, and didn't recommend it, so I hadn't gone. He didn't believe in going to movies, but made an exception for John Wayne, and he was pretty disappointed in ol' John this time out. He'd admired him since he did a movie called *The Fighting Seabees,* the outfit my daddy was in during the war, and Daddy somehow had the idea he was a clean-living, stand-up man, like he played in most of his movies, but I'd read *Photoplay* and knew he'd been married several times and drank and smoked like a fiend. I never told Daddy, though. I didn't want to tarnish his hero. I don't think he's gone to the movies again.

After the movie we had spaghetti at a little place in the Village called Tavola Calda. It was run by a guy named Alfredo, who liked to sit and hang out with the customers and was kind of a bore, but it was Christmas Eve and he bought us each a glass of wine, so we were nice to him. Then we came back to bed. I'm an optimist, I guess, because I was always so attracted to Aurelius and always had such high hopes for the bed thing, and somehow it just never turned out right. He was beginning to really get into what I did for him, and I totally understood Mrs. Digby saying she liked doing it because it was one of the things she did best, but like her, each time, I found myself getting more resentful of him never returning the favor, and I saw why her marriage to Mr. Digby ended after a year. I didn't bring it up again, though. I had too much pride. Another thing that was beginning to get to me was he always took a shower before bed, no matter how late it was, and craftily invited me in with him. It was fun at first, getting all soaped up and slippery together, but I secretly thought he just did it to erase any trace of my natural smell, and that took some of the joy out of it. I had no idea what his natural smell would be, since I'd never smelled it. I never met anybody who took as many showers as he did, and I'd had to get a big bottle of bath oil to soak in my tub since the hot water and soap of all those extra showers dried out my skin. I have to admit I sometimes wistfully thought about Tripp and how he always complained I bathed too much. He would be totally disgusted with me now.

I rubbed my eyes and heard the sound of the shower going. Of course. I turned over and put the covers over my head. He came out rubbing himself with a towel.

"Hey, little girl, get up. It's Christmas!" He came over and dragged the covers off me. "Santa came last night and brought you some goodies."

"Okay, okay!" Under the little tree we'd put up was a pile of beautifully wrapped packages, and I felt bad—my one small package of the silver-and-leather bracelet I'd gotten for him seemed small and mingy in comparison.

"Wow, sweetie, you didn't have to get me so much! These are so beautiful! Did you wrap them yourself?"

"Of course I did. Well, open them, girl!"

"Aren't you going to get dressed?"

"I won't if you won't."

So, stark naked, I tore the gifts open one by one, and every one was perfect. There was an antique dusty-blue velvet bed jacket embroidered in silver thread and trimmed in lace, a lovely mother-of-pearl necklace carved in a peace sign on a delicate silver chain, and a set of three African bracelets made of hammered silver. The biggest box I saved for last, and it was an antique black velvet quilt pieced with green and rose and gold and blue silk, hand-stitched in amber. It was all so exquisite I wanted to cry. I did cry a little.

"Oh, Aurelius, you shouldn't have gotten me all this. Everything is perfect. Just perfect."

I leaped on top of him and hugged him. We fell on the floor and might have made love again, but I really didn't want him to have to take another shower, so instead I handed him his bracelet, which he opened up and put on and said with real enthusiasm that it was the best present he'd ever gotten. We kissed, and it truly was a beautiful Christmas morning. Maybe the next time in bed would be better. I went back to my place, got dressed (after a quick bath in oil), and we went out to Joe Jr.'s for breakfast, then we walked around the Village for an hour or two, just happy to be out in the cold sunshine, happy to be young and together. Everyone on the street looked at us and smiled. I guess we stood out, but I loved it and so did he. The way we looked together was part of the attraction for us.

I called Mama and Daddy from a phone booth, and everyone was there, so I talked to the aunts and uncles, Lucille and her husband, Jim Floyd, who had just gone into partnership with Mr. Wilmerding of Wilmerding's Funeral Service, which would now be Wilmerding and Hawkins, and talked to Tiffany LaDawn, who chattered into the phone telling me about some bear or whatever that Santa had brought her. I couldn't believe the kid could talk like that. It felt like I'd been gone a year.

"I hate it that you're by yourself on Christmas, Cherry," Mama said. "I wish you could have come home."

"I'm not by myself, Mama. Aurelius is here with me. He's the sweetest man in the whole world, and he got me so many beautiful things for

Christmas. I'll write and tell you about them. It's costing too much money to go over them all now." I'd written Mama about Aurelius, of course, told her he was a musician and how handsome he was, but not the most pertinent things, like that we were sleeping together and he was black. I figured that would take care of itself all in good time.

"Oh. Is he standing right there? Let me talk to him. I'd like to wish him a merry Christmas."

"Uh, well, okay." Great. This was stupid. I couldn't think of any reason not to let her talk to him, not without hurting his feelings. I'd just let it go and see what happened. She'd have to find out sooner or later. I handed the phone to him.

"Hello, Mrs. Marshall. Merry Christmas. You've certainly got a beautiful daughter. She's standing out here in the sunlight, and she looks like an angel. She showed me your picture and I can see where she gets her good looks from." He was smooth, talking in that deep caramel voice that melted me. I wondered if it was melting my mother.

"Yes, we're out here in the park. . . . It's cold, but it should be cold. It's Christmas. . . . Um-hmm. Yes. . . . Excuse me, Mrs. Marshall." He put his hand over the phone. "Oh, honey, do you have more change? I don't have any and the operator says time is running out." I dug around in my purse and handed him some coins. "There. Sorry. . . . Yes, she sure is. . . . I'm proud of her, too. . . . She's going to be famous, that's for sure. . . . I will. . . . I'll do my best. Do you want to say good-bye?" He handed the phone to me.

"So, Mama, isn't he charming? He's real good-looking, too."

"Cherry, is that man black? He sure sounds like it. What kind of a name is Aurelius? Where is he from? Who are his people?"

"I love you, too, Mama. I'll write you tomorrow. Y'all have a great dinner. I sure will miss your chicken and dressing. Oh, the operator is cutting in again. Tell Daddy I love him, too. Bye."

"Well, I think that went well. Your mother is a sweetheart."

"What did she say to you?"

"Not much. Just to keep you out of trouble. I said I would try, but that'll be a hard thing to do."

"You better believe it. The only question is who's going to keep *you* out of trouble?"

When we got back, Mrs. Digby had her door open and invited us in for eggnog and cookies. I ran up to get her present, a pink silk camisole and tap-panty set, and Aurelius gave her a bone-china teacup and saucer with a lily-of-the-valley pattern, which she opened first and cooed over, giving him a little kiss on the lips, which got her all giggly.

"Wait until you're alone to open mine," I said. "It's only for the eyes you want to see it."

She opened it anyhow, her mouth dropped in delight, and we all laughed. Her eyes sparkled and I could see the old showgirl peek out of her.

"I'll save this for a *special* occasion."

"Maybe for some Italian?"

"You never can tell, can you?" She had a twinkle in her eye, and by golly it wouldn't surprise me if she really did have an Italian or two in her closet.

Aurelius had to work that night, so I went over to the loft for dinner with Sal and Lale. They had ordered a turkey dinner complete with all the trimmings—dressing, sweet potatoes, gravy, apple pie, the works—from Balducci's, the best gourmet food store in the Village. There were twelve of us at dinner—some models I knew, a couple of photographers, and friends of Sal's. As far as I could tell, Lale didn't have anybody special as his date, although a few of the girls were simpering around him like the pea brains they were. There I go, buying into the dumb-model thing, but these ones really were.

Lale and Sal had put up a ten-foot-tall Christmas tree and decorated it with what looked like the booty from a Mardi Gras float, tons of sparkly ropes of beads, glass balls, and twinkling lights. It was gorgeous and was the perfect size for the high ceilings.

I had managed to finish the portrait, and after dinner, we all gathered around for the unveiling. I sat Sal down in a chair across from it, and Lale put his hands over his eyes. Then I whipped off the sheet and everybody cheered. It was Miss Sally, in Technicolor, wearing her red sparkly Marilyn Monroe dress like the one from *Gentlemen Prefer Blondes,* feather tiara and all. It nearly drove me crazy painting those sequins, but it was definitely worth it. Sal just sat there and tears came into his eyes. Finally, he got up and hugged me, holding me and rocking back and forth.

"It's the most beautiful thing I've ever seen. Thank you, thank you, Miss Cherry."

"When are you going to do mine?" Lale asked. Everybody else said they wanted theirs done, too, so I just said I'd do them when I had time, which would be never. It was like that at school, every girl wanting me to draw a picture of their boyfriends. You just can't keep doing it for free. One of these days maybe I'd do them for money, but right now this one was for love. Sal had done a lot for me, which I could never repay. He couldn't take his eyes off it.

"I'm going to put the sheet back on it if you don't stop staring at it and talk to us," one of the girls said. He laughed and popped open a bottle of champagne, but I caught him sneaking looks at it the rest of the night.

After everyone left, Lale, Sal, and I opened our presents. My big one for Sal was the painting, but I gave him the African batik anyhow, which he seemed to like, tying it around himself like a sarong and doing a little dance. Lale put on the silver-and-leather necklace, and gave me a small kiss on half my lips. It was going to be full on the lips but I turned my head a fraction at the last minute. It was weird—my lip tingled where his touched it, and both of us were a little embarrassed. Then he handed me a small box. It was the size of a ring box. In fact, it was a ring. Not a fancy ring, certainly not an engagement kind of ring, but a wide silver band set with a cool moonstone. It fit my right middle finger like it had been measured. It was so beautiful, so comfortable, that I didn't want to take it off. It was just the right amount of expensive.

"Lale, it . . . it's . . . perfect. Thank you so much." I looked up at him and his eyes were the very color of the glint in the stone. He leaned down to kiss me and this time I turned my face toward him, feeling a stirring down inside that I couldn't stop from happening. Our lips almost touched, I could smell the sweet champagne of his breath, feel the heat from his skin, but Sal, who had been looking at the painting some more, came over and clapped his hands just in time.

"Break it up, break it up! Don't get all mushy on me, guys. Cherry, you haven't opened *my* present yet!" He dragged out a huge box, the size of a major appliance. I collected myself and was half grateful for the interruption, half annoyed. Lale was just annoyed, and grumped over to get himself another glass of champagne. I ripped open the paper. Inside was a smaller box, and inside that was a smaller one.

"What on earth . . . ? Sal, this is ridiculous! If there's a tiny little box in the bottom of this thing you will be in so much trouble!"

On the boxes went, more paper, more unwrapping, until finally one the size of a dress box revealed black and gold tissue paper. I delicately opened the paper and there was an exquisite antique dress from the thirties. It was done in chevrons of alternating black and gold sequins on fine net chiffon, had a plunging neckline in front and back, and could have been worn by Jean Harlow or Carole Lombard.

"Oh, Sal. Oh, my gosh. Where did you find this? This is the most beautiful dress I've ever seen in my life. It's so delicate, I'll be afraid to wear it."

"You save it for a special occasion, my sweetheart. I got it from a friend of mine named Harriet Love—isn't that *delicious*? She has a wonderful store in the Village. I throw a lot of business her way and she owed me one. I wanted to get you the shoes to match, but well . . ."

"I know, I know. You don't have to rub it in. People were tiny back in those days. Poor nutrition. I don't see how they kept from falling over, trying to walk around on feet the size those Chinese footbound women had. You tell Harriet Love I'm there as soon as her doors open tomorrow."

The three of us hugged, Lale now over his pout, then we finished off the bottle of champagne.

41

VOGUE

Dear Baby,

Did you have a good Christmas? What did Leo get you? I wish we could just pick up the phone and call each other, but it is so hard with no phone in my room. You can always call Mrs. Digby, though, if you really need to talk to me and I'll go down to the corner and call you back.

Big news! I went to *Vogue* on Monday and met with Diana Vreeland! I had no idea what to expect, but Suzan said if she called me in, it was because she wanted to use me, and I should make a memorable entrance. She is the most vibrant person I have ever met, so I tried to dress up for it. I wore a chamois skirt with a handkerchief hem, my new green lace-up boots, a huge turquoise squash-blossom necklace I got at the flea market that weighs about ten pounds, and a hunter-green turtleneck sweater. I had a scarf of black and rust and turquoise and green wrapped around my head, and two big turquoise bracelets on my arms that were so heavy I felt like I was lifting weights. She said I looked *divine,* her favorite word.

I have to say I was a little nervous, not the least because of something weird that happened right before I went in, which I'll tell you about in a minute, but first I have to tell you about Mrs. Vreeland. Her office walls are painted in bright-red lacquer and she has leopard-skin carpet over all the floors. Not real leopard skin, of course, though I bet she would use it if she could. There were walls of black lacquered bookcases, the furniture was black lacquer, except for a couple of good wicker chairs, and there was a *huge* cork inspiration board with tons of pictures and scraps of things she sees and cuts out from everywhere. She had my Diamonds & Ermine ad up there, which thrilled me no end. There was a wonderful portrait of her in profile behind her desk. She really is the bravest woman I know, to have her portrait done in profile with that nose. I thought at first she was ugly, but the more I'm around her, the more beautiful she becomes. Beautiful is not really the word. More like overwhelming. Do I sound like a girl with a crush? I guess I am. Because she really wants me to do stuff for *Vogue*!! We talked about several layouts she's planning, a big one she wants to do in *Russia*! Can you believe it? I never even took French in school because I figured I'd never travel outside the U.S., and now I'll be going halfway around the world. I really had limited horizons then, didn't I? Mrs. Vreeland went on and on about Russia for thirty minutes, and I wish I could remember everything she said, she has such a . . . baroque . . . way of talking and she *adores* Russia so much. She described the onion domes in great detail, ones like those on St. Basil's in Red Square that look like they're made out of Christmas candy and others that are gilded in pure gold; the White Nights of spring when it never gets dark and people walk their babies in the park at midnight in what seems like eternal blue twilight. Everything looks like a painting then, deep cobalt skies dotted with stars and washed with light toward the horizon, outlining dark-green Maxfield Parrish trees. All the buildings are painted sherbet colors of pink, golden yellow, pistachio green, and pale turquoise with trim like white cake frosting. Leningrad is the most beautiful city in the world, next to Paris, she said, built on canals, but Moscow is earthier, heavy, strong, and dark, and is the soul of Russia. We'll go to both places. She sees me in the deep snow in a birch forest, and in those little weathered moss-green and cerulean-blue dachas, the ones right out of *Peter and the Wolf* that are trimmed in unpainted wooden lace. It will be a lot of fur coats and incredible clothes, of course, and a white horse will somehow be involved. That was important to her, me on a white horse in the snow. I was afraid to tell her I had only ridden one those few times at Cassie's. I'll just have to fake it. There will be a whole team going, of course, I'm not the only model, and *Richard Avedon* is going to be the photographer! I keep having to pinch myself—it is so fantastic it doesn't seem real. The pictures won't be in the magazine until the winter issue next year, but she has to do them early to take advantage of the snow. She also wants to do a bathing-suit layout for summer with my old friend Ron Bonetti as the photographer. He's been doing more work for them and this will be a big deal for both of us, kind of a trial, I guess. We'll go to Miami and shoot on the beach with the pastel Art Deco buildings. She likes the idea of such a pale person as me out on the beach, hiding under umbrellas and hats, scarves and sunglasses, trying to escape from the sun while being right under its eye. She also has this great idea of me moon-bathing on the beach, under a full moon at night, the waves shining silver and reflecting on the dark sand and palm trees. Remember Tripp once said I looked like I was made on the moon? I know, I have to stop thinking about Tripp. I will. I promise. Anyhow, that Miami one we'll do right after the New Year, as soon as the moon is full. It's so weird how these things work. They're always shooting the next season in the middle of the opposite one—summer in winter, fall in spring. I don't know really how they know what is going to be the fashion that far in advance, but they always do. It's like some kind of telepathy they have, these designers doing things that are all in sync with each other, like suddenly everybody at once decrees midis are in style, or gauchos or empire waistlines or whatever. Although how much of a secret can their designs be, really, since there are tons of people who know what each one is doing and I'm sure everyone has their spies? Anyhow, I feel like I have my ticket to ride on the rocket and am standing in line.

Which brings me to the weird thing that happened right before I had my appointment. I had a couple of hours to kill, since I had a go-see earlier, so I went to this shop downtown called Love Saves the Day. It's a crazy antique clothing shop that also sells a lot of other stuff, costume jewelry, old Fiestaware and used toys like Barbie and G.I. Joe, and is really cool. I picked out a few things and went to the dressing room, which was behind a door curtained off into two cubicles, to try them on. I had my clothes off and was putting on a rayon print dress from the forties—you know, the kind with the zipper in the side, which is a little hard to get over your head, so I had it half over my head with my arms sticking up in the air, tightly pinned, when someone came into the other side. I heard sounds of them undressing, and after a couple of minutes the curtain between the cubicles swooped open, and standing there was a naked man. A really *good-looking* naked man. Holding a huge penis. I was in such shock that I couldn't move, even if I wanted to, since I was stuck in the dress, trying to get it off up around my shoulders. Thank goodness he didn't try to touch me. He just stood there and said in this cute French accent, "Don't you tink I am beeg? Don't you tink I am beautiful?" I was working as fast as I could to get the dress off without screaming. I said, "Um, yes, you're big and beautiful, but I have a boyfriend and I'm not interested in going out with anybody new. So let me get dressed, now, please, and shut the curtain." He smiled like he didn't understand a word I said and repeated again, "Don't you tink I am beeg? Don't you tink I am beautiful?" "Are you from Paris," I said, trying to buy myself some time as I threw on my clothes. "You sound like you have a French accent." He only repeated what he had said before, and still he didn't come closer. By this time I had gotten my clothes on and gathered up my stuff, so I squeezed by, trying not to touch him, and said, "Well, nice talking to you. I have to go now. I have an appointment."

I slammed the door shut and ran out to get help, but the only other person in the store was a little old lady who was at the cash register. I hated to scare her, but I had to tell her there was a naked man in the dressing room flashing himself. The two of us waited for him to come out, practically standing up on the balls of our feet ready to run, but he didn't, and we didn't know what to do. She couldn't leave the store and I didn't want to leave her there alone with him. So she suggested I run next door to the coffee shop and get the cook. He was a big tattooed muscled-up guy in a sleeveless undershirt and paper cap, a stained apron tied around him—a huge hunk of comforting New York man. He went to the dressing room and pounded on the door. "Hey, buddy," he said, "you gotta get out of there or we're calling the cops." The door opened right up, and out came the most perfect man you've ever seen. He looked like Alain Delon, wearing a three-piece suit and a snap-brimmed hat. He carried an umbrella and a briefcase, and had a newspaper tucked under his arm. He ducked his head, tipped his hat, and walked out the door just like a gentleman of your acquaintance passing on the street. The cook shook his head, muttering to himself, then went back to his coffee shop. While the old lady and I collected our wits, we talked about all the crazy things that had happened to us in New York.

Finally, I left, and leaning against the wall a couple of doors down, was a pimp-looking guy wearing a purple satin shirt who growled as I walked by, "Hey, honey. Want to f***?" (You can fill in the blanks.) I just about died. I couldn't believe it. I mean, what are the chances of running into two nuts in fifteen minutes? Even in New York? I kept on walking and he didn't try to follow, but a half-block later I realized . . . I'd left my portfolio in Love Saves the Day. My heart dropped into my stomach. I'd have to go back and get it. I had to have it for Mrs. Vreeland. So I took a deep breath and walked back, past the guy, who obviously took it as a sign I was interested in his proposition. When I came out again he was there, in front of the store waiting for me, and started walking down the street beside me. I looked straight ahead, trying to concentrate on something other than what he was saying, when a cab with its light on miraculously drove up. I leaped out into the street, flagged it down, practically getting run over, and jumped in. As the door shut and I was safe, I said to the purple-shirt guy, "Don't you get slapped a lot?" He just shrugged and said, "Yeah, but I get f***** a lot." Then he walked on, whistling a tune.

So anyhow, my blood was good and pumped by the time I got to *Vogue*. In the cab, I spritzed myself all over with Chanel No. 5, like Mrs. Vreeland had advised, to cover the flop sweat, and then had my interview. Is this a crazy town or what?

Now it's nearly midnight and I am going to take a hot bath (in oil) and go to bed. I haven't heard Aurelius come in yet. The weird thing about living right next to him is that we know what the other one is doing, and I'm not sure I like that. I have no idea where all this is heading, but I do really like him. I just have to ask myself if I love him, and the answer to that, according to Mama's rule, has to be no.

Please write soon and let me know what is going on with you and Leo. Do you have to ask yourself if you love him?

I know I love YOU,
Cherry

42

LEAVING FOR OZ

The highway from Little Rock to New York seemed as long as the yellow-brick road, except Cassie didn't have a wise scarecrow, cowardly lion, or kindhearted tin man to keep her company. No little dog Toto. Just her Blue Bird of Happiness sitting on the dashboard. It hadn't been at all hard to leave Nick and the big empty house. She just wrote him a note and left. He might not even see it until the next morning.

What a life it would be to be married to a doctor, never seeing him, always playing second fiddle to the hundreds of patients who loved him and thought he was God Almighty. No wife can ever give a man that. Not that Nick had suggested she marry him, but he'd taken off early again last night and they'd gone out for dinner at a nice Italian restaurant. He told her about his marriage to Nicole and how, yes, he had done a little surgery on her. And how she had left him two weeks before her thirtieth birthday.

"So what kind of surgery did you do on her, if you don't mind me asking?"

"As a matter of fact, I did her nose."

"Ah. Wasn't that weird, operating on your own wife?"

"Not really. When I operate, all I think about is the work at hand. You have to."

"You really love doing noses, don't you?"

"I'm the *Michelangelo* of noses." He used a funny Italian accent and tried to smile, almost made it.

"I'm sure you are, but for me, I don't know. The whole beauty thing, with the expensive clothes and plastic surgery and all just seems so . . . empty and silly."

"Most people don't think that way. Some women will do anything to be beautiful, always did. Back in the eighteen-hundreds, they used to faint from pulling their corsets so tight it cut off the blood flow. Some of them even died from kidney and liver failure. A little nose job or face-lift is nothing compared to that."

"I know you're right. My ex-boyfriend is making a fortune as a model in New York right now. Maybe I just don't like what having good looks does to people. Anyhow, I'll just keep the nose I have for now, so you might as well give up on that one."

"You don't have to get your nose fixed. You're a beautiful girl, just like you are. I always have to try to make someone that little bit more perfect. I'm also clumsy with women. I haven't dated that much since Nicole left. I don't have the time for it."

"I guess you didn't have time for marriage, either, did you?" He didn't answer. "I'm sorry. That was rude. You've been nice to me. I appreciate you letting me stay at your place, but I'm going to have to get on with my life. I wish you luck in finding a woman who can deal with a husband who's never there."

"Maybe that's why doctors have such high divorce rates."

"Yeah. It's a good thing they make so much money." He did smile at that.

He brought her home, then went to the hospital and came in late, as usual, but this time she was awake and heard the doorknob to her room gently turn. He waited a moment, tried it again, then went away. She fell asleep, knowing he wouldn't be back.

She left the next day, a note on the stove, his dinner warming in the oven.

Dear Nick,

I couldn't wait around to say good-bye. Thanks for everything.

I hope you find your dream girl. Maybe a nurse would understand.

I'm sure there are a lot of them just waiting for you to look their way. I know of one brunette O.R. nurse who was sure mad when she thought I was with you.

Adiós,
Cassie

Then she got into the Thunderbird and headed east, her heart beating faster at the proposition of seeing Lale again. The only thing she had to go on was Cherry's address and a map of Manhattan she'd gotten in a bookstore in Little Rock. Wouldn't Cherry be shocked when she opened her door and Cassie was standing there? Maybe Lale would be in her room. Maybe they'd be in bed. She wouldn't think about that.

One thing she knew, though, is that they *would* be surprised when they saw her.

43

MIAMI MOONLIGHT

By the time the plane touched down in Miami, I felt like an old hand at air travel. I didn't know what a big *Vogue* shoot would be like, but this one must not have been a big one, because it was just me and Ron Bonetti, a funny little gay guy named Gerard Robinson who was the hair and makeup person, and the editor who was paying the bills and overseeing everything, a woman with heavy bangs and thick glasses named Rita Todesco who seemed like a weird choice to work for *Vogue,* since she wore long black shapeless dresses and sensible shoes, and seemed like she didn't give a hoot about fashion. I guess she was good at details. Permits would have to be gotten, I suspected, for shooting on a public beach, and other things I couldn't even imagine. Ron brought most of the props and stuff.

Ron said that Mrs. Vreeland had called him into the office a few days before and told him what she liked most about his photographs was the *sensuality* in them. She knew he could capture the *feeling* of the ocean air, the *scent* of the sea, the *texture* of the sand, the *grit* in the bathing suit. She wanted the *heat* and *masculinity* of the sun to come through in every shot, as if it was seeking out this delicious pale morsel to ravage, and she was running from it. She told him her ideas for *moon-bathing,* the contrast to sunbathing, and how the cool light of the moon should make *love* to me and I should *surrender* to it, rather than hide under wraps, as its light moon-tanned me into whiteness. Ron did her voice perfectly, with a word in practically every sentence emphasized. I was okay with the moon, but a little bit worried about the actual time spent out in the sun because, no joke, after trying and failing miserably for years to get tan when I was a teenager, I always got a horrible blistery burn every time I went swimming. I hated suntan lotion, especially Coppertone, which made me feel sticky and yucky and the smell brought back memories of the sharp chlorine of the public swimming pool or the fishy tea-colored water of the lake, and the inevitable burns. I always had a feeling suntan lotion was somehow bad for you, too, maybe even poisonous, since your skin drinks the chemicals up and puts them into your bloodstream. People who make that stuff don't really care how safe it is, as long as it works. The bottom line was that I just didn't get out in the sun much unless I had on a hat and long sleeves, and if I went swimming I'd dip in and out and then lie under an umbrella. I was never much of a swimmer anyhow, and besides, it ruined my makeup. That was something I never wanted to be seen without, and swimming with my face in the water was definitely out, so really, why bother?

But Mrs. Vreeland's visions of the shots were beautiful, and I think she also picked Ron because he was a master with lighting. These ideas sounded like they would need a master to pull them off. Mrs. Vreeland didn't worry about how something was going to get done—she just saw it in her head and figured we would find a way to make it happen. She apparently liked the small jobs he'd done for her, and this was his first big opportunity to do editorial. He was totally pumped, and so was I. Like Ron said the first time we met, we were going to be together in *Vogue*!

Gerard I met for the first time at the airport. He was little but muscular and had really short hair, which was kind of weird when everyone else had long hair. He was dressed all in black, a sleeveless T-shirt (showing off fresh bright tattoos of roses and fighting cocks with big tail feathers), tight bell-bottom jeans, and a black leather jacket thrown over his shoulder. He seemed pretty laid-back, but then he'd obviously done it all before and was probably jaded by travel. Rita didn't say much at all to us, just introduced herself and then went to the gift shop and got a bunch of magazines and candy. Just before we went through the line to get on the plane, Gerard pulled out a package and asked me if I'd carry it in my bag for him, that he didn't have enough room in his own, so I said sure and crammed it in, although I didn't have all that much extra room, either. It was a little cheeky of him, I thought, but he was the one who would be doing my face and hair and we had to be together for four days, so I was nice about it. He had a transistor radio clipped to his belt with an earphone and was bopping up and down to the music until I had to nicely ask him to stop it. He was beginning to get on my nerves. He was even shorter than Ron, and I felt like the center pole in the circus tent as the four of us picked up our carry-ons and got in line for the plane. The guy at the gate was going through some of the bags, and opened Gerard's and Ron's, but waved me on through with a wink, which I returned.

I had a terrible time with the small amount of leg room on these planes, and couldn't cross my legs unless I practically jammed my knees into my mouth. I had to sit at an angle, legs out partway into the aisle until the food cart bumped into my legs a few times, then I made Ron change seats with me and I got the window. He had no such problems. Gerard and Rita sat behind us, Gerard still listening to the radio. I don't know how anybody can stand having racket in their ears all the time. I need a little peace and quiet, especially in a plane, which might fall out of the sky at any minute, so you need to be able to hear any unusual noise it makes.

"Boeuf Bourguignon or Chicken à la King?" I voted for the beef and the stewardess put down a little plastic plate with some kind of meat smothered in brown gravy and Crayola-bright carrots and peas on it.

"Boeuf Bourguignon. Hmm." I eyed the gray meat. "Looks like the old Swanson Salisbury Steak TV dinners we used to eat back in the fifties. They were part of the Amana food plan that came with our freezer."

"I think it *is* the old Swanson Salisbury Steak TV dinner from the fifties. They got a great deal on the leftovers when Amana discontinued the food plan." Ron sawed away, trying to cut his beef, which was hard, given how small the plate was and how little elbow room we had.

We ate it, drank our drinks—Coke for me and vodka for Ron—in the small flimsy plastic cups and burped a little. I guess with that tiny kitchen the stewardesses had to work in we couldn't expect real food.

"I have something to tell you, Cherry," Ron said after the stewardess picked up our plates.

"Sounds serious."

"Becky left me."

"Oh, Ron, I'm so sorry. What happened?"

"She fell in love. With Grace."

"Grace?"

"Another woman."

"You're kidding."

"I kid you not. Ironic, isn't it? I'm the one who had the career with beautiful women, and all the time I thought she was jealous of me, she was doing the same thing."

"Well . . . if she was . . . like that, why did she marry you in the first place?"

"That's what women do. They get married and have kids. Except we never got around to the kids part. I just thought she had a low sex drive. The woman she's with now has two. Kids, not sex drives. Becky and Grace can both be mothers. Kind of confusing to have two mothers, though, wouldn't you say? It's weird."

"Yeah, that would be a little confusing. Which one would be the home-room mother? Would they take turns baking the cookies? But then, I guess life's weird in general. Everybody's just got their own kind of weirdness. Are you okay?"

"I'm okay. I mean, I've known for a long time it had to end—it was just a shock that this is the way it went down. Frankly, it's not losing Becky so much as it is changing all the habits. You know, when you live with somebody, you're connected by a whole string of experiences, each one a thin cord—like she knows how to make your eggs, what kind of underwear you wear. Your music. Your bad dreams. The time she went with you to the emergency room when you cut your finger. All those cords wind into a thick rope that holds you together, and when you break up, it's like somebody took an ax and cut them all at once. It's a shock. You have to start all over again." He paused, looked at his hands, flexed his fingers. He didn't have a wedding-band crease because as far as I knew he had never worn a wedding band. Not in front of me anyhow. "So how's *your* love life?" he finally said.

"It's great. I'm seeing Aurelius Taylor, the saxophone player I told you about. He's the sweetest guy in the whole world."

"Uh-oh. Sweet. That's the kiss of death, like a girl saying about you

'He has a good personality,' when you really want them to say you're a sexy big hunk o' love."

"He *is* a sexy big hunk o' love."

"Liar."

"Stop it! He is, too."

"Suuure, he is. I can tell by the excitement in your voice."

"Oh, shut up. What do you know?" He was so annoying. The worst thing was that there was truth in what he said.

We stayed at the Albion Hotel, a few blocks off South Beach, a beautiful old Art Deco hotel. I had my own room, but we had to use it for the hair and makeup. It was warm, and I hadn't realized how heady the soft Miami air would be, or how exotic the palm trees were, which I'd only seen in pictures. Shucking off my coat and putting on sandals and a slinky silk dress, I felt like I was in some movie like *South Pacific* or something.

The first night, we all went out to a Cuban restaurant, which I loved because it had rice and pinto beans and pork, which I grew up on, but also exotic stuff like fried plantains, which were kind of like bananas only not as sweet. There was great Cuban music and we all danced, except for Rita, who went back to the hotel early. I guess part of her appeal for *Vogue* was that she wasn't a party girl. Gerard, on the other hand, was a wild man on the dance floor, flinging me around and then disappearing like a whirligig into the crowd to dance with perfect strangers, leaving me alone at the mercy of every guy who wanted to cut in, and I began to wonder if he might be on something. I had given him back the package he gave me to carry on the plane, and when I asked him what it was, he said casually, just like he was ordering breakfast or something, "Oh, it's drugs. LSD. Ether. Pot. A few uppers and downers. Poppers." Ether? Was he going to give himself an operation? What was that all about? I nearly freaked. I'd had all that stuff in my bag and if I'd been caught, I'd probably be in prison! He was *not* going to get me to carry it back on the plane, so he might as well forget about that. I bit my tongue to keep from telling him off, because we still had to work together, but after this shoot was over, no way, José, would I ever do him any more favors.

The first morning went all right—the sun was out, the beach was beautiful, and the bathing suits and hats were cute. Rita was still in one of her black dresses, but she'd added a straw hat and big sunglasses and changed her orthopedic shoes for orthopedic sandals. Some of the shots were in the water, which was a lot colder than I thought Florida water would be, and Rita waded right in and put Band-Aids over my nipples, which stick out anyhow, but *really* stood up when the cold water hit them. Can't have nipple bumps in *Vogue,* I guess. It was pretty embarrassing. Then a big wind blew up, and the sand just about wrecked everything. It's hard to look into the camera and be sexy with sand blowing right in your eyes. We had to keep stopping and redoing the makeup, especially the lip gloss, which got like sandpaper and gritted in my teeth, and Gerard had to stand and hold a big silver reflector to keep the wind out of my face and give it more light. He was almost lifted up and blown out to sea a time or two, but finally the wind died down enough to get the shots. We worked all morning, then stopped for a nice lunch by the pool at the hotel. I felt like a glamorous ad for some exotic drink or something, out there in a fuchsia bikini, big hat, and sunglasses, drinking my fruit drink, eating little sandwiches, just like in the movies. I could get used to this. Then we went back upstairs to my room to redo the makeup, and Gerard pulled out a pair of scissors.

"I think we need to cut some of that hair off, Cherry. You would look much better with a cute, short do."

"Uh, I don't think so, Gerard. Mrs. Vreeland didn't say anything about me cutting my hair, and I just got it grown out from a bad haircut my cousin gave me when she was going to beauty school. I don't think Clairol would like it if I had short hair, and I do a lot of work for them. Let's not cut it." He was acting a little weird and for a minute I was afraid he was going to attack me with the scissors anyhow. I'd worked too hard to get my hair to grow out to let some hairdresser I'd just met cut it all off on a whim.

While I was talking, he pulled out a handkerchief and poured some liquid from a metal bottle onto it. Then he stuck a corner of the handkerchief into his mouth and started sucking on it. It smelled sharp and astringent. The room all of a sudden seemed too close. I was getting woozy-headed.

"What is that you're doing, Gerard?"

"Ether. Want some? If you only take a little you get the best high. Too much and you pass out, but what a great sleep!" He laughed, a high-pitched sound that was slightly demented.

"You want to cut my hair while you're high on ether? I don't think so." I got up and opened the window and took some deep breaths.

"Okay. Want to see my new tattoo?"

He pulled up his shirt, and across his belly was a rainbow that plunged down under his waistband and ended . . . well, I could imagine what the pot of gold at the end of the rainbow was.

"That's lovely, Gerard." He started to unzip his pants. "But I don't need to see the end of the rainbow. Listen, I really need to go to the bathroom. Why don't you take a little break, go back to your room and have your ether, and then I'll call you and we'll get back to work? Okay?" He shrugged and went out of the room, sucking on the rag.

"*Ron!* Get in here!" I screamed into the phone, and Ron came running in.

"You have to get rid of that guy. He's going to get all of us thrown in jail. Call Rita. I'm not working with him. I'll just do my own makeup—I'm better at it than he is anyhow. I don't want to see him again, please."

"What did he do? Calm down, Cherry." When I told him, he was in a worse state than I was, and I was calming down. He called Rita and the upshot was that Gerard was back on the plane that afternoon. I don't know what he did with the drugs. They're probably clogging up the pipes at the Albion or making some poor fish stoned.

Anyhow, the moon-bathing shot went well, and Rita even loosened up and wore a beige dress. I was so tired after the night shoot, though, that I didn't want to go out, so we just had a little dinner in the hotel dining room. Rita ate with us, then excused herself.

"Stay and have another glass of wine?"

"Sure, Ron. How are the pictures? Getting some good ones?"

"Oh, yeah. Lots of good ones. This is going to be big for both of us. When we get back to New York, I have some great ideas for tests. You know Guy Bourdin?" I shook my head. "He's incredible, one of the best. He's been doing these dark, sinister fashion shots. Real moody stuff. I want to take them even farther. Get this: There you are at a roadside hamburger joint in the middle of the night, wearing an Oscar de la Renta evening gown, jewels, makeup, nails, hair done up. The guy behind the counter, a greasy-spoon kind of guy in a dirty white apron, is making a burger for you, and in the bushes to the right, a guy in a black mask is lurking, holding a gun."

"And then what?"

"What do you mean? That's it. It's a fashion shot."

"A fashion shot? Ha. Fashion *shot.* Get it? You made a joke."

"Of course it's a fashion shot. Look. It's a story—there you are, in an expensive evening dress, out in the middle of nowhere at night, eating a greasy burger, looking fabulous and bored, all by yourself, and there is a guy waiting to . . . what? We don't know. Is he going to rob you of your jewels? Kidnap you? Wait until you go and then rob the burger guy? What are you doing out there in the first place? See? It sets up this air of mystery. You write your own ending. You gotta love it."

"I do kind of love it." Actually, I did. I always liked a good mystery. And I figured it was weird enough to be right up Mrs. Vreeland's alley.

"Or how about this one . . . you're holding a raging dog on a leash, a Doberman or pit bull or one of those. He's baring his teeth, lunging at the camera, and you hold the leash with all your strength with fingers and arms covered in rows of diamond bracelets and rings. You have on an exquisite evening dress by Bill Blass, which is in danger of being shredded by the dog at any minute. Your hair is wild, your teeth are bared, too, with the effort of controlling the dog. Like it?"

"Not so much. Maybe not lunging dogs, Ron, although the concept is great. Maybe you could get Rhonda for that one. It sounds more like her kind of thing."

"Okay. Maybe I will. But what do you think? Think Mrs. Vreeland will go for it?"

"I think Mrs. Vreeland will love those. As soon as we get back, let's do some tests and I bet she gives us sixteen pages."

She gave us twelve for the sun and moon shots! I couldn't believe it. Mama would die.

44

THE FIRST DAY

Hitting New York traffic after days of boring freeway and hamburger joints was a shock. As she came in on the New Jersey Turnpike, the skyline appeared, like a hazy mirage in the clouds, then she went down into the darkness of the Lincoln Tunnel and was shot out into Manhattan traffic. There was so much to try to see all at once, so many cars coming at her from all directions so fast, that Cassie had to pull over at a gas station on Eleventh Avenue, catch her breath, and study the map. It looked like it would be pretty easy to find Twelfth Street. The streets were mostly laid out like a checkerboard, and numbered. She pulled back out onto Eleventh Avenue, took it slow, and tried not to flinch when a car whizzed around her, like the driver was in a demolition derby. She turned on Fourteenth and headed down Seventh Avenue and started looking for a parking place, which turned out to be not so easy. Maybe it was a sign. All the way, the closer she got to New York, the more she realized she dreaded seeing Lale and Cherry. She had made a mistake in coming, but it was too late. She couldn't turn around and go back now. She'd come too far. If nothing else, she just wanted Lale to look her in the eyes and tell her he didn't love her, never had, and she should go home and leave him alone. At least she would have heard it straight from his mouth. Why couldn't men ever be honest with a woman? Instead of breaking up with them, clean and tidy, they just stopped calling. One of her guy friends had done that to his girlfriend, and when she told him it was a chicken thing to do, he said he knew it, but he didn't want to hurt her feelings and she'd get the idea if he never called again. It would be easier. Right. Easier on *him*. At least Lale wrote her a note and left her the car and sent the money, so he wasn't all bad. She couldn't have loved him as much as she did if he was all bad. She wouldn't have been in that much pain if he was all bad.

She drove around the block of West Twelfth Street for the umpteenth time and, miracle of miracles, a car pulled out, and she grabbed the space. It was not at all like she expected New York to be. Somehow she didn't think there would be any trees here, just cement and tall buildings. The houses looked old and like the ones she'd seen in movies that took place back in the 1800s. The street was tree-lined and cleaner than she thought. Snuffy had told her how dirty the city was. Snuffy was her fount of information about New York, since he came so often, but he didn't get to every single place in the city. Just the liquor warehouses.

She stretched, got out her coat and purse, and walked down the street toward the address on the envelope of Cherry's last letter. She stood in front of the house, a red-brick four-story building that looked much like the others on the street, started to go toward the door, then changed her mind and walked on past it to the corner of Sixth Avenue. Now that she was here, it wasn't so easy to just knock on Cherry's door and confront her. Maybe she'd have something to eat first. That would settle her nervous stomach. She went into a coffee shop called Joe Jr.'s and sat at a booth by the door.

"What'll it be, miss?"

"Hamburger, please. Tomato, pickles. No onions. Salad on the side."

"What to drink?"

"Do you have Tab?"

"Sure.

He wrote it all down, yelled out the order to the cook behind the counter, and laid down a fork, spoon, and knife wrapped in a paper napkin. He filled a glass with Tab, set it down in front of her, wiped up a little spill.

"Thanks. Do y'all have any lemon?"

"We do." He put a couple of lemon wedges on a small plate and set them down. She squeezed them into the glass. He watched her.

"You're not from around here, are you?"

"Why, how can you tell?"

He laughed. "You don't sound like you're from around here. Where you from?"

"Arkansas."

"No kidding. I know somebody from there."

"Really? Who?"

"A pretty model. Big girl. White-blond hair."

"Is her name Cherry?"

"That's the one. You a friend of hers?"

"Yeah. I'm Cassie. An old friend. I'm here to visit her."

"You are? I thought she was off on a job. She told me this morning she was going to Miami to shoot some pictures for . . . *Vogue* magazine, I think. She left right after she had breakfast. Her usual. Scrambled eggs and cheese Danish."

"Yep, that's her usual, all right. Do you know when she's coming back? I kind of wanted to surprise her."

"I don't know. Why don't you call up the magazine? They could tell you."

"I might do that. Well. If she's not home, maybe you could tell me of a good cheap hotel to spend a few days . . . what was your name?"

"Oh, I'm Tony. Sure. Try the Chelsea. It's on Twenty-third between Seventh and Eighth. Just up the street."

"Thanks, Tony. You're a big help."

"Arkansas grows some pretty women, that's for sure. Maybe I'll take a trip down there one of these days."

"You do that. We're just hanging off the trees."

Cassie ate her burger, then went to the phone booth and looked up *Vogue* in the book. The address was 420 Lexington Avenue. Maybe she should go there instead of calling. She doubted anybody would tell her anything on the phone.

But first she needed to get settled, clean up, collect herself. Think a little more. She made her way north and found the Chelsea on Twenty-third Street. It was a tall but not-too-tall building with wrought-iron balconies and strange, different-size dormers and windows on the top, and looked like something she could afford. There was a parking space right in front, a good sign, so she went in and rented a room. The lobby was shabby but homey, a huge old iron staircase rising up the middle, but the room she got was nothing special. It was painted a drab green color, with an old four-poster bed, a small dresser, a table, and a little TV with rabbit ears. It had seen a lot of traffic, that's for sure, and the bathroom was out in the hallway—she'd have to share it—but the price was right. She unpacked her few clothes and washed up, then got her courage together and went out to face New York.

The streets were numbered, and with her map she didn't have much trouble finding 420 Lexington. She'd find out when Cherry was coming back, and maybe they could tell her how to find Lale, too. He'd been in the magazine plenty of times. They could at least tell her which agency he was with. It would be best to take things slow, not just land on him the first day she got here. She had to keep her head together about this, not just go off and make a stupid mistake.

The big glass doors with *Vogue* printed in gold script on them were a little intimidating. The carpets were clean and soft, and the air had a perfume that smelled like class. Cassie wished she had worn something besides sneakers, jeans, and a turtleneck. She had on her best coat, a quilted white car coat with a fake-fur lining, but after being dragged around in the car, it needed a cleaning. She hadn't thought about putting on makeup, since she usually didn't wear any, but the girl at the desk was made up and dressed to the nines. She had never felt more like a hick. The girl glanced up at her, then looked again, eyebrows raised to her hairline, like she was viewing a wet river rat.

"May I help you?"

"I hope so. I have a friend who is a model for y'all, and she's off right now on a job, in Miami, I think. I just needed to know when she's going to be back in town. Her name is Cherry Marshall."

"I'm afraid we can't help you. There are a lot of models who work for us, and we aren't allowed to give out any information about them."

"I know you have to protect them—my goodness, I can see there must be all kinds of crazy people who would love to meet some of them—but I'm an old friend of hers from Arkansas, and she would be really happy to see me. I know where she lives—I just need to know when she'll be back in town. That's all. Really."

"Sorry." The girl pretended to go through a drawer in search of something. Cassie tried again. She had come too far to just walk away now.

"Look. I'm not a crazy person who's after her. If you can't help me, maybe you can get somebody else who can. It's a simple thing I'm asking."

"Nobody here can help you. Now please leave." It was horrible. Cassie was on the verge of tears. To come all this way, get so close, and have a nasty little girl treat her like she was trash was more than she could take. She was trembling with anger.

"You are the rudest, *snootiest* person I have ever met in my life!" She was trying not to cry and whirled around to go, almost running over a small woman who was coming in the door. The girl at the desk snapped to attention, and Diana Vreeland took a step back.

"I'm so *sorry,* Mrs. Vreeland," the girl said. "Do you want me to call security?"

Mrs. Vreeland stared up into Cassie's face, which was blotchy with tears and anger. Her eyes lit up.

"My God! That nose!"

"My nose? My *nose*! What is the *matter* with you people? I can't believe a total stranger would say something about my nose! So *what* if it's big? What's it to you, lady? If you've ever looked in the mirror, you have a pretty good-size honker yourself! And what's wrong with a big nose anyhow? It works. It breathes. It smells. Are people going to be attacking me from here on out unless I get my nose chopped off? I can't believe this!" Now she was crying for real, on the verge of hysteria. She ran toward the door, but the voice stopped her.

"Stop! Come back! Dear girl, I wasn't criticizing your nose! Come back. Please."

Something in the voice made her stop, and she turned around. The receptionist was poised on one foot, phone in hand, ready to call the guard. Mrs. Vreeland gave her a signal and she put the phone down.

"Please. Come into my office. I want to talk to you."

Cassie wiped her eyes and followed the little woman into her office. She gaped at the red walls and leopard rug. What kind of place was this? What was the woman going to do to her?

"Sit down. Please." The voice was kind. Cassie sat on the edge of the wicker chair. "First of all, you are *absolutely* right. I *do* have an enormous honker. Much bigger than yours. I know *exactly* how you feel. I have always had to overcome it, and yes, there were people who thought I should have it reduced. But do you know why I never did? Because the nose is the instrument of *sensuality* that controls the entire face. It is the interesting *larger* nose that expresses the senses and the character and projects the *person* more than the smaller nose. *Anybody* can be beautiful with a small nose. But it takes a woman of *great* charm and wit to be interesting with a *big* nose. I have that. I cultivated those qualities with a lot of hard work. You, my dear, I believe, could do it, too.

"Think of the parts of the nose, the septum, the columella, the iliac bone. The nose is a complex structure. The flare of the nostrils, the height and shape, give a *resonance* to the face that anyone with a smaller nose just doesn't have. I have a friend who is a *beautiful* countess, and she will *only* be photographed in profile because she loves her nose so much. It is her trademark. It is as high in the middle as a church steeple, and she is *ravishing.* She has been married five times and has so much money she could never spend it all if she devoted herself to shopping twenty-four hours a day. So you must not believe I was belittling your nose. Not at all. In fact, I've been searching for just such a nose as yours. I would like to photograph your nose for our magazine."

"I . . . I'm not a model. I'm . . . Cassie Culver. I just came by to find a friend of mine, Cherry Marshall."

"Ah, Cherry. *Wonderful* girl. Pity her nose is so small. She has her own unique qualities, though, no? But of course you're not a model. It makes no difference. You have the perfect nose for our story."

"What story is that?"

"It will be about plastic surgery."

"Wait a minute, here. Hold the phone. I am *not* going to be a before picture, or a picture of what a girl doesn't want to be. And there is no way I am getting an operation for a magazine story. I just went through all this with a doctor friend of mine, and . . ."

"No, no, no, no. Dear girl, didn't you hear a word I've just said? I don't want you to change one tiny bit of your nose. It is *perfect.* Your nose will be your trademark, too, just as mine is. The article will be about surgery, yes, for those who want to do that, but will also extol the virtues of noses that aren't so . . . manicured." She picked up the phone and dialed a number.

"Dick? I've just found the perfect girl for our little nose essay."

45

THE UNBELIEVABLE

Dear Cherry,

I bet you were wondering when I would send you this letter, because you must have known for a long time it would be coming. I am so ashamed of myself, and I can't tell you how angry I am at myself and at Leo, too. I made him choose, and guess what? You can guess. He chose the Church. What was I thinking? It couldn't have gone on, though, like it was. I've come to realize I was just one last little fling in his life, the dying ember of his youth, before he gave it all up and finally submitted his will to that monster mother who eats her young. I really think of the Church like that. She takes young men and turns them into her drones, the ones that only live to service the queen and then die; after screwing her in the air, they spiral down to earth, dead from the experience. If you ask Leo, he might tell you that *I'm* the queen bee that cut off his balls. In any case, I don't think he has any. I just don't understand him. We had such a great thing going, but when push came to shove, he couldn't leave the mother ship. The new excitement finally got worn off of the dusty room at the old mill. It was cold and not too comfy, and I never got over the feeling that there were ghost eyes looking at us the whole time. Plus, I wanted to be able to go out to dinner with him, hold his hand, and let everyone know we were together. Is that so crazy, to want everyone to know you are in love? His conscience was getting the better of him, too. I mean, how can you sit in that little screened-off room and listen to other people confess their sins and give them penance while you are full of sins yourself? That's another thing I didn't like—being a sin. I mean, okay, I'm up for a little naughtiness once in a while, but to be a black-hearted sin . . . well, that's a whole 'nother level. That's what he called me. His temptress. His sin. I really thought he was different, that he was more open-minded. He knows so much, he's studied human nature, psychology, the arts—he can do anything! Except love a woman, I guess, although he did love me, at least for a little while. I'm sure of that. I think finally it was Father Bennett who got to him. I almost know when it happened, because one day we were doing fine and the next he and Bennett had to go to a conference in Little Rock. I can just see it now, the two of them alone in the car, Bennett working on him all the way. He never liked me, that's for sure. I was up at the abbey once in shorts and he walked in while I was doing pottery. You should have seen the look on his face, like I was the devil himself sitting at the wheel with my hooved legs spread, throwing a pot. I admit the shorts were my white ones, the *short* ones, but still, it was summer and nothing had even started between Leo and me then. It was just percolating. But ol' Bennett has a strong sense of percolating, that one, and he probably knew even before it started that it had started. Ah, well. It hurts. It hurts so much, but in the final analysis, I don't think I'd want to be with a man who felt guilty every time he made love to me. That's not what it's all about. I want a man who is my equal, my partner, who can love me and not think of me as something dirty. I guess those Catholics are right when they say give them a child until he's six and he's theirs forever.

On the brighter side, I went up to Lost Acre Hollow and reconnected with Scipio Jones—remember me mentioning him? He was named after this famous black lawyer who helped a lot of young men who had been falsely accused of some stuff and they were going to hang them, which was the usual procedure back in the early 1900s. Scipio loaned me a book about it, which is really interesting. I invited him to come and demonstrate for my class, which he did, and was a big hit with them, even the Kluxer kids, who were amazed at how he could throw a perfect doughnut. He doesn't talk like a black man at all, or even a southerner. He went to school up north in Rhode Island at RISD. What he's doing down here is a long story I'll tell you one of these days, but the bottom line is that we are friends. JUST friends, for now, although I guess we have to do everything as twins, you and me, even have black boyfriends. If it ever progresses to the point that I find out details, I'll let you know if he is anything like Aurelius. I hope not—no offense. He isn't as much a nut for bathing, I don't think, since he works making pots all day and only has a cold-water shower at his cob house he built in the woods—remember I told you I once took my class out there to see it and we had a project of making little cob houses? The shower is in a little bathroom he sculpted off the side of the house. He says it's good for the soul to take cold showers. It wakes you up, that's for sure—at least I would suspect that it does, never having taken one there myself. I wish you could see the house. I'll take pictures and send. It's one big sculpture in mud and straw, and he has made it look like a giant *face,* if you can believe it. High up near the roof are two round windows he salvaged from the dump, set like a pair of eyes underneath overhanging eyebrows, and below them is a nose with flaring nostrils set with smaller windows he got from a wrecked car. When you're working in clay, you can make the windows any size or shape you want. Right below the nose is the mouth—rather, the door—which is dark red painted wood, and a red wooden tongue spreads out into a small round porch. Inside, the walls are smooth white lime plaster, and the furniture and beams and everything else is made of wood, mostly kept in their natural tree shapes. A long twisting vine with the bark left on works as a banister, running along a curved staircase that spirals up the middle of the house from first floor to the top. The floors are made of clay, satiny gray, and have been burnished by a piece of fine leather and linseed oil. There's not a straight line in the whole house; every room curves and flows into the next one. Upstairs is a bed with white linens like you get at flea markets, the beautiful soft old ones with crocheted edging that took somebody's grandma a year to make. A crocheted hammock is slung across the chasm above the top of the stairs. I have no idea how he gets into it. Maybe it's just for decoration. The kitchen has a neat wooden shelf full of dishes and bowls he made, and a cheery red water pump sits beside the ceramic sink, a blue-and-white-checked dish towel draped neatly across it. It's like a big playhouse, only so much better. He just invited me and my class there once, but I know he will invite me again. I can tell. In the meantime, instead of hanging out at the abbey, I've been going to Lost Acre Hollow and watching him work. I think I must be a pottery groupie. Is that sick? Maybe I just miss Leo and the whole art scene at St. Juniper's. I sure miss the love part. Anyhow, I'm learning a lot about throwing pots, and I get better all the time.

What is happening with Aurelius? I wish he made you happier. We're a pair, aren't we? I wish I could see you and talk in person about all this. Maybe I can come up to New York when school is out at spring break for a visit. Would you let me? I miss you so much. No matter how many men come and go in our lives, you and I will always be together. We're true soul mates, twins forever. Write soon. I know you are having the time of your life, but I dreamed you were in trouble and it was such a real, disturbing dream that I can't get it out of my head. You were standing on the bridge over the Arkansas River, and every time you took a step, part of the bridge would fall in. I was at the end, trying to reach you, but couldn't because of the falling debris. You kept reaching out your hands to me, and I couldn't help you. Please write soon and let me know you're all right.

Much love,
Baby

Well, Baby was right about one thing. I wasn't at all surprised to hear Leo had not given up the Church. Some guys just like having their every waking moment dictated, living in a community where they know more or less what their days are going to be like in advance, having total job security. Kind of like a career army officer. I could see why he wouldn't want to leave St. Juniper's, too. On a smaller scale, it was a little like the European churches we studied in art history class—a big open space where sound echoed off the stone walls, with gothic arches and full-color life-size statues of Jesus on the cross and Mary in a beautiful blue robe wearing her heart on the outside, like a big, bleeding brooch. There were graceful little marble bird-bath things full of holy water that you dipped your finger into and then crossed yourself as you came in the door, red velvet padded pews, and the most incredible stained-glass windows that lit up like jewels as the sun beamed through them. A high domed ceiling held up by marble pillars was the centerpiece hanging over it all, painted with angels flying up to heaven in blue and white and gold clouds, their toes rosy and clean from never having touched earth. I loved the robes and incense and little boys carrying candles in procession. I loved the ceremony and the feeling of being close to God, the tradition that went back almost two thousand years. I nearly always got weepy during mass, even though I was an Apostolic Holiness Church of God and couldn't take communion. I could see how Leo would be reluctant to leave that world and strike out on his own, with no experience for anything but teaching in the Church. It was a world in itself and I understood why he couldn't give it up. Frankly, I was glad it was over, and Baby seemed not much the worse for wear. Not if she was already interested in Scipio Jones. I'd always loved Lost Acre Hollow, too, just over the border in Missouri, about ten miles from Buchanan. It was a tourist place, built to be like a pioneer mountain town, with shops in little log cabins that were set up to demonstrate and produce all the old hill crafts like quilting, fiddle and dulcimer crafting, blacksmithing, gunsmithing, pottery, soap making, sorghum-molasses making, log-cabin building, and everything else you can think of that the pioneers had to do to survive when they settled in the mountains. Mama and Daddy first took me there when I was a kid, and my favorite was a woman making apple-head dolls out of real apples that dried and shriveled up into old people's faces. I still had mine, and every year it got smaller and darker and more wrinkly. Every night in the big auditorium they had a show of the old-time hill music, most of which had been preserved from the early English and Celtic settlers, and went as far back as Elizabethan England. The performers did jig dancing, which the audience could join in on, and it was the best place in the world I could imagine to work. No wonder Baby was smitten with Scipio. What an odd name.

Ah, well. I'd wait with interest to see what happened next. But I wish Baby hadn't said that about her dream of me being in trouble. I hate things like that. We truly believe we were twins in a past life, and it is no surprise she knows everything about me.

The worst of it was, the day the letter arrived, my period was two weeks late.

46

CASSIE AND RICHARD

Richard Avedon reminded Cassie of a Chihuahua, not in an unkind way, but he was small and feisty, full of energy, with prominent eyes behind big glasses. He had a nice smile, though, and tried to put her at ease, taking her coat and ushering her into the studio.

"Welcome, Cassie. Diana tells me this is your first photo shoot."

"I don't know what I'm even doing here, Mr. Avedon. I'm from Arkansas and I've only been in New York two days. I didn't come here for this, and I don't know about this whole picture thing of my nose, anyhow. Frankly, I'm scared y'all might be making fun of me and there's no way to tell."

"Well. That was pretty direct. First of all, Cassie, let me assure you, there is no way Diana Vreeland or I would spend our time and energy to make fun of you. You don't know us, but what possible good would we get out of making fun of a perfectly nice girl? A pretty, perfectly nice girl from Arkansas?"

"I don't know. I can't think of a reason. But I'm still not sure. I was told that New Yorkers were all crazy, and frankly, putting me in a fashion magazine seems pretty crazy to me."

"I suppose a fair number of them are, and I don't blame you for being wary. I bet you were also told that the minute you set foot in New York you would get mugged, weren't you? Did they tell you to get pepper spray?"

"Not pepper spray. But I heard you can get mugged here. Somebody said I should get a gun."

"A gun. Did you?"

"No, sir."

"That's good. You're not going to need a gun, Cassie. What on earth would you do with it if somebody did try to mug you? By the time you rummaged around in your purse and found the gun, took off the safety, aimed, and shot the attacker, he would have already mugged you and be gone. In fact, he would probably have taken the gun away from you. No. No guns."

"I guess maybe you're right. I've never shot a pistol anyhow. My brother taught me to shoot a twenty-two, though. He can shoot the head off a turtle at fifty yards. I'm pretty good myself—I can do it at thirty."

"Forget guns. Did you walk over here? What did you see on the streets?"

"People. A lot of people walking, shopping, and going to work, I guess. Families. Kids. There were some tough-looking guys, though."

"I bet there are some tough-looking guys in Arkansas, too. You know, all those people who live here and walk around on the streets don't get mugged every day. True, once in a while somebody does—I'll be honest about that—and that's what hits the papers. But the chances of that happening to you are about one in a million. Pretty good odds, I'd say."

"One in a million?"

"There are almost eight million people in New York. I don't think there are eight muggings a day. Even if there are, that's still pretty good odds."

"Okay. I feel better. I wasn't really worried about it anyhow. Snuffy tends to exaggerate a lot. He's the one who told me all that stuff."

"Good girl. Now, have something to drink, and let's talk about the picture. What would you like?"

"Do you have any Tab?"

"I don't think so. How about Perrier?"

"What's that?"

"Sparkling water. Like club soda, only fancier. They drink it in France. I brought a case of it back from Paris."

"Okay. With lemon?"

"Sure." He got the drink for her. She took a sip, licked a fleck of lemon off her lip.

"Thank you. This is real good. Refreshing. I'm trying to stay off of Cokes and things like that, and Tab has no calories. I've lost a lot of weight recently and I'm not looking to gain it back in a hurry."

Avedon had been dancing around, looking at her from all angles, holding his hands up making a square with his forefingers and thumbs, like a picture frame. It made her a little nervous.

"I didn't bring any more clothes, Mrs. Vreeland said you'd have things, if I needed them."

"This is going to be good. It's a beauty shot, not fashion, but yes, Diana sent over some clothes. And I have a man here who'll help you with makeup and fix up your hair. He's the best."

"Mr. Avedon?"

"Call me Dick."

"Okay . . . Mr. Avedon . . . Dick . . . I want you to know right up front, I don't know how to be a model. You'll have to tell me everything to do. I don't want you to be disappointed in me."

"You don't have to be a model, Cassie. We'll just make a pretty picture, and then you can leave here and be anything you want to be. You're young and beautiful and healthy. You can use that to buy a ticket to anything." He called out to someone in the other room. "Sal? Come on in here. I have a lovely young lady for you. Let's get the show on the road."

47

THE TALK

Aurelius said he would cook dinner for me the night I came back from Miami. We hadn't talked since I left—it was just too hard on a pay phone—and I didn't know when he'd be at home anyhow. I sure wasn't going to call Mrs. Digby and have her go get him in the middle of the night. I would have to get my own phone one of these days, and so would he. He said he didn't need it because he was hardly ever there, and he had an answering service, a girl who took messages for him who he called several times a day. I thought about getting one of those, but I usually called the agency enough that it didn't matter. If anybody wanted to get in touch with me, they could call them. In a way it was nice not to have to be at the mercy of the telephone, but finding pay phones was hard and keeping a bag full of dimes wasn't easy, either. My purse already weighed a ton.

I had relaxed, unpacked, gone through the mail, read Baby's letter, and just sat with it in my hand, looking out the window. Back home, we used to say, "That girl is in trouble," meaning she was pregnant, and that's just how Baby had put it. I'd never thought about getting pregnant before, which was strange, but somehow I just didn't think I would. I couldn't think of going to the doctor to get birth control pills in Arkansas—they frowned on single women doing that—and Doc McGuire had been my doctor since I was born and I was sure he'd tell Mama and Daddy about it, and probably wouldn't give them to me anyhow. Tripp and I had always been so careful to use something, and Aurelius and I were, too, but there was a time or two when I thought it would be safe, since the only time you could get pregnant was right in the middle of your cycle and this was just after a period. Maybe I'd been misinformed. Maybe the schedule wasn't foolproof. Maybe that's why Catholics had such big families—they had to rely on the rhythm method. Aurelius had rhythm, but I obviously didn't. I didn't know for sure I was pregnant, but I was never late, and my nipples were getting sore. I didn't know if that was a sign or not, but something in me said it was.

He knocked on the door.

"Hey, gorgeous. You don't have much of a tan for being in Miami. How did it go?"

"Great, sweetheart. I think Mrs. Vreeland will like what we did. I hope so. Did you miss me?"

"Of course I missed you. C'mere and give me a kiss." I went over and gave him a good one, then clung to him.

"I think you did miss me." I started unbuttoning his shirt and before you knew it, we were in bed. I tried, I really tried, to do everything I could to please him, and he was obviously pleased, but somehow it ended up the same way it always did, me with nothing but frustration and him with a big ol' smile on his face. He held me and brushed my hair out of my eyes. He was surprised to find them wet.

"What's wrong, baby? Something's not right. I can tell. Did you meet somebody else on the trip? You can tell me. I don't want any secrets between us."

"No, I swear, I didn't meet anybody else. I don't want anybody else, Aurelius. I just want you. But that's the problem. I don't feel like I have you. I don't feel like you love me. You never have said it. Do you love me, even a little bit?"

"Well, baby, of course I do. I love you a lot. It's hard for me to say it. It's always been hard for me to give myself to a woman. I've never been close to getting married, and I'm not sure I ever will be. I guess I'm kind of a loner. I always liked not having anybody to answer to, not having to explain myself to anybody. Coming and going when I wanted to. But I could get used to having you around. I think I could." I nestled into his chest, but didn't say anything. He raised his head and looked at me. "Hey—come to think of it, you never said 'I love you' to me. Do you love me?"

"I don't know. It's all so new to me, coming to New York, this whole different life. Once I thought I was in love with Tripp Barlow, but when he left me to go back to his wife, it was almost a relief. I don't think I'm ready to settle down and get married, either, Aurelius. I feel like I'm just starting my life. Not that I don't love you a little bit—I surely do. You are the most beautiful man I've ever met, and you can wring feelings out of me with that saxophone I didn't even know I had. I don't want anybody but you . . ."

"But . . ."

"But I don't think I'm in love with you."

"That's cool, baby. I understand. We don't have to make any promises to each other right now. Let's just enjoy what we have and not worry about what might happen tomorrow. We're both just getting started here. You're going to be a big star, and I hope I am, too. One of these days we'll be ready to settle down, and if we make it 'til then, we'll be together. We'll get married and have the prettiest babies you've ever seen. Can you imagine? You're the most beautiful woman I've ever been with, you're *scarily* beautiful. My Lord. What has a li'l old sharecropper like me done to deserve a goddess like you? Some angel from de cotton patch done come and visited po' ol' Aurelius and done give him a angel." He started to tickle me, and I broke out laughing.

"Well, you po' ol' thang. You must've done somethin' raight, or you'd still be out there in the hot sun, drankin' out of a gourd while you scrap the cotton bolls to save up and get yourself a new pair of britches! You sure don't have none on now." We started to pillow-fight and it was okay. Except it wasn't, but we'd deal with it another time. He didn't want any secrets between us, but he'd made it clear he didn't want to get married, either. I would never, like Cassie, try to drag a man to the altar with a shotgun. I'd learned that much from her.

Aurelius went to his place to shower, and I took a bath, then dressed and went over. He'd made a wonderful dinner of fried catfish and hush puppies with pinto beans, collards, and sliced tomatoes. I groaned with pleasure. This meal was going to be the orgasm I couldn't seem to have with him.

48

THE GUIDING LIGHT

"Salvadoooor! Salvador de Vega! Where are you?" Lale burst through the door, yelling at the top of his voice. Sal flushed the toilet and ran out, alarmed.

"Lale? What's wrong? Are you okay?"

Lale grabbed him and swirled him around the room, singing at the top of his voice, "Some enchanted evening . . . you may see a stranger . . . you may see a straaaaanger across a crowded room."

"Well, you've flipped. You've finally flipped. To what do I owe this exhibition of exuberance? And *when* did you learn the lyrics to that song?"

"You play the dang record night and day. How could I *not* learn the lyrics?" He let him go and whirled around. "You'll never guess what I got today."

"A big booking to go to Europe for *GQ*?"

"Well, yes, I got that yesterday, but something else. Guess. I'll give you a hint. It's not modeling."

"I have no idea. What did you get today?"

"A part on *The Guiding Light*!"

"A *real* part? Not just a pretty face dancing in the crowd? Not an under-five?"

"Nope. It's more than five lines. It's a six-month contract, and if they like me and the story line goes they might make it more. Maybe even a three-year contract. Six hundred smackaroos a day."

"Oh, Lale! That's so *great*! How did this all come about? I didn't even know you were up for anything."

"Woman who's the casting director saw the Diamonds & Ermine. What she wanted was a James Bond kind of guy, because with that voice-over they all think that's how I talk, but when she met me, she kind of liked my real southern voice even better, so they're going to make the character a southerner. I'll be a mysterious stranger who comes to town, and nobody knows I'm really a P.I. who's looking for the heir to a fortune. Of course I fall in love with the star of the show, or she falls in love with me or whatever, and I don't know how it turns out. I don't think the writers even know how it turns out—they just write it as they go along."

"What'll happen to your modeling career? You can't just quit now."

"I can do both. I only work three days a week. They don't care over at Ford. It'll help with the image if I'm a big soap star, too."

"Well, let's break out the champagne! May I give you a congratulatory kiss?"

Lale laughed. "Sure. Why not?" Sal leaned in and kissed him gently on the lips. A tender, sweet kiss that lit a spark and surprised them both. They leaned back and looked in each other's eyes. Something had been building in both of them all these months and that sweet little kiss wasn't enough. They kissed again, this time longer, with more feeling, as if they had waited a lifetime for it. The kiss became hotter, as the spark grew into a flame and finally roared into a fire.

They wrestled their clothes off and barely made it to the big red satin bed behind the curtain before their hands were all over each other.

After a long couple of hours, they lay exhausted.

"Well, now I know what it is y'all do. I never quite could figure it out before," Lale said, lazing back on the pillows.

Sal laughed. "You seemed to know what you were doing. You're a quick study. Not so different than it is with a girl, is it?"

"Yeah. Sure it's different. They don't have beards. Or peckers. And they have tits."

"Tits, tits. What is the big deal about tits? Cherry doesn't have any and you seem to like her."

"I do. I like her a lot."

"More than me?"

"I like you both the same. In different ways. Most of the models don't have tits, either, come to think of it. Cassie used to have great ones. Did I ever tell you about her, really?" Sal snuggled up under his arm. Lale hugged him close. "She was fat. I hated that. At least I thought I did. But it's crazy, now sometimes I wish some of the women had a little more flesh on them. It's downright painful to bump up against bones all the time. There was this one girl who was so bony, I was twisting her shoulder bone one night in the dark, thinking it was the electric blanket control. To tell you the truth, I kind of miss Cassie sometimes, as nutty as that is."

"Really?"

"Really. Why, is that weird or something?"

"You know how there are no coincidences in this life? I believe that. I think that everything that happens to us happens for a reason, and we might not know what it is at the time, but it's all connected, on some big scoreboard in the sky."

"What are you talking about?"

"Well, like, for instance, that driver, Smitty."

"Snuffy."

"Snuffy, stopping at the very same truck stop where I was, that fateful day back in February, which is nearly a year ago, my goodness, and me finding you, and then you coming with me to New York, where we ran into Michel Denon . . ."

"You don't have to recite my life story. I get what you mean. What are you trying to say?"

"Well, I was going to tell you tonight, but today I worked for Richard Avedon, a last-minute-favor kind of thing, on this girl who is doing a little job for *Vogue,* and you won't believe it, *but* . . ."

"But what? Are you trying to make me strangle you?"

"The girl was named Cassie Culver and she was from Arkansas."

Lale stared at him in stunned silence.

"Are you making some kind of joke here? Because if you are . . ."

"I am not. I would never kid about something like that. But she wasn't fat at all. She was thin. And beautiful. She did have a rather large nose, which I gather was the whole point of the shoot. Diana Vreeland saw her somewhere, pounced on her to be in an article about plastic surgery—a 'Do You' or 'Don't You' kind of thing. Cassie is going to be the 'Don't You.' She's a sweet girl, only been in town two days, fresh off the farm."

"I can't believe it. She did come. What an idiot I am." He got out of bed and started to put on his clothes. "Where is she staying? Did she say?"

"She told me everything, including that she was looking for a certain ex-boyfriend named Lale Hardcastle. I neglected to tell her I knew you, of course, but I'm quite sympathetic to talk to, as you know. The secrets I have under my hat would . . ."

"Come on! Cut the chatter! Where is she staying?"

"The Chelsea Hotel. I don't know how she picked that place. Every artist in the world lives there. Andy Warhol's gang lives there, for Pete's sake. Does she have some kind of connection here? In town two days and working for Avedon? What's her story? She can't be as naïve as she seems to be."

"Oh, yes she can. I've got to find her." He headed for the door, then stopped in his tracks and turned around. "Listen, Sal. What we done this afternoon stays between you and me, okay? I mean, I'm not a homo—you know that. Don't you?"

"Of course I know that! Who do you think you're talking to? You *know* I can keep a secret. We'll just say it was an experiment, all right?"

"Right. An experiment."

"Everyone is entitled to one experiment in his life, don't you think?"

"Right."

"Be home for dinner? I'll make fried chicken."

"Sure. Great. See you later."

Sal lay back, a big smile on his face. He'd known from the day he set eyes on Lale he could get him if he just took his time. It was that radar thing, whether anybody believed in it or not.

49

THE LITTLE BLUE FAIRY

I went back and slept in my own bed after the dinner with Aurelius. I told him I was tired from the trip, and it was the truth. But I really just needed some time by myself to think everything through. What if I was pregnant? What would I do? I was just starting out in a big career, just beginning my life. I'd have to move back to Arkansas and be in disgrace, because I couldn't model and take care of a baby, too. If I came back home pregnant with a half-black baby and no husband, I don't know if Mama and Daddy would ever get over it. They loved me more than anything in the world, and they had been so afraid of me coming to New York, sure that I'd get in some kind of trouble. I just pooh-poohed them and thought I was so big and tough and was immune to anything the city could throw at me, and here I'd gotten caught in the oldest trap in the world. I wouldn't blame them if they threw me out and never spoke to me again. I didn't think they would care so much that the baby was half black—they'd love it anyhow—but everybody else in that little town would. If I moved back there and had the baby, nobody would treat the little thing like they should. He or she would have an uphill fight every step of the way. Who would ask it over to play? Who would it date? With the best Christian will in the world, you can't change people who, a scant hundred years ago, had slaves and thought black people were like smart livestock who didn't have souls. My generation was enlightened by Martin Luther King and the whole civil rights fight, but all the while I was growing up, all we heard in church was about how we had to help the poor savages in Africa. We took up love offerings for the missionaries who came back from there with slides of half-naked natives all painted up with feathers in their hair, the little skinny kids with bloated bellies and flies all over their faces. In the movies, ever since I could remember, all the blacks were portrayed as cannibals or somebody's maid or a stupid Step'n Fetchit kind of guy saying, "Yassuh, boss. I sho will shine yo' shoes. I shine 'um up good!" Or Butterfly McQueen blubbering, "I don't know nuthin' 'bout birthin' babies!" and Scarlett slapping the fire out of her. It's horrible, but it was the way we were brought up. If Aurelius came down there with us, we'd be shunned in the politest way, but shunned all the same. I couldn't imagine him even wanting to go down there with us. He'd grown up in it himself and he knew how it was. Like he said, men had been hanged for doing a lot less with a white woman than we'd done. In New York, I'd felt so free and didn't care what people thought. Maybe, if I was honest with myself, I was showing off, so proud that I was open and above all the petty racism that it was almost racism in reverse. I liked walking down the street with Aurelius, seeing the looks on people's faces, the admiration, the slight shock, the envy. I liked how we looked together, all dressed up in our finery, and how we looked when we were naked, our pale and dark bodies wrapped around each other in front of the mirror. The baby would undoubtedly be beautiful, if it looked like a mix of us. Maybe it would be a girl with pale-coffee skin and blond curly hair. Maybe she would have green eyes like me. Or it might be a boy with caramel-colored skin and dark brown eyes, a nose like mine. He would have a beautiful megawatt smile like his father and be a musician or a dancer or an actor. Whatever he did, he would be a big success. We could live in New York and after a while my parents would get used to the idea and come and visit and bring toys for the baby. It was a lovely dream.

But the reality was that we didn't want to get married, neither one of us. If I told him I was pregnant, he probably would marry me, but I didn't want that. I wanted to go to Moscow and be in *Vogue* on a white horse in a birch forest in the snow and meet a man—black, white, Asian, or mixed, it didn't matter—who turned my blood to fire and gave me the kind of orgasms that Tripp used to. Except this one would love only me and not have a wife he hadn't told me about, or hang-ups about showering after having sex with me, or have anything at all to stop him from loving me. I couldn't think about spending the rest of my life with Aurelius and never again having that feeling like I was whooshing down the mountain in a lava flow, blown out of a volcano. My life would be sitting up with the baby, waiting for him to come home from some gig, worrying when he didn't show up, once in a while hanging out in a smoky little jazz club and waiting for him to finish a set. I'd have to learn how to love jazz and drink bourbon. There's no way to spend your life in a smoky jazz club, only half liking the music and drinking a single glass of white wine. I couldn't imagine a life like that. I would become old and bitter and always wonder what would have happened if I hadn't done it.

But the alternative was horrible, too. *Abortion*. What an ugly word. As ugly as the word *murder*. Cassie wouldn't get an abortion, and look what happened to her. What would have happened if she had? I knew. She would have forever been sorry, paying a price, and even though it turned out the way it did, at least she knew she did the right thing and wouldn't go to hell. Which I surely would. If I could even find somebody to do it. It was illegal and you couldn't get a real doctor to do it. Girls went to quacks who stuck wire coat hangers and knitting needles up them without benefit of anesthesia or cleanliness. I'd known a girl my sophomore year at DuVall, another art major, who disappeared one day and didn't come back to class for six weeks. When she did, we all gasped when we saw her. Her skin was whiter than mine, even, a pale shade of green, and she was so weak she had to sit down every five minutes. Somebody had to help her carry her books to class. She'd had an illegal abortion and they almost killed her. I didn't know details like where or how, but we heard she nearly bled to death and had to be rushed to the hospital, where they gave her six pints of blood. They didn't treat her all that well in the hospital, either. Hospitals didn't look kindly on girls who tried to kill their babies. Neither did her parents, who'd kicked her out, and she'd had to get a job in the cafeteria to pay for her schooling. She had the look of a dog that had been beaten one too many times, and she dropped out that year. I lost track of her.

I tried to sleep, but the room was hot, and I flung off the covers and lay with my legs out. I must have dozed off, because it seemed like there was something flying around the room, some kind of bug. It made a funny little tinkling noise, not like a bug at all, and it looked blue. As crazy as it sounds, a little blue light was flitting around the room, like a fairy. I knew it was my imagination, but there it was. And there was something familiar about it. It flew from a shadowy corner to the window, then came and hovered right over my head. When I closed my eyes I saw it and when I opened them it was there. I knew what it was. It was the soul of the little baby who had started in my belly. It was trying to decide whether to come in or stay out. I know in my heart that's what it was. I tried to pray, but I didn't think God would listen to the prayers of a girl who didn't want her baby. It felt like the prayers got to the ceiling, bumped against it, and then, like dried leaves, crumbled and drifted back down on me. Maybe I could talk directly to the little baby's soul. "Dear sweet little baby. I want you, I do. Just not right now. Could you come back later? Is that possible? Can you come back when I meet someone I love who would be a good daddy for you and we could be a family? I selfishly, so selfishly, want to go to Moscow and Europe and be famous and make a lot of money. Enough money to make life easier for you and to get Mama, your grandma, wonderful designer clothes and bring her to New York so she can be part of your life. She would love you so much. My daddy would love you, too, although he wouldn't take any money from me. He griped about the cashmere sweater I got him for Christmas and said I spent way too much, although Mama said he wore it. Oh, my sweet baby, I'm so wicked. I know it's wrong. I do want you. I do. Can't you wait just a little while?'

The little light flitted and twinkled and tears ran down my cheeks as I somehow tried to find the words to pray to God without Him thinking I was a horrible person, although I knew full well that He knew my heart better than I did, and I guess I fell asleep because the next thing I remembered was the sun coming in the window of my room and I had to get up to go do a job for Macy's.

50

THE HOGS

Snow was falling on the glass roof of the pool house. It had been another bad weekend at Sneden's Landing. Suzan had confronted Freddy about the latest model he was screwing and he had gone off on her again. Would she never learn to keep her mouth shut? Probably not. She didn't care about the physical act anymore, but the girl was a newcomer who was beginning to flaunt herself all over the agency, treating Suzan with condescension, lording it over the other girls, who more than likely had screwed him themselves, but knew enough to keep their mouths shut about it. It didn't look good, and she was going to have to let her go, which was too bad since she had the potential to be a good moneymaker. Unfortunately, Suzan's tirade got a little heated and she made the mistake of slapping Freddy. Fortunately, her resulting bruises were all on her arms and back, not her face. She rubbed herself well with Arnica gel and put an ice pack on the worst of the bruises, then took a bottle of cold Chardonnay to the pool room to sit and look at the water as snowflakes began to cover the glass. It was her favorite place to think, and looking at the cool blue water soothed her. It had been a good

Christmas, all in all. The party had been a tremendous success, a little bonus being Diana Vreeland discovering Cherry. Freddy had made a big show of giving Suzan a sable coat in front of everyone, which she could have bought herself if she had wanted to waste the money. It was her money that bought it. Her money, not Freddy's, no matter whose name was on the secret bank account. How had this happened to her? How did it happen to any woman? You make a wrong decision and are too proud to let the world know the truth, so you stick it out. Except everybody in the industry knew. They all knew and they all felt sorry for her, but what could they do? Beauty was a trap. Everyone wanted to be you; everyone thought beauty was the magic elixir that led to happiness and wealth. If only they knew. She envied ugly girls sometimes. They never had to put up with men sniffing around them like dogs and using them as pretty accessories. Somebody once told her that the Jewish rabbis all had the most beautiful wives. It gave them more status. It wasn't just rabbis who wanted beautiful wives. Every man did. The trouble was that once they were married, the beautiful girlfriend became the wife, and they had to pursue another, younger, more beautiful girlfriend. One was never enough. And once you got past the perfect features and perfume, every woman was the same. They all wanted a man who would love only them. They all had demands. Some of the lucky ones, the smart ones, the charming ones, lasted longer. But too bad if looks were all they had. Looks were a gift that came and went before you could say "face-lift." She would be forty in a few days. After forty, no matter how beautiful or charming or smart you were, in the eyes of society you were off the board. Men might say, "Yes, she's still beautiful, but I can get somebody just like her twenty years younger." In the society columns, over the years, you went from being "the stunning Suzan Hartman," to "the beautiful Suzan Hartman," to "the handsome Suzan Hartman," to "Suzan Hartman, the woman who used to be a model." Your jowls begin to sag just that little bit and your eyes don't seem as open and bright anymore. The enamel on your teeth gets thinner and yellowed, no matter how much you brush. If you manage to starve yourself and stay thin, your neck goes to granny strings, and your hands start to look veined and bony, like a Halloween witch's. If you got a face-lift, like so many women she knew, it changed as you aged. Noses traveled off-center and continued to grow in unnatural ways, old faces pulled too tightly looked like masks. There were whole troops of them at Quo Vadis every day for lunch, little old mummies in Chanel suits, low-heeled patent-leather shoes, and baggy silk stockings. She could see it all starting now. She was too skinny. In the nude, her hip bones stuck out like the poles of a pup tent, her stomach slung low between them, her pubic bone jutting high. Her breasts were tiny sacks, useless appendages that would never suckle a baby. Her butt was beginning to go flat. She needed to put on a few pounds, but she couldn't make herself eat. It was the habit of a lifetime, seeing food as her enemy, forcing herself to starve to fit the tiny clothes. Ah, well. Wine was full of calories. She had to allow for that. So what if she'd never be twenty again? Who wanted to go through all that crap endlessly? In fact, who wanted to do any of it anymore? She was so tired of playing the game. What would Freddy do, she mused, if she disappeared again? If she just packed her bags and moved so far away he would never find her? Where might that be? Alaska? Somewhere in the Amazon jungle? The Near East? She smiled, thinking of going to one of those places where the women wore coverings over their entire bodies, and nobody ever knew what they looked like at all. A whole half of the population were black ghosts. She could just see Freddy over there, running down the street, lifting all the sheets, looking for her under them, the women screaming and beating him over the head. She'd read of one country, Afghanistan or one of those, where the men would actually beat a woman if the wind happened to blow her sheet up and display a little ankle. The men in those places were horrors. Freddy would fit right in.

His voice broke into her reverie. He was calling for her. What now? What else could he do to her? She ignored him.

"Susan? Where are you? Susan?" He was drunk. Well, that wasn't unusual. She was well on her way, too. Another half bottle ought to do it.

"Suz*an,* Freddy. I'm out here by the pool."

He came out, red-eyed and staggering, holding a bottle of gin.

"Where is it, Su*zan*? What did you do with the money?"

"What money, Freddy? What are you talking about?"

"I had four thousand dollars in my desk and it's gone. Don't play innocent with me. It was in my locked drawer. You've been in my locked drawer."

"Maybe you forgot to lock it and one of the kids took it. You're always flashing that wad of cash around them."

"No, the drawer was locked. Someone's been in it."

"Well, it wasn't me. Go to bed and let me have my wine in peace. You owe me that much at least."

"You have that backward. It's *you* who owe *me*. I made you what you are today. I'm the one who made Suzan Hartman! You were just one more pretty little twat—from *Arkansas,* no less. A high school dropout. You didn't even go to that hick school where they called the Hogs. But you were a Hog caller. A phony Hog caller. That's all you were, a pretty little *phony* Hog caller! Whoo, pig, sooooie!"

"Don't make fun of the Razorbacks, Freddy."

"Wooooooo, pig, pig pig pig, soooooooie! Whoooo, pig pig pig, sooooie!"

He was standing beside her chaise, yelling right in her face. Mustering all the dignity she could, Suzan got up and walked away, leaving him standing there still calling after her, "Woooooooooooo, pig!!! Wooooooooo, pig, sooooooooie!"

He was so carried away with his rant, so staggeringly drunk, that he didn't see the wine bottle sitting by the chaise. He stepped back and stumbled over it, his slipper falling off. The bottle of Bombay Sapphire he had been holding crashed to the floor, breaking into shards, and he stepped on a piece, cutting his foot. He tried to catch himself, but lost his balance, and, arms flailing, toppled into the pool, striking his head on the edge as he fell. A small slick of blood colored the tile where he hit, as he sank like a rock to the bottom of the deep end. Suzan turned, waited for a moment, then walked back to the pool.

"Freddy? Stop fooling around. Come back up here this instant! Freddy?"

Suzan stood looking down into the water, waiting for him to come back up, but he didn't. Blood floated up through the water from his head in a lazy rivulet.

"Well, stay there, then, if you're going to be like that. I told you not to make fun of the Razorbacks."

Then she picked up her bottle of wine and went to bed.

51

MRS. DIGBY'S SECRET

Lana and I were doing a shoot for Bausch & Lomb sunglasses with Neal Barr, the sweet, wonderful photographer who I'd worked with for Vanity Fair. The first shots were sophisticated, me in a black knit dress that molded to my figure, a wide-brimmed hat, and big black glasses, a cigarette in a long black holder, Lana in a gold evening dress, her hair in an up-do, wearing a pair of gold gradient lenses. Then we did girl-next-door ones, with pastel headbands and T-shirts. It was a routine job, but nice. I'd been a little anxious all day and Lana could sense something was the matter.

"Are you okay, Cherry?" she asked when we were alone in the dressing room.

"No. I'm not okay, Lana. I think I might be pregnant."

"Oh. That's awful. Is it Aurelius?"

"Of course it's Aurelius! I haven't been with anybody else."

"What does he say?"

"He doesn't know. I kind of sounded him out on getting married and he is in no way ready to do that."

"Do you want to?"

"No. I'm just not ready. I have twelve pages coming out in *Vogue* and a big trip planned to Moscow. And I don't think I love him enough to marry him. Oh, Lana, I'm so stupid! I've made such a mess out of things." I started to cry, trying not to mess up the eye makeup that had just taken an hour to perfect. With an iron will, I pulled the tears back in. At least enough not to totally wreck the mascara.

"Well, it's no big deal. You'll just get an abortion. I've had three."

"You've had *three*? Why?"

"Oh, you know. I get sloppy sometimes. Heat of the moment and all. It's really no worse than having a tooth extracted."

"I wouldn't even know where to go for one. What do you do?"

"Are you kidding me? You mean you don't know?"

"Of course I don't know. How would I know?"

"You're living in the house of the best abortionist in New York. I just thought you knew."

"Who? Mrs. Digby?"

"Of course Mrs. Digby. She's famous. All the girls go to her. She's clean and discreet and she cares about us. You should talk to her about it."

Mrs. Digby. I had no clue. I mean, there were occasionally girls going in and out of her house, but that was to be expected with all the young people living there. Once late at night, I saw a girl leaving as I was coming in, but didn't think anything about it. Now it all made sense. She had certainly been around the block enough to know the route. Mrs. Digby. Who would have thought?

52

CASSIE AND LALE

Lale saw the old T-bird sitting outside the Chelsea Hotel. Sal hadn't been kidding. Cassie was here. What had he been thinking all these months—that she was just going to quietly fade away and he would never have to see her again or face what he did? His heart pounded as he stood in the lobby and asked for her. The desk clerk, a small, bored man in a striped shirt, looked in a ledger and gave him a room number. Instead of taking the elevator, to give himself more time, he climbed the huge vertical tunnel of stairs, each stair seeming like it was ten feet high. The hallway floor was black-and-white tile, and the door was painted a dark brown, thick paint, a hundred coats of paint, like you could peel it off and roof a house with it. He listened, and there were small sounds coming from inside. She was there. He knocked. The door opened and a woman who he had never seen before answered. She had cornflower eyes like Cassie, but they had makeup on them that made them look twice their size. She was slim. Her cheekbones jutted out, her nose thin and high. She stared at him as if she didn't recognize him, either. Then she stood back and he walked in.

"Cassie? Is that you?"

"You knocked on my door. Who were you expecting? How did you know I was here?"

"Sal's a friend of mine."

"Oh. Really? Small world. Well, come in and find a place to sit. It's not very big."

She was slightly in shock and nervous, but trying not to let on. It was unreal that he would just come knocking on her door. She had rehearsed this moment so many times, but now that it was here, she wasn't ready for it. He pulled out a chair from the table. She sat in the one by the window. Golden afternoon light came in and highlighted her long honey hair, touched the shoulders of her blouse, a white cotton lisle embroidered with flowers of red and green and blue.

"You look so . . . so different." He couldn't think of any words big enough to say how beautiful she looked, and didn't think she'd believe he meant it anyhow.

"So do you."

There was a long silence. They sat and stared at each other, like strangers who had wandered into the wrong room at a party.

"Sal said you were modeling for Richard Avedon. After you'd been in town two days?"

"Yeah. It was kind of a fluke. It's a long story."

"I have time."

"Do you? You never had time before."

"Just tell me how you got Avedon to take your picture."

"I told you, it was a fluke. Diana Vreeland saw me and sent me over to Dick. . . ."

"Dick? You're calling him Dick?"

"That's his name. Anyhow, I went up to *Vogue,* trying to track down Cherry, since I didn't have your address, and Diana Vreeland saw me and sent me over to Dick to do a picture for the magazine. It was no big deal."

"So, let me get this straight. You walked into *Vogue* and Diana Vreeland decided to put you in the magazine, just like that? Is that what you're saying?"

"Pretty much. Yeah."

"Is that why you lost all that weight? To come up here and be a model, too?"

"No . . . I lost weight because my baby was sick and died and I didn't have much of an appetite. You do know we had a baby girl and she died, don't you? Aren't you interested in that? What does it matter that somebody took my picture?" There was nothing he could say. "Were you ever going to call me, Lale? Ever? Or did you think it would just all go away and I'd forget about it?"

"I thought about you a lot. I did. I sent money."

"Yeah. Thanks for the money. I mean it. I couldn't have paid the hospital or doctors without it. But you made me feel like I was nothing, Lale. Like I was just some girl you happened to knock up. You didn't leave much of a trail, did you? You made sure I didn't have any address or phone number for you. So I figured I'd find Cherry, who at least gave me her address, and then she'd lead me to you. The two of you seemed to know each other pretty well. Funny, isn't it? The two people who were my best friends in tiny little ol' Buchanan, Arkansas, come to New York and find each other."

"You have the wrong idea about me and Cherry. We're just friends. I swear."

"That's what she'd say, too. But I know what I saw on the TV. I saw it in your eyes, Lale. You don't have to lie to me. Not anymore."

"I'm not lying. I like her a lot, but, Cassie, that was acting. We were what they call 'in the moment.' At that moment we were in love, for the cameras, and . . . I can't really explain it . . . when the camera turned off, so did we."

"It's okay. I understand. If I had to choose between Cherry and me, I'd take Cherry, too. The only thing is, I just wish you had told me you didn't want to get married instead of letting it get so far and then running off and leaving me like you did. I wish you had written me one time to say you were sorry, or that you were okay, or to acknowledge I was there. You'll never know what I went through. Half the town thought the baby wasn't yours. Your mother saw to that, and where did she get that idea?"

"I'm sorry. You don't know how sorry I am."

"Yeah. Me, too." She reached for her purse. He flinched, as if he was afraid she was going to pull out a gun. Instead, she handed him a small stack of pictures.

"What are these?"

"All that's left of Lalea. I thought you ought to at least see what she looked like."

The first picture was a shock. He stared at the little ruined face, trying to keep the horror out of his eyes. There were four, each one slightly worse than the one before, as more tubes and needles were added. Tears came into his eyes. He handed them back to her.

"Cassie . . . I'm sorry. You don't know how much. I came over here to see if I couldn't somehow . . . do something to make it up."

"How can you do that, Lale? Can you turn back time and stay with me? What would you have done if we'd gotten married and Lalea had been born just like she was? Would you have taken your turn sleeping at the hospital, looking at her every day, sick with worry, knowing she was going to die? Or would you have taken off then? If she'd lived, would you have gone back to work with your daddy raising watermelons? Would you have stayed with us and been happy driving a tractor and eating out once in a while at the diner? How long would you have stayed in Buchanan, Lale? Can you answer me that, truthfully, for one time?"

"No. You're right. I probably would have left, no matter what. I couldn't ever be happy there. I know it. And you wouldn't have been happy with me, either."

"That's the first honest thing you've ever said to me, and you know what? You're right. I wouldn't. You did me a favor. You taught me a valuable lesson, Lale Hardcastle. It was an expensive one, but one well learned. So I ought to thank you."

"But you won't."

"No, I won't."

He handed her the pictures. "Can I keep one?"

She hesitated, then handed one back.

"I guess so. She was half yours." The air was thick with all that was unsaid.

"Thank you." He put the picture into his shirt pocket, then stood up. "Why don't we get out of here for a little bit?"

"Why not? Want to take a little ride in the T-bird? You haven't seen it in a while. You'll find it's cleaner than it used to be." Cassie put on her coat and slung her bag over her shoulder.

When they got to the T-bird, she handed him the keys. "Want to drive?"

"Sure. I'll take you to a place like you've never seen before. It's one of the most beautiful places in the city. I go there a lot, sometimes just to wonder at being here and to think."

He headed all the way down Seventh Avenue, turned left on Chambers Street, miraculously found a spot, and parked the car.

"I'm glad you have the car. I don't need one in the city. Taking the subway is a lot faster, and you don't have the hassle of always trying to find a place to park. We'll walk from here."

They started over the Brooklyn Bridge walkway. It was a sunny day, but cold, and there weren't too many pedestrians. They walked to the exact center of the bridge, stopped, and looked south, toward the Statue of Liberty, her arm holding high the torch of freedom. Red tugboats churned up white wakes as they plowed the river, small boats zipped in and out; ferryboats lumbered from the Bowery to Staten Island; big barges eased into the piers at the foot of Brooklyn Heights, unloading their cargos from faraway places, with names, she imagined, like Marrakech and Zanzibar. Cassie took a deep, cold breath.

"It's a picture postcard, come to life."

"I thought you'd like it. There's no other view like it anywhere."

They leaned on the railing, looking out at the sparkling water, the sound of traffic humming under their feet.

"I can see why you'd want to be here, instead of Buchanan. It's a whole different world."

"Yeah. It is."

"You're not ever going back, are you?"

"No. I might visit Mama and them. But I'll never live there again. What are you going to do? I mean, are you going to stay here and try to be a model? It seems like you got a break awful easy. But then, I guess, so did I. It happens like that, sometimes. You either hit right away, or you never do."

"No. I don't want to be a model. I couldn't anyway. Dick said I'm too 'special' for the magazines. I think he meant my nose. This was just a one-time deal, for an article about plastic surgery and choices. You'll see it when it comes out. He said if I wanted to, though, I could probably work on Seventh Avenue, as a fitting model for the designers. They don't care, really, what you look like if you fit the clothes."

"Are you going to try? I mean, if you're going to stay, I could probably help you, you know, somehow. Cherry would help you, too. She's always been on your side—I just want you to know that."

"Yeah. I know. I'm not mad at her. It's hard to keep a foot in two places. It must be exciting, living in this world."

She looked at him then, her eyes as blue as the water.

"If I stayed, would you want to see me? Even sometimes?"

He hesitated. That hesitation was all she needed.

"It's okay. Don't worry. I'm not going to stay. This place is beautiful, but it's not for me. I can't see myself standing all day like a glorified dummy, letting somebody pin clothes on me so some other, prettier girl can wear them. I need to get back to the diner, back to the real world. Bernadette needs me, and so does Mama. In fact, I think I'm going to check out of the Chelsea and leave right now. I can find my own way back. Tell Cherry I understand. And I wish her luck. Take it easy."

And she was gone, long honey hair blowing in the wind. Lale stood and looked after her until she was out of sight, until the cold made him move.

53

THE DUNGEON

"Mrs. Digby? Can I come in for a minute?" It was late at night. I'd been trying to get my courage up to go and talk to her all evening, but kept putting it off. Aurelius was out doing a gig at a place called the Loft in SoHo, and wouldn't be back for hours. I told him I had to get up early for work, so he didn't expect to see me. It was now or never.

"Hello, dear. I've been expecting you. I made some chocolate chips. Pecans on top, just like you like. Thank you so much for introducing me to pecans. It's not something I'd ever have thought to do, but they really do make the cookies so much better. That added little nutty crunch. Would you like tea? A little milk and sugar?"

"Yes, thank you. Why were you expecting me?"

"Oh, I don't know. Just a little feeling I got. I get them from time to time. I'm a little psychic, you know. Now. Here's your tea. What can I do for you?"

"Well. I don't really know what to say. I mean, Lana told me . . . I mean . . ." I started to cry. "I'm, um, I guess I'm what you would call 'in trouble.' And I don't know what to do."

"I see. Does Aurelius know?"

"No. I don't want him to know."

"But don't you think he deserves to know? I mean, it is partly his child, too."

"Yes, he deserves to know, but he doesn't want to marry me, and I don't want to marry him, and oh, Mrs. Digby, I'm so miserable. I'm going to hell, I know it, but I just can't get married and have this baby now. I can't. I'm just not ready. I'm so stupid."

"I understand, dear. Believe me, I understand. It's happened to many a girl before you, and you won't be the last one. It happened to me, on more than one occasion. I was lucky. I had a wonderful woman who knew what to do, and I didn't suffer so much, although after the last one I was never able to conceive again. I'm not quite sure why. Scarring, most likely. I felt like it was my just deserts. I wouldn't have made a very good mother anyhow. You have to know that there are sometimes complications, such as infertility. It's something you should not take lightly. Are you sure you want to do this?"

"No. I'm not sure at all. But I'm sure I don't want to quit this career I have here. I feel like my life is just starting. It's selfish, I know, but I can't help it."

"We are all selfish in some ways, my dear. Which is not necessarily a bad thing. It just means we have to look out for ourselves. And you are on the verge of becoming a big model. I can promise you that. You have a wonderful life ahead of you."

"I do? You can see that?"

"I can see that. Although sometimes what I see can change, it's pretty reliable."

"That makes me feel a little better. If I were to . . . do it, what . . . I mean, how . . . what do you do?"

"Well, I think it's best I don't go into all the details, but it won't take long, and there will be a bit of discomfort involved. But that's good. Pain is good. Pain washes away the sin, don't you think? Sort of a penance. And the pain won't last forever. The wonderful thing about our bodies is that we remember we had pain after it's over, but we can't for the life of us recall what it felt like. You're a young healthy girl. You should be fine. How far along are you?"

"About a month. A little less, maybe."

"That's good. You don't want to go too long. I personally won't do it after two and a half months. By then, it looks too much like a baby.

Now it's just a mass of little cells. Not a baby at all. Do you want some time to think about it? We can go downstairs now if you want, and I can examine you."

I took a deep breath. "Okay. Let's do it now and get it over with."

We took the basement stairs, by way of a door I had never seen in Mrs. Digby's apartment. The steps were wooden, old and creaky, and ended in a little stone hallway that was so low I had to duck my head. She, of course, had no such problem. It was lit by a bare bulb and was a little claustrophobic, but then what was I expecting? We came to a door with a round brick top, and she took out a key and opened it, flipped a switch, and a light came on in a little room that was clean but grim, a twin-size bed in the middle, a sink, and a cabinet. The ceiling was brick, and the bed was the old-fashioned iron kind with bars for a headboard. The paint was worn in the places I imagined a girl's hands would grip. The brick walls were thick. No sounds would come out of this room, no matter how loud.

"Lie down, my dear. Let me take a look. Don't be embarrassed. It's just us girls here."

I lay down and awkwardly lifted my dress above my chest. My belly was still flat, but my breasts were a little bigger. The nipples were a bright pink and looked more than ever like giant jellybeans on little white mounds of flesh that were just beginning to swell. She had a lamp with a strong light, and a little stool that she rolled to the end of the bed.

"Scoot right down to the edge, my dear. That's a good girl. This won't hurt. I'm just looking."

She stuck that metal thing inside me that was always freezing cold, to open me up. I started to tremble a little.

"Yes, you are most certainly pregnant, dearie. And I think you are right, not quite a month. This will be no problem."

I was shaking pretty good now, and my breathing was coming hard. I was so scared. The room was too small and there were no windows. It was what a room in hell might be like, staying forever in a tiny brick room with no air and no sunshine. A room like the one in the back of my head where I had shoved all the things I would think about later, all the bad things I had done since I came to New York. They were all crowding around me in the iron bed in that little brick room. Mrs. Digby had taken out some kind of instruments I didn't want to look at too closely. She got up and washed her hands at the sink for a long time, then dried them and sat down again.

"I can't tell you how important cleanliness is. Do you realize that in the last century, more women died of childbed fever in hospitals than they did at home? That's because the stupid men doctors would go down to do autopsies and who knows what all, and then come up and deliver babies without washing their hands. Can you imagine? They thought, I suppose, well, my hands are already a mess, might as well just get them good and messy before I take all that time to wash. My goodness, common sense should have told them *that* was a mistake. Still, that's why a lot of girls today get into the messes they do—people just don't take the time to properly wash. I was taught well, I can promise you. The woman who taught me did all the girls for Ziegfeld. She was the best. Now this is going to pinch, just a little."

By this time, I was really shaking. I felt something cold go inside, and a pain like a hot poker went right through the middle of my stomach. I screamed—I couldn't help it.

"Stop! Stop, Mrs. Digby. Is it too late? Did you do it yet? Please stop. I don't want to do this. I can't."

She stopped, withdrew the instrument.

"I'm not done, dearie. Are you sure you want me to stop? You'll still have the baby, you know."

"I don't care. I can't do it. I'll just have to figure out something else."

She wiped me clean, and I sat up on the side of the bed, shaking. It was wrong. It was so wrong to be here, doing this. I hadn't seen the little blue fairy since that one night. It might be in there. No matter what happened, I was going to have to face the consequences of what I had done, and if it was meant for me to have this baby, so be it. I would find a way. I'd do something. I could take a leave of absence and get somebody to take care of it while I worked. I'd get my figure back. Other models did it. Cassie had gone through with it. I couldn't face Cassie if I killed this baby. I heard myself telling Cassie, the night she drove her car onto the railroad track, "Killing a baby is the worst sin you can commit. It's an innocent little thing and it doesn't have any say in it. Let the baby live!" I couldn't kill the baby. I couldn't.

"Are you all right, dear?"

"Did you hurt the baby?"

"No, I don't think so. I barely touched you. Let me look."

I lay back down and she took another look.

"No, you're fine. If you're sure this is what you want, then just go upstairs and take a couple of aspirin. You'll be okay in the morning. If I can help you, or if you change your mind, just call. I'm right here."

"Thanks, Mrs. D. You've been great. How much do I owe you?"

"Nothing. You don't owe me a thing. Just take care of yourself. I'll see you tomorrow."

I went back upstairs and collapsed on the bed, crying. I needed to call someone, but who? I couldn't call my mother. She would be so disappointed in me. I couldn't call Baby. She didn't have a phone. I couldn't tell Aurelius, not yet. Or Sal. Or Lale, God forbid. Lana would think I'd lost my mind. But I needed to talk to somebody.

I went downstairs to the pay phone on the corner by Joe Jr's. The night was cold but clear. There were cars on the street, but not too many. I dialed a number. It rang several times, and a familiar voice answered.

"Hello?"

"Forgive me, Father, for I have sinned."

"Who is this? Cherry? Is that you?"

"Hi, Father Leo. How's the sin business?"

"Good Lord, what are you doing calling me in the middle of the night? Are you all right?"

"Not really." I started to cry. I told him everything, what I had almost done, and how miserable I was. About Aurelius and Mrs. Digby, the whole thing. He listened, and let out a big sigh.

"Oh, Cherry, my darling. You poor lamb."

"Am I going to hell, Father Leo? What am I going to do?"

"Maybe there's not any hell. I think we make our own hells, right here. One thing I do know, is that the God I serve is a God of love, and He loves you. He loves you and that baby, and no matter what happens, He will take care of you. He would never send you to hell for making a mistake. We all make mistakes, every single one of us. That I know. I thought I was on my way to hell, too, and who knows? Maybe I still am."

"I hate to tell you, but I know all about it. Baby's my best friend—you know that."

"Of course I do. I knew she'd tell you. She had to tell somebody. It's not the kind of thing you can keep a secret. Is she still angry at me?"

"No. I don't think so. I think she understands. I understand. You had to do what you had to do. I mean, I think the whole celibacy thing is nutty, but like you said, if you want to play on the team you have to play by the rules. She'll get over it."

"I'm sure she will. She's still a kid. But will I? I do love her, you know. Quite a lot."

"She knows you do. And you'll get over it. If you don't, then you'll just have to rethink things. There's nothing that says you have to stay there forever."

"No, I think I will. It's too late for me. I thought I could break out, but those ties are strong. As strong as a marriage vow. But you—what will you do?"

"I don't know. I'll play it by ear. If I can call you up once in a while, that would be great. Is that okay?"

"You call me anytime. I'm here. It's my job."

54

THE RIVIERA

Aurelius took me out for dinner at a restaurant in the Village called the Riviera Café. It was on Seventh Avenue, not too far from our house. The night was warm for January, and if you could see them, which you couldn't very well because of all the lights of the city, there were stars in the sky. We strolled along, arm in arm, not saying anything. I was going over in my mind how I was going to tell him about the baby. Nothing seemed right.

"You're awful quiet tonight, baby. Is anything the matter?"

"I'm just not feeling too well, sweetie. I'm okay. I had a long day of work today. Catalog. It's the hardest thing, changing wigs every shot, I don't even know how many changes of clothes. They get all they can get out of you."

"Well, we'll have a nice glass of wine and a good dinner and you'll feel better."

We sat down and had our wine, and I looked at the menu, but nothing appealed to me. I felt sort of sick at my stomach. I finally ordered the swordfish, which was unusual for me, since I'd never eaten it, but nothing else looked good, either.

"I've been waiting to tell you," he said when we'd gotten our food, "I have some good news for you. I've been offered a part in a play."

"Really? That's great. What play?"

"*A Raisin in the Sun*. They're taking a cast on a tour across the country. It's the Sidney Poitier role, baby. It's a real role, not some hood or lackey. It's walking in the steps of ol' Sidney himself!"

"Wow! That's so great, sweetheart! But that means you'll be gone a long time, won't you?"

"Yeah, that's the only bad thing. I'll be away from you. But we knew we'd have times like this, didn't we? I mean, you get trips to places . . ."

"Oh, absolutely. We knew we'd have to be separated sometimes. But we'll get back together when you come home. Won't we?"

"Of course we will. You bet we will! I'll miss you, baby."

"I'll miss you, too, sweetie. But we'll write. And call."

"Yeah, we'll write and call. Are you all right?"

I felt really sick. And something was acting funny with my vision. I thought I saw some kind of big bug flitting across the room. A blue one.

"Excuse me, honey. I have to go to the bathroom. I'll be right back."

It seemed like the blue fairy was leading the way to the tiny bathroom, flitting down the dimly lit corridor. I closed the door and locked it, then leaned over and threw up what little of the swordfish I had managed to get down. Then I had an urge to sit, so I turned around, pulled down my pantyhose and sat. A spasm took me and I strained. I heard a small plop and when I wiped, it was blood. A lot of blood. I looked in the toilet and there in the bottom was a small clot of blood, about the size of a nickel. I looked around the room, but the tinkling sound had gone. The blue fairy, the little soul of the baby, had gone. I was all alone. I started to cry.

"Thank you. Thank you so much, Jesus. Forgive me, please forgive me. Please give me another chance. Please let this little baby come back to me again one day. I love it so much. I love you so much. Thank you, thank you. I'll do better. I promise I will."

I leaned against the wall and sobbed until there were no more sobs. I wadded up toilet paper and put it in my panties to catch the flow. Then I fixed my makeup and went back out.

"I'm not feeling so well, sweetheart. I started my period."

"Oh, well, then let's get the check. I'll take you home."

"You're the best, Aurelius. I do love you. I really do."

"And I love you, too, baby. I do."

55

GOOD-BYE, FREDDY

There had never been so many good-looking women all in one place at one time. Campbell's funeral home was packed with them, all wearing black, weeping, hugging, giggling behind their hands. The open coffin sat at the front of the room, black and shiny, like a limousine, ready to take Freddy to his eternal rest. Or whatever. The preacher was a pompous man with a balding horseshoe hairdo who looked like his shirt collar was a size too small. He had never met Freddy in his life, but stood at attention, goggle-eyed at all the models. He kept hugging Suzan, who caught my glance and rolled her eyes. Suzan had asked me to sit with her in the front row, along with Gina and Liz and the rest of the staff. I think when the chips are down, you need somebody you can trust, and I might have been the only one she knew for sure who hadn't slept with ol' Freddy. We were all totally in shock, of course. The morning of his death, Suzan said, she had come down and had her breakfast, thinking Freddy was still asleep, like he always was at that hour. When he wasn't down by noon, she went to his room and saw his bed hadn't been slept in. The car was in the garage, and there was fresh snow, no tracks leading anywhere. She ran from room to room, and finally went out to the pool house, where she saw him floating, blood on the side of the pool. A bottle of Bombay Sapphire gin was broken on the floor, along with one of his slippers, and it was pretty evident he'd been drunk and just tripped into the pool. His blood-alcohol level had been off the charts when they did the autopsy, and the coroner said the cut on his head had probably knocked him out. He'd drowned. After she found the body, Suzan, of course, went into hysterics and called the police. The doctor came and gave her a sedative, and Gina came out and helped her get back to the apartment. It was such a tragedy. Such a waste. But we'd all seen Freddy drunk around that pool, and knew he was an accident just waiting to happen. Nobody was that surprised.

After the preacher spoke, we all filed by and lay our hands on the casket one last time. Freddy looked good, all clean and shaved, wearing a nice Armani suit with a red silk tie. He had a little smile on his face. Suzan was the last to go up. I waited for her a few respectful feet back. She leaned down and kissed the cold face, then took something out of her bag and slipped it into his hands. It was a blue bottle of Bombay Sapphire. She turned, as they closed the lid, and waited while they rolled the coffin down the aisle. We walked out behind it, her holding on to my arm.

"Well, that's over."

"I'm so sorry, Suzan."

"Are you?"

"Well, kind of. But I'm sorry it was such a shock to you."

"Yes, it was a shock. But I'm not sorry at all. I'm free."

"What are you going to do?"

"Oh, I'll keep the agency. But I think I'll go to Paris for a long holiday. Gina can keep things going until I get back. She runs it all anyhow. I might think about starting a branch of Suzan Hartman in Paris—who knows? Would you want to go with me? There's a lot of work for girls like you in Paris. Can you imagine, the girls from Arkansas take on the City of Light?"

Paris! A lot of my friends in the agency had been to Paris. In fact, most girls went there for a year of seasoning when they first started. They came back home with fat portfolios of tear sheets and much more polish and sophistication than when they'd left. We'd just found out that Diana Vreeland had been fired from *Vogue,* which seemed impossible, like God being fired, but she had. My trip to Moscow was not going to happen. No white horses in snowy birch forests for me. Maybe a little time in Paris was just what I needed. Suzan's eyes were shining. She looked a lot younger, somehow, softer, more relaxed. There was a quality in her I'd never seen before. She was happy.

"You know, Suzan, that sounds like fun. I'm kind of at loose ends right now. I'd love to go, if it wouldn't be forever. I love New York so much, but then I've never seen Paris."

"And Paris has never seen a couple of girls like us."

ACKNOWLEDGMENTS

Many people have helped me along the way to writing my second book, none more than my doctor, Arlan Fuller, who kept the old machine going to complete the task. Without him there would be no book and most likely no author. My sons, John Buffalo and Matthew; Matthew's wife, Salina, and their daughter, Mattie James; my stepchildren, Susan, Danielle, Elizabeth, Kate, Michael, Stephen, Maggie, and their spouses and children; as well as my sister-in-law Barbara Wasserman, her son, Peter Alson, and his wife and daughter; are the best family there is. I couldn't have done any of it without them. I thank my host of friends, Aurora Huston, Susan Shinn, Christina Pabst, Natasha Stoynoff, Sarah Keathley, Diane Fisher, Dwayne Prickett, Carol Mailer, and Carmel Borders, among many others, who told me with absolute sincerity that they stayed up until two reading my drafts, and Dan Skelton, who is a poet, a critic, and a friend. My dear father, James Davis, passed away while I was writing this book. I miss him and his dry wit and loving charm and wish he were here to read it. He would be shocked, but would be proud of me anyhow. My mother, Gaynell Davis, will read it and be proud, but will still be shocked.

Great thanks to the powerful Random House; its publisher, Gina Centrello; my beloved editor, David Ebershoff; Diana Fox; Jynne Martin; Carol Schneider; Janet Wygal; Stephanie Higgs; and all the rest of the gang, for giving me the tools and the freedom to do this book.

A special warm thanks to John Taylor Williams (ol' Handsome Ike), my agent and friend, who believed in me before I did, and kept my courage up when the days got long. Thanks to Hope Denekamp, Ike's assistant, who is always there for me.

What fun it was to relive that period when I was a young model, through the many books and magazines that went into the research of *Cheap Diamonds*. I am grateful to Jackie Thurik for finding the period magazines I needed. Besides *D.V.,* Diana Vreeland's autobiography, another book that was most helpful in researching Mrs. Vreeland was *Diana Vreeland,* by Eleanor Dwight. Thanks, also, to Michael Gross and his wonderful book *Model,* and to Richard Kostelanetz for his book *SoHo: The Rise and Fall of an Artists' Colony. High on Rebellion,* by Yvonne Sewall-Ruskin, was a gold mine about Max's Kansas City, where I have spent the odd evening or two. So many other books that I can't enumerate them all added spice to the mix.

Last but not least, I'd like to remember my dear late husband of thirty-three years, Norman Mailer, who showed me what being a writer means, and who had the wisdom to let me do it on my own. I love you.

AUTHOR'S NOTE

This is a work of fiction. Most of the names, characters, locations, dialogue, and plot are the products of the author's imagination and are not to be construed as real. There are, however, places in New York that once existed, and some that still exist. Several well-known figures are mentioned by their real names, and, with utmost respect, the author has taken the liberty of creating dialogue for these characters, most of whom she has known in at least a passing way. But their words should not be construed as actual comments by the character—with the exception of Diana Vreeland, whose exchange with Cherry on perfume was adapted from her autobiography, *D.V.* (Alfred A. Knopf, 1984). A writer of fiction has only three sources of information from which to draw: real-life experiences, research, and imagination. The author has drawn from them all, and, like Dr. Frankenstein, was inclined to occasionally borrow the odd characteristic from people and places in her life to toss into the mix of entirely different characters or situations. However, none of the fictitious characters in *Cheap Diamonds* is based on an actual person, and any resemblance to living people is entirely coincidental.

CHEAP DIAMONDS

Norris Church Mailer

A Reader's Guide

A Conversation with Norris Church Mailer

Random House Reader's Circle: There are some very interesting similarities between your life and that of our protagonist, Cherry Marshall: both of you grew up in Arkansas and came to New York in the 1970s, both of you modeled, both of you are artists—the list goes on and on! Could you talk a little bit about how much of you there is in Cherry, and maybe highlight some of the ways she's different from you?

Norris Church Mailer: Cherry is definitely a part of me, but she is not me. We had a few similar adventures, but her story is certainly not mine. I did model for a few years but was never as successful as she became because I was married with a family and just couldn't do the traveling that's involved if you are to become successful. Wilhelmina wanted me to go to Paris for a year, as a lot of the new girls do to get experience, and that I couldn't do. So I did jobs in New York, and basically quit when I got pregnant with my second son, John Buffalo. I made Cherry an artist because it is something I understand, but she could have as easily been something else.

RHRC: Would you say you see some of yourself in each of your characters?

NCM: Of course. Even the villains have to come through my sensibilities, so I try to put myself in their position and make them as human as possible. Nobody sees himself or herself as a villain; they only see their side of the story.

RHRC: Why did you choose to embody so many voices in this text, instead of just staying in Cherry's head? There are portions narrated by Lale, Cassie, and even a cabdriver. How did this challenge you as a writer?

NCM: In my first book, *Windchill Summer*, I used two voices, too: Cherry's first-person narration, and then an omniscient third-person voice, because Cherry couldn't possibly know what was going on with the other parts of the story. I find this happens often in fiction, the usage of more than one voice, and it works for me.

RHRC: You chose to intersperse the narrative of *Cheap Diamonds* with letters the characters send to one another. What do you think this adds?

NCM: I wanted to bring back Cherry's home and friends in an immediate way, and the use of letters lets me do first-person for them, which is always more intimate than the more distant third-person.

RHRC: As someone who lives in New York today, what was it like to write about the New York of the 1970s? It seems it couldn't be more different, with artist-only lofts in SoHo and struggling artists and musicians living in the West Village. Could you elaborate a bit on that experience?

NCM: I moved to New York in 1975 when SoHo was just beginning to become more than a warehouse district where a few artists lived and worked. You could still buy a huge loft for $25,000 in those days, and if we bought real estate, we would now be rich. I did in fact rent a loft on Canal Street and was part of the SoHo scene for a couple of years, as the shops and galleries moved in and I had shows in a gallery called Central Falls, which is no longer there. It was one of the most exciting times in my life, mainly because I was young, but also because of the tenor of the times, the way the city was changing, opening up.

RHRC: Just out of curiosity, I have to ask—was the scene at Max's Kansas City based on your personal experience? Did you really see Andy Warhol, Robert Rauschenberg, Roy Lichtenstein, Lou Reed, David Bowie, and Debbie Harry all in the same place?

NCM: I did go to Max's Kansas City a few times, but it was a few years after the hottest years of the sixties and early seventies. I have met a lot of the people I write about, maybe not all at Max's, but I know people who hung out there at that time who told me stories, and I read a wonderful book by Yvonne Sewall Ruskin called *High on Rebellion: Inside the*

Underground at Max's Kansas City. It is an oral biography with pictures and a gold mine for the time.

RHRC: Cassie's narrative is a very important part of this book, but it is very different from Cherry's. Why did you choose to give Cassie such a strong focus?

NCM: I like to have two stories weaving in and out, finally coming together in the end. Cassie and Cherry were from the same place but had different goals and lives. There were, and still are, a lot of girls like Cassie, who get pregnant young, marry, and become old much too soon. By knowing Cherry, Cassie discovers for herself that life doesn't have to be about marrying the perfect man.

RHRC: In the end, you don't allow Lale to become a two-dimensional villain but, rather, make the reader sympathize with him. Do you think he is deserving of redemption?

NCM: I think everyone is deserving of redemption. Though not everyone is redeemed. But I tried to put myself into the shoes of a nineteen-year-old boy who is caught up in his sexuality, like every boy, and who can't stand up to the consequences. He will ultimately either be happy or not, but he had to be true to himself and live with the choices he made.

RHRC: You grew up in the Free Will Baptist Church, which is fairly similar to the Holiness Church Cherry attends. When you first came to New York, did you have some of the same reactions that Cherry does—for example, the way she feels when confronted with the drugs and overt sexuality of Max's Kansas City?

NCM: Oh, sure. If you grow up in church from the time you are on your mother's breast, you believe what the grown-ups tell you—in this case, that you will burn and sizzle in hell for every sin you commit. No matter how sophisticated you become, how little you believe the teachings, you can never truly get away from it. It is one of my themes, how destructive fundamentalism really is, how it teaches negativism and retribution, not love, and has nothing to do with what Jesus said, which was to love your neighbor. I do remember my preacher saying that if we drank one beer or had one glass of wine we would go to hell. I was terrified every night before I went to sleep that I had done some sin by mistake and would die and go to hell. It was terrifying for a child.

RHRC: *Cheap Diamonds* deals a lot with issues of race and homosexuality. Cherry worries about what her family will think about her dating a black man, and Sal is beaten up by a drunk and angry group of homophobes. How important was it to you to discuss these issues in the book?

NCM: These were key themes in the book, as 1970 was a time of change for both homosexuality and racism. Our generation thought we could change the world, and in fact some places did change, but not everywhere. I wanted Cherry to be in a place that was totally different from the small Arkansas town she came from; I wanted her to have all the new experiences she could.

RHRC: To me, this book is about staying true to yourself—from Cherry's eyebrows to her Southern accent to the nose Cassie decides not to fix, which then lands her a spot in *Vogue* and a photo shoot with the legendary Richard Avedon, characters are rewarded again and again for being themselves. Is this a message you were trying to get across in *Cheap Diamonds*?

NCM: I never really set out to preach that, but I think it's good to stay true to yourself. But that takes different forms. I have nothing against cosmetic surgery or hair-dying if that will make you feel better about yourself. Maybe that's the real you.

RHRC: Was your experience of writing and publishing *Cheap Diamonds* different from that of *Windchill Summer,* your first book? When you began writing *Windchill Summer,* did you have the general plot of all three books in mind? I'd love to hear about your process.

NCM: I knew when I finished *Windchill Summer* that I wanted to continue Cherry's story. There was a natural progression that was in tandem with my own life, although, I stress, it is not my own story. I actually did an intermediate book that was Lale and Cassie's story and Cherry's romance with a black man in Buchanan, the little Ozark town where she practice taught. At the end of that book, she goes to New York to become a model, and then there would have been a third book about the modeling world, but my editor at Random House convinced me to combine the last two books, so that's what I did. Now there might be a third chapter to the trilogy, when Cherry goes to Paris for her year abroad. But I have no real idea; I never work with an outline or even a complete story. My characters seem to write my books for me as I go along.

RHRC: Did you have to conduct research to write this novel, or were you able to write it out of your own personal experience?

NCM: Both. Memory is a treacherous friend, and I found I misremembered a lot of events. One great tool was old fashion magazines, which are a gold mine for researching a period. You get to read about all the then-current fashions, movies, books, music, and trends. If I wrote about an article in *Cosmopolitan,* for example, there was a real-life one in the issue I mention. I also did a lot of research about SoHo, music from the era, and the modeling world. This was a wonderful, fun book to research.

One thing I'd like to address is the fact that both Cherry and Lale made a success of modeling rather soon after they began. It has been said that's not realistic, but the reality is, if a young model doesn't begin to make money soon after joining the agency, he or she isn't kept on for long—usually for only a year or so. It is not unheard of for a model to get a job on her first "go see" and become famous in a few months. In fact, it happens a lot. That wasn't my own experience, but I saw it happen over and over. Jessica Lange started at the same time I did and really never worked much because right away she was sent to audition for *King Kong* and got the part. We were all so excited for her, thinking it could happen to us. And to some of them it did.

RHRC: If you had to make up a list of books for a reading group, what would you include?

NCM: There are so many writers I love, but for contemporary writers, I would put something on it by Adriana Trigiani, Elizabeth Berg, Doris Kearns Goodwin, Barbara Kingsolver, and Amy Tan. I would add a Norman Mailer, a William Kennedy, a Don DeLillo, and a Phil Roth. I would also include Eudora Welty and Ernest Hemingway, Tolstoy and Dostoyevsky, F. Scott Fitzgerald, and Margaret Mitchell. I have eclectic tastes, and love mysteries by P. D. James, Ruth Rendell, Mary Higgins Clark, and Sue Grafton. I'll read a new Walter Mosley or Ken Follett. I love writers who send me to another era and place, like Diana Gabaldon, and I just read *The Tenderness of Wolves* by Stef Penney, which I liked a lot. I read a lot, as you can gather.

RHRC: Could you share any advice you have for aspiring writers out there?

NCM: When you begin a novel, just remember that nobody ever has to see it if you don't want them to. Don't write with anybody in mind, like your mother or your preacher or your best friend who might think the character is based on her. This is your story, and while there might be elements in it of people you know, you will not do an exact portrait of anybody. It's too limiting. You would be constantly bogged down with trying to determine if the person would really have said that or done this.

Reading Group Questions and Topics for Discussion

1. Cherry's good looks and choice of career often get her into trouble. How did the author undercut the idea that modeling is all glitz and glamour? Was there anything in the novel that went against this notion?

2. What did you make of Cherry's relationship with Aurelius? Do you think Cherry ever really loved him?

3. Religion plays a big part in this novel. Discuss Cherry's internal conflict when confronted with morally questionable situations—does it seem as though she is choosing between her past and her present?

4. If you were to pinpoint the novel's essential theme in only a few words, what would it be?

5. What insights did reading *Cheap Diamonds* give you into the New York City of the early seventies? How did it seem different from New York today?

6. Early on in the novel, Suzan tells Cherry that "friendship takes a backseat to love every time." Did that turn out to be true in *Cheap Diamonds*? Have you found it to be true in your own life?

7. Did you think Cherry betrayed Cassie when she didn't confront Lale right away about abandoning her and the baby? What would you have done under the same circumstances?

8. In her professional and personal relationships, Cherry confronts some of the most pressing issues of her time—race and homosexuality.

How does this naïve girl from Arkansas come up against these issues? Does her perspective change over the course of the novel? What does this suggest about the era in which *Cheap Diamonds* takes place?

9. The author embodies more than one voice in *Cheap Diamonds*, from Cherry to Cassie to Baby to Suzan to Sal, even a cabdriver who appears for only one scene. What is the effect of this multiplicity of voices? Which voice did you find most effective, and why?

10. When Cherry and Baby thwart Cassie's attempted suicide on the railroad tracks, Cassie says that her "guardian angel" must have sent them. Then Sal suggests that Lale's guardian angel must have arranged their chance meeting at the truck stop, which led to Lale's success as a model. "Don't you believe in fate?" Sal asks. What role does fate play in this novel? Do you believe that certain things are predestined?

11. In what ways did Cherry grow and change over the course of the novel? Do you think she let her success as a model, and the preferential treatment that came with it, go to her head?

12. Dramatic irony is a literary term used to describe moments when the words or actions of the characters have a different meaning for the reader than they do for the character, in most cases due to the fact that the reader knows something the character doesn't. One example of dramatic irony in *Cheap Diamonds* is when Suzan winces because of the pain in her ribs and claims she "slipped on the bathroom floor." The reader is immediately cognizant of what's happening with Freddy, but Cherry doesn't seem to catch on. Can you think of other examples of dramatic irony in the novel?

13. Which character did you most identify with and why?

14. Do you find the title of the novel an apt one? What do you think Mailer was trying to suggest?

15. Identity is one central theme of this novel—many of the characters have their identities questioned and challenged by others. Is there a message about staying true to oneself that you took away from your reading of *Cheap Diamonds*?

16. If you could ask Mailer a question of your own, what would it be?

17. *Cheap Diamonds* is the second book in a trilogy that began with Mailer's 2000 book, *Windchill Summer*. What do you think will happen to Cherry next? What would you like to see happen?

Photo: © CHRISTINA PABST

NORRIS CHURCH MAILER is the author of a previous novel, *Windchill Summer*. Raised in Arkansas and now a resident of Brooklyn, Norris is the mother of two sons, two stepsons, and five stepdaughters, as well as a granny to ten.